Amalina and the Midnight Gift

Episode 3 in
The Count at Play
& Slaughter series

C.L. Holmes

Bad Hound Press

This one is for Dick and Dario,
masters of the F.N.T. and the S.A.F., respectively

Other books in the series:

Amalina and the Secrets of the Wailing Castle

Amalina and the Palace of Pleasure

Amalina and the Midnight Gift
Episode 3 in The Count at Play & Slaughter series
© 2019 C.L. Holmes

Bad Hound Press
A Division of Giant Dog Books
www.giantdogbooks.com
All rights reserved.

ISBN-13: 978-1-949043-16-7
ISBN-10: 1-949043-16-9

Cover, design and layouts by Dominic Wilde

Episode 3

Amalina and the Midnight Gift

Prologue

Old and Ancient Friends

The ancient castle was so old and worn it appeared to have fused with its towering perch, as if in some inanimate bid to become one with the eternal mountains. The castle's owner, while not half as old, had grown ancient in his own way, surviving long enough to outlive everyone he knew from childhood—the enchanting detritus of brothers, sisters, cousins, wives, lovers, friends, and even those countrymen of his generation he'd never met—the countless rains, winds, and merciless time having hosed them clean from the rocks. He alone clung on and could now claim only one person as his contemporary, an acquaintance perhaps older than the castle itself. Perhaps, as rumors went, even older than the mountains themselves. An acquaintance who seemed to effortlessly defy age and time and whom the old man's servants feared; feared as much as they loved and cherished the old man and his ancient castle.

This fearful acquaintance arrived one night, pushing through the outer doors as if he owned the place, but otherwise politely announced his presence, and asked to be shown to the master of the house.

"What are you doing here?" The old man's voice was both surprised and pleased, if a bit hushed and gravelly from his growing infirmity. Unseen by the old master—and more importantly, undetected by the visitor—the servants crept behind the dark red curtain which separated the bedroom from the rest of the master suite. The servants were half bent over, each wishing the other would make a parting in the thick, dusty drapes so they could watch over the scene; but dreading the other would do just that. Their limbs shivered as they listened. "I wonder," the old man said, "why have you come?"

"Why not?" The visitor's voice was deep and resonating. And it would have sounded almost predatory in its confidence, its ease, its slickness, if the servants weren't already familiar with its owner and his purpose. He was a man to be feared above anything else, of course. Which was why their bodies shook at his presence. But they could comfort themselves he was there for their master, not them. His voice rumbled gently: "I'm overdue in this visit, I think, from the looks of it. But I'm here."

"And still," their master's voice returned. "Why? You had no inkling I was ill. That I lay on my death bed."

"No I did not. I came to tell you something important."

"Ah? What is it? But I deserve nothing from you."

"Of all the people I've ever known," said the visitor, with a tenderness never heard before from this one, "you deserve the most. But this is not a gift. It is news. News of your oldest friend."

"We're still friends? I'm so glad to hear it."

"For as long as we can keep our bodies together we will be friends. Now be quiet, old friend, and listen to what I have to say. It will please you very much."

The servants traded curious glances.

"I'm grateful to hear it," said the servants' master. "Ah, yes, now I see, something has changed in you. Something's changed …"

"I am trying something *new*."

"New. Good. That means you are alive."

. . .

"Allow me to continue before you are no longer so," the visitor chided impatiently, but with a fond grin. "Please, let me tell you quickly."

The old man waved his hand in a gracious gesture for his visitor to do as he wished.

The visitor, his skin pale white, his hair thick and dark brown—almost black—and pulled back from his forehead and scooping over his head like a helmet, his large, depthless brown eyes locked on the old man, he lowered himself to the side of the bed, and reached out a hand from below his black cloak to touch the old man's shoulder in a gesture of reassurance. There was something in his eyes like a flame, though burning much hotter and brighter in those large glassy eyes than the simple reflection of the nearby candle.

"I've taken your advice," said the visitor. "At long last, I have taken steps to become what you have long wished me to be."

"This *is* good news. A blessing to these dying ears."

"Watching is not the same as existing," he began to recite. "Existing is not the same as living. Living with friendship is more nourishing than a cold separation from humanity."

The old man nodded, a slight smile of satisfaction tracing his lips. "Go on."

"I have broken from my past. I've freed her—my wife—from the hands of that scoundrel in the cemetery. Secured her mortal remains. Only I know her location now. And having seen to her safety and quiet rest, I have reached out into the world and have made connections with families in the western kingdoms."

"*Outsiders?*" said the old man, as his eyebrows lifted in surprise with a brittle, papery sound. "Not like you, my old friend."

"Even now I have operatives traveling through Italia and the French territories, spreading my name to the royal courts and high nobles. Their daughters are being groomed for my own court."

"Your own court!"

"I am opening my castles. You should see the high castle."

"You own a castle? I did not know."

"I didn't tell you?"

"No, my friend."

"Well, there you are."

"A castle such as mine?"

"Many such as yours. Many even older."

"I suppose I should have known," said the old man. "Why wouldn't you own such things? Why couldn't you? I suppose this court of yours will be marvelous to behold."

"I have vowed to come out of the shadows. So now I do. And I have sworn to live as you have wished me to."

"How is that?"

"Happily. Acceptably. Humanly."

"You thrill me before I die. You are not just telling me this to be kind?"

"The time has come, my friend. I have renewed my life. I shall live as life is supposed to be lived. Full of experience and the sharing of thoughts, learning and pleasure. The reign of cruelty is abandoned. It is left like a sword on the field of battle. Because all war is futile, and love is genuine and pleasurable."

"I should never have thought it could be, but it is. What has worked this miraculous change in you?"

"You."

"And what will you get up to in your new Ardeelian court, with all these ripe plums of the west?"

"What you in your youth could only dream of."

The old man let out a mortal groan, his eyes closing and his body writhing.

"You've come to torture me," he said with a laugh, at last.

"Are you sincere, my friend? This news wounds you?"

"As always, my ancient friend, you know everything and yet understand so little. Here is the truth: I regret the leaving of a life I should wish continued. But I regret nothing I have done, and I am pleased you will have for yourself what I only now wish to relive."

"You were the best man I've ever known."

"Your words so very pleasant. I know death must be close."

"Before it takes you, know one last thing: with my old wife buried, from these succulent fruits—the plums and peaches and cherries which I will refresh my court—I shall secure a new wife. A woman to share my life in this new era."

"For love," the old man sighed. "Yes. Eternal love."

"This pleases you, too, my old friend?"

"If only you could have found this happiness sooner so we could share it while I was in my prime."

"I was a fool," said the visitor, remorsefully. "But it is my time to learn and show my understanding."

The old man nodded. After a thought he said:

"Can I offer you something to eat?"

"You've forgotten my partialities, my dear, dear friend?" said the visitor, wiping his upper lip, revealing a long, sharp, canine tooth.

"Not at all. I'm overstaffed these days. And I was considering letting go a few. I should think at least one of them would be to your taste."

"I believe you're testing me." The visitor looked to the closed curtains. He could hear the clamping of knees and the chattering of teeth. He could smell the sweat of fear exploding from the bodies hidden behind it.

"Come here you two," the old man called breathily to his servants, beckoning them into the chamber. "I know you are there, and I wish my friend to see you. Come and show yourselves to Mr. Tepsji."

"Count Tepsji," the visitor corrected with a playful, and toothy grin. He watched the curtain with interest.

PART ONE
THE BOOK OF ERIS
(LATE SPRING, EARLY SUMMER)

1

The Carriage

In the carriage again; Amalina Dalca's head and shoulders pressed deep into the seat cushions, while her legs cast across the compartment so her feet could rest on the opposite bench. Her skirt was off and she relished how her bare legs bounced against each other with the swaying motion, and savored how the sunlight streaming through the open windows played warmly on her skin. Her eyes were half-closed and a smile was on at least one corner of her lips, thinking of a life that existed behind her.

Hansa's castle was the best castle of all. So went her thoughts. Hansa's castle—one of the foreign castles she'd visited a couple years ago, during her very first trip into the world beyond Ardeel—was not only large, and high, and decorated pleasantly, and was cheerful, and had great views in all directions, and had surrounding groves of fruit trees that were ripe when she visited, its crowning grace was its overstuffed stable of horses. Now that Amalina could ride this majestic animal she could appreciate with a growing connoisseur's taste the temper and character of its different breeds.

But Hansa's had not been the most colorful castle, she reflected now, her casual thoughts finding a new track. The most colorful were the ones she'd seen this year, this time out, and belonged to the princesses (or their families, anyway) in the southern Italian provinces, where the mediterranean sun, even in winter, pulled the colors off the walls and waved them around like gaudy flags. It was stunning, even if sometimes difficult to look at. Amalina's home country was richly colorful in its seasons, of course, but Amalina had never witnessed in Ardeel this variety of shades, and ones touched with such immeasurable vibrance; not in nature, village, city, or castle.

Even so, Amalina decided, with her lips lightly pursed, no matter how amusing and lively the homes she'd entered this year (or last), *her* castle was the best compared to all. Better even than Hansa's. Not to be smug about it. It was simply true.

She could not wait for her new friends to come see for themselves.

. . .

This year, unlike last year, Amalina did not suffer a sudden bout of shame that she was not a true princess, that she was an imposter at best, or, at worst, a deceiving criminal who might be leading these women into mortal jeopardy. Instead, when the threat rose of a thought that she was not who she pretended to be, it was cut off by the vision of a pair of handsome eyes, and a wall-like chest of brilliant red wool, and a head of lush dark hair, and the feeling of strong arms around her. *Ivanti!* He had recognized her! And she had recognized him! And both had been a thousand miles from home and yet somehow found each other in the sprawl of attendees at the ball. Found each other, *can you believe it!* The idea of fate or destiny didn't enter into Amalina's thoughts. Only a great unquestioned satisfaction that Ivanti Ion Vokent—*Lieutenant* Ivanti Ion Vokent, military adjutant to the renowned general of a renowned regiment of a renowned army—the hometown boy she had once loved with abandon (secretly in her heart), who had never paid much attention to her (or anyway, the sort of attention she had wanted), was suddenly, in the pressing crowds of the French Court, before her; and he regarded her fondly with those beautiful eyes, and with his large, strong hands had taken her up and thrown her into the air, a whoop of elation causing everyone to turn.

Amalina sat up with a small gasp.

"Stop!" she called out the window. "Stop!"

She charged out of the carriage while it was still slowing, trying to catch hold of the handles that would help her onto the rider's bench.

"Ms. Dalca!" cried the man, looking down from the bench. "Where are your clothes?"

She glanced down at herself in dismay. "Oh! … foolish …"

Amalina reappeared on the bench minutes later wearing her old plain Ardeelian dress—which was getting much too small for her, she had to admit. She was still growing and wouldn't be able to fit into it before long.

She sat next to the driver, Genadie, a small rat-like man with long dirty, greasy hair and perpetually dingy, mud splattered, threadbare clothes. He smelled, too, but she'd grown used to it over the years, and now his smell was just familiar. Comforting in the right circumstances. She took the reins from him and hurried the horses on. The overwhelming thoughts of Ivanti trailed off safely behind them.

"What brings you up here?" rasped Genadie in his scratchy voice. He was pleased when she snatched the reins from him, and sat back with a relaxed smile of his own. He crossed his bone-thin legs at the ankles.

"Thought it was time to relieve you," said Amalina. "I don't know how you stay awake, riding almost day and night."

Genadie shrugged and chewed on some millet he kept in a small leather bag on his belt.

"Where are we? How much longer before we get home?" she asked.

"At this rate? It could still be another week. Or more. Depends how bad the roads are. Spring can make a mudpit of the countyside."

"Another week!" Amalina flapped the reins and drove the horses faster.

The road was level and dry. Without the mud which could catch and bog horses (and whatever they were hitched to), and without the deep, dangerous ruts that could break a wheel or an axle or otherwise derail a carriage's progress, she felt safe to push the team, and so she did. Genadie was comfortable with how they tore along and positioned himself to have a nap, turning down the brim of his hat to cover his grimy face. But of course, Amalina understood, she wasn't driving them as fast as Genadie often did. He could sleep very easily at this speed, and so he did.

The faster they sped the more Amalina was forced to pay attention to the horses and their clattering harnesses. The faster they sped the more she had to adjust herself to the shifting of the driver's bench, as the carriage rumbled to-and-fro underneath it. The faster they sped the more she had to mind the road and any obstacles that needed avoiding. The faster they sped the more distractions there were to free her mind from thoughts of intense joy and love and of Lieutenant Vokent. And the faster they sped, the sooner they would arrive at Amalina's castle.

The road angled upward inside a portion of hills, and then wound around the sides of the larger, higher upthrusts of land instead of summiting them. She was driving the horses so fast, and in such a daze, she didn't bother to slow them in the curves, at times bringing the wheels up on one side. It was rousing. Not something to fear. So long as Genadie didn't wake to give her warning, they were safe. As they lurched and angled to the right, nearly dumping him off the side, Genadie could be heard snoring.

The horses and carriage were rocketing so recklessly fast, and Amalina so out of her mind, she almost did not notice, as they ripped around a bend, the fallen tree blocking most of the road. In shock, she flinched. But then she pulled the reins, coming out of her seat to do so, and yelled for the horses to stop. The horses, quicker than Amalina to perceive the impossible impediment, tried to bring everything to a whinnying halt a few feet before impact. The only other option was to dive off the road to the right, and plunge down a steep embankment. She didn't know which it would be. And instead of closing her eyes, she goggled in amazement at what was going to happen.

The carriage stopped short. Amalina couldn't grab hold of a rail, or, in the last moment, nab it with her toe. She launched off the front of the rider's bench. And was saved only by Genadie, whose gnarled and crooked fingers caught her at the waistband and retrieved her.

In the huffing-puffing aftermath, their pounding hearts in their throats, and as the horses, more quickly recovered, tottered their carriage forward at a walking pace, Amalina and Genadie noticed the other carriage. It was down the steep and deep embankment on the right, broken in half, one of its wheels thrown off and away, the others shattered and deformed by the fall.

• • •

"We should see if anyone's down there," said Amalina, still panting. "See if anyone's hurt."

"Nevermind them," said Genadie. Though he too couldn't help but stare down into the wreck of broken wood planks and twisted straps of metal.

"Someone could be hurt."

"They'd be dead with that fall, Ms. Dalca. Look to the horses."

The horses, far down and attached to the front half of the broken shell, were stiff and still and flattened out weirdly against the side of the embankment.

Amalina pulled the reins and brought their carriage to a complete stop. Genadie huffed, but continued to sift through the site with a heavylidded stare. Nobody can pass a place of disaster without pausing; without attempting to process its details; to comprehend it; to envision themselves within it and hope to see an escape for themselves.

"Let's go see," Amalina said. Before Genadie could protest, she'd thrown the reins at him and was jumping off the rider's bench.

"Hello!" she shouted from the edge of the road. She tried in French and also in a German dialect. "Is anyone there?"

There was no answer. She looked for limbs sticking out of the spaces in the shredded carriage. All she could see were boxes and other bits of luggage. Some larger crates had obviously been strapped to the top of the carriage in netting that was now torn, and those crates strewn deeper into the ravine.

Genadie took Amalina's hand and they scudded carefully down along the rocky slope. Amalina calling to anyone who might be inside. Anyone still alive.

She saw a boot—a light tan boot—as she reached the tail end of the carriage. The boot was sticking out from underneath the front half, much further along. The boot was tangled in the straps of the reins, the rest of its owner crushed between the carriage and the rocks.

"Hello! Hello!" she called to it. The boot did not move. "Hurry, Genadie, the driver!"

Genadie didn't hurry, but helped her downward, his lips set grimly straight in his grizzled face, his eyes glinting with dark recognition of the mortality of the situation.

"I think not," said Genadie in a low rasp.

Still they went, and Amalina pushed at the boot with the tip of her toe. It was like touching a dead dog, or a dead deer. It moved and mashed in a fleshy way. But also in an unresponsive, solidly dead way.

"Should we try to get him out?" asked Amalina. "He needs service and burial."

"Others can see to it. We'll alert the authorities at the next station. Still have a long way go, little one."

Looking round towards the back half of the carriage, Amalina noted a large oblong plank that seemed to be a different color from the carriage's wood. A piece from a large box that had once been inside the main compartment. With the stresses of the drop, the box had fallen out and broken apart. There were many, many boxes and cases thrown and toppled and busted and scattered down the slope; bits of all sizes and makes and ages. This carriage had been a transport, then? and not carried passengers?

"What are you doing?" Genadie called, watching her work through the debris but not looking to assist.

"Going to see if anyone's under this mess."

"Don't."

Amalina turned to Genadie, startled by his voice. Though it was weak and almost whispered, it felt as if the words had penetrated her chest. A tear had welled up in the corner of her eye at the sadness of this scene. Genadie's coldness made her indignant.

"I'm going to. Whether you want to help me or not."

"Don't."

Genadie's lips hadn't moved. In fact, at the sound of the voice, his eyes widened in surprise.

"What?" she asked.

"Do not move this board," whispered the voice, from underneath. "Don't even touch it."

• • •

Amalina and Genadie stared at the board. It was long, wide and thick and made of heavy wood, but not polished or finished in any way. Though it must have once been a part of a box by the ravaged nail holes at either end, it looked like it was pressed to the ground and that nothing—no box, no body—could squeeze under. The board would have been the last thing she would have gotten around to lifting, if at all. Because it seemed impossible someone was—or *could*—be there.

"You're under there?" Amalina asked, matching his heavily accented German dialect. "You're alive."

"Yes ... My driver?"

"Dead ..."

"The clumsy idiot."

"Are you injured?"

"I am just fine. Leave me alone."

"But ..." said Amalina. "You're buried."

"I said I am just fine. And I ask that you leave me alone."

"Your voice is very weak." Which was true, despite how deep it penetrated into her body when he whispered. There was nothing like that sensation that she'd ever known, except for ...

Amalina looked to Genadie. His arms were folded and his expression had only become grimmer. What was that look in his eye? Worry? Fear? He was thinking the same thing she was.

"You're …" Amalina began. She did not finish the thought.

The man did not reply.

Amalina went to the board, she began to shift it.

"No!" But it was just a hoarse, whispered gasp than a shout. "Do not!"

"But I need to see."

"See what? Leave me. Leave me!"

She stood there, thinking.

Genadie said in a low voice: "Perhaps, Amalina … "

Amalina leaned over and tried to peer under the edge of the board. She had visions of a man with ghastly white skin and large, dark eyes.

"You don't want me to move the board."

"That's a good girl."

"Because you cannot tolerate the sun," said Amalina, almost like a question.

Silence was her answer.

"Amalina, we should leave the fellow alone if that is what he wishes."

"There are cracks in the board," she said. "It isn't fully sealed at the edges. Does it hurt?"

There was a pause. Then, from below: "I said leave me alone."

"It's not even noon yet, sir." No matter how she turned her head she could not see under the parting of the board. It was difficult to resist the temptation just to throw it aside. "It will be a very long day."

No answer. She might have heard him swallow a very dry swallow. But it might have been some dirt shifting nearby.

"There will be others passing, maybe," she said. "Others who might not hear you. Or might not understand or obey you."

As before, silence.

"Would it help if I buried you a little?"

"Ms. Dalca, come away from there," Genadie warned, sternly.

"What is that?" whispered the man below the board.

"We can bury you a little. Make it look like the board isn't even there. They might not see you, I mean the board … if someone were to come down here. So you won't be disturbed."

Silence.

"Would it hurt you if we did that?"

"It would not."

"Would you be able to breathe?"

"Do it, girl," said the voice, definitely now. "Quick."

Amalina looked up to the top of the ridge. Their carriage was still there, and no other traveler had yet appeared. She then searched for a tool to dig with, pushing and kicking through the debris.

Amalina spotted something. Just in front of her. A book bound in vivid red leather. So much like the red leather-bound book she'd once seen—and read—in the deputy sheriff's office; The Secret History of the Sheriff of Korr. For a second she thought this was it. But of course it couldn't be. That book was locked in the sheriff's office practically on the other side of the world. So what could this be? she wondered. She brought her face close, and saw there was no title.

"What are you doing down there?" Genadie called.

"What are you waiting for?" asked the voice.

Amalina straightened with the guilt of a discovered thief. It's not like she was about to steal the book. Was she? She cleared her throat and patted the dust off her clothes.

She found a short piece of splintered panel and began carving out dirt and transferred it to the board, starting at where she thought his feet were. Genadie ambled closer, then searched around and found a shovel attached to the carriage's rear end. He handed this to her and took her jagged panel to help with the process. By his expression he wasn't pleased to be doing this. But the fear hadn't left, and he would reluctantly help her.

"Good," said the man. "Good."

"Who are you?" Amalina asked as they got near the top of the board. "What's your name?"

"I could ask the same of you."

"But I asked first."

"I've forgotten my name. It matters not. Just finish. You have my gratitude."

• • •

It took some time before Amalina and Genadie discussed what had happened at the broken carriage. Not because Amalina wasn't dying of curiosity (and could barely keep from talking), but Genadie had withdrawn into one of his odd, thoughtful silences and it was best not to disturb him. That evening, when Genadie had run the horses so ragged they'd collapsed, forcing the two to stop for the night, the conversation really got going. It would be some hours for the horses to recover, Genadie made up a campfire and then traded guesses with Amalina as to the identity of the strange man they'd encountered.

However, any mystery about the strange man was settled when he stepped up to the fire. Amalina gasped. Genadie fell off the stone he was sitting on. His crooked hand flew to his belt. To the hilt of his dagger.

The man was broad-shouldered, almost squarely built, with dark skin and dense, tightly curled black hair. Though his features were thick and somewhat stunted, he was handsome in a roguish way. He wore a white, blousy shirt, with a gaily patterned vest above that. His pants were a strange yellow and fed into high boots. He looked like a gypsy.

"Who are you," he said, his voice much deeper and more powerful than earlier, but with the same peculiarities and accent. This was he. "What is your name?"

The strange man's eyes roved from Genadie to Amalina, an amused smile playing on his lips.

"Amalina, sir," said Amalina, recognizing already she was in the presence of a very familiar creature. Not a real *human* man, but something else. "And what is yours?"

"Him," the man pointed.

Amalina identified Genadie by name. Genadie wiped his hand across his mouth, looking uneasy.

The man smiled. Even in the campfire's uneven light she could see the long, sharp teeth.

"You know me," he said.

"No."

"You are familiar with me? You've heard of me?"

Amalina shook her head. "Would you like something to eat or drink?"

Genadie made a face but she already regretted making the offer.

"How did you know what to do?"

"You are Strigoi," she said.

"What's that?"

"Strigoi. You are a Strigoi?"

The man shook his head and sat down on the rock Genadie had vacated. Genadie scooted back nervously, not taking his eyes off him.

"I haven't heard that word in a while. You're from the east?"

Amalina nodded.

He smiled again. The sharpness of the teeth seemed more pronounced at this close range. And the look in his eyes said danger.

"There is no such thing as what you mentioned," said the man. "Those are legends. Folk tales."

Amalina made a face.

"But you know something," said the man. "Something about me. That is why you knew what to do."

She nodded.

"Both of you," he said, as if this particular facet, that they both knew, was remarkable. "Both … But you two don't know me well enough. Or else you wouldn't have done what you did and turned your backs to me. You would have taken away the board and let me perish before your eyes."

"Oh, no," said Amalina. "We wouldn't do that."

"My first thought, Amalina," he said, "Was when night came, and I was free, I would hunt you down and kill you."

The way he said it was so straightforward, as if relating a friendly story, that the threat didn't make a full impact.

"I could never allow someone to live who knew who—knew *what* and *where*—I am." He looked from the fire to Amalina, his eye wandering up and down her whole figure, and then stared so fixedly into her eyes it felt like his gaze pierced right through her head. "And it would also be quite amusing to reward my saviors with a cruel betrayal."

He laughed at the thought. It was a high, bright laugh. It made Amalina shiver.

"But then I thought to myself: How is it they know me, and yet I have never met them? How is it they could know me and not only allow me to live, but they would—the both of them—help me do so? And not ask for a favor in return (which would have made it understandable, if also predictable)? Who *are* these people? I must know. I should not kill them but ask them some questions."

"We told you our names," said Genadie, his hand still on the hilt of his knife.

"Your clothes," said the man, looking at him. "And that carriage … rather old. Sir, you are from … ?"

Amalina and Genadie said nothing. She looked to the carriage to see what about it stood out, what informed him. But she returned her eyes to him, before he could attack. If that's what he was winding up to do.

"Yes, you're from the land beyond the forest; cradled within the mountains," he said, growing every more interested, smiling cleverly. "What is it? A land of many names. You know, I remember when some people still called it *Ultra Sylvanum*. Oh, I know it well.

"You're from Ardeel," said the man, now using Amalina's native language. He didn't have so much an accent anymore. He sounded just like one of the gypsies Genadie would hire from time to time, the ones that would also, from time to time, roam through her own village. "You're from Ardeel. You are servants to someone such as I am, I think. Tell me, what does he call himself?"

Genadie shook his head lightly to Amalina, asking her—begging her—to say nothing. But when the man swung his look to Genadie, Genadie said: "We are not."

"You are. Tell me the name. But I would not know it, would I? Describe his appearance to me, so that I can form a picture in my mind."

"But it is useless," Genadie's voice scratched confidently. "First, sir, we are not from Ardeel, sir. And we do not serve someone like you. We've heard stories, of course, sir. Our people are superstitious. But, I assure you, sir, we don't know anyone like you. No, sir."

"I don't believe you. No, it couldn't be true. You serve someone … someone *else*. It is the only explanation. You are being cautious. Perhaps he—or is it a she? Well, you've been trained well. And you obey. Both of you. It *is* both of you, acting in concert."

Amalina and Genadie were silent. They would not commit themselves either way. Amalina felt a blush and a sweat she hoped the darkness hid and the heat of the campfire explained. If only he would leave, she could start shaking.

"Strigoi," he muttered darkly, and shook his head. "An echo from the east. And then this fails to explain why you would help me."

"We'd help any traveler in trouble," said Amalina, clasping her hands and trying to look innocent. "That is our way."

"You are such good and benevolent people you would help me? Even if I was one of those non-existent things you've accused me of being?"

"We did help you, sir. Didn't we?"

This man suddenly roared with laughter.

"If this were true, and you were that decent and virtuous, I would be forced to kill you. Out of principle."

Amalina said nothing. She couldn't move her mouth to speak. She couldn't even look over to Genadie to see how he was taking it.

"This is interesting." The man stood up. "I need strength after what I've been through, but you two I will not harm. No. I thank you for your kindness. Though I would warn you away from kindnesses to strangers in the future."

"I told you so," said Genadie, after the man left and Amalina began to shake. "And why did you tell him our names?"

She answered with her own question: "Why didn't we remove the board?"

• • •

"You may not believe what I told you," said the strange man the next night, as he appeared before Amalina and Genadie as they stood outside an inn. "Anyone can lie these days."

Amalina and Genadie gawped. Genadie had driven the horses so hard for the rest of the previous night and the whole day onto sundown—killing one whole team of horses and having to summon a new batch (using a strange little flute he wore around his neck)—had rode so many hard miles that they could not believe this man was now here before them again. Somehow he had tracked their path and over such a long distance. It seemed impossible, even if he possessed the full powers of Count Tepsji, their master.

"But this isn't the place to talk," said the man. "Let's go inside. You look very tired. You can fortify yourselves with food and drink."

"What do you want to talk about ... with us?" asked Amalina, genuinely curious even in this strange man's presence. She took her mind off him enough to eat a piece of roasted chicken, which the man paid for with odd looking coins. Genadie restricted himself to nibbling nervous handfuls of his millet.

The man smiled broadly.

"What I am is what your master is."

"Master … " Amalina choked as she moved to protest.

"Which is to say, we are what our creator is." And at this statement, Genadie grumbled. But the man didn't seem to notice and continued his own thought. "Or what he was. This was a long time ago, and I haven't seen him in centuries. He could be dead. Or, like your master, in hiding."

Genadie swung his head to look at the far side of the room, his jaw flexing rapidly as he ground the grains between his teeth. The man paused, noting the action.

"You will be interested to read this." The man took a long, flat book from behind him, as if by magic, and set it onto the table. It looked rather plain, though it was bound in red leather. It was the book Amalina had seen in the debris of the crash. The one she had been tempted to pick up, to take. Now here it was before her, being pushed at her. "You can read, can't you?"

"Very much so," said Amalina. Then on a second thought. "What language?"

He opened it to the first page. It wasn't printed but handwritten. The letters were roughly laid down, like the lettering of a literate laborer. But the words were legible enough. And the writing seemed educated. It was in the native Ardeelian language.

"Can you read it?"

"Yes, of course," said Amalina.

Genadie flashed a curious glance over to the page, then nodded resentfully. This action the dark man marked with his eyes, as well, before continuing on.

"In here you will find everything you need to know about me. That you think I am a strigoi reveals how little your master has admitted of him- or herself to you. Now you will know your master and I are indeed in body the same, no different in our manner of existence. Just as I assured you last night, but you chose not to believe. And you—the both of you—by reading this book, will know *what* we really are."

"Who wrote this book?"

"Me."

· · ·

"Read it," Amalina insisted as she handed the book to Genadie.

"An encyclopedia of lies," he said, batting it away.

"What's to lie about? It's his history. From a harmless child to the victim of a monster. A monster that has killed many people—just as our Count has.

He says what he's learned, and what he truly is, Genadie. He *is* just like the Count—" Genadie almost snarled at this, but left it as an unpleasant uptick of his left nostril "—and the Count is like him. If you ever hoped to understand him."

"Don't get any ideas of understanding our Master. Master is master of all, and can be anything he wishes. What he wants you to understand of him he will reveal to you."

"Well," said Amalina. "Maybe this book is the way he's revealing himself to us."

A cracking sound came from within Genadie's closed mouth. She assumed it was him chomping a loose grain and not one of his teeth.

"You were supposed to be sleeping not reading," scolded Genadie.

"How could I help but read it? It has answers."

"Are you going to be able to stay awake?"

"I won't be able to close my eyes until we've reached the castle. That man may have given us this book—a generous thing to do—but knowing what he is, I don't care to be caught off guard."

"Smart girl."

"Read it," said Amalina, putting the book on the seat inside the carriage compartment after Genadie climbed in. "Just give it a try. So I can have someone to talk to about it. I can't stand thinking I'm the only one who knows."

Genadie made a face. "It's getting late. We've stopped for too long. Go, before I climb up there myself."

"Do you think the horses will last?"

"Should get them through the morning, anyway."

Amalina climbed up on the riding board and with a shout and snap of the whip drove the horses. Genadie had the ability to motivate a whole pack of horses to speeds she could not comprehend, which left them spent and dying. Amalina could only get them to a decent gallop, a speed she felt less comfortable using at night where her vision was limited. She pushed them a little harder now, though, trusting the horses would keep them on the road in their own self interest.

They had to keep moving. Both Amalina and Genadie had agreed. The way the man would appear every night, wherever they set camp or stopped at an inn, had set their nerves on edge. It seemed at each encounter the man was warming to them, for what purpose they couldn't fathom. And it seemed just as easy he could, at the turn of a thought, kill them both. He'd already said they knew too much about him. And now he had provided them a book that explained his every mystery.

There was also the unspoken fear he was following them, and he would continue to do so all the way back to Ardeel—and to the high castle.

Amalina didn't remember if she or Genadie had originated the idea, but in some whispered conversation they'd decided to push on fast, and never for a moment stop. Only to get fresh horses, or to trade positions, would they ever let the carriage rest. This man could not surprise them with another visit if they were always in motion. They could only pray—Amalina to Heaven, Genadie to his Master (who he believed to be the worldly incarnation of Zeus, father of the Greek Pantheon)—that no wheels or axles broke.

They'd rode so long and so fast, that the few minutes they paused in their flight, the lack of jumbling and rocking to and fro felt unnatural to Amalina. She was only satisfied once they were back under way.

Amalina snapped the whip and pulled the blanket over her shoulders to keep herself warm. The lamps on either side of the carriage did not carve out much of a view. She fixed her gaze on the passing greyish dirt rather than peer into the black ahead. Anything could emerge from the darkness, and her imagination (supplemented by folk stories, and more concrete examples of mystical and monstrous horrors detailed in books she'd read in the castle) drew their leering, gibbering and writhing likenesses in the air where the lamplight failed to show her something more natural.

"You best take care," said the strange man in a soft voice. "There is a sharp curve some miles ahead. Many carriages have been lost there even in the daytime."

Amalina swallowed hard and tried not to scream. Though she stared straight ahead—glancing only once at the strange man's orange velvet knee to make certain he was now there on the bench beside her—she felt her eyes were popping out of her head.

"Thank you, sir," she choked.

"Ten more minutes I think," he said, keeping his voice low.

"Thank you, sir," she returned again, softer. But why? She should say it loud. Very loud, so Genadie would hear. That was the whole point of placing one of them on the riding bench and the other inside the carriage. If the man somehow caught up to them and attempted to kill them while in full flight, one or the other, not being in the same location, might stand a chance of escaping, or make ready for defense. That strategy would only work if both knew when the man was in or on the carriage.

The strange man seemed to know this by speaking in a hushed, confidential way to Amalina, reserving this conversation for them alone. Genadie was not to be disturbed. But maybe he had another reason to keep it private.

Sound the alarm, she thought; but didn't.

"You are father and daughter?"

"What? Who?"

"The man you are with: he is your father."

"Not at all," said Amalina, wrinkling her nose. "Not even."

"That sounds absolute. Where *is* your father?"

"I don't know anymore, sir. I left home, you see."

"Where is your home?"

"A farm, sir. Nowhere special."

"You left home and then you took to your master."

"We have a master, sir, it's true. But not what you mean. He is nothing like you. He is just a normal man. One of us. Though, I mean, nothing like *us*: he is of a good rank and very wealthy. Heaven has favored him."

"I see. Where is that again?"

She gave him the name of the city Genadie had told her to say.

"Oh, yes. And this man you are riding with: he is what to you?"

"A friend. Well, not even that. Just another servant for the Count."

"Count," the man murmured, savoring his first taste of information. "What is his name?"

"Graja Volescu." A name she'd heard somewhere and sounded important. She'd have to tell Genadie later, just in case he was interrogated.

The man shook his head. "Never heard of him. Tell me what he looks like, so I can get an image of him."

"But, as I said: he's just a man. Nothing like you. Nothing like in your book."

"You've read it?" said the man, sounding amused, but still low enough not to alert Genadie to his presence. "You know who I am."

"Just a little," she whispered back.

"Do you believe what you've read?"

"Shouldn't I?"

"Some people would think it is too fantastic. People who, as they say, have never in their life encountered someone such as myself."

"Too fantastic? As fantastic as someone boarding a speeding carriage in the middle of the night?"

The man nodded and smiled again. She was now able to look at the lower half of his face. That was enough. The teeth. She vowed not to look into his eyes.

"The turn is coming soon," he cautioned lightly. "Do take care."

"Why have you come, sir?"

"Because I have trusted you—the both of you—with my book. But, to think of it, there was no saying either would read it. Or that you would believe what you have read. And so, realizing my mistake in being so forward, I have come to give you another gift." His voice became serious. "But this one is for you alone, and you should reveal it to no one. Not your master nor your friend in the carriage. Do you understand?"

"I think so."

"Do you understand, little girl?"

"Yes, sir."

The man held out his gloved hand. In his palm was a short, moderately thick stick with unevenly knobbed ends. On a second look, even in the dim light of the lanterns, it looked something like the cleaned thigh bone of a duck.

"What is it, sir?"

"My gift to you," he said. "Take it and keep it yours. And believe that I shall know if you betray my trust should you reveal it to anyone. Your friend. Anyone. Even your master. Especially your master."

"The Count," said Amalina.

"Whatever he chooses to call himself. This relative of mine, so to speak. Because I know it is so. Do not protest. You are only honoring your fealty to him by trying to conceal the truth. But you've already revealed it to me. And you've proved, so I think, that he was not as honest a fellow as I am. He hasn't exposed himself to you in his entirety the way I am willing to. I have put in your hands my complete story, haven't I? Withholding nothing. And now I trust to your possession—and protection—this precious gift. *Only for you, little girl.* That is my rule. Even *he*, the master you serve, is not to be trusted with this item. If you do reveal it to him, I will know, and it will lose all its *power.*"

"Power?" she asked.

He touched his forefinger to his lips, reminding her to keep her voice low.

"Your master is very powerful. Believe what I am telling you. But he can't control what is out of his reckoning. As you know, our senses are very keen. We can see, smell, hear, and feel for miles. But with this," he held the stick out so that she could take if from him, "you disappear. All you have to do is hold it lengthwise between your teeth, and you become invisible. Nobody on earth, not any creature, not even *he* can detect you. And you may do anything you wish. And should you wish to know anything about him, to verify what he is—what I said he is, and all I say he can do, and what created him and what can destroy him—that you can gain the full measure of what he is without him knowing you have done so, then you have the token with which to accomplish such a thing."

She clamped the stick between her teeth. It tasted like an old, dusty chicken bone. She felt nothing.

The man's eyes widened, but he continued to stare at her.

She'd looked to his eyes!

"It won't work on me, of course," he said slowly, his eyes roaming over her body. "I am the one who worked the magic and gave you the object. But try it carefully on others, and you will see I have given you a very powerful gift indeed. Something people would kill to possess. So tell no one, and guard it as if your life depends on it. Because it does."

Amalina took it out of her mouth, and fiddled it close to her eyes.

"What is it, exactly?"

"The bone of a boiled-down black cat. Who knows why that animal is the most effective in creating this device, but who knows why *anything*?

Things are as they are. Read the whole book, you will understand soon enough. Just remember who gave it to you."

Before he left he asked, almost shyly: "And ... are there more of you?"

"Who?"

"Servants. For your master. Or is it just you two?"

"A whole house full. He has an army."

The man's eyes went very, very wide.

· · ·

Amalina did not tell Genadie about the magical item, but in the morning, at a waystation near a dark forest, she did mention the strange man had come to her in the night, even with the wagon at full speed. Genadie nodded but seemed distracted. He held onto the man's book with a tight grip, his knuckles white, and his nervous eye twitching and blinking. He'd read it. At least some of it. And he hadn't liked what he'd learned; about the creature this man was; and that the Count—his beloved master—might be the same sort of being. No matter how powerful these creatures are, just the thought that there were more of them, even *one* more of them, besides his master, meant that his master was not unique. Just another creation.

Genadie tried to dispose of this problem with an offhand comment: "Whatever Master chooses to be, it is his wish. Just as anything else he chooses to do, or what actions to take, it is beyond our reasoning. But why not, if he should descend from the heavens, select the body of a creature most powerful?"

"But what are we going to do about this stranger?" asked Amalina, trying to get Genadie back on track. "He has followed us halfway across Europe. Who knows when he will decide he wants to kill us, or worse? Or what if he follows us all the way back to the castle? What then?"

"I don't know how he tracks us, but we will do our best to lose him," said Genadie. "I will hire a team of men to drive this carriage on the southern highway. Keep it moving on, day and night, all the way to Istanbul. We will hire a new carriage of our own, with normal horses from the common market. They may be slower and need to be changed out frequently, but we will be shed of everything of our Master's, besides our own bodies and personal possessions."

"Will it work?"

"We'll know tonight, won't we, Ms. Dalca?" His words were confident, but his expression hadn't altered from its sour cast.

"How much of the book did you read?" asked Amalina.

He didn't answer. He hurried away to get their daylight's business accomplished so they could set off immediately.

Amalina had plenty of time to try out her magic gift—or to get rid of it—but she kept it in her pocket and pretended it wasn't there, and concentrated on prayers to lose the man.

After two days and nights and still the incessant stranger had not bothered them again, they were confident they'd gotten rid of him.

2

A Ready Force

"I'll tell you what, *former* low constable Attila Bronk, if you want an army, a proper army, you'll need firearms and cannons. And as you know, I'm the only commander in the south who has those things in ready supply. And since there isn't a proper governor seated in Tsobl who can tell me to use them on you rabble, if Hak Vogoneyevic, your proposed champion, can present to me a ready force … well, they may call it treason up in Tsobl, but you talk a good game, Bronk, and I'll let you have them. Have it all: pistols, muskets, cannons. As long as you can present said ready force."

Attila's moods were impossible to read. His outward temperament was lead; his eyelids always sitting at half-mast over his irises, as if he were drowsy or bored. An artful construction on his part, because he was rarely drowsy, and with his perculating mind never bored. But because his lids were lowered, and his eyebrows staunchly set as a straight black fur on top, and his lips forever untroubled in any direction, nobody could tell how happy he had grown over the last few months, unless they noted how much faster he moved in recent days, or the frequency his right hand snuck to the left arm to steady its nervous jitter—even when he had fulfilled, as he did now, his greatest wishes and ambitions: *A load-out of advanced weapons!* And for the ambient quality of Attila's facial *inexpression*, nobody could detect how unhappy he would become just a couple minutes later. And it was an incredible depth of unhappiness, sunk by a force of misery so profound it plunked him from highest peak of ecstasy to limitless abyss in the space of ten seconds. His face remained the same.

One minute earlier: he was drinking from a goblet, tasting a truly excellent wine the innkeeper provided him, though he kept reminding the innkeeper water was all he wanted. The wine heartened him, and the sight of Hak Vogoneyevic's followers crowding into the inn's public room fortified his spirits. The faces around him were smiling and upbeat, a small flame of their own ambition lighting their eyes. And then came the general of the south western army promising to add to the fortunes of Hak's forces. A supply of the most needed equipment for an assault.

But half a minute later, an old man with white hair—slicked back at the side of his head—stepped forward; eyes flameless; his mouth drawn into something stern. Attila noted his mouth, and without anything else to go by assumed the old man was someone Attila hadn't encountered in a while: A challenger.

"I suppose you're that Bronk fella," said the man, ignoring the southern general and the general bouyant mood of the crowd.

"Attila Bronk," he nodded.

"Gone east to get the eastern boys shaking their pitchforks, eh?"

"Former low constable of Tsobl," Attila informed the man. "I am no mob-enciter, but a man of the law—"

"*Formerly.*"

"Still am," countered Attila, looking bored, though feeling the exhaltation of renewed challenge, and no irritation at being called 'former' twice by two seperate people in less than two minutes. A new heart to be snared, he was thinking, a new mind to be enthralled. If a southern general's heart can be won, and apparently it had, whose could not? "I've only relocated my office, sir. I am the representative of Sir Hak Vogoneyevic."

"Right," said the old man, rounding the final moment of Attila's complacence. "You need to talk to him."

Something bad had happened.

The old man's tone was damning. Attila read him for signs again, and from the old man's assured stance and his bitter, disappointed-father-like stare, he knew something *very* bad had happened. Most assuredly.

His emotions plummeted like a shot goose, making him feel queasy, immediately exhausted. To anyone in the room watching him intently, he hadn't even blinked.

But he left the inn soon enough, leaving the pleasing goblet of wine unfinished.

. . .

"You won't be kind enough to elaborate on your statement?" Attila asked the old man, in one form or another, for the tenth time. "It will be another night before we arrive at Jolescu. I should be prepared for whatever situation I might find there.

The old man acted as if he hadn't heard, keeping his horse a full length ahead. As if he might want people to think it was a coincidence they were riding on the same road so close together; no association between them. He hadn't yet given his name.

By observation—by his clothes, by the color of the dried mud on them and the straw caught in it—he was a farmer from outside of Jolescu. Attila would have assumed the old man was considered useless, an errand-runner or landowner's idiot, but the clothes were fresh (so to speak), and he carried himself with an inborn dignity, and held a confidence and wisdom that radiated out of his eyes. His voice, so solid and judgemental, announced he was a man with a mind; driven by personal concern and a deep obligation to some principle to ride for days to deliver this message.

"If you love Sir Vogoneyevic," said Attila. "You help him by aiding me."

No answer. Did he shrug his shoulder? Or had a fly bit him on the neck?

"I assure you," Attila persisted. Then, feeling a slight desperation: "There was *some* reason you came to me."

"I was told you were a man of few words," said the old man over his shoulder. "That you were iron-nerved. My stupid son-in-law chatters less like a trapped squirrel than you."

"However, you told me I need to talk with the nobleman I serve, sir. But you didn't say what I need to tell him, or what we are to speak about. This naturally leads to questions."

"Do you hear the sea?"

"What is that?"

"I said, Bronk: Can you hear the sea?"

Attila knew he could not. The nearest and largest body of water was a lake miles away and separated by mountains. Even the river wasn't close enough. Still, he cocked his ear to the air to humor the old man. "No. Or did you mean the river?"

"Can you hear the river?" the old man returned irritably.

"Well, no."

"Have you ever been to the sea? Seen it?"

"I don't think so. I've no recollection. Have you?"

"The sea can lift waves as tall as a mountain, and reach out of its home and swallow villages."

"Comforting that we are in the mountains, then."

"*Yes*," said the old man. He hammered that word hard. Then, with a leathery creak, he turned in his saddle to glance at Attila. The eyes were judging again. Disdainful. "Yes it is comforting. And how disagreeable it would be for me to rage through these mountains, crying of an impending typhoon somewhere. Terrifying the women and children and driving the men into a frenzy of anger, when nothing can be done about a tidal wave. In truth, the awesome wave will never strike up here in the mountains, but at the shores of the sea. Where we are not, you see."

"You feel I'm raging in the mountains against the sea?"

"You've done worse than that. You've not only troubled the people, but you've set the men, convinced them, to ride *down* to the sea. And, in fact, you've asked the sea to rise to meet them. A two-man catastrophe you are."

"I understand," said Attila with a nod, his bored eyes looking off to the horizon in a sarcastic gesture lost on the old man's back. "You want me to talk to Sir Vogoneyevic so I can remove him from Jolescu and let your people be—"

"Too late," the old man snapped bitterly. "Our fair mountains are no longer the sanctuary they were."

"Then what?"
The old man rode on.

Return to the High Castle

Turning off the mountain highway and entering the village of Netz, Amalina stared down from the driver's box to the iron cage, which hung off a pole at the top of Netz's main street. The cage had once held the rotting corpse of a revolutionary. Later it was stuffed full with flowers. Flowers beloved by the high castle's first visiting foreign princess. The cage was empty now and swung vaguely on a breeze. Next to it was a square wood sign which read, to the point: Netz.

"We aren't stopping are we?" asked Amalina, not wanting to.

Genadie, who'd kept quiet after their encounter with the strange man, agreed. "I should think not."

"The horses *are* tired," Amalina pointed out, because she felt obligated. Foam had built up all over the harness-team's shoulders and rumps. Their breaths were heavy. If these horses had been the weird specimens Genadie summoned from the wild with his little flute he wore around his neck, their exhaustion would not be much of a consideration. Though they'd still draw unfavorable interest from the citizens of Netz, who would recognize unbridled cruelty as the wheezing, shivering team, reduced to hide and bone tromped gloomily by. Still, those weird horses would get them to their destination, without question. But this team of horses had been purchased on the regular market: they were less hearty and they could fail at any moment. If they didn't take care—if the horses should collapse—it could be another day or more before the castle was reached. Amalina and Genadie wanted to make it to the castle before sundown.

Though the strange man had been lost hundreds of miles back—lost most certain now—Amalina and Genadie, with yet another nervous night's ride behind them, and the morning's sun breaking over the mountainside, shared a feeling they'd still be safer inside the High Castle, under their master's protection, than out in the world on their own. To stop early would tempt fate. And it was easy to imagine the stranger bowing to them once again when night fell; he asking where their master lived.

Discounting the cage at the highway turnoff, Netz had not changed since Amalina had last seen it. As the people's heads turned to stare, she recognized many of the faces and remembered their names. She lifted her hand in a tentative wave, unsure if it was proper. Her wave was met with mystified looks, or squinted eyes as if the object was trying to identify the subject and coming up short. After a time the carriage rattled out of the village.

Beyond Netz was the long, gently undulating stretch of plain with farmhouses dabbed here and there. In the distance the plain doglegged around the upthrust shoulder of a small mountain. The small mountain shielded the much further off, much higher placed castle of Count Tepsji; the high castle; his Palace of Pleasures. The shielding mountain's base was covered in a forest that resembled a dense green carpet which had wrapped itself comfortably there and gone to sleep.

Amalina took a breath. The spring air was still so crisp and light. It hadn't yet thickened into the valley's summery soup you had to chew through to get a breath. She was glad she hadn't missed this better part of one of her favorite seasons even though the year was so far advanced.

The fang-like mountains had already reminded Amalina that she was nearing home, which had sent a confusing signal of warmth and trepidation down into her body and limbs. She knew the approaching landmarks would remind her of all the things that had come before. But even knowing so, at the sight of a certain farmhouse and its outer buildings—now burnt into a sad heap—she remembered Kralov and his men, who'd used the place as a base of operations before heading up the road to confront the Count, carrying in their cart the secret weapon which might have destroyed him.

Rounding the shoulder of the mountain, she recalled her desperate charge over it atop her horse, White Snow, which had died in the race to the castle, the victim of a vicious pack of wolves led by a great black wolf. The last she'd seen of the horse, it was crying out as blood flew from its flanks, the pack tearing into its body with abandon. The red of its blood matching and complementing the vivid red/orange of the encompassing autumn leaf background. And she'd barely escaped the same fate, having lucked into an escape route, then smashing down the pack leader's massive black head. Hopefully for the second and last time. Her shudder at the dark mortal memory was fast replaced by the same elation she'd felt when she'd finally made her way out of the forest, safe and still alive. Because she *was* still alive. Fighting the next fight.

All these stirred feelings fell away when the mountain passed behind her and the road extended out like a thin thread which then climbed the steep rise to the high castle. The high castle. The castle stood near the summit, in all its cold majesty. And now came the flood of excitement that had visited her once before, the time she'd returned from her first European excursion.

Amalina's castle!

Well, it was Count Tepsji's castle. But since the western princesses (and their families) were led to believe a lady princess—named Katarina Tepsji, the Count's niece—lived there with him, and since Katarina was really Amalina, by a trick of logic the castle became hers.

Amalina sighed.

Genadie felt the same rush of homecoming and urged the horses on, his narrow eyes glinted and his grizzled chin worked back and forth, trying to hold back a smile.

As before, Amalina now thought of all the plans she had for the castle. How to build and improve it. This was why her castle was superior to all the other ones she'd seen and visited: She could take whatever bright fashion she liked from those she'd visited and add it to hers, and even expand from there, and polish things with an Ardeelian touch just to make it convincing that the place had always been that way. It would become glorious.

The only drawback to her plans were the castle's two main servants: Georg, the chief of the household, and Abraxa, head maid. An impossible man and an awful woman; husband and wife. Twin terrors who jealously sought the Count's approval and attention. And who loathed Genadie and Amalina as rivals, because Genadie and Amalina had resided in the castle and served Count Tepsji long before them. Fitting like spoons in their envy, hatred, and contempt for Genadie and Amalina, those terrible two heaped derision on their perceived adversaries in the presence of the Count whenever they could. They were as one, as well, in their fawning obsequiousness before his feet. They almost outdid Genadie in that last aspect.

And remember, she thought with a brief frown, Georg's extended family were also in the castle now, gumming up the courtyard, and halls, and hallways. Incomptetent as servants but serving well enough as Georg's unquestioning loyalists.

It was disappointing to consider, but the Georgs were a necessary feature, and only lightly tarnished Amalina's excitement. Fortunately for her it was as easy to dismiss them and all their headaches as it was to overlook the Count's own monstrous habits. And even ignore the sinister secret of the castle itself. It was easy to turn a blind eye to the blemishes of what now felt like home to her, especially when concentrating on her ambitions for it.

As if to demonstrate Genadie's thoughts were running along the same lines of hampered anticipation, his thin lips twitched a couple times disagreeably, and the light in his eye receded and he suddenly looked wary.

"I think we can keep them under control this time," said Amalina, with an optimistic lilt.

"Who is that?"

"The prickly pair," she answered. "Georg and Abraxa."

"Ah," he said. "They won't keep me out of my room as they did before. I swear I won't let them do it."

"You deserve to be inside."

"Master gave me my room before they ever even *knew* of the high castle." The room he was referring to was a small ground floor closet, which had been a perceived promotion from his hovel, a repurposed smithing shack outside the main building but within the inner courtyard. My, how he'd cherished the day he was allowed to rest his head inside the main building with his master, even if it was only to get inside a closet.

Georg and Abraxa had cruelly banished him back to the hovel when they came to work for the Count, for no apparent reason other than to remind him of his lowly station. "Well, we've done well for Master—" Genadie gulped nervously here "—and they can't deny me my, as you say, Ms. Dalca, *deserved* place."

"We'll work together, you and I. And we'll keep them under control."

He made a face, as if remembering something. "But what about the rest?"

"As long as Georg minds us his relatives will be nothing to worry about."

"I wasn't speaking of Georg's people. I meant *them.*"

Genadie pointed to the castle, like she should see something there. Amalina squinted but couldn't tell what it might be.

"Can't you see them?"

"I don't … " she shook her head.

Something flashed along the top of the castle's wall. A reflection off two small figures.

Soldiers.

Oh, yes, she thought: The army. She'd forgotten about them just now. Who was it who'd come with them? Some mad looking general that the Count had knighted into his service. Their sworn duty was to protect the Count's body and the castle itself. They had rode in during Commander Kralov's assault and had thwarted the hoped-for overthrow and execution of Count Tepsji. Besides Abraxa, Georg, and Georg's family, there was now a sizeable army housed in the stone walls of the high castle. It was certainly beginning to give off the air of a *genuine* castle. So much different than the once abandoned hulk she'd lived in that long, lonely first winter, with only the Count and Genadie as companions.

Also different now was the castle's surrounding wall. All the damage to it from Kralov's explosives had been repaired. And the two large, solid doors which had been shattered to splinters had been replaced by fresh treated lumber, studded and ornamented with spikes of metal to make it look dangerous and foreboding.

The soldiers on the parapet called down for identification. All the letters of introduction and state papers, which could have proved who Genadie and Amalina were (and where they were from), Genadie had destroyed to protect their true identity against that strange man—should the strange man have killed them and then poked around for clues in their belongings. They didn't even have the old carriage that might speak of Tepsji's property. They were without identification.

Did they have the password? snapped the soldiers in annoyance.

Amalina and Genadie glanced at each other. Then they shrugged.

"Go fetch Georg," said Genadie reluctantly, in a bitter tone. "He'll tell you who we are."

"Who?" said one of the soldiers.

"Georg! Georg! Or that wife of his, Abraxa. Or if you dare to wake our Master, ask our Master Lord Tepsji, and see if he doesn't recognize the names Genadie, or Amalina—"

"—Mouse," Amalina interrupted. "He calls me Mouse, mostly."

"Or, easy enough, *metal heads*," snarled Genadie impatiently to the soldiers with the shiny helmets. "You can simply open the doors for Princess Tepsji. If you really don't recognize her, you had better learn who she is quick."

They took none of Genadie's suggestions. One went away and then reappeared with their general. *The General.* What was his name? He was a giant of an old man. He had a block chin and thick, wild, wavy hair of someone a quarter of his age. He grimaced down at them, blinked once, turned and left.

The doors opened. The men with the shiny breastplates and helmets, with shiny weapons at the ready, stared cautiously at the carriage entering. Amalina spotted at least twenty soldiers of war, decked with armor and uniform colors, spread out at different posts and stations around the courtyard, and out-buildings, and main building. And along the parapet of course.

Despite the soldiers' hardened, glowering looks, when the doors shut and the thick bolts thrown into place, Amalina felt much safer than she had in days. Because these men, even if they didn't know it yet, were there to protect her.

All the same, as the carriage slowed near the main building, the soldiers closed on it in a tightening circle; swords drawn, spears lowered. The tips of the spears reached out as if to tickle Amalina and Genadie, or skewer anything inside the carriage's main compartment. Genadie growled his objection.

"Where's the princess?" one of them barked.

Genadie pointed to Amalina.

"Come down from there."

When they did so, one of the soldiers steered them to the side of the main building; against the wall, not through the front doors, swords and spearpoints encouraging their participation. At the stone wall, the commanding soldier said:

"On your knees."

"What?" started Genadie. He was answered by two spears rushing to his breast. He took a step back to avoid them and struck the wall. His nervous eye ticked several times quickly.

"Your knees. Now."

Amalina knelt, her knees feeling the hard stone. It was uncomfortable. Genadie joined her there.

"Head to the ground, arms out."

"What?" exclaimed Amalina.

But then they obeyed. Genuflecting first to the hovering weapons, then spreading out prone. The grey stone was cold against the tip of Amalina's nose. Her breath came back at her, trapped between her face and the ground.

"Why are we doing this?" asked Amalina in a decidedly neutral voice.

"Stay down."

She understood what the soldiers were up to when she heard the carriage door open and then came the sounds of luggage being handled. They were inspecting for assassins and powder kegs.

"Princess?" asked a voice above them. "Why were you riding on the bench with this animal?"

"Call the Master here," said Genadie. "Bring out Georg and Abraxa. I assure you, we will be vouched for."

"Bring your general back out," said Amalina. "He'll recognize us if he sees us again. Up close. He must remember us, though we only met in passing."

"Never mind *him*," countered Genadie. "Call *the Master*. Call Master!"

There was no answer. The position became uncomfortable and difficult to bear. Amalina felt her body shaking. The sun became a summer's sun and she began to sweat on her back and chill on her front. It might have only been minutes, then twenty minutes. The inspection was already done. The soldiers milled about, mumbling between each other. It felt like hours.

Someone stepped between Amalina and Genadie. Heavy feet ground the thin grit beside their heads. Then waited there. She heard heavy breaths.

"Metal heads?" said the deep voice. She recognized the voice as the one she'd heard before leaving for her European tour. The rumble of the old, fanatical General. *What was his name?* He continued: "Disrespectful. Are you comfortable down there?"

"No," answered Amalina. Her voice was dry and faint. Not as forceful as she'd hoped.

"You're not a real princess. You're no *true* relation to his eminence."

"It's my role when traveling, or at home when foreigners are visiting."

"Your *role*, of course. But you are not a *real* princess."

"No."

"We haven't had one of those in Ardeel in nearly half a century. I can remember the last one. You can't, I wouldn't think."

"No."

"They don't ride on top of carriages, or wear common dresses."

Amalina didn't know how to answer that, so she said: "But it is my role, assigned by your master."

There was a long silence as she listened to him breath.

"Metal heads," the general said again in disgust.

. . .

The last time Amalina had been in the high castle's entrance hall (*l'entrée grande* as it was known) at its highest glory, not only had it been overstuffed with flowers to gratify the floral passion of the Count's first official princess from the western kingdom, Lisbet Spaarvierlet, and had sported a long central table dripping at its sides and corners with a massive, perpetual buffet, so that the Count's guests could, at their whim, descend from their rooms—even in the middle of the night—and gorge on the overly-indulgent cornucopia of the Count's kitchens, but the hall had been packed with Georg's extended family; tripping over themselves in their services, or over their children playing games under their feet.

No more.

When Amalina and Genadie—Genadie lugging a bag he'd rescued from the debris of Amalina's trunks, to keep it from the soldiers—entered *l'entrée grande*, they found it stripped bare of flowers and food. Clean and austere now, the long, tall, cavern-like space had been swept and scoured to an unnatural clarity. Not just its stones, but even the table, the several tapestries, the suit of armor (attached to the wall), the mantel of the gigantic fireplace, and the always-present plain lead cup (and its supporting pedestal). All held a shine as if they had been polished, or covered over with a glossy sheen.

The fireplace was bare. No wood in the grate, when normally there would be a raging fire. Only a few torches attempted to bring light to this massive chamber.

It was a strangely cool reception.

Even Genadie, who was circling the room with his bag, appeared thrown and wary.

Where was Georg and his people? or Abraxa? Amalina wondered. Were they hiding? Without Georg's nephews, Ham and Gul, who were the castle's regular footmen, coming to greet them and perhaps provide a jovial buffer, Amalina dreaded the first sight of Georg or Abraxa; what insults either (or both) of those miserable people might hurl at her. She braced herself. Already picturing their angry faces behind doors or around corners.

She stumbled forward and gasped in surprise. Instead of the terrible two, she noticed the Count suddenly towering behind her.

4

The Imperfect Report

"Tell me about the western kingdoms," said Count Tepsji, who was laid out on the velvet divan, stretched out exactly as he had been last year when he'd received the previous report. His fingers were steepled together with their tips resting on his lips, his large brown eyes pointed to the ceiling, half closed. If he were a cat he would be emitting a complacent purr.

"Italy was nothing like anything I have ever seen," gushed Amalina, forgetting the last few awkward minutes: of being collected by the Count in the empty entrance hall, and being shepherded hastily to his private study; no time for hellos, or needless questions on how he was getting on. It was simply away to the study and then everyone took their places. And now it was just as it always was.

Amalina stood before the recumbent, cat-like Count. Genadie stood at Amalina's side, his bag at his knee. His hand ready to dart inside the bag's open mouth. The Count, pale with ink black hair slicked back on his head, ready to receive, his eyes ticking back and forth, as if to see what Amalina was to recount for him projected onto the ceiling.

"Why, sir, they love art and food even more than we do," she said. "It's as if they worship them on the same altar as ... the same altar as, uh ... well, nevermind that. And they are a very inventive, creative and clever folk. I understood from books Venice was a city that floats on water. But to actually see it. And to explore their streets in thin black boats, instead of carriages pulled by horses—"

"No horses, I'm sure the smell was much better for it," the Count put in.

"Not necessaril—"

"However," interrupted the Count, prompting her, "the dear *lady princesses?*"

"Just one last thing before I get to the princesses," Amalina insisted, with a hint of desperation more than apology. Because, to her dismay, she was now finding it difficult to focus: she knew she must present her full report on the young ladies she'd met in her travels. Present it to Count Tepsji, the man who had funded the venture. And she'd been trained how the report should be delivered. And she had assumed—had pictured in her mind—that on her next opportunity to recall these women in detail—the occasion which was now, here, *this minute*—the details would fall out of her mouth in the most satisfactory way. She wanted it so. Anything to ease the awkwardness of her life with the Count.

Unfortunately, because of her encounter with the strange man and the revelations in his book, and the fact that she now felt she understood the Count better, knew secrets he was keeping to himself (and he had thought she might never learn), his dreadfulness was weakened in her eyes. *He* was weakened. Last year, despite his incredible power—enough to destroy hundreds of men with his bare hands—at times he could strike her as something very silly. And presently, looking down at him on his couch, elongated like a sunning pet confident in its command over a household which seemed to whirl around for its own satisfaction, he could have been so again. However, she being secretly loaded with new information, he became something much different: No longer simply a monstrous evil creature, nor something straighforwardly so silly: just *something else*. This change preoccupied Amalina. And she knew her report wasn't going to come out as smooth as she'd planned. She needed to buy time as she struggled to put her thoughts in order.

"What do you have to say to me, other than what I wish to hear?" asked the Count with mild amusement touched with impatience. Just as easily he could have come off the couch and slashed her throat. Or thrown her into a wall for inconveniencing his pleasures. But either action would have prevented him learning what he wanted to know about the princesses.

"Well, sir, let me tell you about—"

Genadie started. He shifted quickly on his feet as if about to leap. Amalina thought he was going to jump in front of her; to defend against the Count's attack. He'd done so before on another occasion. And he'd almost died for it, receiving a measure of the Count's fury from which Genadie had taken months to recover. Then she saw she was mistaken. The Count was still worked comfortably into the couch, and Genadie had not intended to leap between them. He was looking at *her*. Even now his eyes burned toward her, his lips shifting nervously.

Why?

What was Genadie upset about?

Then Amalina realized Genadie had thought she was going to tell the Count about the strange man and the book. His mind had been covering the same ground as hers, and he'd assumed she was about to blab.

The Count looked between the two, wondering with irritation what was passing between his subordinates.

"*In Venice*," began Amalina, at first toward Genadie, to calm and assure him his assumption was wrong, then turned toward the Count to throw him off, "they have a peculiar practice of disguising themselves with masks. Fantastic masks, covering the whole face. You can't tell one person from the other, rich or poor, young or old (though the clothes might help there). And sometimes a lady will dress as a man, and a man will dress as a woman. It is an amazing sight, and difficult to imagine unless you see it yourself. If you ever get there, you will find it very exciting."

. . .

But of course he *wouldn't* be visiting Venice. Not any time soon. That was the whole point of this operation: Amalina would meet those high-stationed ladies of the western kingdoms, who the Count could not meet himself, and lure them to Ardeel. Bait them with the promise of something exotic, wealthy, and waiting for them in the east with welcoming arms.

As the Count had once confessed to Amalina (in one of his long, rambling diatribes), he trusted no housing but his great castles made of stone, which were fireproof and which protected him from the sun—whose rays could kill him. Nor had he confidence in any transportation other than that provided by his own limbs, which would carry him only so far in a single night. Until he purchased the right properties, and built a well-spaced string of castles to allow him to escape from his land's encaging mountains—racing from one secure fortress to the next before daybreak, like a meek animal leaping rock-to-rock to cross a raging river—he would summon, and entice, and connive to his castle what he desired from the outside world.

. . .

However, at her impossible suggestion for the Count to visit Venice, he did not look a bit resentful. Instead he stroked the side of his face where a mustache occasionally resided. It was a soothing, self-reassuring gesture. His eyes were half-closed again.

For Genadie's part, his body retracted to a half-crouch, and he stared at the floor, unable to look at Amalina or his master.

"I've heard something about this practice somewhere," said the Count in a contemplative tone. "The masks. They employ them in a celebration of some sort?"

"Every day, sir. Day and night. Anyone who feels in the mood becomes a masker."

"It would seem to me, yes … an invitation to incredible mischief." He smiled, obviously considering some mischief he would enjoy.

"It makes communication very easy, you see," said Amalina, finding her own interest, hoping to regain focus—for her and the rest. "Everyone is in a receptive mood, because everyone is a stranger, and those they meet in a shaded corner or on a bridge seem full of fun and mystery."

But at this statement, just when she hoped to recover, she was transported to the undulating world of gondolas, and palazzos, and blinding days, and midnight walks, and mysterious fogs, and unexpected alcoves, and smooth, wet marble, and clams and octopus on a plate, and balsamic vinegars and herbed salts, and focaccias and ciabattas and ciambellas (what interesting breads to a former baker!), and subtle perfumes, and prosecco by the bottle, and cloaked bodies held close together against the chill, and curious, hushed whispers, and faces hidden and laughing; and suddenly reexperienced the same giddy sensation she'd felt in the Carnivale atmosphere of Venice; which then communicated immediately to her flights of merriment wrought by the Paris celebrations; which then rocketed through a pastel-postered passage to the memory of young Lieutenant Ivanti Ion Vokent; dressed in his handsome uniform, his great warm smile sending beams at her, and her dizzy joy of being in his arms, spinning round.

This left Amalina even more diverted than before. She carried on, though rendered woefully inadequate to her purpsose. For Count Tepsji's sake, she spoke hazily of: the Lady Princess Maria Lazedo; the Lady Princess Angelina DiSigordo; the Lady P. Ara Pluma; L.P. Pia Lampeda; L.P. Gina Ninovetto; L.P. Gina Colveni; the sisters Alamera; daughters Medici; daughters Strozzi; cousins Larizzi, etc.; and then on to France: Marie DelaCroix; Selene Pique; Katherine Lenore; etc.; but each one she spoke of, though she had enjoyed their company, and had been left with the strongest images and senses of their character upon leaving them, were now difficult to recall. It was like trying to see them through a milky veil. Before her eyes were not the memories of princesses, but the dimples of Vokent, the wide shoulders of the proud soldier who now seemed to return her interest, the surprise of the boy she had once so loved, grown into a man-of-the-world. Not a permeable layer. Amalina struggled along.

Genadie, too, was having trouble in his designated task. At each princess named he pulled from his case a vellum swatch with a portrait drawn on it. But he shook his head as he fumbled through the selections, unsure he'd located the right girl. He sheepishly pushed portraits in the Count's direction, flagging it in the general area where he understood the Count's eyes to be; unable to look for himself whether he placed it in the right spot; unable, it seemed, to look directly at his beloved Master. An inability arising not from his (routine) unrestrained adulation, just as one can't stare directly into the sun, but from embarrassment, or shame, or dismay.

"What's the matter with you two?" asked the Count after a couple hours of suffering.

Genadie collapsed and wailed.

"We should have waited until tomorrow," explained Amalina. "It was a long road for us, and we are more tired than expected, sir."

The Count stared as if unable to process what she'd told him. His eyes jumped back and forth between Amalina and the weeping, convulsing Genadie.

"To be honest," Amalina continued, feeling the pressure to speak to dispel the awkward silence, "we weren't received here at our castle very well, either. Your general was particularly rude."

"You will say nothing more—much less *against*—my good General Marosh. Do you understand?"

"Yes, sir."

The Count nodded with satisfaction.

"But the general was pretty mean—"

The Count shook his head.

"And also," Amalina tacked quickly, "maybe if there were something for us to drink. Or to eat."

"I suppose that's true. Yesss. I had forgotten about such *needful things* for you darlings."

He seemed content with this finding and stroked his non-existent mustache.

"Sir?"

"Yes, Ms. Dalca?"

"I would have asked for a meal to be made, but I didn't see anyone inside the castle. But … *could* we have something—? … um … perhaps Georg or Abraxa could get something for us?"

"Who is that?"

But it was the last distraction he would tolerate. He pushed Amalina's recitation-of-the-princesses to full speed until the ordeal was over. Amalina and Genadie were sent out of his private study, mouths dry, stomachs knotted, minds leaden, while he pondered which western gems to invite to the castle.

5

The Warm Replacements

"Where are Georg and Abraxa?" Amalina asked Genadie, as they returned to the echoing entrance hall.

Genadie shrugged indifferently, pulling along his case of tiny portraits as if it were filled with boulders. He still couldn't take his eyes off the floor, his mouth slanted unhappily in the black stubble. "I hope he ate them."

"Why did you almost leap at me in there?" she whispered as they put distance between them and the Count. "What did you think I was going to tell him?"

"You know very well what," he grumbled. "Good thing you are a smart and quick girl, eh? And that you didn't."

"I told him exactly what I was going to tell him," Amalina rankled. "Don't you assume to know what I think. But what if I did tell him? What's the matter with that? You know we never did talk about what we should do about … about *him*."

He made a miserable face: "*Him*."

"The stranger …" she said softly, "and his book."

Genadie took one of his crooked hands away from the case to chop it through the air. "Nothing! We say nothing about it, because they mean nothing here, you understand? It is foolishness. All of it. Absurdity, end-to-end. I should have burned that book. What was I thinking? … Where did you put it?"

"You aren't burning it."

"It can't stay in this castle. It is an insult to Master."

"I haven't finished reading it. Did you?"

"Give it to me. I will dispose of it."

"We're going to show his book to the Count. *And* we're going to tell him about the man who gave it to us."

"I suppose you're going to shelve it in Master's library, too?" Genadie looked disgusted. "So that others might read it and begin to question. And start to have doubts?"

"Is that why you're looking down, Genadie? Are you now having doubts about your Master? … because of what you read in the book?"

Genadie whirled on Amalina, swinging his case around like a giant flail and pointed his meandering-jointed finger in her face. He hissed: "You see? Lies believed! Slanders countenanced!"

"Don't point your finger at me!"

"It must be destroyed!"

"Is everything all right?" said a round faced young man at the foot of the stairs. He wasn't suited in armor or wearing the colors of Marosh's army. He wore a plain brown jacket and pants, clean and well fitted. He also bore a light polite smile. An effort to show that he *was* concerned about the ruckus in the hallway and meant to help, but also that he didn't want to be drawn in on the wrong side of whatever might be happening.

Amalina and Genadie stared at him. Genadie let his case settle to the floor.

"Can I help you?" said the round faced young man. "Would you like to know the way out? Or were you just arriving ... or were you ... were you just visiting with ... *him*?"

"Hello," said Amalina. "Who are you?"

"I'm, um, I'm the footman, miss," he replied. "And the steward. And the all-round servant. Oh, also, the, uh, head of staff. Yes, that too. And you are?"

"Amalina. And this is Genadie. We are—"

"But of course you are!" he shouted with delight. He came forward. As he did so, while letting forth a flurry of words, he motioned with his hands that he was about to take up Genadie's case for him. Genadie fended off the young man's hands and clutched it protectively. "I should have known. I'm so very sorry! I was given your description by the ... uh ... well, by Count Tepsji." Here the young man's hands were fended off. "And his description fits you to perfection." As the fending off continued, the young man looking confused. "But I was surprised. And I didn't hear you come, either." Now the protective clutching commensed. "I should have thought I would be alerted by one of the house guards." The young man straightened up with an understanding nod and grin to Genadie, but still not allowing the word-flurry to break. "Well, I'm sorry, of course. I'm so busy. There really is not much in the way of staff here besides me, so I can't be everywhere at once and sometimes arrivals or other things are missed. But come along and take the lead and show me where your rooms are." He motioned them onto the stairs and began to climb. "I think I know by having peeked into them, but I can never be too sure; there are so many—as you know." He stopped and took a breath. "Amalina! Genadie! Well, well! He said you'd be back at some point. And here you are!"

The young man's smile was the infectious kind. Amalina was already smiling. Half of Genadie's mouth was shaped into something receptive as well. He peered over the young man with one eye, while his nervous one twitched and blinked.

"Please don't take any offense," said the young man, turning up the stairs again. "Offense, that is, that I said I was head of staff. I understand you both have been here for some time. But I was told it *is* my title, and, well, I'd always hoped I would make 'Head of Staff' before I died. So I can't help but claim it. Though I can assure you I don't *want* it."

"Where are we going?" asked Amalina as they climbed the stairs.

"Oh! Very sorry! But I did say I wanted you to lead me to your rooms, didn't I? And now here I am leading *you*. To nowhere in particular I suppose," he laughed cheerily, then led them down a hall. "I suppose you know this castle much better than I. I've gotten lost many times. And I'd have gotten lost again right now without a doubt, when I'd hoped to bring you straight to your rooms so you can have a rest. I take it your belongings are in the courtyard? or still on your carriage? Just show me to your rooms and I'll bring everything right up. Leave it all to me, Genadie and Amalina. Yes, if you've just arrived, which you *must* have, then you'll want a rest. I'm sure, I'm sure. Back from France is it? The whole other side of the world! That's a long enough trip to take the rush out of a spring river, eh? Yes, you *are* very tired. Very tired.You must be."

His steps were high, as if he were always stepping over sleeping dogs, and his body was faced forward so that he had to be constantly looking back to talk to them, which he did. And he never lost the smile, though it became a little more manic the more he talked and talked and talked.

"What's your name?" Amalina asked him.

"Who is this?" said a woman coming down the hallway from the opposite direction. She held a torch and shielded her eyes from its glare to get a better look. She also adopted the young man's smile. She wore a puffy-rimmed hat that was chased around with lacing and had lengths of cloth falling down over her ears and looping around her neck. Where the young man's color was an almost uniform faded brown, hers was a dim dark green.

"Amalina and Genadie!" cheered the young man. "They're here!"

"Oh!" It looked like she wanted to clap her hands in delight, but then realized she was holding the torch. "Back so soon! How wonderful!"

"Yes, I am Amalina and this is Genadie," Amalina nodded. "But we don't know your names, I'm afraid."

"Pils," said the young man.

"Anka," said the mature woman.

Now they stood in silence, looking each other over. Amalina noticed that the two had moon faces and short, rounded noses. But they didn't look related. And both looked nothing like Georg, as his blood-related staff did.

"But who in the world are you?" said Genadie, putting his weight on his back foot and craning his neck up, making him look like he had a hunched back. "Where are Georg and Abraxa?"

Pils and Anka consulted each other with a glance.

"Who are they?" asked Anka, politely.

"You don't know them? You've never heard of them?" said Amalina. "Or seen them in this castle?"

They shook their heads at the same time, with mystified expressions.

Pils asked helpfully: "Are they one of General Marosh's staff?"

"No. The Count's servants." Amalina held back from mentioning Georg was the head of staff and Abraxa was the head maid, considering these two had just claimed the titles. "Let's see, there was Ham and Gul, and ..." Amalina named the members of Georg's family she could remember, while the two continued to shake their heads.

"They were employed here, milady?"—Amalina flinched at being called a proper lady—"In *this* castle?" asked Anka.

"They were the Count's servants," Amalina insisted. "There were nearly fifty of them."

"Besides you two," said Pils, "as far as I understand it, *we* are the only servants at all."

• • •

Georg and Abraxa were no more.

It was impossible to fathom.

"Pils and Anka?" said Amalina, as much to familiarize herself with their names. They nodded to her, their smiles wide, genuine and gentle. "Well, I suppose if we could get to our rooms and have a rest."

"Oh, of course, of course," Pils voice rang merrily. Now he stepped to the side. "You lead the way."

"Here," said Anka. "I'll take my lady. Pils, you see to Genadie. Then let's fetch their belongings and get them settled." It sounded like she was proposing a race. "We'll have the General's cooks whip up something delicious when you rise."

"Which way to your room, sir?" Pils asked Genadie, eager to get the race started.

Genadie stared in disbelief. Then his eyebrows rose high on his forehead. He stifled a laugh, which came out like small puttering grunts.

"I'm downstairs," said Genadie. The one smiling side of his face joined the other and spread. Even his hunched posture appeared to loosen. He gained an inch. He took the stairs, waving with a barely-muted eagerness for Pils to follow, the bag no longer an encumbrance. It was a race between them now, and it would lead to Genadie's cherished closet room.

• • •

"I'm on the other side of the castle," Amalina told Anka, taking her in a direction that would get them there.

"Milady," Anka began, "I promised a meal at your rising. But when do you rise? Do you follow the ... uh ... his ... uh ... that is to say, the Count's hours? Or do you wake in the morning and sleep in the evening?"

"What do you do?" asked Amalina.

"Pils and I sleep when we can. He … uh … that one … you know, Count Tepsji … He prefers the night to the day. But we're at his call at all times. Not that he requires us too much. Ah, you must know what I mean. You are more familiar with his house affairs."

It seemed difficult for Anka to mention the Count by name. Also, neither Pils nor Anka favored him with over-the-top appellations. No 'His Eminences', no 'The Almighty One's, no 'Zeus's. So unlike Georg and Abraxa. Or Genadie and General Marosh, for that matter.

"You and Pils are quite a surprise," said Amalina. "How long have you been here?"

"Not long. A number of months. Maybe a little less. It's difficult to keep track of time. Days are nights and nights are days."

"And how did you come to be here?"

Anka's smile shook.

"Oh, if you don't want to say," hurried Amalina, "if it's too difficult, please don't mind my questions, and don't feel you have to answer then. I was just curious."

"Our master needed our services no longer. He was dying, you see. And he gifted us to his closest friend, who is the … uh … Count Tepsji."

"Do you know who the Count is?" asked Amalina, looking for Anka's reaction.

"A titled gentleman of the noble order, I suppose."

"Or should I say, do you know *what* he is?"

"Well, of course I do, milady. He is a horrible monster. A creature of the highest evil who has plagued these lands since time began. Or some centuries, from what I understand. Nasty, foul, terrible thing. But you know."

The old woman had said it so matter-of-factly, and her smile just barely dimmed as she said it. For the content of what she said, she might have spit on the ground at the end of it, but contented herself to make an obscene gesture with her free hand.

"May he soon die," Anka concluded. She noticed Amalina's expression. "Oh, I hope you aren't bothered by my saying so."

"Feel free to speak your mind, Anka," said Amalina, non-commitally. "I just … I'm used to everyone worshipping the Count as if he were a saint."

Anka shook her head with a look of disgust. Now she spit. It was a large and thick glob. "That thing belongs in hell. Never a good word about … *him* … will you hear from Pils and I."

"You know," Amalina whispered, "he might very well be able to hear you."

Anka spit twice more, making it louder and a heavier glob each time. Her only regret: "Oh, now I suppose I'll have to clean that all up."

"I'm surprised you're here, Anka." Amalina clarified: "That the Count would allow you to be here."

"We are a gift from his dearest friend. And no matter what we think of him, Pils and I, we pride ourselves in our service. It was our master's wish we serve this creature to the best of our abilities. He was a great man, our master. We can only hope to do him honor and serve impeccably." Then she added with a wink: "We also want to live, don't we? It is Ardeel's Saxon strain which strive and persist in the face of every—and any—*thing*."

"Still, it's surprising," said Amalina. "We had an invasion of revolutionaries last year. They almost killed him—"

"Why didn't they?" Anka blurted. "Oh—em—forgive me … "

"So it's strange he'd allow inside his castle someone with such open hostility toward him."

"Well, he isn't afraid of much, is he? He loved our master genuinely, it seems, and honored his wish. And Pils and I are as meek as lambs, aren't we? And then there is the General and his men to keep us honest. And you understand, I wouldn't say these things straight to his face, anyhow. If he chooses to listen in on me, that's his fault."

Hearing these words, Amalina felt it was now three against one inside the castle: Her, Pils' and Anka's enmity toward the Count, weighted against Genadie's abject slavering. But really, thinking about it, it was three against two: Amalina, Pils and Anka against Genadie *and* Count Tepsji. But then again, it was three against hundreds, because she couldn't leave off General Marosh and his soldiers. Amalina stopped counting. Her burst of enthusiasm bursted.

"This is my room," Amalina said. Anka rushed to open the door, but she was there first. The room looked untouched since the last time she'd been in there. Months ago.

Over half a year.

Anka entered and bowed, and motioned for Amalina to get comfortable.

Amalina had another thought.

"No," said Amalina, with a jolt. "Let's get back downstairs. Fast."

• • •

The last Amalina had seen of Genadie, he was racing Pils for his old room, she thinking he couldn't wait to reclaim that cramped storage closet before Georg and Abraxa miraculously reappeared to block him.

But now she realized it might've been a different race altogether. With Amalina and Anka heading upstairs, and Genadie having the good excuse to go downstairs—towards his old closet, yes—as he reached the lower floors of the castle, he was heading closer and closer to the carriage and their belongings. He could, if he wanted to, nab the leather-bound diary.

If Genadie gets his hands on it!

Genadie was so clever and ruthless. He'd spotted this opportunity long before Amalina woke to it.

"Wait, milady, wait," Anka called after Amalina. But Amalina distanced her quickly and wound down the stairs fast enough that she reached *l'entrée grande* while Pils and Genadie were still inside.

"But that isn't even fit for anything more than storage," she heard Pils say. "I thought you must be upstairs. Are you sure you aren't upstairs? At the very least, sir, you should be in the regular servants quarters. But that doesn't sound right ..."

"Yes, Genadie," Amalina said brightly, as she came upon them. "Take one of the rooms upstairs. You deserve it."

Genadie looked to protest.

"If I have a room upstairs, so should you," Amalina said as she passed them. "Don't be shy."

"There are so many rooms," said Pils. "I can't see how ... uh ... *he* could refuse you. He praises you often. And holds you in such high regard."

"Master ... praises me?" Genadie whimpered and almost lost his legs. He wobbled. Pils took his arm.

Amalina was already out the doors, Anka bustling just behind her, out of breath. And maybe Genadie hadn't been intent on getting the book. Maybe Amalina was the shrewder one. While Genadie was back inside the castle, recovering from the shock of his master's esteem, Amalina made her way to the strewn pile of bags and boxes and crates, where the soldiers had created it and then abandoned it. She would be the first to reach the book after all.

The carriage was gone. The soldiers had returned to the parapet, staring alert and puppetlike out into the forest or down into the valley below. She couldn't believe it was still daytime. Though the blue overhead was turning purple, and it would soon be night, Amalina was still very visible; and so were her actions.

Amalina pretended to take inventory. She pulled up a case buried under several others, causing them to topple. She quickly opened it and pulled out a dress which was wrapped around the book. She handed the oddly-bunched dress to Anka who, out-of-breath and unready for its surprise hardness and weight, bobbled it.

Amalina was about to take a chance. But she felt she could trust the old maid. More than she ever could Genadie. How determined the little rat was to make the book disappear, she couldn't risk hiding it in her own room just for him to sneak in and ferret it out. And Anka was no partisan for the Count.

Amalina was about to take a *big* chance. But she was confident.

Or should I? she thought, one last time.

"Anka, inside this dress is a book. Genadie doesn't want the Count to know about it. He wants to get rid of it, but I don't think that's a good idea. Will you help me hide it?"

"What kind of book is it?"

"Don't read it yourself. Don't even look at it. It will be for the Count to decide what to do with it."

"Is it a bible? He made me leave mine behind."

"No. For what you have to do, what it is is unimportant. Just take it away. And don't let Genadie know I gave it to you. Or what you did with it. Same goes for Count Tepsji. Don't even tell me where you hide the thing. Just go now and put it where it will be safe, and where no one will find it. Bring it to me when I ask for it."

"Oh." Anka burbled, dumbstruck. For an anxious second, Amalina began to worry she'd supposed too much about Anka. But maybe, Amalina realized, her own mysterious behaviour was just too much of a surprise for the old woman, having met for the first time just minutes ago.

"I can explain later," said Amalina. "You can trust me. We're of a like mind, you understand, regarding our Count. But go now before Genadie comes out here, or the soldiers start wondering what we're doing and we begin to look suspicious. Oh, and I wouldn't talk like you did about the Count around Genadie. *He* would take offense." Amalina winked.

"Yes, Milady," said Anka, still lightly baffled. "I suppose I shouldn't go in through the main doors, then?"

"Go around through the kitchen, I think," advised Amalina, her body tensing, imagining Genadie coming out the front doors any second. "I'll return to my room and rest. Thank you."

Anka eyed Amalina once over. And then nodded, with a smile crimped by caution.

. . .

"What did you do with the book?" Genadie demanded in a low scratchy whisper. "Ms. Dalca, it was given to both of us. It isn't fair you should hide it from me."

"He didn't lend it to us to be torn up," answered Amalina. She was rummaging through her drawers, making sure her newer outfits were on top, or had first positions in the standing closet.

He protested: "I have no intention to tear it up."

"Or burn it."

Genadie had no comment. He turned away.

"The minute you declared your interest in destroying that book, Genadie, was the minute it became mine alone."

"Every second that abomination exists inside this castle it sets down evil roots that will harm us all."

Amalina shook her head in disbelief. "You've some imagination. Go get some sleep. You'll come to your senses. And don't bother peeping around my room like you are. I'm telling you, I hid it where you will never ever find it."

Genadie snarled like a small, unhappy animal.

"You shouldn't waste your time searching. Instead, let's figure out when to tell the Count about the book, and the man who wrote it; and just what we should say about them."

"Whao!" Genadie flopped onto the floor as he howled, his face turning red beneath all the grizzle and grime, his greasy hair flopping to and fro. "Whao! Whao!"

The door opened, Count Tepsji entered. He stared down at Genadie and his lip curled in distaste.

"Master!" Genadie gyrated his body round, his outrage spun into supplication. "Master! Master!"

"You've had your rest already?" said the Count, bemused.

"I don't need it, Master," Genadie declared. "I am always at your service."

"*I* haven't rested yet," said Amalina.

"But I see you've found some energy that was lacking earlier," the Count carried on. "You have recovered sufficiently, in any case. I would like the letters to fly immediately. I have made my selection."

"Who?" Amalina asked him, immediately trying to picture which new friend she might hope to see again.

"All of them."

Amalina and Genadie stared at him. "All of them?"

"After the last year's paltry response I will now spread my net as wide as I can."

"It might appear a little desperate," said Amalina. "And, sir, not every girl gets along with the other. If one should find out you invited someone she doesn't like it might discourage her."

In the prolonged silence he smirked, waiting for Amalina to bring her thought to its conclusion. He didn't necessarily see the problem.

"It would be a pity," she said, "if the lady who might be discouraged is the one you would have preferred. Maybe, sir, a round of invitations for those you desire the most, and who you know are on good terms with each other. So one might encourage the other. Then another round later, after the first have confirmed their interest or disinterest."

The Count walked to the window. It seemed an automatic movement. He stopped when he realized it was still daytime and the burning sun was sealed off by a slim board. He turned back, his expression petulant, pouting his frustration at encountering an unforeseen, but entirely sensible, impediment.

"Then I must think some more." It sounded more like a question. An angry one. "You didn't inform me of the princesses' petty prejudices, Ms.

Dalca. Something you should have made clear if you knew such a dilemma would trip me up."

"I didn't mean to. But I really didn't think you were going to propose *all*—"

"Shall I have the deliberations out here in Ms. Dalca's room, then?" He asked himself; Amalina and Genadie ignored in his private debate. "Or in my private chamber? My private chamber, I think. Yes, I think so."

The Count shot through the door so hard it slammed shut with a cracking sound, and shuddered open on its stressed hinges.

Amalina began to say: "He didn't hear what we were talking about—"

Wham!

Amalina and Genadie flew from the Count's arms and hit the divan—the divan in the count's private study. They both tumbled over it and onto the floor.

It was the Count's habit to seize whoever he wished at a given moment, and in the snap of a finger deposit them in the room he wished them to be. Easy for him, disconcerting and disastrous to his transportee. The individual's body was left humming, pained and nauseous, and if they hurtled into something unforgiving, possibly killed. That hadn't happened yet.

Amalina rose to her feet, feeling dizzy. She might have recovered quicker if she wasn't already exhausted.

With an impatient sneer the Count set himself on the couch. But his pose was deliberately uncomfortable and he looked out of place, wearing his house clothes instead of reclining inside his customary leisure gown.

"The writing material is at the desk." The Count motioned toward the large desk. A stack of vellum pages waited opposite a larger stack of preconstructed envelopes. Between the two sat the ink bottle and pen with the fancy plume, nib cutter and kit (with its red silk ribbons and scissors and salt shaker), and blotter and wax candle for sealing.

Genadie leapt from the floor to the desk. Amalina rubbed her sore ribs.

"Draw the list," the Count instructed. "Then we will select the first round, then the second. Leaving perhaps a third if necessary."

A knock sounded at the door. It was soft, tentative.

"Ms. Quiet?" His words, directed at the door, came out more like a statement of fact.

"Uh—yes."

The Count bid Ms. Quiet to enter. The door opened only very slowly, and not all the way. And then Anka (who must be Ms. Quiet) appeared into the room piece by piece, as she shuffled crabwise from behind the door. Amalina recognized her immediately, but then almost let out a gasp when she saw in the maid's arms the book. Genadie also started in his seat, and spun his head to gape at Amalina. Amalina turned back to Anka as the maid took two steps toward the Count.

• • •

Anka's eyes were lowered and locked on the floor just below the Count's feet. She had not yet looked up, and it seemed from the way she spoke that she still didn't know anyone else was in the room.

"Sorry to bother you, sir," she said in a timid voice. "Heard your door close and knew you were here."

"And what have you to tell me, Ms. Quiet?" asked the Count.

She shrugged her shoulders and the book pushed forward as she did so.

"Well, I suppose I must tell you something—as I know …" she suddenly blurted at the end, "*I* should *tell you*." Her eyes came up to look at him directly. "I would never disobey or create mischief for mischief's—" her eyes ticked to the side and then locked on Amalina. Her eyes flashed, her face puckered in, her shoulders shrank. Her eyes diverted to her feet quickly, her round cheeks blushed with guilt. "Oh! Oh! Oh, well … what can I say, but … " She looked up again, her eyes turned away from Amalina to regard the other side of the room, only to find Genadie at the writing desk, which launched her through the same startled motion as before. "Oh! Oh! Oh!—"

"Is there a problem, Ms. Quiet? Are you quite all right?"

She glanced guiltily from Amalina to Genadie and then lowered her gaze directly to the book held over her chest.

"I didn't know the others were here. But I guess I'm not ashamed to say it in front of everyone. I'm no tell-tale, sir. I'd say anything I have to say to their face before I'd said it behind their backs."

"You're being remarkably talkative, Ms. Quiet," said the Count, grinning thinly as he was drawn into the developing mystery before him. "You've come to tell me something about someone?"

"Amalina—"

"Mouse?" the Count shot in quickly, and his head turned like an owl's between his shoulder blades, and fixed Amalina with a penetrating stare, a wide greedy, tooth-filled smile glowing underneath. Amalina fell back at the sight. She felt something solid jump up into her throat.

"Er, Mouse, yes," said Anka. Her eyes were firmly nailed to her feet now and would not look up, though her head moved in a conversational way, shifting the hat around. She shrugged the book forward again. "This book here. She gave it to me and told me to hide it. You told me to do anything she asked of me, but I couldn't decide on a good hiding spot, and since you know everything, I thought I would come to you, sir. I would tell you what I was up to, so you would be properly informed, as you like, and you could tell me where best to hide it."

The Count's head spun back round and peered at the book curiously.

"Mouse, who are you hiding this book from?"

"Genadie, sir," said Anka. "That's what she said. She wanted to hide it from Genadie." Here she hesitated and trembled. Then: "But, in truth, she meant everyone else besides the two of us—her and I—I figure. Even ..."

"Me?" The Count sounded amused again, but there was an underlying shadow in his tone.

Anka shrugged and then nodded. "The truth, sir. Can't go wrong with the truth, isn't that so, sir? You can tell, sir, I'm not lying to you at this moment, yes, sir?"

"What is it that should be hidden from me, Ms. Dalca?"

"Not hiding from you," said Amalina. The words hopped out of her body before she realized she was speaking. She needed to wedge a defense in before the situation got any more out of her control. His head spun back round, his chin resting on his right shoulder blade. Amalina's body rebelled at so unnatural a sight. "Anka's mistaken. I just didn't want to disturb you with it, sir. Not right away. Not until the time was right."

"Oh?" said the Count, mercifully turning his body toward her so that it matched the direction of his face. "It appears now is the time, Ms. Dalca."

Amalina said in qausi-apology: "This could have kept til the selection was over and your mind was free to contemplate other matters."

The Count said nothing more, choosing to glower at Amalina with his unnaturally large eyes. His grin had frozen into a disturbing rictus.

"The book," she continued. "We—or rather, *I*—found it."

"You wished to keep it to yourself," said the Count. Then he shook his head. "But, no. You said it would come after my selections were made. Given to me only then. *Not* as a gift. A matter for my contemplation. What would I need to contemplate, Mouse?"

Amalina was accustomed to the Count's self-referential way of speaking and sounding things out aloud. She waited until he was quite done and ready to receive the next bit of information. Normally it would bore and annoy her. But now it gave her time to think. She was already blushing and sweating from guilt, and her stomach knotted at the thought of Anka's betrayal.

"Let me start at the beginning," said Amalina. "So you understand better, sir. I found this book in a wreck ..."

Amalina described coming upon the destroyed carriage along the highway.

"Aha!" gloated the Count. "Did I not tell you that these things can happen? And that a fragile carriage is the most dangerous way to travel for a man such as I?"

"You couldn't be any more right, sir," said Amalina. Genadie stood from his chair and then sat back down. He gripped its side with white-knuckled fingers, making a face as he did so. He knew what she was about to say. She went and said it: "Because in fact, sir, there was—in that crash—a man such as you."

"No, Master, no," Genadie slavered on his chair.

The smile on the Count's face flickered and his eyelids dropped halfway closed.

"Such as me?"

Amalina told the Count how the man exhibited the various strengths and weaknesses that he himself possessed. She spoke of the stranger's relentless pursuit (leaving out that the man might actually be much faster than the Count by the incredible speed and distance he'd tracked them), and how he'd tried to discover how they knew of his kind, and whether they served such a man, and still more questions about the man he assumed they must serve. She assured the Count they told this stranger nothing he wanted, that Genadie had destroyed anything he might use to place where they were from and where the Count lived. And that they'd finally lost him along the way. But during his pursuit, he'd given them this book. A diary to read. To understand the creature that he was.

"Creature?" said the Count.

"I can't remember what he said exactly. But that's what he meant."

"Have you read it yet?"

Amalina glanced at Genadie, then she shook her head. "No."

The Count stared at her doubtfully. Then he slipped forward to the book still cradled in Anka's arms and stroked it cautiously—as if it might be spring-loaded with a trap, or that it might be laced with silver.

"Ms. Dalca," said the Count. "You did not read this book?"

"We were driving so fast, sir, I didn't have time even if I wanted to. But I thought you should know first, before I did, considering what he'd said to us."

"Why was he allowed to say anything, I wonder?" said the Count to himself. "Why, when you had the chance, did you not kill him? It would have been so easy to do. So easy … "

Amalina shook her head. "Honestly, sir, I don't know. It just didn't occur to me."

"No. Of course. Killing is not in your nature." The Count made a face. "But I wasn't speaking to *you*."

"He was nothing like you, Master!" Genadie groaned as he slid to the floor. "Because nothing *is* like you. Because you are above all, Master."

"That is without question. But your flattery doesn't answer what I asked, does it?"

The room's air seemed to quiver and redden, especially around Count Tepsji.

"He is a lower being, Master. Not worh your consideration, Master. He was a charlatan, a nothing. An imposter. You have other concerns and you should forget about him, Master."

"You could have killed him. If you had killed him then I could have more easily forgotten about him."

"Yes, Master. But I don't ... I don't know why I—But I didn't even want to stop there, Master! It was Amalina's idea to check for survivors! She was the one who saved him, even when I begged her to leave!" Genadie twisted on the floor as he moaned and lamented. Amalina felt sorry for him. "But ... In truth, master, I can't answer you, because I just didn't think about it at the time! I didn't *know* I could do anything against him! The memories ... *Memories* ... forgive me!"

They all sensed the mortal blow about to be struck. Amalina could not watch, and could not believe Anka's shamelessness, as the old maid's eyes doubled in size and her mouth shrank to a dot, while her body shook as she anticipated something horrific about to happen to Genadie, but not taking one step to stop it. A white-hot anger swelled in Amalina's chest against the treacherous Anka, who—while perhaps having solved Amalina and Genadie's quarrel, and as well relieved outright Amalina's quandary over what to do by just delivering the book to the Count—now proved so cowardly in a moment so crucial for a fellow servant. Until Amalina noted she herself was also stuck in place.

The Count extended his hand to Anka, ignoring Genadie entirely. Anka made a small noise, her knees knocked and her eyes rolled as if she were about to faint. Then, after a moment, she snapped up, realizing this wasn't a gesture spelling her doom. She gratefully handed him the book.

As he opened its cover, the Count said with a mirthless downturn of his lips, "Now let me see ..."

6

The Open History of the Strange Gentleman

The strange gentleman's book was a loose gathering of his thoughts; committed to the written word as it came to him; during a desperate scramble, apparently, in an hour he thought was his last, and he didn't want to leave the world without providing for the future generations this gift: a record of his being there. But his name never appears.

It mentions little of his previous life. The period of normalcy before becoming the new being. He'd been born into a family of poor migrants whose only benefit to him was laying a bedrock of superstitions, and their practice of rudimentary magic—which never seemed to work. And he hadn't climbed much out of his low condition when the change took place. A transformation he regretted at first.

Cast out of society, driven from family, friends and close associations— that is, the living—by sunlight and by so many uncommon weaknesses: extreme vulnerabilities bared as he randomly encountered them. Unaware they would strip him of strength or his very existence until he lay agonized in some cave; scared, confused and possibly dying. He listed them in order. His words captured the personal horror at every new discovery.

It was blood, human blood, which sustained him. Revived him. Empowered him. He made no excuses. It was a condition forced upon him, just as much as the pathetic, itinerant existence he'd been born into. And it was with this last trick of thought he justified what he did to survive. God had made him poor, and by the same divine hand he had been elevated above humanity. He could not question the laws of the universe. He became the terror because providence had made him a terror.

Terror personified.

During one entry he tried to recall all the innocent souls he had killed (the not-so-innocent souls and those who died in their attempt to kill him he would reserve for a later time). His victims were nameless for the most part, but they lived in castles and wore the finest silks and velvets—which he gladly tore through, with relish; or they existed in camps of threadbare tents, or down in the depths of abandoned mines and decked in the saddest shreds of clothes—obscenities he tried to ignore as he committed his required savagery.

He described the elation experienced throughout his entire body— *through every cell and fiber*—after he tore through the throats or thighs—or wherever on a body he could find a vital flow of blood—and swallowed the spout of his foodstuff. It was a sensation beyond relief. Beyond carnal ecstacy, though that is what it necessarily was. The power he received felt as if it exceeded his physical limits. As if it dissolved him and made him one with air and time.

He could lift any object. He could hear any sound within ten miles. Smell any odor within five. See any object perhaps to the end of infinity, so long as it were in line-of-sight. He could run as fast as lightning (in short bursts). He could dematerialize and slip his body like a mist anywhere he wished. Or better, he could solidify, and shape himself into any beast living—be it the largest elephant or the smallest insect—the caveat that it was always easier to mimic a creature whose blood he had partaken. And with his transormations he came to understand the language of animals and insects. To converse with them. He could gain knowledge from them, reason with them and employ them. He could withstand and heal most any damage to his form, as long as it wasn't delivered by one of the elements that were his bane.

His new life—his reign of terror—began simply enough. A process which he described as he understood it: The gaunt, hideous creature which had invaded his camp one night, had torn his throat with a precision that exposed his veins but did not sever everything there. It dined on his blood as it poured out of his body, his limbs secured by its overwhelming strength and the gentleman's own abject paralysis at this horror. He grew faint and felt his life passing. The creature seemed to suck every last drop from him, even turning him upside down and squeezing him. Still he retained a queer consciousness throughout the process, at some point feeling disassociated from his physical form.

In the end the creature cut its own wrist with its fingernail (which had transformed into an enormous, razor-sharp talon). It fed its blood into the gentleman's mouth, and he felt its hot liquor crawl down his throat and begin renewing his life. Expanding him. The creature left with the laugh of a sly criminal, and with no explanation for why it had done what it had done. On that night he had been reborn. Changed into something new, something old, and something strange.

• • •

From her readings on arcane creatures, direct observations of Count Tepsji, and clever surmise, Amalina might have predicted most of the book's revelations, no matter how sensational. But its most intriguing claim she had never suspected, and it overthrew her guesses at the Count's core nature: the Count's being—*if* he shared the same origin as the strange man—was not the result of a curse, or a product of his deranged and unsettled spirit, or gained by arrangement with infernal forces, or was a naturally formed pestilence, or was a divine creation sent down from heaven as punishment—

nor, as Genadie would have it, was he Zeus descended from Olympus. Instead, the Count was once human, and a malevolent force had made him its victim, and transformed him into what he was.

This was an incredible shock.

Amalina knew that even if the Count hadn't yet read every word in the book, he had read enough; knowing most of its secrets from personal experience, of course. But now, in a head spinning thought, she knew that he knew everything that she now knew about him. And as she sat at his desk, scratching a new letter on the vellum, and he lay on the couch a few feet away, one leg thrown carelessly over the other, contemplating the ceiling silently, she could almost hear his thoughts thrashing the furniture inside his head.

This diary had done more than strip away his mystique and remove his claim as a unique entity. It had, with its matter-of-fact details, exposed his genesis as one of *victimhood*. He had been inferior to another. Unthinkable. And with the author's frankness regarding his fear of destruction, his terror at being confronted by those various items that could deprive him of power and life, it did more than suggest, by the power of transference, a mental fragility within the Count, it exposed real nerve endings, where his carefree demeanor had led her to believe there were just blunt steel ends. It painted the Count with humanity; a confirmed and absolute, almost delicate, vulnerability. Like a magnificent leaf dangling on an old tree.

These things were now in his head, just as they were in her head. And his concern could not have been more evident than when he asked her, not once, not twice, but finally, for a third time, as she came to the end of her sealing the small stack of envelopes with wax: "You did not read anything in this … this book? Not one word?"

"No, sir," said Amalina, for the third time. It was easier to lie with her back to him and while concentrating on perfectly centering his royal seal on the hot wax blob. "Oh, no," she said as she squished the small carved stone into the wax. "I forgot the ribbons."

. . .

"You weren't tempted," asked the Count on their way to the aviary, "just to open the cover?"

It was night and they took the long way through the courtyard. There was a torch every ten feet, with a guard in full armor standing alert next to it.

"Was there something you wanted me to read, sir?" Amalina asked in return, huffing heavy into the air to see if she could catch sight of her breath. The mountain air was very cold this evening. It woke her.

"Ms. Dalca, I am familiar with your curiosity," he said. "It's how I found you at your window that one night when we met. I also know your fondness for reading, which is why you were the perfect choice to organize my Great Library. Receiving into your hands a rare book such as the one this mysterious man gave you, and with the possibility of learning from that book the particulars of a species which he purports that I am one ... How could you resist?"

"Maybe. If there'd been more time, sir. We were trying to race from him, remember? And maybe if Genadie hadn't been there I might have."

They climbed the dark steps inside the outer wall. Count Tepsji was unusually silent and patient as he walked behind her.

"Where is Genadie?" asked Amalina. "Shouldn't he be doing this?"

From the short rustle of cloth, it sounded like the Count shrugged. She didn't look back. His expression would probably be the same as earlier in the day, when he'd explained that Genadie was no longer needed.

． ． ．

At the time, with his eyes nearly shut, and his mouth slack at the corners, the Count had pronounced: "A new strategy of mine. Better the invitations not originate from me, personally. And cleverer still that they are written in your authentic, childlike hand, which your friends will recognize and warm to. What's more inviting than a request from a dear friend? A superior idea. An oversight on my part. And a satisfying explanation for last year's inadequate response."

Amalina agreed.

"I hope you spent generously this time out," he'd added. "And you did not hide the gold coins—and the size of your ample purse—from your acquiantances out of misplaced modesty; so that everyone detected my generosity and considerable wealth."

"Within reason," she replied. "And taste."

"No reason to bother Genadie, I think," he'd concluded.

． ． ．

The aviary was a large, vaulted room. It housed the homing pigeons with which the Count maintained correspondence with his minions. It also sheltered—coating its ceiling like an immense fur blanket—hundreds of dark bats. When she opened the door and thrust in her candle, she was met with a warm breath of feathers, fur and dung. The room seemed to shift as they entered. Squeaks and chitters came from above. A cheery greeting on the return of their master.

Amalina choked back a gasp. Shifting restlessly on the long, high counter—the counter now clear of the birdcages she and Genadie had carried the Count's previous supply of pigeons bound for the western princesses—were at least twenty of the dark shouldered, greasy-feathered, cruel-eyed pigeons she most disliked. They were the pigeons dedicated to the Count's local correspondence. They were the ones who brought to the castle the small slips of paper the Count read and then pasted into various books in his secret message chamber, which was in his hidden storage vault below the castle's main building. The birds were ugly, imperious creatures.

Amalina couldn't bear to watch what came next. She placed the candle next to the window, which she opened now, and tried to keep her eyes to the bits of forest visible in the moonlight. While she distracted herself by imagining the vicious wolves prowling within the woods, the Count, as was his way, hunched himself down and brought his hands before him like they were the thin, scaly feet of a bird. His lips took on a beak-like shape, and his eyes rounded like tunnels, and he burbled and cooed at the pigeons. In this manner he assembled half of them for a flight.

"Should we use *them*?" asked Amalina of the birds. "They are a bit scrawny and unsightly."

"They'll do," said the Count, at first cooing, booping and warbling, forgetting to speak in a proper human tongue. "The ladies will never lay eyes on them anyway. No sense in delaying just to acquire a longer ranged sort. He won't mind if I use his birds."

He?

Amalina wasn't quick enough at the moment—so overcome as she was by the loathesome pigeons on the counter and the chittering bats overhead; and the Count's semi-transformation—to ask who the Count was referring to. In fact, the question didn't occur to her until the pigeons were sent into the night, invitations tied with silk ribbons to their legs, and the bats following after to escort them all the way to the Ardeelian frontier.

He? she wondered later. He who? She had always assumed the ugly birds were Count Tepsji's property. So who did they really belong to? By necessity they had been grown and groomed to fly to the high castle. But they were meant to be in someone else's coop, to be released when this person wished to send word to the Count—and the birds would have been content doing so for their natural lives.

But now the Count had simply hijacked half for his own purposesm, with his own orders—delivered directly in their own pigeon language—for them to head far west.

He who? she continued to wonder. He who?

• • •

Perhaps because Amalina had caught this curious piece in the Count's words—tugging into the light a corner of a minor mystery—and somewhere in her sleep-deprived head she finally realized she really *was* back at the high castle, returned to the land she belonged, with all its various internal concerns, she was visited in the night by a dream she hadn't had in months. A nightmare she'd forgotten, and was startled to be confronted by once more: Lucinda Skeldar bounced through the rye, only her head visible as it rose above their blonde crowns, her dark brunette hair bobbing merrily at the action. And she was singing the song Amalina didn't like. And she was coming straight for Amalina with a smile but a fixed stare. And it didn't matter what the girl was singing. She was saying something else. Secretly. Demanding. *Kill the man responsible for my death, Amalina. Kill him. Give me justice. What are you waiting for, Amalina? It's been so long. Kill him!*

Amalina woke in a sweat, her covers knotted and thrown off the bed. Lucinda's song still haunted her ears. And Lucinda's demand pressed on her mind. The Count had killed Lucinda, of course. That was the very first time Amalina had seen him; had learned of his existence, as he tore the poor girl's throat before Amalina's eyes.

And the poor girl still wanted revenge.

Right, Amalina thought with an exhausted sigh. Lucinda, now in heaven, couldn't know Amalina had long ago given up the idea of killing the Count.

Her intent was to overhaul the castle.

· · ·

In less than a week the Count lost his patience and called Amalina away from her sketching of castle improvements to write up the next round of invitations.

"It hasn't been long enough," said Amalina, annoyed to have been drawn from more important work. "Could the birds have arrived at all? And then it'll take longer, you know, for any return posts. And that's after giving them time to think over the matter."

"I don't need the counseling of a small child," the Count smirked.

"I'm not a small child!"

"I've lived a very long time—"

"So you've said before … sir. But I'm not a small child."

"To me everyone looks like and acts like—and *is*—a small child. Hm, I don't wish to be put into one of my Mouse's famous delay tactics. Sit down and write out the next set. I've noted the families I wish to be contacted next. This time the wording will be less round-about. I wish these not to be veiled invitations. Perhaps more insistent."

"Desperate," Amalina interpreted.

"Well, you're right," said the Count. "I imagine there will be a longer string of correspondence than what we enjoyed last year." The Count was referring to Lady Princess Lisbet Spaarvierlet, who the previous year had arrived almost as fast as her letter declaring she'd accepted the invitation.

Her haste in arriving, driven by her father's hope that pretty Lisbet would snare and enfiance the wealthy noble before any other princess—and thereby rescue the Spaarvierlets from debt—was matched by her haste in leaving the castle; after experiencing an invasion of the Palace of Pleasures by the revolutionary Commander Kralov and his band of rebels, who'd been determined to exterminate the Count and all his guests. The Count reasoned, "Word will have gotten out about the minor bloodshed—and exaggerated, of course. I despair any rational family will now hesitate to throw their daughter eastward. Round after round of subtle negotiations are inevitable, it follows, even if the families are as debt-ridden as the Spaarvierlets. Thus we must remove any subtlety from our end. We are lonely—"

"We?"

"—and company over a winter might be too much to ask, especially away from a princess' own family. But poor little, dear little, Katarina Tepsji has only her uncle, who is a man of political, civic and economic occupation and seldom available for company, and could use a friend by her side to enjoy the beautiful scenery, etc., etc. You get the idea."

On a scrap of paper the Count had written in his cramped, spidery handwriting the names of seven more ladies.

"Still, it's a little *early*," said Amalina. "The first birds might not have—"

"A family will know if they are willing to risk their daughter the moment they read the invitation. Allowing two days for hesitations, and another for calculation, planning and arrangement. Lucky for us we don't ask for their sons, who are more properly engaged in learning the management of their lands or chasing after the next war, and so more difficult to let go of. A daughter is a loose article looking to be applied to its best bid and its capacity. But they will have to make a quick decision to beat the rains and then the winter. Or everything will be put off until spring ..."

Amalina started writing the first letter in her practiced style. The Count's words—*we are lonely … sons … chasing after the next war*—brought to mind Lt. Vokent and Amalina scratched her blown sentence. She pushed aside the paper and started fresh. She didn't look over to the Count, but she could feel his impatient eyes on her back.

"As I was saying, Mouse," he continued, the strange man's book thumping in his hands. "The first families will have decided within a week from receipt. So it's only sensible to get off the next round now, without waiting for the first to reply. The second will receive theirs after the first have already made up their minds, one way or another. And it gives those who come second a chance to reach us before winter if they really try."

"Yes. It has nothing to do with desperation at all."

"No." Earnesty rang in the Count's voice. He was somehow unaware of the sarcasm steadily trickling at him from the direction of his desk.

. . .

That night the Count cackled covetously before the open aviary window, as the last of the evil-eyed birds took flight. Their tiny silhouettes tracing westward across the moon.

7

The Giant

Hak Vogoneyevic was a giant even by mountain standards. A blond-haired, well-tanned, rock-muscled giant. A simple giant. A family-man giant, who had been reduced to poverty by flouting his noble birth to marry his commoner sweetheart, Gug. And he'd been quite content in his diminished status. But then he was rescued from embarrassment and ruination, was removed from his wife and his two children and given a new and grander purpose by former low constable Attila Bronk. As the plan went, Hak would take up his revered Vogoneyevic ancestors' fighting mantle, and tilt himself, with a grand army of the Ardeelian common folk at his side, against the greatest menace of them all: The Count of Ardeel. Only a simple giant of true heart and of immaculate virtue, and from a blood-line of the greatest fighting stock, could bring down the Count and free the Ardeelian people.

After the battle of Vogoneyevic Fields, where Hak defeated four armed and armored soldiers bare-handed, word of his ascendance spread. And though the government promised a bounty against him (and Attila), and some of the folk were tempted to take it, Hak's status of a people's champion grew. As did his popularity. And before long Hak was being invited into the territories and homes of true national patriots. From these beginnings sprung the spokes of the war engine that would roll against the Count.

Hak was not a man of words but was genuine and was loved. And in little time was rumored to have killed twenty or thirty mounted soldiers with his bare hands—*'though shackled with iron chains, three strands!'*, so it went.

After a while, he could be counted on to labor without the help of his master-guide Attila, winning the confidence of whoever he met and drawing in recruits on his own. And also train with more experienced fighters, learning the art of hand-to-hand and armed warfare. This freed Attila to travel and quietly work the political angles for the coming struggle, solidifying the allies and planning the crucial supply of the army once in motion.

This was how Attila had left Hak: a virtuous champion coming into his own.

"Where's Sir Vogoneyevic?" asked Attila as he entered the small hamlet outside Jolescu.

"Bronk! Bronk!" cried a handful of the peasants, overjoyed to be in the presence of their hero's right hand man. The only thing that kept them from pulling him down from his horse and carrying him aloft to Hak, with cheers rising from all around, was their awed reverence for the former low constable. He was quiet and mysterious, almost like an obscure saint. He quit his horse and with his predictable bored expression walked in the direction they beckoned, feeling only a few daring hands dart out to touch him in places. The old man who had brought him to Jolescu remained on his horse and was left alone.

The inside of the home where Attila was led was dark except where the fire burned in the hearth. But the laughs and hollers and overwhelming stench told just how crowded it was. The space was full of jumping and swaying dirty, sweaty bodies. Cups were being swung, their wine falling onto the floor or into mouths indiscriminately.

The outside crowd's cries that Attila had arrived died in the room's commotion. All attention was devoted to revelry. And even the cause of it, Champion Sir Hak Vogoneyevic, was lost in it and not the center of it.

His eyes adjusted to the darkness, Attila spotted Hak caught in a network of supporting arms, jumbling breasts and kicking legs. Faces with shadows for eyes, and open caves for mouths flew about him, shouting and singing. Hak had an innocent smile sliding off the corner of this face, his eyes looked saggy and bleary, and as if he couldn't tell you where he was if asked.

Attila moved with little resistance through the crowds. He had the ability to slip through openings and create passages with the slightest pressure, and pass through them like a sword through cream. The revelers swirled off as he made his way to Hak, unaware anything had changed in the room. But when Attila tried to take Hak's hand and move him to a private corner, the giant sat right down onto the floor, taking some bobbing chests and laughter with him.

Hak was too heavy for Attila to manage.

"Sir Vogoneyevic," shouted Attila over the song. "What's happened? What are you doing?"

"I'm in Jolescu," the giant answered some other question, his eyes listing to the floor, sounding lost. Sounding as a child to a parent, shame barely hidden in his defiance. "What's wrong?"

. . .

"I expected you to be a man," Attila said above Hak, who was now half-sitting, half-lying in his bedroom, hands petting lamely at the straw, head leaning against what looked like a pig trough. "A great man of the people."

"Then why'd you pull me away from them, sir? I had 'em right there with me."

"I said a great man of a great people," he said with his half-lidded, dull expression. "Not a sodden ape of the nation's beer barrel wastrels."

"You can't say those things to me, sir. About me *or* my people."

"I certainly can. I've sworn myself to the truth, Sir Hak Vogoneyevic. And I have spoken very plainly what I see."

"The truth is, sir," said Hak, righting himself and speaking very slowly. "I have done *a lot* for you, sir. A whole *lot*."

"What you've done, and have been doing—until I left you on your own—is for yourself, your family, your country … and should have been for your dignity. Stop drooling."

Hak wiped his mouth with a laugh. If his eyes could have slurred, they would have. They slurred up at Attila. "I mean is, Mr. Bronk, I've done a whole lot I never would have wanted to do."

"Become a hero to your own people and lead them from oppression? Did you know we have received the promise from a southern general to deliver his arms *to you*—that means true weapons of war: muskets, cannons—if you present yourself and your men, and I mean good fighting men, in battle readiness to him? Now, tell me how that is to happen in your … wickedness and dissipation? What the hell has happened to you?"

"You said you've never killed a man." Hak pointed his limp finger at Attila's face, which ended up targeting the low constable's knees. "That's something I would have liked. That's somethin' I woulda *had* for myself … if it wasn't for *you* … coming to *me*."

"I see where you are headed with this. But I was not born into a family of martial champions, as you were."

"I don't think you were born at all, Mr. Bronk. I think you were hatched. A chicken you are. A real chicken."

"If I killed half the governor's army single-handed, I couldn't rouse the spirits of the Ardeelian people. You could do it by simply speaking to them. Did you hear me about the muskets and the cannons? Those are for you, if you can put two feet on the ground and prove yourself."

"I've killed men, Mr. Bronk. I've cut them down and destroyed them."

"And you are very good at it."

"And I am very good at it," Hak agreed with a drunken burble. "Isn't anything to brag about, Mr. Bronk." He laughed. "Even if you like doing it."

"You like killing now?"

"Why don't you come down here and hug me, for all the nightmares you've given me. Then you'll find out."

"When I brought you out, I had hoped you'd raise a national army of liberation. What I see here: You're splendid to lead your countrymen to the cask, and inspire them to drown themselves into drunken oblivion. For pity's sake, if you don't right yourself, and fast recruit double the men we have, we can say farewell to the southern general." Speech done, Attila shook the parting of his cloak. "Wine simply doesn't agree with you," he added diplomatically.

. . .

"How's papa?"

"Goodness, what are you doing here?" said Attila, looking bored but clutching at his trembling left hand. He looked down on the tufted blond head of Hak's son, Man. Even more bothersome, Hak's wife Gug and daughter Lija—and apparently the new family dog—stood a few paces behind the boy.

"Came to see papa, Mr. Bronk. All of us. Even brownie dog."

"Yes. And who is manning the farm?"

"The neighbors have been real nice to us and mama. Mama has it all worked out, Mr. Bronk. So she said we could visit papa. It's been real long and we miss him. Can I see him, Mr. Bronk?"

"Did your mother send you to ask me, instead of asking me herself?"

"She still wants to kill you for taking papa away from us for so long."

"I don't *want* to see him," said Gug from her spot. "But he should meet his son. And I came along to see how someone dedicated to truth will lie to a child."

"I have no intention of lying to anyone," he said, attempting a gentle pat on Man's head to test his mother's reaction. Her general aspect didn't change, but he thought he detected the softening of something—maybe several sinew.

"Well, answer his son," she said. "How is his father? Or better yet, show us to him."

Attila took a second appraising look at her. "Ah, you've already been here, haven't you?"

"Show us to him, or him to us. Let's see how my Hak has been transformed—by your steady hands—into the savior of this country. It should give Man inspiration."

On a third appraising look, he decided that he was wrong, and that, sarcastic though she was: "No, you haven't been here yet. You haven't seen your husband."

"We've spent a good week tracking the Hope of Ardeel and getting here, relying on charity and support by the families who would join his side. We've just arrived. Now show his son to him. Or is there something wrong?"

Attila stepped forward, his eyes lowering as if he might fall asleep. "Did you say 'the families who would join his side'?"

"Everyone it talking about that idiot and his pet donkey."

"Mr. Bronk, is papa okay? Can I see him now?"

Attila patted him on the head again, and spoke over it: "Had those families sent someone to see him? To join with our forces? To train?"

Gug eyed him warily. "Some did. Some promised they would."

"Promised? How many promised?"

"Mr. Bronk, can I, sir?"

"You don't have enough already?"

"An army needs to be as big as its mission. And this is perhaps the greatest challenge ever to face Ardeel."

"Mr. Bronk?"

"You mean besides the invasion we lost to your people."

"Mr. Bronk?"

"Mrs. Vogonoeyevic, one look at my age, and you will know I was not even born when the invasion happened. However, this will be an even greater challenge, to be sure."

"Mr. Bronk?"

"But when Sir Vogoneyevic succeeds—and he will, I'll have you know we are about to receive the full armament of the southern army—it might remedy the pain suffered by your people during that episode, by proving to the government who wields the true power now."

"Mr. Bronk?"

"I don't understand half the things you say, and I doubt Hak understands half of *that*. But you've cast your spell and I hope you are not hoping to do the same to me. Please answer the boy now."

"Yes, Man? What was it you wanted to know?"

"Where's papa going?"

Hak was out of his room. He was staggering toward the inn.

"Papa! Papa!" called little Lija.

"Papa! Papa!" called Man.

The dog barked and trotted after him.

Gug singed the back of Hak's head with a look, while shaking her own.

"What's the matter with papa, Mr. Bronk?" asked Man.

"Needs some rest—"

"Bring 'em out!" shouted Hak toward the inn. "Bring 'em all out! I shall lick every one, ha, ha!"

"He was celebrating and is a bit …" Attila stopped talking.

At least twenty drunks piled into the street at once. Hak grabbed four of them and began to reenact his single-handed victory at Vogoneyevic Fields on their heads. The drunks laughed, even the ones being struck—until they realized they were in an earnest fight and began to protest and battle back.

Attila slipped next to Gug. "I admit I neither understood nor appreciated your value to the cause, Mrs. Vogoneyevic. And I would never ask of you something you would disapprove. However, perhaps, if you would like to keep your family close together, you could move other people with your story and your children. Stir sympathy for not just a good family man—" Hak seemed to break a man's jaw here, Hak redfaced and bellowing like a boar "—but his whole family would be a good encouragement. They couldn't expect your young son, Man, to join the battle, of course, but his charm would allow others to consider *their* sons."

Men circled Hak and laughing all the while tried to pull him off the other trodden examples. "I've done it!" Hak yelled victoriously. "Done it again! Nobody can stand against the Vogoneyevic might! Ain't that so, Mr. Bronk? Mr. Bronk, where are you? Hey, isn't that brownie dog?"

"An army has coffers," Attila continued in a side whisper. "Even one as small as ours. And I understand you have neighbors helping with your harvest, but we could supplement you, or outright pay you if you would—"

But Gug was pulling the crying Lija and protesting Man back the way they'd come.

"The truth is I can't be everywhere," he hurried after her. "And you exert an influence on him I cannot. If only you would. Please, Mrs. Vogoneyevic. Please. Please, Mrs. Vogoneyevic! Come back, Mrs. Vogoneyevic!"

8

Feather and Claw

"Come down to Netz. I will meet you when I see you sitting for a three course meal in the Prancing Stag." The letter was not signed. The calligraphy was excellent, with impressive flourishes, and in its artistry disguised the true hand of whoever might have written it. The messenger who delivered the letter said the small boy who had given it to him refused to—could not, or would not—admit who had paid him to engage his services, and had only asked, outside of instructions, "If the beautiful Princess Tepsji was truly returned."

It was intriguing enough to revive Amalina's spirit after a month's boredom during her confinement in the high castle. She understood that it was probably not one of her friends from the west quickly snuck into Ardeel requesting a private reunion, nor Lt. Vokent trying to surprise her. But it was *someone*. And that someone was daring enough to communicate with the Count's niece directly, and mysteriously. Daring, indeed. Who could it be? Was it a man or a woman? And why a three course meal? And why the Prancing Stag? There was only one way to find out.

But, of course, there was no possibility to do so.

"You can't go to the village, girl," said General Marosh, glaring at his captain for bringing Amalina into his command center.

"I must."

"I don't see it that way."

"I was invited. The princess was invited, and I am the princess."

"You're a princess only when another princess is here and you have to play your role."

"But I'd be playing my role, General Marosh, don't you see?" said Amalina. "I'd be going as the princess."

"This invitation was not sent by a princess."

"How do you know?"

Marosh clenched and flexed his great, bearded jaw and looked down at her in frustration. This was not the behavior he would tolerate from one of his men. But she was not one of his men. She was an important possession of his beloved master.

"If it were a princess, she would have let you know. Nobody travels hundreds of miles to play coy. And, anyway, there's been no foreigners arrived in Netz. At least none who would be interested in you, or would have call to be interested in you. So."

"*Someone* sent this letter," she persisted.

"If I didn't know it was impossible, I would suspect you'd had the letter sent yourself, as an excuse to leave the castle. But it *is* impossible, and I know you understand you will not be allowed to leave under any circumstances."

"Ridiculous."

"You may feel you can be bold with your life," said Marosh. "An attribute I'd appreciate in one of my men. In you it is a pain for me. I can't risk your safety against his Highness's wishes."

"I'm not in your army. I don't see why I have to ask you for permission to leave."

"Then why did you?" he chuckled. "Because I control the doors."

"Count Tepsji controls everything."

Marosh fell to his knee, dropped his head and nodded gravely. His huge hand came up to touch the X carved into his forehead. "Yes, girl, the Grand Knight of Ardeel, king of all the world, controls everything. But until his Excellency returns to the castle, I am in charge here. And when he returns, he will find you as safe and sound as his castle."

As a parting shot, Amalina said: "Well … *someone* is going to be upset when I don't meet them in Netz."

"I imagine it will be the proprietor of the Prancing Stag," he answered dryly, "who hoped to lure you to a three course meal in his establishment in order to court favor with Count Tepsji, and to impress the village with the level of his clientele. And make some money at it."

"You have to take me down to Netz," she told Pils. She gripped his arm and pleaded with her eyes. "Someone has written to me. And they are waiting to meet me. And I won't know who until I go."

"How would I take you to Netz?" asked Pils, looking apologetic. "I'm not allowed out of the castle. Not even while the Count is away."

"Don't you have to get supplies? I can sneak into the back of the wagon. Nobody will know as long as you don't tell anyone."

Pils shrugged. "I don't get supplies, Ms. Amalina. The General's staff sees to all of that, didn't you know? They control everything coming in and going out of the high castle and are the ones who get to travel to the village. I haven't seen the outside of these walls since I arrived."

"Maybe Genadie could arrange something."

Pils looked doubtful but didn't say anything to discourage her. "I haven't seen him around, really," he commented neutrally.

Which was true. Ever since the day Anka delivered the book straight to the Count, Genadie had kept to himself. Shrinking at everyone's approach, hiding himself away. Not even continuing with Amalina's language lessons (more Italian and more French), except to growl with his back to her that she was adequate and could study on her own. Who knows what he was getting himself up to, then. He didn't even have to take care of the animals anymore. General Marosh's people had seized every prime duty in the castle:

the kitchens, animal husbandry, the stable, the well, the plumbing (such as it was in that time), gathering wood, chopping wood, priming torches, the smithing, wall defenses, perimeter patrol, hunting and foraging, provisioning and resupply. It was all accomplished with solemn martial rigor and twice-cleaned-and-polished uniforms. And a redundancy of at least two soldiers and one weapon at the ready. Pils and Anka were allowed their services inside the main building, which didn't amount to much after Marosh's heavy take. So it would seem to have left Genadie nothing to do but to stew and twiddle his fingers and toes.

Amalina went to Genadie's closet-room, intent to make peace with him and get him to demand a trip to Netz. The closet-room was cleared out. She supposed Pils had finally convinced Genadie to take a real room. However, after a short search, he wasn't in the main building.

The aviary!

Amalina snapped her finger and tore up to the loft.

The bats had returned and jostled against each other in their sleep when Amalina entered. But she had sensed Genadie rather *wouldn't* be there when she was already halfway up the stairs, and wasn't too disappointed when the bats were all she found.

Genadie had to be somewhere, of course. There was no way he had gotten out of the castle under Marosh's watch. Even the waste outlet from the upper story toilets, which Princess Spaarvierlet's young brother Aklan had discovered and through which they'd helped his sister's people escape the castle when it was under siege, had been barred over by Marosh's engineers. Unless Genadie had taken some secret route only he and the Count knew about. A possibility. But still, she couldn't imagine Genadie quitting his Master. He'd nearly reduced to a puddle of quivering tears the last time the Count had left the castle for a long stretch. He would never voluntarily leave. It would be his death, she figured.

Coming down from the pigeon loft, Amalina saw Anka. Overcoming a lump of anger in her throat, she called to the maid and asked her if she knew where Genadie was.

"You're sure you want to speak with him?" said Anka with an even voice and a polite smile. Her eyes announced her ample awareness that this was the first time they were actually speaking since the incident. *But all's fine*, her old eyes said. "I'm not certain he wants to speak to you. No," she laughed a laugh of pity, "I don't think he would at all. Don't you think?"

It was hard enough to face Anka after her unexpected betrayal. And now her pity at this first conversation turned Amalina's stomach against the woman. Someone who, on another gut level, she still considered *could* be on her side. An ally against the Count. An accomplice. The discomfort in Amalina's organs, not knowing which way to go, made it impossible to face the maid. She looked at the ground and turned to walk away immediately.

"Oh, please, I'm sorry."

Amalina halted, looked over her shoulder. Anka scurried up close. "You're still mad, Ms. Dalca? After all this time? I wish you wouldn't be."

Amalina's unspoken outrage boiled up so fast it surprised her. "I told you I didn't want anyone knowing about the book, Anka! Not until I told you to bring it out. Instead you brought it right to *him*!"

"Of course, of course," said Anka with an easy voice. "By your age, Ms. Dalca, I'd say I've known this awful man for more years than you've been alive. You'll forgive me if I tell you I know better how to conduct myself around him. What I did did no harm to anyone, and dispelled something that could have turned very unpleasant."

"Things *didn't* turn unpleasant?"

"Worse then, if you please. I mean worse with the Count. And if you'll hear me out, let me explain something you're unaware. When you gave me that book, if I wasn't already confused enough, General Marosh had seen the whole thing. He'd watched you hand me the book, the dress, the all of 'em. And he followed me from the courtyard. Followed right behind me. Watching. Really pressed the stones with his feet, to let me know he was there and watching what I was up to. So you understand now."

"Oh."

"I mean to say, where was I to hide your book, then? What was I to do under such awful scrutiny, milady, and I not understanding what was happening? Bring the book right to the Count is what I did, so there should be no mistake to the General that you and I weren't up to no good—or at least I—and he couldn't later speak to the Count on what he'd suspected us doing behind his back, and get that monster thinking awful things before we had a chance to have our say about it. I think I handled the situation the best it could be handled, yes I think so. That's all I can say." Anka's eyes were not exactly pleading for friendship but more insistent that Amalina not take it so hard.

Amalina shrugged. It'd been almost a month. How long could she hold a grudge?

"I can only tell you I've a lifetime of experience in my head. Keeping myself well and alive. If you're smart you'll trust me," said Anka.

"And Pils, too?"

"If you like," she said, her smile warming as Amalina lips turned softly up at the corners. "He's a little younger than me. But trust *me* even more than him. *He* does. You'll see what I mean."

"I'll tell Genadie the same, if he'll ever talk to me again."

"I don't think he will. Talk to you, that is. You saw his face. Oh!"

"But it's been almost a month," said Amalina, echoing her previous thought. "How long could he hold a grudge?"

"Maybe I'm wrong," said Anka with a charitable smile. "You know that one better than I. But you *did* see the way he looked at you, when I ... Well, when the Count saw the book. And started to read it. As I said ... Oh, dear!"

Amalina thought: regaining Genadie's confidence might be more difficult than how Anka got mine.

Still, Amalina was pleased. It seemed she and Anka had broken the chill between them.

One day passed. Then another. Amalina was tormented by Lucinda Skeldar in her dreams, demanding revenge, and in her unguarded waking moments by Lt. Vokent, flagellating her passions. But otherwise she was consumed by the promise of the mysterious invitation; its purpose and who could have sent it.

Amalina didn't know how long the letter's offer was good for. A month? A week? Had it only been for that very day? She didn't want the opportunity to pass. If Amalina really wanted to see who had sent the letter—and she really did—there was still an option open to her. This she began to contemplate. To contemplate quite seriously. Only, her thoughts were broken by soldiers calling from the battlements, and the sound of the castle doors being opened.

. . .

There was something unsettling about the man who drove the plain cart into the courtyard. He was small, dwarfed by the several stacks of birdcages rattling behind him in the cart's bed, but he was solid, as if he were as thick as he was tall; compact, not fat, and more square than round. He wore black clothes, black gloves, black boots, swung a thin black whip, and wore a black hat with a long brim. The blackness of all this getup seemed to feed directly into the black-green-gray lines and wrinkles that featured on his darkened, sickly-green-gray skin, as if they were all somehow attached and connected. The lines and wrinkles being the more interesting ends of the material. His face was buried inside all the lines and wrinkles, with only his long arching nose, toothy sneer, and angry brow ridge protruding aggressively from them. His eyes were sunken, white, shard-like slits, with constantly shifting pupils that seemed to favor the corners. He wasn't the least bit intimidated by Marosh's men, skittering off the bench of the cart and making his way very purposely, in an automatic way, toward just where Amalina had come out. She slid back, hoping he hadn't seen her, but close enough to observe. Yes, he moved as if nothing around him mattered much. As if he were the only one in the castle. Nobody except the Count, not even General Marosh— who strutted and bounced as he walked—moved with such uninhibited confidence. As he passed by Amalina, unaware of her in the shadows of the entrance, she saw the larger lines and wrinkles on his skin were just examples of smaller lines and wrinkles covering his face, almost like a patterned tattoo, but naturally formed on a layer of congealed grease. A bizarre, putrid raisin with a cunning look. A sly, sloshy apricot pit with legs. He had the appearance of the world's evil compacted into its densest form.

She followed behind him at a safe distance, unable to resist.

Without an armed escort, he went straight to the aviary.

The aviary! she remarked.

After a moment inside, she heard him mutter: "What? … What? … Where? … What has happened?"

She was drawing closer to the room, but then quickly doubled back and hid inside a closet. The man scuttled like and angry insect from the aviary and down the stairs. She followed the sounds to *l'entrée grande*. There he had cornered Pils.

"Where, I say," his high-pitched voice knifed at Pils, the young man looking surprised and puzzled, "where are the birds? What has happened to them?"

And when Pils couldn't answer—and Amalina kept out of sight—it wasn't long before the man was in the courtyard, thrusting his little arms at General Marosh, as if he didn't notice the General was almost twice as tall has he, and wore both a sword and a pistol in his belt. Marosh looked down at the man, arms crossed across his massive chest.

"What do you mean you don't know what's happened to the birds?" the man chastised Marosh as if he were young Pils.

"The birds are his Excellency's charges. What do I know of them?"

"I came to retrieve fifteen. There is only one!"

"I dare you to question His Magnificence with the same impudence you're trying with me."

"You think I won't?" This startled Marosh. "Well, wake him up and I'll do it. There are supposed to be fifteen and there is only one."

"He isn't in the castle," Marosh announced in a low voice, and wary look.

"Then why did you bother offering me to talk to him?"

"It wasn't an offer," said Marosh. He turned to walk away.

"Where is he?" the man demanded.

"If the King of All wanted you to know, you would know."

"Don't walk away from me! I came to get fifteen birds. Look at my cart! Fifteen cages! I came all this way with fifteen cages. Yet there's only one in this castle! You tell me how that can be."

Marosh waved a dismissive paw at him.

"How am I going to fill all those cages with just one bird?" the man shouted after him, his eyes pinning Marosh's back.

"Cut small."

The more lusty of Marosh's men began to laugh, but then recovered themselves and hid their humor behind a serious mask. They straightened up and slapped their weapons into place.

The man watched Marosh until the general turned a corner and walked out of sight. The man's eyes were narrowed and his crooked grin grew, rucking up more wrinkles as it spread and sliced. Then, still staring with Marosh gone for almost a minute, the man finally shook his head and his legs turned his body. He went to the cart and counted the cages. Then he shook his head again. He looked up at the sky and measured the time by the sun's placement. He shook his head again.

When he next turned, Amalina tried to hide herself, but he'd already seen her.

His eyes fixed on her. They stared for a long time. Where the Count's eyes were large and held a hypnotic fury when he pleased them to be that way, this man's eyes felt like cold pins into her face, her eyes.

"You," he said in his thin, high voice. "Who are you? But aren't you …? Who *are* you, girl?"

As he spoke, a flicker behind the pin-like eyes told of another conversation going on inside his head. What was being discussed she couldn't tell. But later she would feel as if she were being evaluated.

"Katarina Tepsji. The Count's niece."

"Eh?!" he fell back. Then he sneered more obviously and leaned forward. "Oh, is that so? Well, where is that uncle of yours? Where are my birds?"

"They're his birds. I wouldn't know. Why do you want them? *Are* they yours?"

"I came for fifteen. There is only one."

"That's what I heard."

"Heard, did you? Where is your uncle?"

"I don't know."

"Well, what am I to do?"

"Who are you?"

"I haven't time for this." The man scurried past, muttering: "I can only take what I can take … Who knows what happened … I don't have time."

"Who are you?" she asked as she followed him. "Are they your birds, sir? Where are you from?"

He didn't answer, but stopped at one point to warn her with a look.

"You tell your uncle," he finally said, "I brought fifteen cages for fifteen birds. But there was only one when I arrived. What happened? First he hordes them, now this? Will we have to train up a whole new flight? Whose cost there?"

Amalina looked at him blankly. "Where are you from? What's your name?"

"He'll know it," said the man, bothered. "Let me get to my business, what there is of it. No more time to waste before the day is wasted and I'm not on the road." Then he rolled his eyes and shook his head. "Oh! Oh, feather and claw."

He pushed past Amalina and made his way back down to his cart. There he picked up a long pole with a hook on the end of it. He used it to pull a cage off the top row and walked it toward the main building.

"Now that I think of it," she told him, "I might have seen some in the north tower garrett. It's cool there with the windows open and I think they like it."

"Feather and claw," he said morosely.

Amalina disappeared upstairs to her room. She took her thin cloak and the lightest formal dress she owned. As she ran down the stairs she folded them in her arms until they were a flat square. When she reached the courtyard she slowed and peeked out to make sure she would be unobserved. Marosh's soldiers had returned to their look-out positions, or were otherwise staring off in directions of possible intrusion. The man's cart was disregarded.

When Amalina entered the courtyard, eight pairs of eyes fixed on her. Or that was as many as she could count. She held the package of her cloak and dress hard at her side and she went to the horse at the front of the cart. The horse was only a little less appalling than the pigeons. It had a blond coat that was dirty and matted and smelled poorly. She patted it like it was a prize winner and cooed here and there, admiring its cloudy eyes and avoiding the knots of flies at his chewed ears. She carried on this way, sweating that she would be caught by the man before she could do what she needed to do, and waiting patiently for the soldiers to get tired of her and look away.

When she was being ignored, Amalina slipped around to the back of the cart. She lifted the cage that had been underneath the one the man had taken. She tucked her dress and cloak below it. But it made the cage sit a little too high compared to the others. She shifted out the cage and placed the dress and cloak (with the dark cloak on top), into the central cage sitting behind it. She patted the package of material down and breathed a quick prayer that it would be overlooked in the shadows. She closed the cage door and then set the first cage in front of it. Even knowing it was there, the dark square of fabric wasn't easy to see.

She sighed and returned to the horse, patting and singing softly to it. A couple soldiers looked up and eyed her suspiciously. She must have looked suspicious, too, the way she stared back at them, her face flushed and sweat dropping along the side of her face. But they didn't move to question her, they must not have seen what she'd done. They didn't notice she was no longer holding the square.

When the man with the figgy wrinkles came out of the main building, he had returned to his clever, sneering expression. His eyes darted around, and only for a moment rested for any length of time on the upper row of cages, as he fit the one containing the single motley pigeon into the open slot. He threw the pole alongside the stacks in the back of the cart, then went straight for the driver's bench. Before he could flick his thin black whip, the soldiers came forward and called to him to come down.

Amalina's heart beat fast. Had they seen what she'd done, after all?

The soldiers looked through the bars of the cages. But their eyes were shallow and they were grinning. The first soldier was poking his finger in the air toward the cages.

"What are you doing there?" said the man.

"Counting," said the soldier poking his finger. "13, 14, 15. Fifteen cages."

"Yes."

"That's what you arrived with. All empty."

"That is correct."

The soldier poked his finger out once.

"And that's one bird you're taking?" said the soldier.

The man stared at him, not comprehending.

"You came with fifteen cages," said the other soldier, "but you're only leaving with one bird?"

They were mocking him.

He stared poison at them. A poison strong enough to push them back to their positions, regretting they'd said anything.

But as soon as Amalina knew what they were up to, she'd run back inside the castle. It was time. Here was someone leaving the castle in a transport that had room to carry her. And there was really only one direction he could be headed. She had to take the chance.

She darted into the nearest closet and then pulled from her pocket the strange man's magic bone.

9

Nothing to Worry About

"Remember when I told you," said Krom, the general of the southern army, to Attila Bronk, "the assembly had not yet elected a new governor; some bastard who would order me to use my weapons on Hak Vogoneyevic, his army, and yourself? I received word this morning the new governor has been sworn in."

Attila nodded, looking somewhat distracted or disinterested. He hummed acknowledgement under Krom's sustained gazing. Then: "Oh. Who is it, then?" When Krom told him, Attila's eyebrow twitched, and he said: "He finally attained his purpose."

"Eh? What's that?"

"He got what he wanted."

"You know him."

"Without doubt," said Attila. "He used to be the high constable. Sat right above me in the order of things. Should be interesting for him to learn how the structure has changed in the country he is about to govern."

"You being his underling," said Krom, "should piss him off to know what you're up to. It would be a shame if he were to order me to use my weaponry against you."

"Before you hand it over to Sir Vogoneyevic," appended Attila.

Krom frowned and rubbed his chin. "I was urging you to make real this offer—my loan—before a new governor was installed. Now that we have a rump in the chair, makes it more difficult to excuse my actions. You see, before, I could claim there was a lack of power, and the instability led me to accede to the leader of a stronger army in my region. Now I have a confirmed head above me to answer to. And more importantly, still no sign of a stronger army."

"He will be here today," said Attila. "I promise you. With the strongest army you have ever witnessed."

"Well," Krom laughed. "I was a small child at the time, but I *did* travel with the excursionary force into Ardeel. That was something. And what I will say to mollify the new governor, when he learns of what I've done, I can't think."

"I will have a word with the governor."

"Especially if I've handed over my arms to a simple gang. I hear that Hak is a great man, kills five men for lunch, ten men for dinner and holds two hundred men at the ready. I also hear Hak has fallen to the cup, has been spoiled by his fame, and surrounds himself with no more than twenty thugs and no fewer than forty whores."

"Well, you should never listen to rumors. But I'll tell you he is a young man coming to his glory."

"I don't know how I'll excuse myself to the governor and the assembly," he murmured again.

"The assembly is nothing to worry about, and I've already assured you the governor will be mine to handle."

"I don't see how. I am his general and you are not."

"Sir Vogoneyevic will be coming today. Believe me. Let's not let our tempers get the best of us at this great moment in our history."

"You talk a good game. But where is Hak?"

"Have another drink, General."

. . .

Attila did not let his nerves show, even in the greatest test of his nervous system yet. Human hunting parties, treachery, imminent execution was now a light fluff compared to the gamble playing out. Would Hak Vogoneyevic arrive at the head of an impressive army before the general of the southern army gave up on him?

"Gug is watching," Attila had told Hak. "And Lija and your son, Man. They are watching you."

"Where?" Hak had said blearily.

"You think I'm letting her near you?" said Attila. "Do you want Man to see you as a drunk?"

"Then they aren't watching, are they?"

"Listen, Sir Vogoneyevic, there is little time now. Zsolt Marosh has fortified the castle in Netz. We need all the armaments we can get, or we might not stand a prayer against the Count. First we have to get through Marosh, before we even face the true enemy."

"You've said this a hundred times."

"And we can get the armaments we need if we just present an army that is at least adequately trained and at least twice the size of Marosh's, and has a Vogoneyevic at its head who can at least sit up in a saddle."

Hak had belched and put a hand over his eyes.

"If you do not do this, Sir Vogoneyevic, you will lose an army, destroy the family name of Vogoneyevic forever, and be refused into your home in Baibey Valley because, I remind you, Gug is watching."

"I can do all that, Mr. Bronk, just by sitting here getting drunk? Sounds much easier." But he yawned and stood and patted Attila on the back. "Why don't you trust me, Mr. Bronk? Why don't you ever trust me? I killed them soldiers bare-handed, didn't I? When you didn't think I could. And I can kill anyone that gets in my way."

"Well, that's a start, isn't it? Now we have two weeks to train you to fire a rifle. And shape your followers into a disciplined body who can face down Marosh. And then we have to march them down to the waiting general to pick up our weapons and supplies and supply wagons, before we can begin to finish what we started so long ago on your farm."

"The farm," Hak sighed, his eyes closed and teetering on his feet. He bowed his legs to steady himself. "Is she really watching? You don't think she knows about the—"

"She's a woman. She knows everything. But at least she hasn't abandoned you yet. As long as you accomplish what you promised her you'd accomplish when you left her—"

"It's your fault I left, Mr. Bronk."

"It is fate. I am just the instrument."

"Do you really believe what you say, Mr. Bronk?" Hak didn't know sarcasm, his simple eyes looked to Attila for assurance that he indeed believed what he said.

"As long as you begin training, and you arrive at the general's fortifications in time." He didn't add: *Otherwise, it is* my *fate to be humiliated to death.*

And so Hak began his training in earnest, showing his sweat to his followers and making them understand that there was a purpose to his return, and that it wouldn't be easy. That a common effort of superhuman will would be required to pull this off. And he did this throwing looks at odd moments in every direction, making sure Gug was there—or, in case he'd fouled a shot, wasn't.

And only a handful of times had Attila had to pull him out of some foreign bed, after another disappointing lapse into premature celebration.

. . .

If Attila were a nail-biter, his hand would be a series of bloody nubs. Instead, as he stared calmly and reassuringly into the general's eyes, the system that connected his psyche and his soul was a series of figurative bloody nubs. The only physical expression of his nerves, unseen and undetected, was the trace of cold damp fear lacing his body. "Any hour now."

"Did you hear about the massacre at Fornescu?" said the general, conversationally but with a sidelong glance.

"What's that?"

"Shame. I thought that might have been Hak at work."

"What happened?"

"First the castle was destroyed. That was a bit of a mystery there. Then the whole town was slaughtered. Heads and limbs cut off. Most burned in a bonfire in the center square. Nobody knew until some traders passed through."

"That's barbaric. Hak would never—"

"Well, it would prove something," said the general. "Wouldn't it? Hard to ignore a body that'd do something like that."

"I suppose."

"You don't want to claim it, then? For yourselves?"

Attila thought for a fraction of a second. "No. Hak is a man of the people."

"Don't look forward to pushing up against whatever did that. Would be better if someone else had the arms and had to deal with the perpetrators."

"Yes, it would," Attila encouraged. Then, absently, "It couldn't be the Turks …"

"But, you understand, that'll be something the new governor will be ordering me to investigate. And start using that equipment you'd like to get your hands on."

"Time really is of the essence," Attila noted without emotion. Which Hak would be arriving today? he wondered as time ran out. The hero or the disappointment? Or would he not be showing at all?

"He's here!" a sentry called to the general. "The Vogoneyevic faction."

The General made to stand, but Attila put a hand on his arm. "Have some more wine, General. We have half an hour at least."

"Must feel very satisfying being able to swallow that lump in your throat," said the General. "Why don't you have some wine, too?"

"Sir Vogoneyevic forbids me to partake," said Attila.

"Oh? I don't like to drink alone. Didn't realize I was. Don't like it, Bronk. Let's head outside and have a look at the Vogoneyevic lad. See if I'll be handing my armaments off peacefully. Or if I will be placing him and yourself under arrest."

"Arrest?"

"A formality," said the general. "There's no letting a force of opposition leave my custody, unless I could prove I was intimidated. Only way the Tsobl boys would bless me. So, now, let's go see, Bronk."

"But … you will arrest us?"

"I pray not."

"But you will attempt to arrest us if you are not satisfied?"

"He will satisfy me, won't he? Then you've nothing to worry about."

"You should have been more specific about your requirements and intentions. This was not in our agreement."

"At that time Fornescu hadn't happened."

"And what does that have to do with it?"

"Well," began the general in an apologetic tone, "I have to have *someone* to execute for that crime. A horde of drunken blackguards would do the trick. And make me look pretty good and timely and thorough."

The lump in Attila's throat which the general suggested a moment ago appeared.

. . .

"It's not going to be as easy as we thought," Attila whispered.

"How do I look, Mr. Bronk?"

"Like Adonis and Mars combined. And so do the men, thank Heaven."

"Like my clothes?"

"Ready for review, you should be in a painting. Where did you get them?"

"Mother heard what I was getting up to down here. She sent me grandfather's old uniform. A little small, but it fits smart, don't you think, Mr. Bronk?"

"But as I was saying. There is to be a competition."

"Sounds like fun. It's been a boring march."

"Immediately. The tilting grounds are being set."

"All right," Hak looked serene or utterly oblivious.

"You think the men are capable after a long road?"

"Ready for anything, Mr. Bronk."

"You notice how I am not asking what took you so long, Sir Vogoneyevic?"

"Has it been long?"

"I've been marinating with General Krom for nearly half a week, with the threat of the agreement fermenting or spoiling hanging over us."

"What?"

"We expected you three days ago."

"Thank you for not asking, Mr. Bronk."

"As I said," continued Attila, his eyes at half mast, "There will now be a tournament of sorts. Several tests of skill. You and your men are allowed to lose only one to his—"

"We will win all of them."

"That's what I was about to suggest. We can't allow him a single excuse to renege."

"We will win all of them. What are they?"

"Some are easy enough. Five of our strongest fighting men will wrestle with five of Krom's to submission."

"Me. I can beat them all. Won't even need to remove my fancy jacket."

Attila nodded. "As I thought. Though your mother might want you to remove the jacket out of respect. Then five of the most skilled fighters will come at each other with swords, to the blood."

"Me."

"Are you sure?"

"They won't ever touch me. But I *should* remove my jacket, just in case someone gets lucky."

"Five of the best riders will charge at cabbage heads and rings, then try to unseat Krom's men."

"Horses?"

"You know how to ride?"

"Maybe we'll let him have that category," said Hak.

"Unadvised. Nobody in the ranks?"

"I'll ask around. But I'll do it all myself if I have to. Nothing to worry about, Mr. Bronk."

Attila cut Hak a look. "But then there are to be five men against five men in a test of marksmanship. Targets at 250 yards."

"Me, again."

"I think you have some better small game hunters."

"It will be me, Mr. Bronk. Nothing to worry about. I'm telling you, Mr. Bronk. I wish you wouldn't look at me like that, Mr. Bronk."

"You can't do everything yourself."

"These men look up to me. I have to show them I'm the best of all."

"A good commander knows when to reserve himself and delegate."

"What?"

"Let the others have a shot. It'll make them feel better."

"You think I can't fire a rifle good?"

"I think that such a shot isn't required of you. And 250 yards is a pretty far shot, indeed. And you'll be aiming at cabbage heads."

"Sounds like they don't like cabbages much."

"We can't afford to lose a single match. Are you sure you won't take a substitute?"

"I'm doing it."

• • •

As it happened, Hak Vogoneyevic (with jacket set aside and folded on a chair), wiped the field clean of all-comers in the physical match; knocking them down like bowling pins. Then, in the swordsmenship category, he bruted them and treated them like bowling pins, too, never mind the blades. Hak's army sent up a hurrah. Attila should not have doubted Hak's ability on a horse, either. But he never would have suspected pure brutality could be just as effective as finesse. The cabbageheads and rings and Krom's cavaliers fell to the ground like so many more bowling pins.

As expected, General Krom harrumphed doubtfully at the routing of his best soldiers, sent a signal, and the waiting regiment, fully armed, neared the playing field. "Not all these tests are of equal weight, you know," he informed Attila. "Weighted twice is the last. For above all, the rifle commands the field before the charge. If you aim to take on Marosh, you will be facing the best on that score. Fail this, low constable, and well ..."

A message had just arrived before the tournament, another castle had been destroyed in the south. An abandoned or otherwise unoccupied castle, but mysterious vandalism nonetheless. This made General Krom all the more keen to hold onto his weapons, and find an easy scapegoat.

So now Attila lay under the review stand, with his keen eye tracing a line over the rifle barrel at a cabbage set at an upward angle some 300 yards away, with Hak Vogoneyevic standing some yards between the two. Hak, in front of Attila, clumsily hefted Krom's musket, trying to make the operation look as easy as a round of bowling, his dumb confident face projecting dumb confidence. His massive shoulders blocked the action of what he was doing after that. Who knew where Hak's shot would go, but Attila's had to hit the cabbage dead center and burst it into so many pieces—the double difficulty of firing at the exact moment when Hak fired or the game would be up. Attila studied Hak's back, and waited for the motion he had seen and noted on so many occasions: the slight upward motion of the shoulder (Hak's movement certainly altering the position of the barrel to send the ball wide), which meant the hero was pulling the trigger. So Attila's aim was split between Hak's large, sun-browned shoulder and the green vegetable in the distance. If his shot wasn't timed properly, the ruse would be discovered. If his shot was not accurate, instead of zipping past Hak's arm, the ball might bury itself in Hak's blond head.

At that horrible moment, Attila's left hand began its familiar vibration, and his upper lip grew a sweat. The trace of damp fear was more of a soggy blanket over his limbs now. And the barrel began to dip and wave, just as Hak's shoulder dropped.

10

Invisible

Amalina had already given the magic bone its chance. In the doldrums of the past month, knowing Genadie was furious at her, and she was furious at Anka, and everyone was avoiding everyone else, and the Count was locked in study with the strange man's diary, she had plenty of space within the castle to play and practice.

With the bone's first try came its first, and most disappointing, surprise.

Put it between your teeth, the man had said. You will become invisible.

Alone in her room, Amalina held the bone before her eyes using the tips of the fingers of both hands. She studied it, rolling it in her fingers, wondering how it could work such magic. It must be infused with something more than ordinary bone and marrow. It didn't look it. Though the strange man had said the bone once belonged to a black cat, it definitely looked like an old duck's leg bone. Solid and not hollow. Pitted and dull gray. Not anything magical. It looked like something that is swept into a corner after a feast.

Put it between your teeth.

It would work, just as it had on the wagon. It *had* worked then, when she put it in her mouth, hadn't it? The man had looked at her, and kept looking at her, and said it didn't work against him. But there had been a feeling to it, a slight ripple of energy across her skin. Like a cool breeze. She didn't remember if she had looked down at herself. At this point she only remembered trying to avoid his stare, but being drawn toward his eyes, which gazed so powerfully at her.

Amalina ran her tongue around her mouth. It felt dry. Her teeth became itchy at the thought of biting down on the bone; something she might ordinarily do, absent-mindedly, during a meal. Playing around with a leg she'd gnawed clean of meat but had not yet been ready to discard.

Was it a trick?

Was it a trap?

Was it poisoned?

Was it a joke and nothing would happen when she clamped it in her mouth—other than the man laughing when he found out?

But she'd tried it already! along the road! Come on. What was she waiting for?

But this time was different.

A duck leg. Or a goose leg. Too large for a quail or a grouse. Or a mouse or a rat. Could it be from a rabbit? No—he'd said it was a black cat's bone, didn't he? So it must be. Wasn't there something about black cats?

What would happen—really—when she put it in—?

With a clickety-clack, Amalina shoved the bone lengthwise into her mouth and bit down. Her tongue immediately lashed forward, as if to stop the bone's momentum, or to taste what was coming into her body. It was a room temperature cool, tasting slightly salty and slighty stale.

Something was wrong.

Something had fallen away in front of her.

Panic pulsed three times as her eyes searched the room, looking for the culprit. Was it the Count? Had he entered her room, flashed in as a black blur, as he would do on occasion? Maybe by following the strange man's instructions and putting the bone in her mouth, it had alerted the Count.

Or was it the strange man? Had the action somehow summoned him—?

No. Her hands were gone. That was it.

And her cheeks. And her upper brow. And the bridge of her nose. Look in any direction and all those things at the periphery, to which she had grown accustomed, was gone. Turning her head she saw that she was no longer there. Only her sleeves.

Her dress puffed out in front of her, and the sleeves, seemingly hollowed open by a wind, moved this way and that with her gestures. The hem of her skirt danced above her animated, empty shoes.

The clothes remained. Amalina was gone.

Amalina felt that electric ripple again.

She took off her clothes. First her shoes, then her skirt, then her dress. It was incredibly awkward as each item vanished and she moved to the next, because not knowing where her limbs were, only sensing them the way one does when one moves about in pitch black, her arms and hands kept missing their mark or banged into one another. Her hands hit her hips, and then she had to move them up slowly to find the edge of her blouse.

Walking was difficult for some reason. She just didn't know where exactly her legs and feet were. And she kicked her feet out, her mind demanding to see them, to prove that they were there in the light and she knew where they were. She kicked the desk chair, and nearly snapped her first three toes on the corner of the bed. She took the bone out of her mouth to locate the small mirror in the makeup box. Only when bringing the mirror to her face did it dawn on her that she was, in fact, naked.

Angrily she put the bone in her mouth, and in the polished brass of the mirror she now saw a blurry view of the wall behind her. She was invisible. But what kind of magical item was this? It rendered her invisible, but nothing else. If she wished to sneak around the castle, to act as a spy, or a saboteur, or a voyeur, or to escape from the castle, she could only do so without wearing clothes, without any protection at all. This would be satisfactory only in the summer. Or the late spring and the early fall, but then only in the days and not in the cool evenings. She could already envision, because she was already growing invisible goosebumps as she stood there in the cold, that her excursions would be very limited, and conducted with the distraction of wrapping and clapping her arms around her for warmth, and dodging anything that might be uncomfortable to run into. And never mind doing it in the wild: She had no idea if her scent was still detectable—in fact she tried to smell herself, but slammed her hand into her nose and could only smell snot and blood for an hour—but she assumed any sound she made was clearly audible. Any wildlife—from insect to bear—could hone in on her and do their worst.

This magic bone was no merry boon for her. She'd only use it, she figured, in desperate circumstances, when the need to lose all her clothes and suffer the indignity of invisible exposure wouldn't ruin all its fun.

Still, that afternoon she decided to give it a full run. She found Anka coming down a hall and waved her arm from around the corner. Anka's blank look and purposeful stride encouraged her to jump out fully in front of the maid. No reaction. Same for Pils. Same for a set of patrolling soldiers. She was invisible.

Back in her room she spit out the drool soaked bone and then wondered why she hadn't followed any of her subjects around longer, to see where they were going and what they might be up to. It would have to wait until next time.

The second try, after shadowing Pils and Anka through their day— Amalina pushing over a couple stacks of clothes being folded by Anka (who she was still on bad terms with at the time), causing the old maid to exclaim, "is that you, Count Tepsji?" and "Just another thing then! Just another crazy thing for poor Anka to contend with, I suppose. Oh, Master, why did you give us this nightmarish burden, I ask you? For your love, then, Master, Anka does it," causing Amalina to feel guilty and like a brute for having done it— and then observing Marosh's cooks preparing meals in the kitchen, followed by practicing sneaking herself through closing doors, Amalina concluded that observed people aren't very interesting and that using the magic bone left her with little entertainment. And a chill.

She was resigned to leave the magic bone alone. Considered it disappointing magic. But then she saw the bird fly up to the aviary. There she found one of those ruffled, greasy, evil-eyed birds pacing on the counter, a little piece of paper tied to its leg. She opened the note and saw the familiar code written there, one that used all the various characters from the dozen or so cryptographs, making it unreadable even if she tried to decipher it using her own stolen codex (from the Count's coding system). But here was an opportunity, she thought. It was daytime. The Count wouldn't be touring the castle until late afternoon at the earliest. She went to her room and copied out the message. Then she stripped down to just her dress; easy to get rid of. Then she found Pils and tasked him to deliver the message to the Count's private study. Around the corner she lost her clothes behind a box, put the bone in her mouth, and followed right on Pils' heels.

The Count was awake and in his study contemplating the strange man's book. He accepted the message passively and Pils left the room as fast as he could. Amalina kept her distance, moving only when Pils was there, and positioned herself close to the fireplace, but poised to follow the Count when he moved to open the cabinet from the wall, opening a secret door that led to his hidden rooms. She was sure after reading the message he would take it to his private message center, to glue it into one of his many books reserved for secret transmissions. It was his habit to keep and treasure such correspondence, or record it, anyway, and he was prompt about it. And maybe she would see him use his stick cyphers to decode the message before her eyes, revealing the method to this tricky one, and just what it said. So she waited there, trying to keep her panting to a minimum, expecting him to rise immediately and escort her to observe this secret rite.

He sat there, unmoving, for hours. As still as a statue. Even his open eyes seemed not to blink, but stare low at the opposing wall. Her body grew cold, her back and limbs began to ache. She shifted close to the fireplace to warm herself. He did not seem to notice. The fire in the chamber died down and he didn't replenish it. The two candles in the stick burned out without reaction. He didn't need either of them to function. And so she was trapped in the private study with the Count, with no light and no warmth, completely naked and knowing she couldn't risk moving or falling asleep or breathing too heavy.

In the morning Anka knocked on the door and entered. She held a torch which was blinding to Amalina after so many hours in the dark. The Count was no longer there. Amalina ran as fast as she could, retrieved her dress, and threw herself on her bed, resolved to sleep for two days and never to use that worthless magic bone again.

. . .

Amalina bit down lightly on the bone to keep in it place as she ripped off her dress. She flew from the closet, not caring if anyone was there to see the closet door open and close on its own. She also barreled through the front doors, causing the sentries there to peek around at who was coming through, then turn to peer into *l'entrée grande* to see who had flung open the doors. Amalina did not see their puzzled expressions, she was charging after the cart heading out of the castle, trying to ignore the pain of her feet hitting the stone and knowing the sound of it was barely covered by the plod of the horse, the creak of the cart's wheels, and the snap of the man's thin black whip.

The massive doors were closing and one soldier was standing within the gap, watching after the cart. Amalina bumped past him and now she was running on the hard brown soil of the road. She didn't know where she was in relation to the cart, and having learned from busting her nose, sent out her right hand gently to feel for the edge of the cart. It was picking up speed, but he wouldn't be stupid enough to run the cart at top speed as he angled down the mountain. So she sped herself a little more, until she caught hold of the back lip of the cart and was comfortable she was at a matching speed with it. With an awkward shove of her legs, she sprang up at the cart's narrow lip, and tried to catch hold of one of the cage bars. Her fingers stubbed and bent back on the cages painfully, but her left hip landed on the rough wood and she rolled into a sitting position, her legs dangling off the back. She blew out a pained breath and moaned, shaking her throbbing fingers.

The floor of the cart was warm but littered with bits of dirt, straw and filth from the birds. And spots so scratched that splinters stuck out dangerously. Amalina swept a clean, smooth patch free and settled in for the ride.

"You wanted those disgusting birds to be gone," said the man.

Amalina caught her breath. She looked through the bars of the cages at the thick square of his hunched shoulders and back.

"Well, good for you. You didn't like them and now they're gone. And now what's to happen, enh?"

The plod of the horse filled the next silence. Amalina got onto her knees and stared at him, waiting. Then she decided he must be talking to himself.

"Can't get word to him, enh? This one will have to do. But the time will be missed. It will be missed, I can feel it … That's a bit touchy … And close … It *is* close, isn't it? Won't it be? He won't pull it off in time. And then what's to happen, enh?"

The man shook his head and cracked his whip three times.

"Who's going to pay the cost for the new flight, enh? And how long will we be down to this one scrawny rat? Feathers and claws, claws and feathers. I'm not riding back and forth for one rotten gargoyle. No. Even if it takes another year. It's on him! What could he have done with them, but eat them. Or maybe it was the soldiers got hungry … I don't know. And now the time will be missed and she will live and what will happen, enh?"

She will live? Amalina wondered.

The man whistled a greasy whistle. "Very pretty. But such a chatter-box. The most dangerous of all. And now this, enh? No birds but one. Very dangerous. Feathers and claws, claws and feathers." Whip, crack!

As the distant bell of Netz's cathedral began to ring, and the sun fell below the edge of the mountain, dropping a soft darkness across the landscape and leaving a vivid red edge on the clouds above, Amalina gently opened the door of a cage, shimmied in, then reached through the bars into the middle cage. It took several tries to nab a corner of her cloak and dress. And then it took some effort, in the narrow confines of the cages, to pull them through.

As she did so, she listened to a song the man began to tunelessly sing, perhaps prompted by the bell or nervousness at the coming of night while he was still on the road. "One white leg, fat and fancy. One white arm, that is my doll. One breast, two breast, plump and pert. All apart, then into the dirt." He sighed. "Too bad. Such a waste. But those delicious lips are too dangerous when they're talking." He began to sing again, "One white leg, fat and fancy ..."

"Almost night, sir!" a voice warned from the edge of the road. They were passing a farm, the farmer had some long instrument slung over his shoulder. He was headed toward his house, its door was open and a yellow glow of fire, and the silhouette of his old wife, was inside. "Almost night."

"Why thank you," said the man, tipping his cap. "I shall be in town before long."

"God speed you. God protect you."

"I doubt I'm pretty enough to warrant your concern, enh? But thank you. And may you and yours be safe this evening, as well."

"God protect you," the farmer said in the distance.

"Heard you the first time," the man mumbled sulkily to himself. Whip, crack! Whip, crack! Whip, crack! "One breast, two breast, plump and pert. All apart, then into the dirt ..."

But night was faster than the cart, and they were under the stars and a sliver of moon before they reached Netz. The man had fallen silent, and Amalina realized that the whole village would be closed up when they arrived. Where would she stay for the night? Who would answer a knock at their door? This wasn't Tsobl, and the superstitions were much worse here. She might have to sleep in a barn or a coop. Or maybe this man lived in Netz and she would have to leave off her clothes and shelter herself in his home. The thought made her shudder. But she didn't begin to put on her clothes in preparation for her escape. Instead she lay to the side and threw her cloak over herself like a blanket.

She gasped when she heard the low rumble of a voice penetrate to the center of her chest.

"You wanted to speak with me?"

Through the cages, Amalina saw the Count sitting next to the man. The man's head was turned so his long nose thrust at the Count's shoulder.

"The birds. What happened to them?"

"I am using them."

"For what?" said the man in surprise.

The gleam of the Count's teeth and the whites of his eyes shown his expression in the low, gray-blue moonlight. He regarded the man with his typical bemusement, waiting to see what the man would say next.

"Someone's going to have to pay for the new flight, enh? Don't you think? Someone is responsible, someone must pay."

"You need fourteen more," the Count said, glancing back at the cages. Amalina's heart pounded. It seemed his eyes looked right at her. Then she realized she was under her cloak, and everything, her cloak and dress, were out in the open. She stifled an urge to swallow, and turned slowly, with the rock of the cart, to get out from under the cloak.

"Fourteen," echoed the man. "There was supposed to be fifteen, and now there is only one."

"You know I can count."

"Well, it was a surprise when not a single feather of them had been returned for months. Then I come to collect, on account of urgent business, and there's only one. That was all I was saying."

Amalina pushed the cloak and dress back into the cage, then sat up, tucking herself into a ball at the far edge of the cart. If she needed to, she would jump.

"Business," said the Count.

"Urgent."

"You've something to tell me?"

"Not yet. But soon."

"One bird should do, no?"

"Maybe one. Maybe two. Maybe even three."

"If it takes three, it isn't urgent."

"Oh, but it is. You know how it goes. This one is a tricky one. Which accounts for the number of birds … which are now no longer in service, enh? *You're* using them."

"If you told me now where—"

"No sir. It isn't set. I haven't a clue."

"I will take care of it."

"It will take months to set up a new flight."

"Just send me a packet of fresh earth from your home. I will purchase the new birds, and I will teach them. It is quite immediate."

"But not as accurate, enh? Sometimes they go off, with that technique."

"Are you old or young?" asked the Count. "I can't tell."

"How long have we been doing business? I should think I seem very, very old."

"Nothing in this world seems older than what I woke up to this evening."

"Interesting thought. However, as I was saying, with *your* way of training, sometimes they go off. You know … can turn *inaccurate* … using your method …"

There was a silence, and Amalina imagined the Count was staring in bemusement at the man again.

"I look forward to receiving them," said the man. The cart rocked heavily. As if the Count had lunged forward and begun to tear the man to pieces. She couldn't help but glance over. The Count was gone, and the man was staring into emptiness. He glanced this way and that, and into the air. After a minute he shrugged and shook his head.

"One white leg … hmm-hmm-hmm." They were coming into Netz.

· · ·

The village was shut up properly, as any Ardeelian village or home was sealed tight when the bell tolled and day turned night. The only place that flouted the custom, as far as Amalina knew, was Ardeel's largest city, Tsobl, where the highest concentration of foreigners and travellers, and the widest variety of prey, caused the superstitions and customs to relax into quaint obscurity.

The cart rolled through Netz. Whip, crack! Whip, crack! The man might have turned his head, observing the closed off doorways and windows and let off a smirking chuckle. There might be a patrol of elders, or a watch set by the deputy sheriff, or maybe a brave soul wandering the streets somewhere. Amalina didn't see one.

It became obvious the man had no intention of stopping. She feared she would now be taken far away if she didn't leap off somewhere before the highway, where he could drive the horse to top speed.

She threw away the cloak and dress. Seeing how fast they fell into the distance, she hestitated to jump. She didn't even know where she was in relation to the ground. But she had to do it. She half-leapt, half-rolled off the cart's rear lip, feeling it scratch her hip, and then she pounded down onto the cobblestones. Sharp edges bit into her skin, but it was the blow of landing that caused her to open her mouth with a small shout. Her eyes had been closed—even invisible, closed eyes shut out the light—and only heard the bone clattering off to her right. When she opened her eyes, in the dim light of a street lamp, she was naked and bruised and lying fifteen feet from her clothes.

The man made a call, and the cart veered to the side and came to a halt.

Amalina gasped and scrounged for the bone. Where was it? To the right? She crawled, scanning the lumpy gray stones desperately. Was it camoflaged amid the gray? Had it fallen into a deep crack? She flailed her hands in all directions, hoping to find it. In the back of her mind she wondered if she shouldn't just grab her clothes and fly to the nearest shadowed alley.

Glancing back toward the cart, she saw the bone behind her. She spun painfully on her knee and snapped her arm forward. The man was coming down off the driver's bench, his face covered by the hat and its wide brim. He had only to look up and she would be there: one white leg, fat and bruised …

The bone clacked between her teeth and she disappeared.

• • •

The man had stopped to rest the horse. He patted it down while it drank from the trough. She stayed long enough to see the cart ride out the gate toward the highway road. Only later did she kick herself for not waiting to see which way he turned. But she was eager to get her clothes on and get some warmth back into her body.

It was a long night. She huddled herself inside a small barn near the Netz pigeon coops. Since the discovery of the castle aviary, she seemed to be permanently linked to those drab-looking types of birds in some way.

When the morning bell rang, and all the barred entries clattered open, she patted herself clean and went looking for the Prancing Stag Inn. It didn't open until mid-morning. It was a proper sort of restaurant, the kind one would find in larger cities and the west. It seemed there were some foreign businessmen who came to eat, and she shared the dining area with them. She was famous enough now that it wasn't hard to convince the owner who she was, and she could promise payment later for a three-course meal now. With all his reserved bowing and straining to please, the owner didn't seem to have expected her to come. He hadn't sent the letter. After she ate the well-made pies and chicken and venison and several greasy vegetables with a bread she could have improved upon, she was well stuffed.

But nobody came to visit. She waited patiently, if awkwardly: nobody spoke to her. It was the natural Netzian fear of a Tepsji; attending to her by bows and winks, mostly. Had this man, the owner, been, once upon a time, one of the crowd who'd tried to kill her and Genadie—thinking she was just a scullery girl—the revenge-bent mob suspecting they had killed the mayor's daughter? Well, it was all forgotten, anyway. She'd toured the town with Princess Lisbet Spaarvierlet later that year, sprinkling around Count Tepsji's coins. Enough to change the Netzian attitude in her favor.

• • •

Had she missed the timing of the invitation? She'd come to the Prancing Stag, had eaten her three-courser, and now she was done, the anonymous penman a no-show.

In the afternoon, after taking a stroll through Netz, up and down every street, thinking she could not eat another bite, she returned to the Stag and ordered another three-course meal, and made sure she was placed in sight of the window. The meal was served with raised eyebrows over polite smiles. She stuffed herself until she felt sick.

On Amalina's second stroll, when she wondered what might be happening back at the castle, and she considered calling at the inn where she and Lisbet had once stayed, she saw soldiers from the castle loading the familiar birdcages—packed with pigeons—onto the back of the old castle cart.

There was no thinking about it. When the men had returned to the front bench, Amalina was already in the bed of the cart, lying lengthwise, her teeth holding the bone, as she removed her cloak and dress. When her jaw began to hurt, she took the bone out and pulled herself to the shadows, ready to replace it if needed. As the night fell, and certain citizens of Netz gossiped around their tables about the odd visit by the barefoot princess, the soldiers sang a somber marching tune.

. . .

Amalina was invisible when they reached the castle. The cart had slowed on the crest of the hill and then stopped at the walls. She wedged her cloak and dress in a loose metal band underneath the cart while passwords were exhanged, then strolled into the courtyard as it rolled in.

"You've taken the whole day," grumped General Marosh with his great arms folded across his chest. "His Excellency has been up for hours."

"Sorry, General," said one of the soldiers. "The birdmaster of Netz gave us some trouble—"

"No excuses!"

Spears were thrust at the men. They dutifully stripped off their armor and presented their scarred backs for more whipping. For variety they were pounded with truncheons.

"And just for that," concluded Marosh, to the huffing, wheezing pile of flesh, "You two will be missing the hunt this weekend."

The poles and hooks were brought out, the cages to be moved to the aviary. Amalina had no plans to watch, tired as she was after the round of torture.

There were too many people clogging the front doors for her to feel comfortable slipping inside that way. She used a side door in the outer wall and made her way to the battlements where she could then use the small communicating bridge to the castle's main building. It was a route rarely used, and she knew, though it was long and circuitous, it would put her on a much easier path to her room.

But before she could reach her room, she tripped over something. She managed to hold the bone in her teeth, but fell hard on the hallway stones. This area was barely lit at all, with light coming from torches at either end of the connecting halls. This midpoint was almost black. What she'd tripped over was something soft, and it trembled under her shins, but was otherwise as invisible as she was in the darkness. She groped around some more, feeling worn cloth and thin limbs.

"Genadie?"

11

Genadie Explained

"Genadie, are you all right?" Amalina crawled around.

"Ugh."

"What are you doing on the floor?"

"Ugh. Ugh."

She ran her hands over him, trying to locate his head. It seemed it might be under one of his spindly arms.

"What's happened to you?"

He moaned and sighed at the same time.

"Let's get you to bed." Amalina tried lifting him, but this elicited a groan of protest, and he felt like he weighed a hundred weight more than she could handle. With a groan of her own, she went to bring one of the torches.

Amalina gasped.

Genadie looked like a bug that had been crushed, with a black-red pool of dried blood encircling him.

"Genadie! What's happened!"

"M-ssster," Genadie breathed lowly.

"Master? You want me to get him?"

"N-n-o!" Genadie's body shook and he flung himself over. His face was one lumpy bruise with red bruises speckled on top. "No mas-ssster. No … m-ssster."

Genadie slowly, agonizingly, tightened himself into a ball. The same way, years ago, when he'd first been laid up in his closet-room after being nearly murdered by the Count. He'd laid there for months, moaning and sighing and looking like a rolled up worm.

She didn't understand what had happened to him now, but a dark idea dawned on her: "Wait, is this … how long have you been … is this is where you've been this whole time?"

"What dayyyy?"

"Did one of the soldiers do this to you?" asked Amalina.

Genadie didn't move. Under his breath he said, "M-ssster."

"The Count hurt you?"

"Mm. M-ssstr."

It *was* the Count! So it *was* just like last time. "But why would he … ?"

Genadie didn't answer.

"I thought you were avoiding me," said Amalina, a strange relief entering her voice. "And you were here all this time … All this time … Oh, I'm so sorry, Genadie. I should have looked for you sooner. Looked everywhere. But I was afraid you'd still be mad at me."

"Ms. D-alca. Uhm-ah. I. ammmm."

"Mad at *me?*"

"Th- bo-ooook."

"But *I* didn't nearly *kill* you over it. Why be mad at me?"

Genadie swallowed heavily. His eyes opened and looked around, then closed.

"So then why'd he do it? Tell me. It couldn't be *my* fault."

"Th-b-k."

"What's that?"

"Th- book, Ms. D-alca. Th- book."

"I understand 'the book'. But what I'm asking is why did *he* hurt *you*, you understand?"

Genadie rasped at length: "Theeee Booooooook."

Amalina stared down at him. She'd seen him in worse condition, but that first time he'd been smashed to pulp, despite his gory wounds, he'd been so positively excited, his pain mitigated by the enchantment of having been brought into the castle to recover. Now he didn't have that novelty to boister his spirits anymore, so he was free to fully experience his misery. With a nod she decided: He'll live, anyway.

"I can't believe he left you like this. You can't lay here. Let's get you to a room."

"Ms. D-lca," he hiccupped as his eyes bulged, "y'r clothes!"

• • •

Once Genadie had been pried out of the pool and was situated in a bed in a small servant's room and was given some broth—and Amalina was fully clothed, of course—she looked down at the frail, shaking, broken body, and felt alongside a maternal sorrow a knot of guilt. If only she could offer him something that might cheer him, the way his first being accepted into the castle had nourished his soul. Now it looked like he could easily melt into the bed like a grease stain.

She tried to engage him in conversation.

"The book," he croaked. "That dam-ned boo-k."

"He didn't attack me for it. Why you? It wasn't your fault. Oh, Genadie, I'm sorry for having not listened to you. At least I shouldn't have trusted it to someone we didn't know. Foolish Anka. And now this. But please tell me why. Say it wasn't my fault."

"It wasn-t."

"It wasn't?"

"Ms. Dal-caaa ..." he sounded sorry for her. "No."

"But I thought you said …"

Genadie shook his head.

"Well then tell me, Genadie, before I burst. How, why?"

After a moment to prepare himself, he said: "He's afraid … I read … it."

"Afraid?" But there was something else to it: Genadie had said 'He' not 'Master'. In his fever, was he forgetting his slavering self? Or was he demoting his god, and slandering him with the commonplace, human-like fault of fear?

"We cann-t question … Master's will," said Genadie, ruefully, with the twitch of a grin to his strained lips. "But there … it is."

"What's he to be afraid of, whether you read it or not?"

Genadie pushed his face into the crook of his arm. "Until now, Ms. Dalca, he's always been … the almighty … Zeus."

"And how would that change if you read the book?"

"You read it … Ms. Dalca," he said. "You know."

"But you've always said he can take any form he likes, and that he chose to be this sort of creature because it's the most powerful on the earth. But he can be anything he likes, because he is Zeus. That was your excuse for him, remember?"

"Ms. Dalca," he breathed heavily, "are you arguing that … our Master is Zeus? Have you accepted … after all?"

Amalina didn't answer. She took a warm, moist cloth and rubbed the blood coating the right side of his face.

"No-ooo," he said slowly. "And you never will, now that you've read … that book. I told you the evil thing … would put down roots. Its roots have broken through … the foundation … the rock that is our … mutual trust."

"I still trust you."

"Not who I meant, Ms. Dalca."

"How could he not trust you? I mean, *you*, Genadie."

"He knows I … lied to him," said Genadie with a whimper. His lips twitched, as if he would cry.

"He must know you lied because you didn't want to hurt him. You've always been loyal to him. And you always will be. Won't you?"

"Have I ever told you how we met, Ms. Dalca?"

Amalina's heart thudded heavily and she felt uneasy at the question, but she didn't know why. "I think I'd remember if you had."

• • •

Genadie drifted off. But when he woke next, it was as if he hadn't, but had gone off to gather some strength.

"It was, of course, many years ago," he said. "When I was just a wandering minstrel. Not a particularly successful one at that … but I was very good anyway. I could sing and play all the favorite songs of the day."

On occasion, Genadie had mumbled some melodies that sounded nice, but his voice was too scratchy and reedy to imagine he could be considered 'very good.' And Genadie's twisted, knotty fingers: what kind of instrument could they possibly work well? His fingers would catch and foul on any strings, and misalign on the holes of a woodwind.

"Don't look at me like that," he said, finding some extra vigor in indignation, and flexing his fingers as she washed them. "I was accomplished on any instrument handed me. And I could sing very handsomely. My only problem was I was short … and proud … and ignorant." He smiled with his eyes closed, like a dreaming kitten (or a dreaming rat, in his case). "Oh, I was intelligent and learned. I traveled all of Europe and parts of Africa and Asia. You can't travel without picking something up, you know. But being smart and learned doesn't preclude ignorance. We are all ignorant, no matter how much we learn. Because Zeus always withholds something for his own."

Genadie sighed.

"Go to sleep," Amalina told him gently. "You get your rest and you'll be better, like before."

"I think not."

"Don't say that."

"Ms. Dalca …" he shook his head. "I did not tell you how we met."

• • •

"I was passing through on my way to the court of the Ottomans. I'd thought it the best land route from Antwerp. It was here I met my lovely maid, Mala, who was the most beautiful woman on any continent, and who thought I was the tallest man she'd ever seen. Silly lass. Her father, the King of the Gypsies, did not hold it against me for beguiling his daughter and allowed us to be wedded. She bore me a son, and then a daughter, and then another son. One child for every year of our love. And she did love me, Ms. Dalca. Though I would be gone for most of the year, playing here and there and living the life of the minstrel traveler. I would track her father's camp down, every year, when I found the time, and we would be together again in each others arms."

Genadie sighed as he had before, when it looked as if he would sleep. But now his eyelids parted, and he stared blankly toward the dark wall, seeing something that wasn't there.

"One year, Ms. Dalca, I found Mala's tribe, but there was trouble. One of the camp's daughters had been killed. Killed in the night by something they called a strigoi. Her father was a powerful man in the camp, and prevailed on the King of the Gypsies to hunt this strigoi down and kill him. But this was no ordinary strigoi. He walked on land, and lived as a normal man. He lived in a nearby castle. These gypsies were foreigners, you see, we all were, and were not a part of the compact between the Ardeelians and their Knight of Ardeel, and we had never seen the written Secret Histories of the land, which tell of the Count's hold over every living person here. We were all ignorant. They thought the beast was something to be put down. The men armed themselves and went to go kill him.

"But before they did, because I would not go with them—because I was even more ignorant, and I did not believe in phantoms, and I thought this was not my fight, and I did not want to leave my love and my children for a fool's errand—they accused me of being a coward, and forced me to drink boiling wine. This is why my voice is the way it is. And I was angry for it. And I hated Mala, though she tried to care for me. All I saw was the destruction of my beautiful voice, the ruin of my livelihood, and I blamed her for making me love her. I swore that she'd cast one of those gypsy spells to entangle me, and now I'd been wrecked like Hercules. And I prayed secretly in my pain that I would be rid of her and her family and everyone. Have them all disappear for my suffering.

"The men left. They never returned. What came next was something too horrible … Too horrible. First the wolves came and killed a number of the women and children. We hid in the wagons and fought them off as best we could—I was still quite ill and somewhat delirious from drinking.

"Then came Master. We watched him as he fell gently from the sky before the campfire. He took each wagon, by hand, one by one, and emptied them onto the ground. Like shaking ants out of a cup. And he killed them. All of them. Even the ones who tried to escape. Even the ones who begged for his mercy. He took pistol fire directly. He allowed them to strike at him with swords and knives. The women. The children. All torn to pieces. Mounds of flesh in a tarn of blood.

"I could not believe my eyes. And by chance, we were the last alive: my wife and my children. We were in the final wagon. So when we saw what was going to happen, we tore a hole in the wagon's side, to sneak away without him seeing. But the wolves were there to stop us.

"'You are a man,' Master said. 'What are you doing here?'"

"I couldn't answer. I was sick, my throat was sore. It was almost impossible to talk.

"'You did not come to attack me, as the others did. Why did you not come after me?'"

Genadie broke off. He closed his eyes. He said, under his breath, "You know how Master is.

"But he would not leave me alone. He was fascinated by me. And disgusted by me. He said he'd seen me before. In this city and that. He'd heard me sing and heard me play. He knew my name. And he accused me of being a coward. He accused me of being a worm. Not a real man for having stayed behind. I wanted to tell him I stayed to protect my family." Genadie choked. "But it was impossible. He asked me, as he does, if I valued my family over him. I did not know how to answer. I shook my head. And he told me I must swear allegiance to him. And though I couldn't—my throat, you see?—I tried to make signs with my hands. It wasn't enough. For my defiance, he broke my hand. Broke every finger on my hand. I screamed, but I did not swear to him. I nodded my head, like so, to show my devotion, I threw myself on the ground in prostration, but he did not understand. Oh, how Master was inflamed. He told me he would kill everyone I loved if I did not swear myself, then and there, with my sweet voice which he knew I possessed, to his service. Tear them apart as he had my hands. But how could I? So he killed them for me. Before my eyes. One by one. First the children. Then my love. As they cried. As they … pl-ea-ded. Only he had missed one. My son. And one of his wolves caught the clever boy and brought him to Master. And Master said he would kill him, too. I had one last chance, if I would only swear myself to him."

Genadie heaved as sigh, and trembled as he let a tear roll down off his cheek.

"I had never seen nor heard anything like … this man. And I understood there was nothing so evil that could exist on this earth, or so uncaring, or so prideful, or so powerful. But I remembered my learnings and stories and fables and legends and myths, and then I remembered: there *was* one. One entity who was prone to walking among man and demanding his praise. Who was mean enough to grant the angry prayers of a tormented soul in order to destroy him. Zeus. Zeus! And I could call his name. I called his name! Zeus! Though it wounded my throat, and I coughed up blood to say it. Zeus! Zeus! Zeus!

"But I was too late. Too late. Mala, everyone … all were gone, save one.

"Master finally understood: Though I was famed for my singing, it was not pride that kept me from pledging myself to him that night, I simply could not speak. My throat, you see. He understood at last … and forgave me. He could not return the rest of my family. They should have told him, you see, what had happened to my voice. Tell him why I couldn't talk." He laughed sadly. "Said it was their fault, you see. But isn't that Master? … And he *has* improved since, Ms. Dalca.

"But he spared my boy. Had his wolves take him away. And Master would allow me to serve him. And as long as I served, he would let my boy live … That was kind."

• • •

"That's just awful," said Amalina. "How can you even look at him?"

"It was so long ago," said Genadie, with a wan smile. "If only they had thought to call his name, as I did."

"They?" He was talking about his wife and children, she realized. "Why would they? He isn't Zeus!"

"If I were to believe what I read in that … that book … he is not. And that is what Master is afraid of, that I read it. That I no longer believe. That I may question him and no longer serve him as I have for these many years."

"The old fraud would deserve it."

"Ms. Dalca," he said, now staring up at her in a reprimanding way. "I have not given the better part of my life for no cause. Master is still Master."

"I suppose so. But what he did to you, and everyone you love. Do you know what became of your child?" Genadie shrugged, gave his head a slight, slow shake. Amalina felt the tears of sympathy falling over her cheeks. And remembered very well just how the Count had threatened to kill everyone she loved if she did not serve him. Perhaps she should take this example as a warning. "But still, I don't know how you could serve him, Genadie. Not after all that."

It was a cruel thing to say, she thought, after having said it. She continued washing him and they were quiet for a while. When she was ready to leave, he looked up at her again.

"You won't tell him I read it."

"No."

"You realize," he said, "this might still be just a test for me. And I should never wish to fail Zeus."

12

Count Tepsji Explained

"**O**h, Amalina, where were you last night?" Anka asked Amalina as they met in a hall.

Hoping to throw the maid off the subject—since Amalina didn't want to say she'd been stranded (and dining lavishly) down in Netz—Amalina countered: "Did you know Genadie was injured? I found him lying in the hall, just after the northern wall bridge—"

"The northern wall bridge …?"

"Here in the building. He was lying there, probably for days, in a pool of his own blood." This thought began to agitate Amalina, and animated her as if this was her primary concern and not simply that she was trying to deflect the conversation.

"He's alive?" said Anka.

"Yes—"

"Is he still there?"

"I moved him into a room—"

"Which one?"

"I don't know. The closest. In the eastern side. Nothing large or fancy," if *that* was what she was worried about, because that was how it sounded. Amalina began to fume for real.

"Is the blood still on the floor? I should have to clean it if it is. Or send Pils to do it."

"Is that all you care about?"

"Oh and here I thought we'd made up, dear. But I asked if Genadie was alive first, didn't I?"

Either from her well ginned-up ire or that she did not want to cede her superior moral position, or both, Amalina returned to the initial question. Or rather *her* initial question: "Did you *know* he was there?"

"We didn't know what to do with the wretch, pretty girl," said Anka, as a kind of admission, apology and explanation, her face showing the strain at trying to stretch the combination. "The Count wasn't here to instruct us, and so we thought we shouldn't do anything contrary to his will. Well, you must understand."

"No. I don't. I put Genadie in bed and have him resting."

Anka shrugged with a contrite look. "Some things Pils and I aren't accustomed to, you understand. Or know the policy … on how to handle certain situations. Yet."

"So then on some things I know better than you do," said Amalina, suddenly magnanimous, and instructive, and without contempt. "You'll have to trust me on this, if anyone is lying near death, help them. Help them immediately."

"This has happened before," she supposed.

"To Genadie quite often. It's the Count's role to harm, and ours to heal as best we can. I'd do the same for you and Pils. I'd hope you'd do the same for me."

Instead of replying, Anka's face went white as she once again considered her mortality in this situation.

"I'd hope you'd do the same for me," Amalina repeated.

"Well, yes, now that there's been proper instruction, of course, milady. Yes. If it means anything, Pils had wanted to move the poor wretch right then. It was my fault I told him not to. It's quite difficult, it's all quite difficult to know ... You know, we served a good man once. A very good man. And we served him well. This one is quite different. How's one to know *everything* when the wrong question could send you ... ?" Anka's pale lips quivered. "But do please understand and forgive. It's easy for one to do great service for someone you love and understand. And tell me, how does one serve impeccably while hating a master, a master you don't understand?All while trying to remain as pleasant as oneself ... while also trying to remain alive ... and in a castle that is all turned around and larger than it should be. It's a difficult thing. A difficult thing. And confusing."

Anka's eyes were blank, she'd really fallen into speaking to herself, trying to fathom her new position in her new place. When she looked up, she saw the sympathy in Amalina's look.

"Well, I hope we're back to friends," said Anka after a moment, muttering more than speaking, "Well, oh ... But as I was saying—yes, I was saying, wasn't I?—the Count was looking for you last night. Didn't know where you'd gotten to. He's waiting for you in his study. You're to go to him straight away when I find you. Right now."

Amalina straightened her dress and swallowed hard.

Anka was one thing. But how could Amalina possibly hide, dodge, or explain her trip to Netz to the Count?

. . .

"You've read the book," the Count stated flatly to Amalina, who now stood before him in his study. "There is no need to lie to me. I know."

Amalina answered him with a sudden deep red flush she couldn't check on her already rosy cheeks.

"In this book, written by this peculiar man you encountered on the road, he recounts in dramatic detail how he was killed and how he was transformed into the—the being—that he eventually became. Did you see him—see him directly, Mouse—perform any of the feats he asserted he could as this altered being?"

"He came to us, night after night," she said helpfully. "No matter how far we rode in the daytime."

"But did he exhibit any of the powers he ascribed to himself in this book?"

"He was deathly afraid of sunlight," she added.

"But I asked you about *powers*, not impotence. And so I ask you for the last time: Mouse, did your peculiar man display to you any of the advantages he claims he has, which you said so closely resemble my own?"

Amalina felt a new blush on top of the old and shook her head. "No."

"The blood rushes into your face to fill your cheeks, your heart beats faster and the smell of salty sweat comes off you when you lie," said the Count. "I'm going to tell you something, Ms. Dalca, and I hope you will pay attention. This is important."

"Yes, sir."

"I've never claimed to be Zeus. That has always been Genadie's daydream. But, also, I've never died," he said. "We've been through this before, when you once accused me of being strigoi. Do you remember when you did that?"

"Yes, sir."

"And what did I tell you? Strigoi was a word invented after I began to exert my power, and the people were confused and sought for ways to explain what was happening. They accused others of rising from their grave to harm the living, to feed off some uncertain energy."

"Yes, sir."

"And invented all sorts of nonsensical attributes to this silly creature they invented. As silly as a fairy tale. *Strigoi*. Strigoi are elementals risen from death. That is the claim. But I *never died!* I was never *killed!* ... as this gentleman was ... before he was transformed ... I am going to tell you something."

After the ensuing silence ran too long and Amalina knew she'd be waiting until morning for him to continue if she did nothing, she nodded.

"I was a young man," said the Count, staring at her, "but my family's power was already being entrusted to me when Bario came to court. I didn't know if he was a slave or a private citizen that my father or mother sent. I didn't know if he was meant to be my mentor or my tutor. For some reason, it was never discussed between us. He was a dark-skinned, white-haired man of staggering charisma, who wore the finest clothes and jewelry. That must have been enough for me. And there never seemed to be a need for him to explain his presence in my chambers, when, in the evening, he suddenly appeared. He told me he was there for a great purpose, and that I was not to speak of him or our lessons to anyone. And I was not to call him teacher or servant, but only Bario, if I ever needed to address him; though he thought I would not.

"In our nightly lessons, he taught me the many aspects of power. He would tell me histories. Ancient histories. Of kingdoms which had once thrived and then collapsed; so long ago that their art and culture are lost to us, or we have forgotten them. His instruction was of cold observation, of why those people had risen to greatness, what their greatness was, and what errors had caused their downfall. From his lessons I was to derive a better understanding of how to navigate the treacherous world of politics and of martial arms, and thereby preserve my family.

"Because his lessons were limited to the evenings, when all others in the house had gone to sleep, I would drift off frequently. Sometimes he would wake me with a thrashing. Sometimes I would come awake in the morning, barely remembering what had happened the night before.

"Only once do I remember him standing behind me, but drawing close. Close enough I could feel his breath on the back of my neck. And then he pressed his mouth against my neck." The Count sighed out of frustration. "I remember *that*. It only happened once, from what I know. But it might have happened a hundred times."

The Count paused to scratch his cheek and tug at his mustache.

"At some point," the Count continued, staring levelly, unblinking at Amalina, "when Bario had deemed me worthy, when I had taken on more responsibilities as a commander in the field, and proven myself as a political chief, he offered me a way to a power which was unlike anything any leader in the world had ever possessed. A personal power. The strength of a god. The limitless attributes of the infinite. He knew I was still young and would not deny his offer. I would, instead, demand to take it there and then.

"The next night he came with a cup, a cheap, common-looking cup, and he told me I would have to drink from it as I took my lesson. What the cup held was thick and as dark as wine, and I drank it down as fast as I could. This happened for some nights. And each day I could feel an energy—not a *new* energy joining me, but my own energy—rising from a centerpoint I did not know I had. My energy increased to the point I thought I would burst out of my own body. Then Bario left the court, without a word to me, and I was alone to discover just how much power he had gifted me.

"You see, Ms. Dalca, I never died. Never. And I would never have thought I was some kind of victim of a predatory creature. Not until I read this book. Now I am subject to anger. That it had all been some sort of game. This man syphoned me. Methodically. And he began reconstituting me with his own blood, which he had me drink from the goblet. This is how my memory of my education and rise to power is now tainted."

The Count added at the end, quickly: "How do you see it, Ms. Dalca?"

Amalina nodded. "You never saw him again?"

"Never."

"And because of this, you never thought there was anyone else like you in the world. You didn't understand what the wine really was. Or that you'd been given a special ability, maybe just through this drink he'd given you."

"Yes."

"And in some sense it is true," Amalina said. "What he told you was true, he did give you power. Even if he left out that it was his blood you drank, and that he was replacing yours with his."

"So you agree, then?" the Count's large eyes pulled at Amalina. "This was a transfer of his own force. Into me."

"If what's written in the stranger's book is true. Or, anyway, if the similarities in his story and what you've said are true. Yes, sir."

"I thought I was the only one," he brooded. She couldn't tell if he meant to sound bitter. He pulled down hard on his mustache.

He flicked his warming eyes at Amalina: "You've wondered why I keep that horrible woman tied to that wheel down underneath the castle. Yes, you asked me as much. Well, did I not tell you it was because she was a creature somehow similar to myself?"

But that doesn't explain why you have her thrown up on that wheel, Amalina thought tartly. *The poor woman. Tortured on the wheel for years. Turning and turning. Screaming and screaming.*

"This book has opened my eyes to many things, Ms. Dalca. It has shone a great white light and discovered for me the secret to which I have long sought the answer ... Or perhaps it has. Yes, perhaps. But there is one way for me to be sure."

"Yes, sir?"

"Come with me, Ms. Dalca. You will help me once again," the Count paused, almost dramatically, but he was really only coming off the couch, "... help me with the woman downstairs."

"The, uh ... The woman downstairs?" she asked, as if she didn't already understand by the knotting of her stomach.

He said with a sly wink and a grin, and a sharpening twist at the end of his mustache: "The horrible one we were just talking about, of course. You remember. The one you personally bound to the wheel, Ms. Dalca. You couldn't have forgotten. Oh, I'm sure she'll be pleased to see you. Come along."

13

The Woman Below

Down they walked through the kitchens and into the cellar. And then further down through the winding stone corridors of branching storerooms and dungeons. And then still further down. Amalina's face pulsed red as a cherry. She was hot. And angry.

It's not fair, she thought. I didn't bind her to that wheel! You put her there. Or Genadie did. I didn't even know about her until I heard the screams. And when I complained about the constant wail that filled the castle at night, you and Genadie tried to deny it was even happening. Blaming me for hearing things. Until you were forced to admit it was real, an actual human wail, when it scared away your guest; which left you needing me to take your guest's place in your schemes! *Then* you admitted it, and *then* you showed me … showed me *her*—spinning and spinning on that mill wheel. Bound there by a silver chain. I put the chain over her mouth, yes. But only to steal her breath and keep her from screaming anymore. And I did *that* because I wasn't given a choice! You made me do it!

All her labored thoughts didn't stay their progress, but only made the route feel quicker. Speeding them somehow to the room deep below the castle. Then they were there. The Count directed Amalina to put the torch in a ring beside the wood door.

"Don't we need Genadie for this?" she asked, a little too smartly.

"I require only you," he rumbled with reassuring confidence. But she could see the tension in his face and the alteration of his expression—the downturned lips and mustache, the hint of wariness to his eyes—to know he was apprehensive. "It will be a touch more dangerous, perhaps. But I must have my answer."

"What answer is that?"

· · ·

Up, then down. Up, then down.
 That is all there is.
 Up … down. Up … down, forever.
 Was that a voice? Or two?
 Yes. Voices outside the door. Familiar voices.
 How long has it been?

Forever?
Or not so long?
An hour ago?
Yesterday?
One hundred years?
Forever.
Up, then down. Up, then down.
What are they saying?
It's hard to hear with the ringing of hot metal against my face.
But I *do* know them.
Are they coming in?
"Don't look directly into her eyes," the low, rumbling voice was saying. "Like before, we must work fast, and let us not take chances … "
How do I look?

. . .

Two years ago, the Count opened the door and ushered Amalina into the room. It smelled of oil and burnt wood and something moldy. To one side of the otherwise empty room was a massive mill wheel, set vertically against the wall, turning and turning. So it was again.

The chains were still there at its hub, and the woman secured behind them. A whithered, ancient body, with ropes of veins and an odd puffiness to the skin that said life was still there. It was difficult to track the woman's head, as it relentlessly made its round from ceiling to floor and back again, but Amalina could tell the eyes were closed, and the face looked more wasted, especially where the chain touched it.

Amalina's legs felt like jelly as she tried to force them, one after the other, to bring her closer to the wheel. Toward the spinning woman. Don't open your eyes, she begged her, as dread caused her to imagine it happening on every upstroke of the wheel.

Behind her the Count was silhouetted in the doorway. With a whoosh he was gone. Then, after a second, there came the groaning of wood beams and the mill wheel ground to a stop.

"Oh, no," said Amalina. The body's head was slanted diagonally downward at the 4 o'clock position.

She looked back to the doorway. The Count hadn't returned.

She adjusted her grip on the metal bar in her hand and then continued forward.

Now there was a snapping of cloth behind her, and a short burst of wind.

"Faster," said the Count.

"Her head's the wrong way," whispered Amalina.

"It might be for the best. It might keep her disoriented. Move along, Ms. Dalca. We can't take too long."

Amalina felt the weight of the bar and shook it. It was flat and narrow, with a bend and notch at one end. The Count had told her what it was for and how to use it. She did so, kneeling beside the wheel, feeling the presence of the body at her side, and used the notch to grab the head of one of the iron nails she'd driven in so long ago. Using some leverage against the wheel, she popped the nail out. If she had been thinking purposefully, it would have been better to remove the nail on the side of the head closest the floor. While it would have been an awkward angle, and difficult to see what she was doing (with the head in the way), at least the chain would have naturally hung down across the woman's face. But freed from the top, she now saw her mistake as the chain dropped free of her face completely, and smacked onto the floor.

The eyes shot open. They looked down/up at her.

Amalina wanted to close her eyes and hold her ears. To tell the poor woman not to send up her wail. But she could only look into those dried out, wrinkled, withered, ancient blue globes that were her eyes.

The face contorted. It made something like retching sounds; as if a stiff leather suit could retch. Her flesh was not able to wail like before. Her mouth had been stopped, its power taken.

"Can you speak?" said the Count from the doorway. He was stooped and staring at the woman's head. "Get out of the way, Ms. Dalca, so that I can see better. No, not that far, girl. You must be ready if she should—"

"You," the sound coming out of the head scratched at him. The skin around the eyes arranged to something quite malevolent, even in its upside-down position. "It's you."

"You came to kill me," said the Count.

"You deserved to die," said the woman. Her body, in pieces, tried to buck against the silver chain. It looked like the links weighed too heavily on her.

"Why?" asked the Count.

It tried to scream. Then: "You did this to me."

"If I didn't you would have tried to kill me again. You *would* try to kill me again." The Count looked scared and fascinated at once. Absentmindedly, he stroked his long mustache.

"*You did this to me!*"

"Ah. I see. You blame me for making you this way. Yes. But … I did *what* to you? When? I don't remember you. Not clearly. There have been so many women. And … Are you sure it was me?"

She wailed and shrieked. Amalina dropped the bar to cover her ears. She clamped down so hard she couldn't even hear the bar clattering on the stone floor.

"Stop," said the Count. "Stop right now and answer me. If you do, I might let you live."

"I don't *want* to live."

"I'll let you have whatever you want."

"I want to kill you."

"Answer my questions, I might give you the chance."

She stared at him. Her face could have used several pints of water to make the tissue less leather-like. The body almost giving the impression of a hide bag. It was difficult for Amalina to look at.

"What do you want to know?" she asked.

"Hmm ... Now that I think about it, I do think I might *understand* ..."

"That isn't a question."

"It might please you," said the Count, "if you understood, too."

"There's nothing to understand but you should die." The woman glanced up at Amalina. She fell back several steps, bringing her hands down to her mouth.

"I attacked you," said the Count.

"Brilliant."

"But, when? Where? I don't recognize you."

"I told you."

"Did you?"

"When I came for you."

"But it was so long ago. You look nothing like yourself, I should think."

"I am quite beautiful, aren't I? Aren't I?" the head almost pleaded between the Count and Amalina. The vulnerability gave Amalina confidence to step forward, finding the metal hammer in her belt, and spotting the small iron nail on the ground. The nail was bent. She sent a shaking hand into her pocket to find a new one.

"Which one, I ask you? Which one were you, woman?"

"Which one? You make me sick—"

"Do tell me again. One last time."

"At the full moon. Near the fair. By the waterfall," said the head.

"Ah," the Count nodded. Remembering, pleased. "*Cascada.* Yes. The fair. Yes, yes. Cluj Sibi."

"You killed me."

"But I did not, did I?" he said. There was a fire in his eyes. "Yes. Yes. Yes, yes. A very big moon. I was famished beyond reason. It had been so long, I had to eat."

"You did."

"And you were nothing. I drained your whole body in one gulp. Very suddenly. Everything—"

"What do you mean I was nothing? I was the most beautiful—"

"Yes, yes. But so small. One gulp, my dear, and you were done. I left you there. As dead as anyone else I have ever ... no difference. No. Except. You were resisting rather viciously, weren't you?"

"Yes."

As he stroked his mustache, his eyes locked onto hers, he gestured with a finger at her. "Yes, yes. You were a like a wolf. Not like the others at all.

You fought, and gouged. And you bit. You bit into me. And you tasted the blood falling from my body."

"You would die with me."

"But I did not, did I? And when I left you for dead, you were not so dead, after all. You ate my blood. Not much, but it was enough. That is why your body was never found. You crawled off and survived. And came to your full powers in the years afterward."

"My full powers," she hissed. She wailed again. "You cursed me!"

"… And came only decades later to find me again, to attack me."

"You cursed me to live like you—something I could never want and never wish—and turned me into this inhuman machine of thirst and ugliness. And I will repay you for it with your destruction! Let me free! Let me free! You promised I could kill you. Let me thank you for my power with my power!"

"Mouse," called the Count, "Now!"

Amalina hesitated. In that hesitation, the woman's body began to shift; just the way the Count's body could twist, and contort, and seemingly vaporize. She was altering herself. The silver chain binding her body robbed motion from the patches of flesh that it touched, but her neck and head were elongating. Becoming something like a snake. Her dead eyes flashed up towards Amalina. Pinning her in place. Then the woman's head came at her. Mouth wide open, growing wider and wider.

Amalina screamed and fell back. She threw the hammer down and braced her hands on the upper and lower lips of the woman's mouth, which had become a howling cavern of teeth. The head shoved Amalina backward and across the floor, the sharp, canine-like fangs stabbing at her skin. She would be ripped apart and swallowed.

· · ·

Suddenly the head was gone.

It was slamming against the floor in the Count's eternal grip. The woman's mistake had been stretching herself—what she *could* stretch of herself—away from the poisonous silver chains. The Count had pounced on her satellite head. He smashed it and crushed it, and he plucked out the fangs.

She wasn't dead, but her dried, haggard head, still tethered by her helpless, drained body, could only put up a mild resistance. He manhandled the angry melon back to the wheel, looking vicious and stern, but always careful to avoid the chains himself. He motioned with his head for Amalina to come.

"Now," he said. "Now! Now! I said to you, now! Mouse, now!"

With the woman's head secured against the wheel, the Count slapped into the wood on either side of her head two of the finger-length fangs.

Amalina picked up the chain's loose strands and ran them around the fangs and the iron nails still in place, running its length across the woman's mouth. Amalina took one nail out of her pocket, and finding the hammer, slammed that nail into place. The chain barred the woman's mouth and petrified her skin all around it. No wail, no howl. Her eyes glared and looked like they were going to come out of their sockets. Turn into two new mouths.

A burst of air and blur of black and the Count was gone. The woman's eyes strained in their sockets. But it was as if the flesh had grown too dry and old. She wasn't as weirdly plastic as the Count could become. The skin cracked as it tried to press toward Amalina.

Then, somewhere within the castle, a lever was thrown, and the groan of massive wooden cogs and wheels, shafts shuddering to life and engaging, resounded throught the walls. And the mill wheel began to turn, taking the head and body with it. The eyes sucked with fear back into the head. They looked all around her, wide, panicked.

After several turns of the wheel they rolled backward into her head, and her whole body shuddered. Then it went slack.

. . .

"Now I understand what happened," said the Count, as the two walked back up from the cellar. Amalina's limbs were shaking and she felt like she was ready to vomit. She didn't know if she would have preferred him to just flash-toss her back into her room, but she also didn't know if she'd surive it. "That woman, you see, was a victim of mine. So long ago."

Amalina nodded, the trembling only getting worse. Before her eyes were the snapping teeth and thrusting fangs. She felt her powerlessness against them. She might have been killed. *Would* have.

The Count carried on: "Well, you asked me, Mouse: what is the reason I had for keeping her here? My answer: To learn the reason she had my power. I thought I was alone, until she came along. She came to kill me, blamed me for what she'd become. I thought perhaps I remembered who she was. I wasn't sure. But ... how had *my* power come to be inside her? She didn't have it when I attacked her. No. I would have remembered that. So I thought perhaps I had misremembered her after all. But I wasn't wrong, was I? I *made* her. Yes, I made her. It was just that I hadn't understood the process ..."

Amalina wondered: *Is he refashioning his memory?* That isn't exactly what was said, or what happened.

Amalina recalled clearly the conversation she had had with the Count (from so many years ago), as she, the Count and Genadie were walking—just as the two of them were now—away from the hidden room containing the constantly spinning wheel with the moaning, groaning woman on it; the woman fastened—just like now—to the wheel by a silver chain; her mouth now gagged and immobilized by a strip of chain Amalina had put across it—just like now—done as a favor to the Count. This memory—and now a feat done twice—gave her a painful pang of guilt and remorse for having assisted the Count in this crude piece of torture and emprisonment of an innocent victim, even if at this moment she was shaking with fear and disgust.

But at that long ago time, the Count had said: "I need her to live until I understand how she became this way."

"But why do you care?" Amalina had asked in return.

And then, most importantly, the Count had concluded: "Because if I knew *how* it happened ..."

At the time his heavy voice had trailed into a mumble which she felt in her chest more than heard. With maybe a trick of her own memory, his words, their low vibrations, came back to her and she understood them clearer. "Because if I knew how it happened," he'd begun. Then: " ... *then I could make for myself another one.*"

• • •

"So now I have my answer," said the Count. "And with it, Ms. Dalca, I have the ability to create my own similar being, if I should want to."

"I suppose, if that is what you'd want," she replied. But he wasn't listening and was obviously lost in his own private thoughts. To jar him she said: "You know, it would have gone easier with her if Genadie had helped us."

He didn't answer. But he politely saw her up to her room.

"Create my own like being," he said at her door, picking up the old conversation as if he had never let it go. "One of my own choosing. Isn't that wonderful?"

14

Governor's Lessons and Lamb

The fat man preferred his lamb hot. He was delighted that he could now eat it every meal if he so wished. And it might arrive steaming on a gold platter without his asking, delivered by the attentive servants now at his disposal. He was no longer the high constable. He wore the traditional sashes and signs of Ardeel's governor-designate.

He'd reached the pinnacle office of government in the land (without being king), and was still young enough to hope for, and achieve, a post back in a more civilized land—if he distinguished himself in his new role here. In the meantime, it was a very comfortable role. He slurped the delicious meat off the fork without even biting, and followed it with a tug of wine from the governor's private stock.

How exquisite, he thought. What a wonderful day. So many responsibilities, and the previous governor had made it appear so difficult. *As long as the cut of lamb makes it to the room still cooking*, he thought with an upward curl of his lip, remembering the first still-bubbling bite, *there's no difficulty at all*.

When, after a contented sigh, he opened his eyes and looked up from his plate, he could not believe who was standing in the room before him. He almost choked on the trailing grease and alcohol and saliva still stirring in his gullet.

The fat man stared. It might have been an apparition. A hallucination.

"Your excellency," said Attila Bronk, with a short, sincere nod. "Congratulations are in order."

"Low Constable," said the fat man.

"No, your predecessor removed me from my post. But you know that, Governor."

"He put a reward on your head." The governor gripped tight the serving fork's handle, privately assessing the utensil's usefulness as a weapon.

"Yes. And now it'll be your replacement, the new high constable, hunting for me; if you direct him to continue your former governor's orders. I'd suggest you leave off that. I will never be caught."

The fat man grunted appreciation at Attila's cool bravado. Of course, all he had to do was call out and there would be an armed guard there to capture his bothersome old subordinate. And, after that, with little more effort than to write out a summary judgment, an execution.

Maybe he wanted to hear out his former low constable, find out what the man was up to. Maybe he knew that by creating a scene he might delay his own agenda for the night. Delay it more than if he just humored Attila. A dramatic arrest forcing him to wait for a fresh plate of sizzling lamb to be cooked and delivered.

"I was sworn in just the other day," said the fat man. "How very prompt you are. You're staying within the city? Or nearby?"

"It happens I was already on my way to Tsobl when I heard about your ascension to the governorship. Something you'd always wanted. Congratulations, again."

"You can stop congratulating me and tell me why you're here. You've managed to interrupt my meal."

"Yes, that was rude. You were enjoying yourself. Lamb, right? And you don't like it cold."

"Why are you here, Attila?"

"I shouldn't be surprised you made the post. But may I ask how you were able to get it? I thought Obermeier had more support in the assembly."

The fat man lifted an eyebrow and grunted again. Then he grinned, and with a wary eye on his former low constable, he forked a bit of the lamb into his mouth. He spoke while eating: "Yes, of course he had the assembly's support ... oh, by the way, in another vote, they will no longer be called the assembly, but rather, now officially, 'the Permanent Council of Ardeel'. It should also interest you that there is a measure, set to pass, that will rename Tsobl to Sobelburg," the fat man zinged this last with a note of triumph. Then he realized it was near impossible to bait a man with no expressions, and so was disappointed. "But to return to the subject: Obermeier did have the *council*'s support. But it was my jurisdiction to investigate the governor's disappearance. And then, what with *that* unsettling mystery of his disappearance, and then word of agitation in the south, and old General Marosh having absconded with a good set of artillery ... Well, both the king and council saw the reason of having a governor experienced in direct control of populations and the enforcement of law, rather than someone like Judge Obermeier, who is simply an intellectual plucked parrot."

Attila nodded at the sense of it.

The fat man winked at him. He took another forkful. "Attila?"

"Never mind me," said Attila with his eternally set, half-lidded, frustratingly neutral expression. "I am now here representing Sir Hak Vogoneyevic. That is my role: Ambassador to the true ruler of this land."

The fat man gagged. He recovered and continued chewing. "How is that? You heard how the council has been declared permanent, and their renaming has begun. So how is it that Hak rules, exactly?"

"It might not be so yet. But it will be. He is blood of Ardeel, and he is its true champion—"

"You should argue that with Marosh."

"That time is coming. But, you understand, Governor, just by saying so you've admitted there are forces here outside of your control. You have the title, and the assembly has made itself a permanent council, but you are still a small boat on a large sea. You command a small crew, but not the waves that surround you."

"Come, Attila," said the fat man humorously. "You're always magnifying your importance; outstripping your real value."

"I repeat: I speak not for myself, but for Sir Hak Vogoneyevic."

"What I mean to say, little ambassador: if you liken Ardeel to a sea, you are only a small mote of water within a vast ocean. At the king's command, you can be thrown into such a tumult you will wish you—or your friend—hadn't stirred the waters."

"The waters have been stirred by so many outside forces, Governor. All believe they hold sway. They will learn their place in the order. This is Ardeel, and these people will be free of *all* tyranny. Sir Hak Vogoneyevic will see to it. Outside forces will fall in line, or they will simply fall."

"You entered my room, Attila, as an outlaw, to issue *threats*?" asked the fat man, pursing his lips disagreeably.

"Before you do anything rash," said Attila, cold as ever. "Just keep in mind that I arrived here in this room just as easily as that plate of lamb. I have freedom of movement unexpected only by those who don't comprehend the rightful—the exact—order of things. Ardeel will always be Ardeel, just as Tsobl will always be Tsobl, no matter how you Sobelburg it. You preside over a foreign system that has been laid down neatly over it, but does not entirely touch it, or control it, and never will."

"You've made your point," said the governor curtly, tired at dealing with those dull eyes. "Anything else?"

"Have you heard about the massacre in Fronescu? Something is happening in Ardeel you may want to prepare yourself for."

As the governor listened in rising irritation, his lamb went cold on the plate.

. . .

It was now the fat man's third service of lamb for the day, and though his day had been a trying one of learning the ins and outs of his new job from administrators and clerks who hadn't been prepared for a sudden transfer of power, and those bureaucrats who were equivocal on whether they were pleased he'd received the position—and not bringing into it Attila's unpleasant surprise—the kitchen and house staff were impeccable. The lamb was as good as the first go round—no matter how it got interrupted.

"My God!" exclaimed the governor, his fork and chunk of meat falling from his hand and painfully into his lap.

"No," said the intruder. In the candlelight: a figure with a huge white head, with large, penetrating dark eyes and a predatory smile, wrapped all around in a jet-black cloak.

"My God! My God!" The governor twisted in his chair. He felt as if he were going to be sick.

"Are you a fool?" said the intruder. He shifted in a slick and easy way that seemed less than human. As if he were part of the air. "Stop saying that."

"Who are you? What are you doing here?"

"You don't know who I am?"

The governor beat his breast to calm his heart. It seemed a mystery until it was not. His mind locked on an answer. His body calmed. A bit. "Ah, yes. You are … You are *him*, isn't it? The Knight …"

"Count Tepsji will do for you."

"What—what are you doing here? What do you want of me?"

"You're the new governor, are you not?"

"Yes. I was just sworn in the other—"

"Didn't the governor who came before you tell you?"

"Tell me what?"

"What to expect."

The governor shook his head. As if to cope with what was happening, his right hand searched for the dropped fork. "I—the governor couldn't tell me anything. He disappeared. That is why I was given his position."

"Ah, yes," said the Count. "Well, this is how things are done."

"How things are done?"

"I wish you'd show me some courtesy," said the Count, his lips turning down.

"Courtesy?" Then the governor scrambled off the chair and he bowed his head to the floor, the way he would if this—this man—were the king. When he was down in this belittling position, something inside him cursed he was doing so. Was he this much of a coward? The former *High Constable*? "Do you wish for something to eat or drink?"

"I can take care of that," said the Count. "Get up. I haven't much time."

"Of course, of course." The governor bustled back into his chair, the blubber of his jowls shaking at the effort. His body remained bowed once he was sitting. His eyes were locked on the desk, the gold platter of meat. So much easier to look at those than at the … creature. "So it is true."

"I don't know how many of these conversations I have had over the years," said the Count with a bland note to his voice. "I always forget what I said before. I have lived for a very long time. But it is always just the same, isn't it? I congratulate you on your title. Then I remind you of what I expect of your people, which was laid out in some covenant or other, I believe. You know about this."

"Of course. Yes."

The Count was silent. The governor was forced to look up. He was met with an expectant stare.

"Sir," the governor added on, hating himself. "Your Highness."

"Well, if the governor didn't tell you what was involved, this is very annoying for me, as I'll have to take longer to explain the situation."

"The situation?"

"It would please me, Governor, if you were quicker to ascertain my meanings than it seems. As I said, I hadn't intended to be here long."

"I'll understand what you have to say. You just go ahead ... with what is needed."

"I will," said the Count. He came forward and sat in a chair facing the desk. He settled into it as if getting comfortable. "I must tell you my expectations: What you are to inform me of immediately, what is less urgent, and what I care nothing about. And how you will conduct our intercourse, the proper methods."

"Yes, yes. Good ... Sir."

"You do understand that you represent the population. It is you I will be looking to for answers. And for restitution if it is needed."

"Yes. Yes, sir. And there is also the, uh ..."

"The what?"

"The assembly ..."

"*You* report to me. *They* are nothing."

"Of course, of course. Um, just so ... well ... you know this already, I suppose. But then, you are ... well, I don't know if it is meaningless to mention, the assembly has been renamed as the Permanent Council."

The Count chuckled with contempt, "You think I care of such things?"

"Yes, that's fine. It's just I was going to ask your opinion on an impending measure   well, maybe it is nothing you care about—but, anyway, a measure before the council; to rename Tsobl as Sobelburg?"

"On your death," stirred the Count with muted rage.

"On my death?"

"This is a measure to assert a Germanic name onto an ancient Ardeelian city, am I right?"

"I suppose it is."

"On your death."

"Yes, of course. Of course." With the fat man's nerves fraying, he also muttered thoughtlessly: "Though how I shall explain to them—"

"There's nothing to explain. It won't happen."

"Of course. Of course. Yes. I understand."

"Or, on your death, your council—or assembly—or rats in the gutters— will be forced to bring forth to me a new governor. Do you understand me? May he be quicker than you. That last one seemed good enough, I think. Why couldn't I have him longer?"

The fat man felt like he was blowing it. That he was completely out of his depth and should never have wanted this position. That if only he had had more time, and been properly informed and prepared for this moment … Who would have thought the governors—that brief line of meaningless, stodgy nincompoops—had conducted direct intercourse with the Knight of Ardeel? But then, that might explain some of the smaller disappointments in the previous men who'd taken the position. "May I ask one more question, Your Excellency?"

"What do you want to ask me?" said the Count, picking at a long canine tooth.

"So … am I to understand you don't know what happened to our previous governor?"

This seemed to incense the Count. He shifted in his chair.

"I know everything that happens to everyone," he said with a low, penetrating grumble. "But not all of it matters to me. And what I know isn't expected to be known by anyone else unless I think they should know it. What you have asked is immaterial. What you need to know is that you are now the governor of Ardeel, but you are not the ruler of this land. And you will pledge your fealty to, and obey, the legitimate authority, which is I."

The lamb went cold again.

· · ·

Exhausted but unable to sleep, the governor snuck down from his bedroom, and cut some lamb and held it on a skewer in the dwindling fire in the fireplace. Then he plated it and returned to his bedchamber with it and a bottle of wine, hoping the snack would put him down for the night.

Someone was following behind him in the hallway.

The person was difficult to see because he was in the shadow and was covered by a heavy cloak. It was not one of the house servants.

"What?" said the startled governor, still moving for his open bedroom door.

The figure motioned him to continue. In a second he understood it wasn't Count Tepsji returning. Neither was it Attila Bronk. Someone new. The governor shook his head and huffed out a breath.

The figure shut the door. The governor placed his plate and bottle on the mattress.

"You understand what time it is?" he asked the figure, lifting his chin and sounding every level of his irritation, even borrowing some that he hadn't been able to express earlier. Only after a moment did he realize this might be an assassin. Perhaps the one who had done in the previous governor.

"Yes," said the man. He pulled down the hood. He had a slender, almond shaped head, with a long nose and a thin spray of dark hair banging down to meet his eyebrows. "I thought it best to meet you discreetly."

"You are a man of Ardeelian blood ... And yet you aren't afraid of being caught out at night?"

"Not many are afraid, here in Tsobl," the man answered. He took off his black gloves. His fingers were long and slender and looked soft.

"I can tell you," said the governor with a warning tone, "This very night, in this very city, the personality everyone is afraid of ... is about. If any hour and any spot one should fear the night, it is this spot and this hour. *This very home.*"

The man looked around him, as if expecting something to form out of the air. Then he brought his eyes back to the governor. "Are you all right?"

"I wish to get some sleep. It's been a trying day."

"Looks like you were awake to me—and you wanted to eat."

"The lamb's getting cold. Who are you, sir? What do you want with me?"

The man formed a small contemptuous smile: "My name is Rosczy. I represent the real power in this country. The highest power in this country. Even higher than yourself."

"Oh?" He couldn't take it any more. He would match contempt for contempt, for he *was* the governor of Ardeel. *Wasn't he?* And this man before him was no extraordinary creature of inhuman evil. He looked like someone's manservant. "Higher than myself is it? Then why are you sneaking in here in the middle of the night like a thief?"

"So you will not be caused embarrassment. I can return in the morning and declare all these truths publicly if you'd like."

"Please," he threw back his head and stared down along his nose, and past his pudgy, grizzled chin. "You're here now. Let's get it out. Tell me, Roszcy, who is the real power in this country? Hm? Educate me. Who is the real power besides its king, its council, its governor, the hero of revolutionary rabble, and eternal creatures who lay claim to this land? Who else?"

"Do not be mistaken," Roszcy said calmly, and confidently. "It is the Cardinal of Netz."

15

The Cardinal's Ring

The Cardinal of Netz applied the poison to his ring by dipping the large, emerald-cut gem into a jar of clear liquid. He used a small rag to catch the drops when he took it out. He didn't think the poison necessary tonight, but he prepared.

When shown the Cardinal's hand, and by the turn of his wrist, the Cardinal forced Bishop Brandt to kiss—instead of the back of his hand, or the tips of his fingers, or along the ridge of his clothed knuckles—the damp stone. Brandt's lips took in the poison without his knowledge, only thinking that he'd escaped the indignity of directly touching the Cardinal's hand—gloved though it was. Now it was only a matter of getting him to eat and drink enough vitalizers to hold off the effects of the poison until later, perhaps miles down the road, and out of the vicinity of the Cardinal and the Cathedral. Though, more likely, the Cardinal would instruct Clement (Rosczy's assistant), with a tickle of his unseen fingers, to serve the Bishop the wine laced with the poison's antidote. There was also a goblet of antidote-fortified water if the Bishop was abstaining from alcohol today.

"Have something to eat," the Cardinal told Bishop Brandt, motioning for the servants to bring a platter of bread, cheeses, cold cuts of sausage and warm beef. "No need to be formal. I am eating myself, you see."

Bishop Brandt thanked the Cardinal for his hospitality, though there was a stiffness to his expression. He began to eat. And he explained, "It was a hard road. Haven't eaten since I left."

"Yes, I've found that's the common experience for most visitors. Well, I'm here to accommodate." After Bishop Brandt thanked him again, the Cardinal said: "But do tell me why you've come. Some news from the archbishop?" The Cardinal had a terrible thought. "I do hope he is well, and nothing's happened."

Bishop Brandt looked at him from the corner of his eye. "Nothing has happened to him. But he has chosen to step aside."

"Step aside?"

"Yes. He feels at his age, life is calling him in another direction."

"At his age? He's only thirty."

"Yes. Only recently finding rank, I believe, by your efforts, yes?"

"I read him his vows. I placed him. As I will do for his successor. But he's only thirty. He has so many years ahead of him."

"I didn't mean he was feeling old. It is rather the passions of his relative youth which suggested to him there are better things to be done with the greener years of his life."

"He doesn't appreciate the power and responsibility of being my Arch Bishop in Tsobl."

"You're disappointed, Cardinal. I'm sure when you appointed him, a man so young, you expected him to serve you for a *very* long time."

The tone hadn't been more than cordial to begin with, now the Cardinal felt the chill in the air. His fingers danced on the arm of his chair, warning off any early delivery of antidote. "You said he didn't step down, that he stepped aside."

"Yes," said Bishop Brandt.

"That would mean he already had a successor in mind? I can't think of anyone better than he—"

"Me. Not that he had me in mind. But he saw the legitimacy of my taking the post, and so."

"But of course that is only his suggestion. I make the appointment."

"Only if our church is beholden to St. Grigori and its cardinal. Part of the decision to pass the title on to me is due to my more orthodox belief that our church's head rests in Rome, not Netz. He felt a return to practical doctrine and common tradition would be suitable for the cosmopolitan church of Tsobl."

"He never shared these ideas with me."

"Did he need to, Cardinal?"

"It just comes as a surprise."

"Yes, I understand your disappointment."

"Nothing disappoints me," said the Cardinal, a bit too quickly and with a ring of anger. "I serve the church and God. And what will be will be. I accept everything that is as part of the will of Heaven. I merely commented that it was a surprise. He'd never said anything like this before. He almost begged me for the position. And now this. He wasn't shoved aside, was he?"

Bishop Brandt's mouth twitched. Then it gave in to a guilty smile. Still, he didn't answer for a while. And when he did he said: "No. This was his own doing. And I don't know what he might have said to you, but he has told me and the other heads of the Tsobl church that he believes in me and my leadership, and he will see to my success in the position."

"Have some more of the sausage," said the Cardinal, arching an eyebrow. "He sent you here to tell me all this? Hm. I think I understand."

"I imagine you do."

"Was there a reason you made the journey here instead of writing me? Was it to see the reaction on my face? If it was, you're no doubt much more frustrated by my indifference than I was disappointed by your news. All things in stride, as I say."

"Interpretation of the written word can be muddled, mistaken and misunderstood. I wanted to make sure that you were clear on what is happening in Tsobl—I mean: in the Church of Tsobl."

"That you are to be the new archbishop, no matter what I say."

"That."

"But that is also if the Pope consents. And you know he listens to my advice. Or he may have ideas of his own."

"I have my own connections, and I will be in charge of that church. It furthers the pacifying and unifying of this country."

"Because your name is Brandt, not Beliscu; you are not Ardeelian blood."

"You see, you do understand. This country has not come together. Not in over half a century. You Ardeelian people have not reconciled—not in any true sense—with the fact that another people rule this land by the right of God."

"Your words sound divisive for someone the Pope would trust to unite a people. Either we are one or we are not, Bishop Brandt."

Brandt shook his head, denying the point, even as he said, after finishing a bite of beef: "There are many changes coming. You salted the wounds of these people with your rhetoric from the pulpit, the men you installed in their houses of worship spread poison and agitation. Perhaps rebellion. But I'm telling you, Cardinal, you can have Netz, but your network of ruin crumbles now. The government will be all there is, and it will be a proper, unified government. As it is, Tsobl, starting after the new governor's proclamation, will be Sobelburg—"

"Sobelburg," chuckled the Cardinal. "You can only press the people so far."

"The people will only be problematic if there is a force that presses back. Someone unwilling to see the future for what it is, and tries to bend back time to a glory and power that people never, ever possessed—not then, not now, not ever."

"I'm surprised you would kneel before me and kiss my hand with the level of contempt you have for me inside you."

"Whatever I think of you," said Bishop Brandt, "I must show my respect for what you have accomplished with your life—even if I stand opposed. You are offended that I can disagree with you without being disagreeable, even willing to bend my knee and kiss your hand to do you honor?"

"Not offended," said the Cardinal with a thin smile. "Delighted."

Bishop Brandt took a bite of cheese. "If you behave yourself, and join with us in our drive for common pacification, you will be rewarded. Well rewarded. We don't see Ardeelians, Cardinal, we see only fellow countrymen; those who support the rightful government of this land."

"Yes," said the Cardinal behind a heavily reinforced smile, "I believe I've made it clear I understand the position of Tsobl—and its new archbishop."

"Sobelburg," he corrected.

"Yes. Not as easy to pronounce with my Ardeelian lips." The Cardinal's smile widened. "Would you permit me to be frank for a moment? I just want to be clear on what has happened ... in *Sobelburg*. The new governor and the assembly—or council, or whatever—has decided upon a high-handed campaign to reinforce its power over this land. One of its strategies is to pare the established church of its native Ardeelian priests and install their own lackeys."

"You can look at it any way you like. There's a profit in viewing it one way, as opposed to another."

"And the Archbishop of the Tsobl Cathedral was removed," the Cardinal continued as if he hadn't been interrupted, "shoved out, rather, so that you could take his place. And the old archbishop—very wisely—suggested you come to me to do a bit of politicking; for your own good and the good of the cause. And to prove your worth to the council by standing up to me."

"He is sensible," said Bishop Brandt.

"Brilliant. He is brilliant. He will go a long way in whatever endeavor he puts his mind to."

"No doubt." Bishop Brandt seemed to become uncomfortable lavishing too many praises on his predecessor.

The Cardinal wished Bishop Brandt good luck in his new position, and told him to give the old archbishop warm regards. He then offered his hand to be kissed. And for a second time he forced the poisoned ring to his enemy's lips.

• • •

"I didn't serve him the correctives," said Clement to the Cardinal, sounding worried he might have missed the signal.

The Cardinal just nodded. "Very good."

By Brandt's size and how much he'd eaten—not including what he might have actually eaten on the trip *to* Netz—he would be dead within five or six hours. It wasn't an exact science, and the Cardinal was no scientist. But he was familiar enough by experience. Since Brandt hadn't asked to stay at St. Grigori, it was logical to assume he would be dying not in Netz but somewhere along the road to Tsobl.

The Cardinal smiled again, and rubbed his gloved fingers contemplatively through his beard; dangerously close to his lips. Another one to die by the favorite trick, thought the Cardinal. And this one probably the most deserving so far. How many did that make? Certainly not as many as claimed by the Monster of Ardeel. But such a comparison was sin to consider. And the Cardinal had good reason for his actions. It wasn't wanton slaughter. And, anyway, it was almost a compliment if he could match the Count in the wielding of power. Of true power. Of life and death.

The Cardinal reflected how wise his young archbishop had been sending the upstart Bishop Brandt north.

Part Two

Transformation

16

The Better Princess

Four months later Count Tepsji summoned Amalina to his private study. He declared with warm enthusiasm, and a dash of drama: "I have made *my selection.*"

His eyes searched her the way a proud, overly-confident and attention-starved entertainer surveys his audience for his wanted—his *expected*—reaction. And he was not the sort of fragile depressive whose face broke into upset pieces—a frown collapsing from the smile, eyes crimping into something wounded and accusatory, nostrils flexing and flaring—when the audience failed to show the sought-for enthusiasm, as Amalina failed to do presently. He was the sort whose face rather hardened at the disappointment; froze over; petrified into permanent glee, as if the recipient of his profound gem had simply failed to comprehend—comprehend the full profundity—of what they have just been blessed with, and perhaps, if allowed another moment to reflect, they will submit to reason and gain the *proper* reaction. But there was, as well, just a glint of something like fear flittering in the iris of the eye. Fear that this secondary tactic was already known by the audience and had been recognized. And all the worse, pitied. *Never pity!*

"Mouse," he said, as she stared at him with her mouth slightly open. "You've heard me?"

"Yes. And ...?"

"You understand what I mean?"

"Of course, sir. You've selected the one you want."

"Yes. Yessss." He wagged his heavy eyebrows over his large, wide, attentive eyes. "It has been some doing on my part, too. But I am certain I have made the right choice."

"Most assured, sir." She assumed there was a reason he'd brought her down to tell her. It might have been that he just wanted to be able to share this ultra-private piece of information with *someone*. He was so like the princesses; at times, in certain ways. And he had limited options when it came to exposing his feelings. But it seemed there was something else. Though her gorge rose in her throat, and she felt a quiver of fear and anger, she was polite enough to ask the most obvious question: "Who is it? Which one?"

Count Tepsji stroked his mustache, a thaw breaking over his fear-frozen expression. It warmed again, it heated. His teeth showed under one side of the mustache. "You tell me who *you* think I have chosen ... who I have chosen to receive my *gift*."

"I can't imagine." Amalina didn't want to imagine. Any one of the princesses would be unthinkable. She didn't really want to know which of her new friends the Count intended to die.

．．．

Unlike the previous year, when Princess Lisbet Spaarvierlet had practically been knocking on the castle's front door before her acceptance letter (to the Count's offer for her to visit) arrived, a much more reasonable exchange of mail and planning took place between the Tepsji's and the parents of the western kingdom's lady princesses. That is not to say that there wasn't a haste built into the process, but reason prevailed. For the most part. Etiquette and decorum's choreography acted like a handsome theatre curtain that falls to mask the stampede of an elaborate stage being set.

Once the particulars of the visits were arranged to everyone's satisfaction, there began a contest between a handful of lady princesses to get to the high castle fast as they could. Winter was approaching, and if they could not reach the castle before yards of snow slapped down over every possible route, it would be unthinkable to send them until the holidays were concluded and spring freed the land. But as the cynical Count surmised in an off-hand comment to Amalina and Pils: the most money-challenged of their fathers would find an advantage in losing the sweet company of a daughter, even one much beloved, even during the year's most solemn season. And the mother would have instructed her child how to use her wiles on the rich and available noble Count during those intimate months of winter shut-in, endearing her to him in the cold stretch, sticking a hook in him and forging a feverish bond between them only a marriage could cure. All accomplished while slower rivals were locked out; at their earliest, making an attempt to reach the castle perhaps even as late as when summer finally dried the roads.

The Italians got the head start. Amalina had visited that region first, and the poorest of the schemers had already been anticipating the invitation. Praying for it. The carriages were already on their way when the last of the acceptance letters were arriving at the high castle from France.

．．．

The first to come was Ragonde la Basca. She of the slight build. The shake. The timid, rounding, searching eyes. Black hair cascading in front of her face more than it did behind, despite the efforts of her personal maid. She exited her carriage in a conservative dress, buttoned up more against the intimidating castle and its foreboding soldiers than September's early bite of cold. She smiled when Amalina met her, but that didn't last. She was greeted by the Count and that was very much enough for her. There was something about him that convinced her she was in the wrong place and with the wrong people.

"You don't find there is something unsettling about your uncle?" she whispered to Amalina, though they were alone. Her fear caused her to be frank even to Amalina. "My driver says he has family from this region, and your uncle has the look of someone from the most horrifying tales. But I dare not say it if you won't believe. You were so charming, Katarina, I would never have thought … But you must see there is something wrong here. Anyone can *feel* it."

"We will hear no more of Princess la Basca," said the Count, later that week. "I wouldn't bother writing her a letter."

"What does that mean?" Amalina asked, taking her quill from the paper. "I'm sure she might come again. And still, corresponding with her will smooth things with Ragonde if I see her again when traveling."

"Her carriage met with an accident. She is dead."

"What!" Amalina began to cry, the image of the Count shifting and blurring through the tears. "You …! *You!*"

"She was a threat. She knew."

"All of them?"

"It was a tragic accident."

"And how can she be a threat to you? She was just a girl."

"A young woman of influence who knew too much." He altered his tone to a workmanlike drone. "Now, we need to be more careful how we proceed. If nothing else is to be learned from our dealing with Ragalona—"

"Ragonde!"

"We neglected an important step, Ms. Dalca. The medicine. Entirely forgot. From now on, after the princesses are delayed after crossing the frontier, where any silver is taxed, impounded, or lifted from them, and any extra pungent articles and foodstuffs discarded on hygienic grounds, they will meet a similar delay in Netz, before coming up to the castle. You will make sure they take their medicine."

He was referring to his homegrown concoction of chemicals that prevented women from experiencing their monthly spells.

"Was that the matter with Ragonde, sir?" Amalina demanded. "Was she in her flow and you were so offended you had to kill her?"

"I'd never have touched her if that were the case."

"She was my friend, you sickening monster." Amalina was shaking and considered running the quill into his chest, just to see if she could do it.

"She was a threat. I couldn't have rumors getting out … To have my plans ruined straightaway … did you *really* like her all that much?"

. . .

Then came Lady Princess Aria Ecci. Also raven haired, but whose eyes were like the edges of weapons, cutting this way and that, and who seemed at once overcome and bored by Netz—where Amalina treated her to the few and inadequate luxuries of the town, and repeated three-course meals at various restaurants, while surrepticiously dosing her with the Count's special medicine laced inside hard candies, which would prevent Aria's body from menstruating. All this before she would be made acceptable and could meet Count Tepsji.

"Fine by me if I never see him," she admitted with a husky voice after two bottles of wine. By her hardened, worldly affectations, or if simply because of her dark skin and slight physical resemblance, Aria reminded Amalina of the tragic Katrina Flauna, who had once come to the castle and been killed. "I'm sure it would be some tragedy for dear babbo babbo if I don't do my best to make your uncle my friend. But why end my travels here, eh? Now that I am free, there aren't enough bulls to make me rest. At least, not yet."

Amalina never understood half the things Aria was talking about, but it always felt like she was being allowed into an adult conversation just to shock her.

. . .

Half a week later they were joined by Margeta la Brichese. The real cold of winter seemed to arrive with her. She looked slightly perturbed that she was not the first to arrive, saying that she always thought she owned the fastest horses and most diligent drivers. She insisted on visiting the St. Grigori cathedral, and attending all services, whether they were conducted by the Cardinal of Netz or a subordinate, rather than waste time in idle chatter.

She reminded Amalina (and Aria, with an accusatory look) of the need to pray before their meals (always three coursers at various inns, insisted by Amalina); and to observe a regretful continence so as to refrain from making gluttons of themselves; and then to feel guilt when eating was done. And three times she mixed up one of the several crucifixes hanging around her neck for her fork.

"You don't seem too happy with Aria," Amalina said to Margeta, in a private conversation.

"I'm shocked you would ask a lady like her to your home. And you seem to comport yourself to her inclinations. Perhaps I didn't know as much about you as I thought, Princess Katarina. I assume your Uncle is better matured, of course. I pray it so."

When Amalina informed Margeta that the Count had an aversion to the church and its signs and implements, Margeta clutched her crucifixes and bible protectively in shock. And she said she wished she had known before she'd come. And Amalina kind of thought the same thing about Margeta. Though she was quite sure she had mentioned, during their time in Rome, the Count's irreligious nature. She was sure of that. And pretty sure Margeta hadn't been so pious.

· · ·

Then came the French: Gillette Arronde.

Happy to have arrived safely and looking for adventure, Gillette reminded Amalina of everything she hoped a fairytale princess would be, and more resembled such a fanciful persona now bundled in her showy, sharply cut furs, and smiling over every new thing she discovered in this foreign land.

"I fear for Samuel," confided Gillette with an extravagant sigh. An odd non-sequitor because she had just been fawning with a particulary globby enthusiasm over the beauty of Netz's solid architecture, city layout, its impressive St. Grigori Cathedral, and how they all fitted so well and picturesquely beside the mountain lake; as if she might die of having discovered them. "Oh, I fear so for Samuel."

"Who is that?" asked Aria, intrigued.

"You will say nothing if I tell you I am already promised to another man? I proposed to him myself. Nobody knows but us ladies here in Ardeel. But if I should do as my family wishes, and take on the Count as my husband, I shall never leave. And with sights such as this to seduce me ..."

"You think you will marry the Count?" Margeta snipped disdainfully.

"My family certainly hopes so. That's why I'm here."

"You haven't even met him."

"As long as *he* meets with certain qualifications," Gillette winked, "it shall pass. Unless I'm to take from your miserable look that I am in for a fight. You want him, too?"

"Absolutely not," said Margeta.

"Then why let it bother you what I do? It should only bother darling Katarina, if she wouldn't want me for a relation. And poor Samuel, who I have promised my eternal love. But how achingly quaint everything looks here. What if I should find myself wanting to stay after all ...?"

· · ·

And Robine Beaujeulle.

Embarassed she had come so late ('after everyone else'), or that there *was* anyone else but her, she was shy to come out of her apartment after arriving in Netz, wishing only to meet with Amalina at first, until Amalina compelled her to join the others. She was living embarrassment; on account that she had been slower than the others; and that she was not as pretty as the others; or as rich as the others; or as learned as the others; or as popular as the others; or as devout as the others. Robine was especially abashed that her parents had determined she was 'below standards', and had sent her as a longshot, to pawn her off on someone who might, by chance, enrich the family coffers. Or, if not, so be it. She had come for her own reasons, too. Just to get out of Paris and visit Amalina, someone she liked. But now there was a cordon of competitors. That the other princesses were, more-or-less, in the same circumstances as she, bolstered Robine's spirits only a little.

"But this is not what I thought it would be," admitted Robine with a whisper of lament.

"How so?" asked Amalina.

"When you were in Paris, we met privately and it was quite fun. Don't you think, with all these other girls, things are just … different? I mean, you are different, certainly, when you are around them."

Amalina could say the same of Robine, who hadn't struck her as shy. But now the girl was in full retreat. Maybe it was the disappointment of having her expectations of a leisurely one-on-one winter dashed. But, though Amalina more sensed it than thought of it (with such clinical dissection), it was Robine's reading of already entrenched alliances that made her reluctant to try to fit in. The young woman was pathologically insecure.

"What are you saying over there?" Gillette shouted from across the table. "Robine, speak up."

At this, Robine became something of a vapor.

• • •

And Isabeau DePense. Her head was a fountain of blond ringlets, looking like a chainmail cap made of gold. She smiled this way and that and at everyone with her pretty white teeth—when she found there were four princesses who'd preceded her arrival. How delighted she was for it. Of course she expected it, she said, smiling. Who *wouldn't* have turned up immediately at an invitation by the cute little countess from Ardeel? And she asked everyone questions about where they were from, and their home life, and then proceeded to tell them what she knew of it herself before they could answer, to test if she was right. And on the street she would point out to Amalina bits of provincial architecture, or construction, or the visible signs of ailment on a passing stranger, and expound on what she had read in a book about such things, or had learned from one of her hundreds of tutors.

"No, no, no, let me guess," said Isabeau, patting her fingertips daintily, eyes growing wide over the latest meal being spread out on the table; this night at the Rock Face Restaurant—an establishment seeming to have sprung up in order to cater to the influx of foreign nobility. "I'd say this is pheasant done up with citrus and plum. And this is a pie of turtledove and yam. And that there is a stew of turtle and," sniff, sniff, "and trout, of course, with heavy pepper or some kind of clove."

While Gillette made a noise of being impressed, Aria snorted.

"Couldn't be more wrong," said Aria. "You've misidentified pheasant from goose. Turtledove and yam from what is clearly rat and turnip—"

"I'm sorry," interrupted Isabeau with a smile. "I don't know what you're saying."

"You seem to know everything else," said Aria, with a derisive sneer.

"Your accent, please?" Isabeau said in perfect Italian, with an immaculate Venetian accent. "It is a litte rough."

Aria repeated what she'd said, very slowly, in French, heavily accented by her Venetian tongue. But everyone understood.

"Ah, you're teasing me," said Isabeau, catching on.

"You don't like the food?" Amalina asked Aria, touching her fork to what she had indicated was rat, sensing there was a hidden complaint within the joke.

"Don't be sensitive," chided Aria. "It ruins the fun."

"But this is so much food," Robine broke in with a shy look, her head slightly bowed, "We keep eating and eating and eating, Katarina. Is it always this way around here?"

"Perhaps there isn't much else to do," said Gillette with a laugh. "At least it tastes good—"

"—tastes *different*—" said Aria.

"—tastes *interesting*," Gillette challenged. "Why don't you try some?"

"But Katty orders so much," she continued. "Yet she eats very little. Have you noticed?"

"I have," commented Isabeau.

"She's just trying to show off to the peasants," snickered Aria, while Amalina blushed. "This is the way she spent her money all around Venice."

"It is a vanity to display your wealth, Katarina," chided Margeta, her lips tightly compacted by disdain to a wrinkled box. "I didn't mention it when you visited, but there is a sin in it, you should know. And I've already made a point to you on this gluttony."

"I only wanted to share," said Amalina. "And what we don't eat is given out and divided among the people here. Those *are* my wishes, and the people are glad enough to do it. It isn't wasted."

"Well, it's still conspicuous indulgence, and profligacy, and a form of gluttony all the same," said Margeta, crossing herself. "And you are getting a little flabby, if you haven't noticed."

"It *is* a little much, Kat," said Aria with a polite grin.

Amalina felt her cheeks glow, while her eyes glanced around for the anonymous invitation writer, hoping he'd appear to explain himself (or was it a *her?*), before she was forced to embarrass herself further by ordering more of these multi-course meals which she could no longer stomach. Or must give up altogether.

. . .

Lastly came Pia Lampeda, who arrived from Italy just when the other Princesses had languished in Netz long enough for the Count's medicine to have taken effect (a fact of which they were still innocent) and were preparing to go to the high castle on the next day.

"Margeta," she exclaimed on seeing the other Roman princess. "You're here?"

"Of course," said Margeta stiffly. "Why not? Lady Tepsji invited me."

"But had I known, we could have come together, like a caravan or something."

"Well, I don't know …"

"Oh, but I wish I had. When did you leave?" When Margeta told her, Pia clasped a hand over her mouth. "What! We left on almost the very same day. I was before you by one day! And yet you arrived before me!"

It turned out Pia had left home before anyone else had. But she was the latest to arrive. "My, what a rough time I had of it. You would never believe. Two of my carriage's wheels broke along the way, at different times, you see. Then my horses fell ill. Then one of my horsemen was accused of stealing some money. Then we were held up—oh, to think of it—held up in the most inbelievable way, by a regiment of the most dangerous thugs, when falseword had been given that we were riding from a territory with the plague and had to sit quarantine! City after city, it was one thing after another. I thought there was a curse on me, how we kept getting thrown off course. Mile posts and signs had been turned to point in the wrong directions at so many roads." Pia sighed.

"And I heard that red hair brings you good luck," said Robine, emerging from her shell because, taking heart, there were now so many *later* arrivals than she.

"Oh, yes," said Isabeau, "that's what is said about red heads in your province, Robine. But it is bad luck in other places."

"I don't think it has to do with my hair at all," said Pia.

"Well, it is *very* red," said Gillette admiringly.

"Sounds like it was an awful trip. It's good you arrived safely, all the same."

It was noticeable Margeta had dissolved into a round of playing with her prayer beads.

Pia sighed in her direction, "Well, Margeta, I wish I'd known you were visiting Katarina, too. We could have gone together."

Margeta looked up from her clattering beads but said nothing.

"She's probably glad you didn't," said Gillette. "With all that bad luck hanging over you."

"We could have kept each other company, though. Isn't that right, Margeta? It would have been nice to have a friendly face and warm company through all that. Why didn't you tell me you were coming, Margeta?"

"You would have felt bad, Princess Lampeda, if I had told you I was, and it turned out you hadn't been invited, too," was her strange answer. "I thank God you made it through your trials, though, and He delivered you safely to us."

• • •

Robine wasn't wrong about how different things were.

Amalina had visited the princesses individually, in their homes. Rarely had they crossed paths with others except at the occasional celebration or ball. So her experience with them had been private. Intimate. With 'Princess Katarina' being just a little oddity from the east, and a small, innocent child at that. Now here were the older girls in direct confrontation with each other, sporting their differences, challenging, jockeying. Some aspects of their personalities changed completely, so that they would be unrecognizable to Amalina if she hadn't met them before but had only read about them in an article.

Where Robine explicitly asked for Amalina's company all to herself, and tried to isolate her when she could, it was Pia Lampeda who accomplished the feat. Maybe because Pia was closest to Amalina in age, or some other factor. But Amalina felt it came down to the princess' unaffected physical intimacy—touching, holding hands, leaning close, embracing, giving pet kisses—that by its directness simply kept their bodies together, creating the closeness Robine so much wanted. Amalina thought Pia's red hair and green eyes and milky skin was quite exotic, and was easily drawn in. The others were driven away in their own turn, and by their own devices: Aria couldn't care less for the close company of any one person; Margeta was as solitary and watchful as the statue of a saint; Gillette was too distracted by her inner conflict of Samuel and the will of her parents, that she might have just as well been back home; Isabeau was too busy lecturing and hooking in the nearest princess to listen to what she had to say, or at least pretend to listen; and Robine, recognizing—or convincing herself with self-pity—that she'd lost the battle for Amalina to the Italian Princess Pia Lampeda, kept at a close, quiet distance, but little more.

Pia would have won out entirely, as it were, if she hadn't—after proving herself unbeatable at cards and feeling emboldened—brought up a subject— and raised that subject publicly—which Amalina had entirely forgotten: in the middle of an introductory hand of Scapone (using Gillette's French-suited playing cards), Amalina wrinkled her forehead in deep concentration. Pia snapped her fingers.

"Katarina," she said, after giving some detailed but cryptic instructions to her maid. "I can't believe I forgot! You were so fast to leave me when you visited, you were gone before I had these made for you. But do you remember?"

The maid returned with a small box. Everyone gathered around. Amalina's pulse quickened and her face turned red, because she knew what was coming. Out of the small box came the small round lenses fitted with little wooden pegs and legs.

"Put them on, Kat," enthused Pia, with one arm wrapped like a constrictor around Amalina's. "Look at the cards and see how easy it is! Tell me my artisans don't perform miracles! Try them on and look! Look!"

Amalina placed the pair of glasses before her eyes. Everything in the room bulged and distorted, especially at the corner of her vision. But Pia was already pushing one of the cards at her face.

"Look! Look! See, Kat! Tell me that isn't *so* much clearer!"

And the card was much clearer. The little red heart was crisp at the edges. The Queen was dressed in something very fancy. And she actually had an expression on her face. Amalina could even see the different color threads woven into the paper.

"What do you think?" cried Pia. "Better?"

All the princesses laughed (happily) and didn't wait for Amalina to answer, but pulled the pair of glasses off Amalina to try for themselves. They all marveled at Pia's present, as Pia explained that she'd noticed the grimaces Amalina made when reading, the headaches she would get, and knew right away that a set of spectacles would do the trick. Eventually the glasses were returned to Amalina, who was forced to try them on again, and keep them on as she played the rest of the game. Margeta said nothing, but the rest— even Aria—complimented her, saying they made her look like an old scribe.

"You don't have to wear them all the time," said Gillette, consolingly. "Just when your eyes grow tired."

"That's right," said Pia, sensing Amalina might not be as pleased as she'd hoped.

"I think you look stupid in them," whispered Robine, later, countering what she'd said earlier, when she recognized there might still be some hope of burrowing in closer. "I don't know what that Italian girl was thinking."

Amalina was thinking the whole time: *How could you, how could you, how could you! I was perfect before you came!*

The wedge of Amalina's disappointment in herself, and her despair—I *do* look like an old scribe … a fat old priest … *Old!*—knocked a comfortable space between her and the princesses for a moment. She slept alone in her apartment that night, using the glasses and seeing perfectly the things she used to see clearly but didn't realize she *wasn't* seeing clearly anymore. And then she cried her eyes out.

It took overnight to overcome. The spectacles were a thoughtful gift and they were *actually* helpful. To find this unhappy and ungrateful piece of her personality existed was a surprise to Amalina, but she knew how wrong it was when, in her dreams, Lucinda Skeldar's head popped above the tops of the rye to remind Amalina, once again, to find her killer, but instead—and in Margeta's voice—she said very clearly: "*Vulgar Vanity!*"

. . .

When Amalina returned to the princesses, they were happy to find their young little Ardeelian friend recovered. Then it was time to move, as one group—nobody closer or removed from Amalina's friendship—into the Count's high castle.

. . .

"Princess Aria," the Count growled like a hungry cat, pulling on his mustache, and regarding her the exact same way he had Katrina Flauna. In fact, they both looked at each other in that particular way the Count and Flauna had exchanged looks. Something predatory, and something private, and something that caused them to laugh in synch with each other—some *knowing* laugh—as they stared into each other's eyes. Their bodies almost dancing, though not. Closing together, but staying apart. It was animalistic. It was sultry.

"Princess Margeta," the Count bowed slightly at the waist, stiffly. She'd reluctantly stowed away her religious trinkets, as she was told he would not abide by them. While this caused her some fits of religious fury and disgust at this heathen family (that her own family had selfishly and insensibly sent her to make friends with), the Count's proper bearing caused her to look down at her shoes, and her shoulders buckled, then fell. He was an alpha wolf taming the pride.

"Princess Gillette," the Count said merrily, moving enthusiastically around her, as if appraising her. His energy transferred into her and she smiled genuinely, with no hint of bashfulness. But she was no shy girl, after all.

"Princess Robine," said the Count in a soothing, soft voice, to the shy one. When she looked up into his giant brown eyes, he tilted his head downward, almost like a young puppy. But he was big. So big. And he nodded at her, and took her hand gently, and welcomed her into his home in the warmest tone. "You have my niece's friendship, and you've come for her. But I hope you will be willing to share a moment or two with an old man who would appreciate your company." Robine melted, with Amalina almost forgotten.

"Princess Isabeau," said the Count. "Tell me a little about yourself." That she did.

"Princess Pia," said the Count. "I hear you almost didn't make it. But sometimes the best things must wait. Sometimes there are trials before the reward. Don't you agree? The easy things in life are the cheapest things in life. And look at this red hair. Almost the color of … of blood!"

Aria. Margeta. Gillette. Robine. Isabeau. Pia. To each one the Count made his introductions, almost cut perfectly to fit their personality. And with each introduction he secured their interest, so that each felt that he was the reason she was there. It was a feat that Amalina, a bystander in the corner of the room, couldn't help but be impressed by. He knew what he was doing.

"Welcome to my home," he told them. "The Palace of Pleasures."

And then, as was his way, he mysteriously disappeared.

17

General Order

A ria. Margeta. Gillette. Robine. Isabeau. Pia.
"You won't tell me who you've chosen," said Amalina, wishing he wouldn't. Willing the Count not to say the name. Thinking she might just plug her fingers in her ears.

"You have your private guess and that's enough," said the Count, enjoying the apprehension he sensed in her, mistaking it for mutually enjoyable suspense. He stood from the divan and straightened his shirt. "In any case, you will know who I've selected in just a moment."

The Count pointed to the study's closed door. Amalina looked to it, her heart pumping, her stomach turning, expecting someone to walk in at his cue. The door didn't open.

"Someone's coming?"

The Count shook his head. "We're going to her. I thought it best I perform the rite where my beloved will be most comfortable."

"Beloved?"

"It's no use trying to pry now. I won't say who it is until we get there."

"You mean both of us? We're both …?"

"Yes," he said with a definite note. "I don't want to make a mistake, and so I will have your assistance. Now, come."

He went to the door and opened it. So then, she thought: there would not be a whir in the air, a blur of black, a slam into Amalina's gut, the breaking open of doors, a tear of wind, and then a rude and painful deposit into some unexpected location. The two would be walking all the way. Amalina gulped. Her collar felt tight.

As if it couldn't be driven home any harder, when they passed through *l'entrée grande* the Count paused, looked thoughtful as he tugged on his mustache, then he went to the pedestal beside the fireplace. He retrieved the dull gray cup that had sat there since Amalina had first arrived in the castle. Just as Bario had done to him, the Count's blood would soon be in it, and that blood would be poured over the lips of some poor girl whose life was sputtering out.

When they headed toward the stairs, they were headed in the wrong direction.

"The princesses are in the other wing."

He put a finger to his lips to let her know she was being too loud. Then he whispered in a rumble that still touched the deeper nerves at her core: "I told you I removed her to a room she would be most comfortable."

"You said it is *her* room."

"It is now." He made a gesture of *never mind all that*. "But we still have another stop on our journey. You have a dress of gold."

"Yes, sir."

"You must wear it. I refuse to have my recollections of this—this scene of divine intervention—be spoiled by careless attire."

As they passed into the stairway, Amalina realized two new sets of armor which were positioned at the doorway were not empty, but filled by Marosh's men; dressed in formal knightly armor and standing guard. Looking back, polished suits were at every doorway, even the one leading out into the courtyard. The metal gleamed in the firelight. Amalina was glad the helmet visors were down: so she couldn't see their faces.

Apparently, all the Count's people within the castle would be well cleaned and suited for his grand moment. This gave Amalina a thought.

"Where's the general?" she asked with a hushed voice.

"Away." His steps were so light she didn't hear them. It was as if he were floating up the stairs. "Why, little mouse?"

"Why can't *he* help you? The old general likes the sight of blood."

The Count turned his head around—his chin resting sickeningly wrong on his right shoulderblade as he looked down at her—an admiring grin opening with his pointed teeth. "True. But this won't be that kind of blood-letting. And you can't imagine the sight of Marosh, or one of his soldier boys, would put any of my ladies at ease."

How true, thought Amalina.

. . .

Nobody was at ease with Marosh. His cloud-like head shoved everyone about. Made them uncomfortable as he showered stormy stares of suspicion (of plots against his Master) and thundered accusations (of disrespect for His Excellency) over every living being who entered the castle. But his uneasy nature was detected long before entering the castle; while Amalina and the princesses were still ensconced in Netz and he combed over his master's would-be arrivals.

Notably, the princesses were not the only personalities to arrive. They brought with them their own maids and drivers and chaperones. These supporting persons came pre-formed, or molded, or otherwise selected by their princesses for their enjoyable presence. Or were tasked by their parents, and their parents' advisors, to keep a princess in bounds. So, they reflected or flew to the dynamic of their mistress and her starting point.

Aria's men seemed to prefer to locate alcohol and box each other. Margeta's people observed a snobbish, quiet piety. Gillette's were frank and somewhat watchful of her; and restraining of her; and fearful of her quick temper with its blows and scratches; and given to daring each other to some ridiculous nonsense for a laugh. Robine's were closeting and encouraging in turns for her, and frustrated by her shyness; and looked longingly at the scenery which they'd traveled so far to see, but could only steal out to enjoy when she wasn't demanding attention. Isabeau's were enduring and patient and bored enough to regard the other princesses as desirable. And Pia's were still exhausted from the trip and didn't account for much.

But as they came to brush up against each other, it was like six clouds closing on each other from six different directions, buffeting and rubbing and merging unsurely. Of course the men on all sides would find ways to gamble and drink and tell stories—as their languages allowed; and somewhere throw a punch. And of course the women would either find fast friendships (seldom), and pick up some new pointers (assiduously), or find fault with everything within the rival's camp (eagerly). And of course, finally, there would be the ones, males and females alike, looking for something quite new: to catch someone's eye, to attract a mate, and slip away under the noses of their ladyships for intense intimacy. And maybe even elope to find a new way for their lives (which would be their utter ruin).

Marosh put a stop to all that. He was familiar with these things from his own household and was only charier with young foreigners—and to him, everyone else in the world was young, and stupid, and rightful of distrust (adding a prejudicial emphasis to men), and he being provincial, these were as foreign as foreign people he'd ever met. He raked them with his presence until they were as docile as sheep to his wolf (he was no shepherd dog; he was not on their side). They pulled themselves tight together within the protective corral of their particular lady's direct company.

By the time they were going to the castle, they were too aware what a long and miserably confining trip they were in for. Especially with Marosh around.

• • •

Before the princesses could go to the castle, there was another week of delay beyond the Count's own timeline. One of Gillette's maids, who had arrived not feeling well, fell entirely ill.

"How's Coterie-Ann?" said Aria, anxious to move up to the castle. "Dead yet?"

"She's on the mend," said Gillette. "But will take her sweet time about it. She *always* does."

"Yes, you can't slug her into fitness," clucked Margeta, making a shrewd observation of Gillette's temper and ease of cruelty toward her servants.

"It *can* be done," retorted Gillette, unabashed. "But the results are less than satisfactory. Still, now I see the reason in our Katarina's unwillingness to have servants. Always getting sick, or dropping something. Or, just when you've gotten used to them, they run off with a lover or die. Neverending."

"Don't give Katarina any ideas she's in the right," sniffed Margeta, "when she is not. A princess needs a proper maid. Nobody's ever heard of a maidless lady of title until this one emerged from the misty rocks of the east with her strange ways."

"I thought she was too poor at first," said Robine.

"But I did have rented maids," said Amalina.

"Look, Princess Katarina," intoned Margeta, getting ready to deliver a sermon. "It doesn't serve you well not being properly served. It gives a bad impression all around. It gives our retainers bad ideas, and really, how can one trust someone who does not trust someone else with their entire being? Rented servants. For show. To placate us. Nothing real."

"Well, you know I'm not poor."

"Then there is no excuse."

"I just like knowing I can do things for myself," said Amalina.

"As I said: Bad ideas all around. Perhaps we can influence you. Growing into a woman as you are in our companionship."

"Are you telling me you don't have your own attendants up in the castle?" Isabeau asked with her telling curiosity.

Marosh shut them all up by entering the room, glaring all around, leaving nobody unaffected, then telling them, with impatience and lightning bolts: "Master sends word. The Palace of Pleasure is *ready to receive*." Then he added without meaning it: "At your pleasure."

"Well, nevermind servants. There is *something* up there," said Gillette of the thundercloud, when he left.

• • •

But there was more than just Marosh at the high castle. There was Marosh's army.

Should any of Marosh's men enter a room or come into view, the royal ladies' eyes roamed this way and that, and not on *them*. And when traveling out of the main building one saw soldiers huddled together, one found a reason to return to the main building, where there were, refreshingly, fewer of them. Or if one was already inside the main building and was confronted by a marching detail, one hurried to another room.

The reason was this. Anka had heard something when she took the cart down to Netz for supplies (in preparation for the first princess, Ragonde la Basca, to arrive), and then blathered unmindfully to the Count.

"I look forward to when these lady princesses show up," she had said, opening the scene.

"So do I, Ms. *Quiet*." The Count emphasized her name in the hope she might get the hint. He was antagonized by some private puzzle he was working out at the time.

"The general's men won't be quite so dull. And we'll surely see the Palace get lively."

"Eh? How do you mean?"

"Never saw one of the general's boys crack a smile since I got here," she said, "unless it had something to do with rough-housing or something low and mean, anyway. But as I was on the cart, I heard them talking. One said to the other he can't wait for the first princess to arrive. Said she will be beautiful, certainly. The other agreed and they were guessing what she might look like. And quicker than anything, don't you know, they were sitting straight up, with great smiles on their faces. Smiling very cheery-like with their eyes, if you know what I mean. The other said he'd heard there were going to be six more ladies. Or a dozen. They didn't know, but you know they were imagining a hundred before the end of it. And thinking they might be able to catch one or another's eye. Oh, one likes blondes, the other likes brunettes. Both thought a red-head would be exotic, and just as well."

"Catch their eye?"

"Of course. Young soldiers, old soldiers. Soldiers are soldiers and a good lusty crew the lot of them. And they always think they can bring down a Queen or a Princess, like in some fairytale. But in their minds they know it will be a Queen or Princess' handmaid or scullery girl, instead. Which'll be just the same and just as well, in the end. Doesn't matter. Perked them up like it was Christmas, when all along this palace has been as pleasant as a common grave. Even gave me the tickles, it did. Should have seen them, sir. This place will pick up lively like." She smiled to herself and sighed womanly thoughts, unaware of the storm gathering on the divan. "Nothing more handsome than a soldier's red cheek and a smile."

The entirety of this exchange Pils reported breathlessly to Amalina.

"And so?" asked Amalina.

"And so you have to see," he gasped. "It's ... Well, you'll never believe. Never. Come, you have to see."

Pils took Amalina by the hand and ran her down to the side courtyard. All Marosh's men had been gathered into ranks and stripped of their helmets, armor and shirts. Amalina heard a low murmuring as she and Pils made their way along the wall to the front of the lines. She realized the murmuring was the multitude of moans and groans of soldiers within their tents further into the courtyard.

At the head of the ranks, General Marosh's eyes were like steel as he glared at the next man to approach his table. There were seven other men behind the table, sitting on chairs, with different instruments before them. There was also a brazier burning on one side with irons stuck into it.

"Think you can steal a princess from our great lord?" hissed Marosh, the red X carved into his forehead nearly glowing like a giant third eye. His hair was thick and wild. Both his hair and his eyes made him look either insane or like an avenging angel.

"No, General. Never, General."

"Are you ready to prove this—and prove it good—to His Excellency?"

"Anything, General. You know I swore myself to you, and of course to the Master of All."

"Sweet words. But the proof is in the deed. So what is your choice?" Marosh waved his giant hand freely at the table.

The soldier pointed feebly to the crooked X that was carved into his own forehead.

Marosh answered the action by setting a human head on the table. He kicked it forward with his boot and then pointed at its forehead. There was an X there.

"This one said he was going to bag a princess," said Marosh.

The general threw another head down onto the table. It had the disfiguring X in its forehead, just as did all the soldiers who'd pledged themselves to General Marosh, and had devoted themselves to the service and preservation of the Count.

"This one," Marosh said, stabbing the X with his finger, "thought there were enough princesses to go around. The Count can *'have only one, after all,'* he said."

The soldier dropped his hand from his forehead, and drooped even at his knees. His face blanched. He looked to his general with dog-like eyes.

"But, my General, I didn't say those things."

"The proof is in the deed. Make your choice. I haven't all day. The men standing behind you haven't all day, and they can't wait to come foreward and prove themselves. Now, what's it to be?"

"But, General … I have a wife." The soldier's eyes dropped tears.

"She'll understand. And approve. What fidelity you prove here to the Count, you prove to her twicefold."

The soldier's mouth opened and closed, his head shook from side to side. His eyes were blinking heavier tears by the moment.

"You will still serve me. You will still serve your true Master, the High King of the Mountains. You will still provide service. You will still enjoy our hunts, man. Long may it last. But make a choice, or I will cut off your head like these dogs and any cowardly deserter."

"Are *you* going to do this—?"

Marosh slammed the man's head onto the table. A long blade he held high into the air, ready to chop down and remove the head with one stroke.

"I'll do it!" cried the man. "I'll do it!"

Marosh threw him onto the ground where three soldiers caught him.

"Your choice, for the last damned time."

"What are they again?"

"Soft acid. Branding. Or castration. You know these men know what they are doing. It won't hurt any more than it has to. You already had your bit of wine, though with the time you're wasting you're losing its effect."

The soldier winced. "I suppose the acid."

"Everyone's taking the acid!" Marosh griped. "We're going to run out soon enough. Are you sure you don't want to go with the branding, to spare one of your brothers the agony? They'll love you more for it."

"No branding."

"Castration, then?"

"Well, I've my wife to think about."

"She'll thank you," he laughed. Then he shoved the soldier into the table and immediately men were on him, rubbing leather cloths or throwing leather sheets on his chest and over his face, though avoiding his eyes and mouth. The men wore protective gloves and hoods and tried to keep a distance from their subject. As they did this, Marosh mumbled under his breath, "As if she will see you again. Or recognize you."

The process was quick and the soldier was given a pat on the back as he stumbled away. His skin looked normal, if a little red from the rub down. But as he stepped toward the tents, his flesh began to crack and bubble. The soldier shuddered and moaned and hugged his waist while trying to keep his hands away from the effected area. His skin hissed. Smoke rose over his shoulders as he disappeared from sight, adding his groans to the men who had already gone through the treatment.

After what Marosh had said, some of the rougher or more zealous men chose branding: to spare one of their brothers from having to do it, to heroically impress everyone with their willingness to commit to the cause, and to aggrandize themselves in the eyes of their General and the Count. They yelled and screamed as the irons went to work, setting patterns to their skin. Some of the men even told the branders what marks to make; another show of cold-blooded bravery. These men were wrapped up like mummies afterward and had to lay down for days to recover, praying they wouldn't develop a serious infection or worse.

Twelve hours of mutilation. There were only five deserters who were caught and executed. Only one man chose castration. Marosh wandered away at this cruel bit of subjugation, mumbling, "Should kill that fellow instead. Any man who would do such a thing has given up hope."

"What use is it around here?" cried the man defiantly at Marosh's back. He had heard the general's comment.

Marosh, whether by wandering away or by design, did not have any of the methods tried on him.

The sight was too much to stick around for, so Amalina and Pils left the courtyard after half an hour. But they ended up leaning out an upper floor window and watched from above.

"My God," cried Anka. "They killed those poor boys I heard innocently talking. Killed them dead, and now this. Why, oh why! How horrible. I never would have said anything if I knew it would come to this. Oh, I wish I hadn't said a thing."

"I wish you hadn't brought me down there," Amalina told Pils. "Why did you? It was horrible."

"I didn't want to be the only one watching," he admitted with some shame.

"They spared the girls and women," said Anka, blowing her nose. "Not sure how you escaped the sentence, Pils. Those men will hate your guts now, for sure."

Pils shook hard at that, but it didn't happen.

And Anka's prediction of a lively house (once the princesses arrived) did not come to pass, either, thanks to her chattiness. The soldiers wore solemn black cloth hoods over their faces, or leather masks, or helmets with all-round visors. They were eerily quiet and presented a gloomy aspect to the castle. Which was probably what had tipped off Ragonde and her people that something was amiss. But the soldiers did not kick Pils in the backside—not even once—when he wasn't looking.

. . .

About the undying hope of man: On two occasions, when princesses were passing into *l'entrée grande*, Amalina noticed a couple of Marosh's soldiers smile—their teeth flashing behind an opening in their black hoods—and then came an exchange of looks between them that said *'look at them, what did I tell you!', 'Yes, and the blonde one is mine.'*

They were the only soldiers in the room, and they didn't know they were being watched or they wouldn't have risked a leer. But also, and this was the point, they were too young to have permanent disfigurement crowd misery into their enthusiastic thoughts.

. . .

The princesses didn't begin to ask questions about the silent soldiers (and their curiously encompassing attire) until the third week of all being together. Questions bubbled up—from the very first day—between the princesses' maids and butlers. And, of course, pieces of the grim facts were discovered and repeated in horror to their charges. But a full question-and-answer on the subject rose up into the higher circle only when there were enough princesses with the hostess to make a quorum: enough to present a united front and feel confident in challenging her.

"Yes," said Amalina sadly, whispering though no soldier was around. "They were made to look hideous."

"My God, why?" said Margeta. "Why in God's name?"

"So they would think no other worldly thoughts than to serve the Count."

"I imagined it to be idle gossip. And it is true?" Margeta crossed herself. "And you allowed it to happen, Katarina?"

"What? No!"

"It is one thing to beat a servant for infractions. But this. Your uncle would be thought of as a Monster. You should ask for heaven's forgiveness." Margeta crossed herself again.

"Sit next to me, Margy, dear," said Aria, with sardonic fondness. "I could use that breeze."

"My uncle didn't tell them to do it. It was General Marosh." A couple of the Lady Princesses moved uncomfortably at his name. Amalina hadn't seen which ones, she just noticed the bristling when she said it. "He's a fanatic, you know. Expects anyone who serves him to be the same."

"Is it just the X on their heads?" asked Gillette. "Like Marosh? Or Xs all over their faces?"

"Burned themselves," said Isabeau. "I've seen it."

"Are you sure they aren't all lepers?" said Robine.

Amalina cut through the gossip and told them it was acid and branding.

"You see," said Isabeau, triumphant.

"So horrible," said Pia. "I can hardly look at them for fear I might see something."

"I told you *I've* seen it," said Isabeau again. "Like fried cheese. If you just look in the gaps, or around their necks."

"The poor wretches," said Gillette weeks later in a renewed conversation on the subject, as the gloomily silent sentries added a palpable grotesqueness to the early winter's pleasant hush. She made a face of disgust. "They shouldn't even be allowed inside the castle proper, they are so upsetting to look at."

"You can't even tell," said Amalina.

"But just knowing ..."

"I think that just makes them more interesting," said Aria, in a sensuous purr. "Mysterious and tragic. I've had plenty of interesting dreams with them. Several of them. At once."

"Only you Aria," growled Margeta.

Aria then said something that made the others laugh in surprise, educated Amalina, and shocked Margeta (as the sensuous Venetian intended to).

"It makes one wonder," Aria continued to purr, "how close to reality a dream can be."

"Don't talk to them, Aria," warned Amalina, seeing the danger this line of thinking was headed. "Don't speak to them. Don't approach them. Don't even look at them. I'm serious. If Marosh found out, you could get them tortured, or killed."

"Katarina, dear," Aria said deliciously, leaning her head back and closing her eyes, "What you say … you just made the dream I will enjoy tonight even *more* interesting."

18

Count Tepsji's Murder Service

Aria Ecci would no doubt find Marosh or Marosh's boys comforting (or *interesting*, as she would say), Amalina thought to herself. She didn't say the princess' name aloud, in case the Count confirmed, by some change in expression, that she was the one who would be dying tonight.

The Count wasn't wrong, after all, thought Amalina: As much as she was terrified about what was to come in just a few moments, part of her mind was spinning with the images of her friends' faces, trying to settle on the one that the Count had chosen for his *ever-own*.

"Besides," said the Count, his words a clear low whisper that penetrated her chest, even though he'd mercifully turned his head back around to watch where he was going, "Marosh does not know this aspect of my romance."

"What do you mean?"

"He knows of my intentions to wed one of our guests, of course. But he doesn't know this other part: Her transition." Following Amalina's surprised silence, he added, "You understand my need for discretion, don't you?"

She couldn't think of a good reason. "He's your best follower, except Genadie—"

"Pssh!" said the Count. He must have meant that for Genadie.

"I thought you trusted Marosh with everything."

"This is a powerful piece of information, Mouse. Had I known of it, I doubt I would have shared it with anyone. Even you. But you came to me with the knowledge of transformation, and you were loyal to me in keeping it to yourself and nobody else. It will remain that way. Our secret."

"But ... won't the general be surprised when one of the princesses is suddenly a ... suddenly like ... suddenly as you are ...?"

"No doubt, when it dawns on him what has happened. But he won't understand how it came to pass. And, in his fear of me and my might, he will obey. He won't ever ask questions."

Amalina thought of the coming task. And her position in it.

"But, sir, I really don't like the sight of blood."

"Close your eyes."

They arrived at Amalina's door. He opened it and motioned her in with a grand gesture.

"I know you're a curious one, Mouse. A very, very curious one, indeed. So I know it might be difficult for you. But you'll know when to keep your eyes closed. And you will if you don't want to see it."

His voice came through the door as she moved to the wardrobe and found the gold dress. It looked gaudy in broad daylight. But at night, reflecting the light of a fire, it smoldered and burned and looked beautiful. It was intended for balls and grand dinners, and any occasion where she was meant to shine.

"But maybe you are less squeamish than you think, my little mouse," he was saying. "You're a mouse after all. Daring. Fearless."

As he said this her eyes caught the sheets on her desk, underneath the glasses. Her cyphers. She had been working and reworking the coded messages, trying to solve them, when he'd called her down to his study. If he stepped inside now, he might notice them. She took the pages and tucked them underneath her mattress.

"So are Anka and Pils," said Amalina, as she covered the movements and riffling of pages with her voice. "So is Genadie. They'd help you without question."

"Ms. Dalca, you are the only one who can help me."

Her eyes rested for a second on a slip of vellum and its mysterious message, before it went under the mattress—and a solution seemed to come to her. But then it went away just as fast. A snap and a spark of light flying away from a fire. Maybe it was a false impression, but she swore she must have caught some of the right thread that would untangle the knot of encryption.

"I'm not the only one," she said as she changed clothes. "I just gave you three good examples of people much better than me. General Marosh, too, if you'd *trust* him."

"But that's just it, little mouse. You're the only one—the *only one*—I can trust."

How wrong you are, she thought. You've no idea.

I'm the scurrying little mouse who hasn't been yours since before I returned. Since before I met the Strange Man. Since before I found Ivanti, even. I am my own agent now. And if I should ever break that code, I am sure I will find a way to turn something important against you.

You don't even know how far it has gone.

. . .

Amalina remembered the feel of the stone floor against her bare feet some weeks ago. And the pounding of her heart in fear and excitement as she walked as gently as she could behind the Count's back—a wall of white linened shoulders. He was entering his counting house, his treasury, on his way to the most cherished place for him: the message center. Amalina knew that's where he would go, she was sure of it this time. And so he did, not even closing the door behind him.

Amalina had been lucky that day. She'd paid close attention to the aviary since the frightening wrinkled man had gone away with his one bird. The Count had accepted delivery of a new flight of pigeons, trained them until they were looking as ravaged and cynical as the ones he'd commandeered. Then he sent them away. Then it seemed the birds began to return. But, upon entering the aviary, she saw that she was mistaken. These birds, as they came in, one by one, looked sleek and better rested. They had a different banding on the leg, with little leather cylinders to contain the wider strips of paper. And they wore little bells that sounded as they flew. Jing, jing, jing. Where were they from?

What messages these newer pigeons carried, who sent them, and whether they were written in code, Amalina didn't know, because Marosh would always be there first. He'd give her one of his fuming looks and she would fall back. The only thing she could glean from these tinkling arrivals was Marosh would capture every message like a jealous lover, and with the most serious expression deliver it to the Count as soon as he woke. And the Count's face would slacken, looking immobilized or dead. And she thought she would die to see what was written that could concern him so.

But she was lucky that day, when she was with Robine in the courtyard riding horses, and Robine looked up and pointed at the circling pigeon. No jing, jing, jing. Amalina flew off the horse and ran to the aviary. The window had been closed. Another stroke of luck. She opened the window and the ugly, greasy pigeon dutifully plopped onto the counter and began looking for something to eat. It was only the second despicable pigeon Amalina could find in the aviary. So they—the evil wrinkled man and the Count— were up to two new exchanges. Amalina grabbed this one quick and removed the thin strip of vellum from around its leg.

Before she could stop herself it was open between her fingers. The handwriting was rough, but it was in code. Some of the more complex characters were missing, so it wasn't the difficult code. She would need only one of the keys to decipher it. But then Robine joined her, out of breath, exclaiming wonder at how fast Amalina had abandoned her without telling her where she was going.

"One might think you were trying to get rid of me," said Robine, becoming moody. "You aren't trying to get rid of me so fast? This was our promised time together. I was looking forward to it."

"Please, Robine, it's just a message ..."

"For you? From another friend?" said Robine, reaching for the paper, angling her head and squinting her eyes to read.

"Oh, Robine." Just when the girl's insecurity and possessiveness had seemed to be evening out. "It's for Uncle."

Amalina rolled up the scrap of paper as best she could to its original state, tied it, and before they could deliver it to the Count, they were intercepted by Marosh. Robine politely fled in terror at the sight of the general. Amalina took the opportunity to go to her room, doff her clothes, and wedge the stale bone between her teeth.

She was just behind Marosh when he handed the little scroll to the Count.

"Another?" the Count said, looking very dead.

"Different, Master. This was one of those *other* pigeons."

The Count lifted his eyebrow as he read it. "It's nothing to worry yourself about, General. Thank you for your service."

"Is there anything to be done about the other matter, My Excellency?"

"Nothing to worry about."

"Master, you expected another alert. So did I. It is only a matter of time."

"Nothing to worry about yet, good general."

"Yes, Master," the general groveled into the ground.

After he'd left, the Count regarded the strip one more time. Then he went below, into his message center, with Amalina following.

. . .

This note was important enough for him to quit his regular business. Now she would see him at work. What he got up to with these special missives.

The book with the shining metal letters AXP sat closed on his standing desk at the bottom of the stairs. He opened it to the last page where the latest strips had been glued in. He now took from the lower drawer a fistful of cyphering sticks. He opened the slip of paper and his eyes ticked up and down from the various sticks until he found the right cypher. Amalina tried following along but the Count was much faster.

The Count growled disagreeably and then Amalina was blown across the floor.

She scrambled around after she hit the far shelf, wondering how she'd been discovered. Wondering when the next blow would fall.

The room was silent. The strip of paper was still rocking back and forth on a stream of air before it settled on the ground.

The Count had done one of his quick disappearances, unaware Amalina had been there beside him. She panicked. Had he shut her into the vault? She clamped down on the bone and ran. The secret door was still open.

Where had he gone to? Was he coming right back?

She went to the strip of paper. It was face down to the floor. She fished around with her invisible hands until she had it in her fingers. In the light she quickly compared it to the cypher stick:

> Too late, of course. Her death will have to wait for another
> opportunity. These opportunities are as rare as diamonds.
> With what you did to the flock, I will remind you, you've
> now squandered a fortune.

Quite a tone to take with the Count. No wonder it provoked him. Maybe he'd gone off to kill the ugly, wrinkled man.

But what was he talking about? '*Her death*'? The ugly little man with his horrible, violent songs, was waiting on the Count to kill someone for him. Why would the Count do it? Was this intended victim the Count's enemy, the ugly man's, or both?

There had been one other bird to arrive from that source since he'd gone away. She checked in the book to see what the previous message was. Maybe it was also in this simple code.

The book was gone. Amalina's stomach knotted. He'd taken it? What—?

She turned and saw it resting in the shelf dedicated to the city of Korr. That's right, she thought. She'd discovered the AXP book on that shelf, once upon a time.

With a spurt of arenaline Amalina grabbed the book from the shelf— stubbing the fingers on her left hand, and scratching the back of her arm on the shelf after that—and brought the book to the light. The last strip of vellum pasted onto the page was in that most complex of codes, using all the unique characters from each of the different cyphers. A code she hadn't yet cracked.

But there were two things that drew her attention closer.

This piece of paper had the little smudge she'd noticed on other strips in the book. Before, in the dimmer light, she'd thought they were fingerprints. Closer to the light, she saw there was some kind of detail to it. She hefted the book closer to the light, and brought her eye up to the page as close as it could get.

It was a face. A hand drawn rendering—with some good style—of a pretty young girl. She was smiling a cupid smile with bright, delighted eyes, under a standard white cap with a braid of hair showing on one side.

Then Amalina noted the writing, in the Count's spidery hand, stuffed into the margin around it:

> In less than a week? Too far away! I will not abandon my lovely princesses on a selfish errand for you! Be patient, or leave me alone! Before this service of murder becomes tiresome! Even to me! ... Keep the money if you will, I can't make it!!!

The Count was venting in the margins. And now, with the newest note, he was informed he'd missed his date and his opportunity to kill. Kill some girl, somewhere, with a cupid smile and a smart braid. Which had brought him a smart upbraid from his client.

A murder service!

It was bad enough that a good Ardeelian general and his men had thrown in on the Count's side. But *this* was even more sickening. Who was that vile, ugly, wrinkled toad that he could think to contract the Count into killing people—sweet little girls—and then he can! The Count had all the money in the world, why would he need blood money? And to commit crimes that had no necessity, no purpose! This had nothing to do with sustaining the Count's life, or restoring his incredible power. It made the Count even more of a villain—he became a heartless assassin!

Once before, she had taken a strip from the book. But then she'd lost it in her travels—purposely, when she'd decided to no longer prosecute the Count for his faults. Now, in her rage, unable to think of the Count partnering with that evil slug for such an indecent purpose, she flipped to an earlier page and plucked out an old message. One with a smudge.

She tossed the book carelessly back into the Korr shelf—which, hours later, she would regret having not replaced more carefully and exactly—and then hurried from the vault before the Count returned.

On the way to her room she waved the dry little strip, in an effort to make it look like it was floating along on a breeze. When she saw Anka and several princesses, including Robine, and their maids in *l'entrée grande*, she let the paper drop to the floor, and kicked it along the edge of the room where no one was looking. Eventually she made it out and up to her room.

She spit out the bone and went to her desk. The light wasn't enough. She opened the window for the daylight to flood the room. *Let the monster come now!* But her hot thought was instantly cooled by the frigid breeze that curled around her naked skin. She wrapped the blanket from her bed around her shoulders and took up the strip.

Yes, on it was the face of another innocent girl. Long dead, certainly. The victim of a foul consipiracy. How long had this been going on?

She remembered the present. That awful present from Pia sitting in her desk. With reluctance she added the glasses to her eyes.

The writing was so much clearer. And now the likeness of the drawing was so obvious, it could never have been a smudge. Oh my, how bad her eyes must be!

It was with the distractions—the effectiveness of the glasses, the knocks on her door, and the entertainments to be planned and accomplished—that diffused her outrage. And so, in later moments, she reconsidered her opinion of the Count: that he might not be entirely wrong in rendering his deadly service. Maybe he was doing it because, though he killed by necessity of nature, he had allowed himself to be guided by others on just who his victim should be. Maybe he considered it less of an offense that way.

And maybe there was a good reason for the ugly man to want these girls to die. She couldn't imagine what it might be, but she had not read the details in his messages. Maybe they were sickly, and needed the comfort of a quick death.

Then she remembered the odious little song the wrinkled man sang: *One white leg, fat and fancy. One white arm, that is my doll. One breast, two breast, plump and pert. All apart, then into the dirt.* Her white hot anger renewed and she would retrieve the slip and all the cyphers and get back to work.

It was all evil! It must be!

She would solve this code. And see if she didn't discover what this was all about!

19

The Lover
or
Count Tepsji's Petite Mysogyny
or
Cold Feet

"Where are we going?" Amalina asked the Count presently, as they continued on toward the waiting princess.

They weren't taking an upward or round-about route from Amalina's room, leading to the visitors' section of the castle. They were going down. Very quickly they were back in the Count's study, then headed for the cabinet. He worked the secret lever, pulled the cabinet away from the wall, and then they were into the vaults. The vaults! His hidden treasury and the message center. She was just thinking of this place, and now they were walking into it. How was this happening? Can he read minds? she worried. Had he read hers and was bringing her to the scene of her crime?

She flushed and sweated.

"Don't be nervous," he said, glancing at her. "It will be over soon enough."

She noted that torches burned in all corners, and candles were alight in the candlestands. He'd intended for them to come this way. They'd been lit long before she'd been thinking of the codes and of her discoveries in here. But before she could relax, her eyes caught the flash of light off of the metal lettering of the AXP book. It sat on his standing desk once more. Closed. But it *had* been moved to his desk again. Maybe some new message had been added. Or maybe he'd discovered she'd been into it, and he had set it there to confront her—

"This way," he said with a mixture of excitement and irritation at having to keep dragging her along. "Please, Ms. Dalca."

The door was open to the stone storeroom. The passage from there led to another, and then another. Everything was open to pass through, with her gold dress rippling in the soft, warm light. And Amalina would have been charmed with the effect on her dress, if it wasn't accompanied by the memory of all that had happened in these rooms. She saw the bearded heads of Kralov's revolutionaries—heads free of the large bodies, or the large bodies free of their heads. Their skin blackened by fire. The white shirts scorched black or soaked red in blood, or both.

The rubble had been cleared away, the damage repaired, and for Amalina it was just a setpiece returned to its original placement, the act to begin again, her mind already replaying it. Instead of shivering, she felt a strange heaviness to her body, her eyes lowered and she wanted to go to sleep.

How long had it been since she'd met the Count in his private study and he'd announced his plans to kill a princess? This feels like a journey, she thought, and it's taking forever. Forever! Am I just dreaming it? An elongating nightmare? It must be.

"Mouse, come forward."

"Do you know what you're doing?"

"Of course I do, Ms. Dalca. What a question to ask me. I've been through it myself before."

"Yes," she said. "Once. Or was it twice?"

"I experienced it once before, when it happened to me," he said. "And then once when I did it—quite unintentionally—to our lady of the market faire, outside Cluj Sibi falls; now the lady of the turning wheel. Oh, what a mistake that was. But that *does* make it two."

"That's not what I meant," said Amalina, feeling drowsy.

"What did you mean, then? Are you trying to delay my moment of tender triumph? Because it looks like you are. Deliberately so. There's only so much night I have left, and my darling is waiting for me. What are you talking about, Ms. Dalca? Come out with it quickly."

"I mean marriage, sir. You were married once or twice before. And now you plan to do it again."

"That is a different thing, and this is a *very* different thing."

"Yes. Altogether different. This is about love."

His eyes widened, as if stunned with delight. Because she'd voiced what was in his head and in his heart. Just come right out and said it, and it struck him hard with a ticklish feather.

"You've said 'beloved' and 'my darling' and all that," said Amalina. "And it sounds very nice, and pretty convincing, sir. But you do you really mean it?"

"I've interviewed them all," he said, suddenly looking defensive.

"Yes. Interview is a good word for it."

"You know how thorough it was."

"Yes, I trust you in that."

"But what?"

"But for a man who doesn't ..."

"Yes? I don't what?"

. . .

Like a bat flitting hungrily over a sleeping herd, the Count had darted at the prone and unaware princesses during their stay. Here and there landing. Sampling. Never letting one have too much of his attention or he might draw them all awake to what was happening.

They were treated to exciting diversions: the fireworks of flowers—in bloom even out of season. The impressive artworks of the Count's Grand Gallery, with its paintings and sculptures and dioramas curated over centuries. Concerts were played by musicians brought up to the castle from all around Ardeel, while the ladies got their exercise in dance. Knitting and sewing was to be had with the finest of cloth and thread the castle provided. Short excursions on foot and on horses were arranged. Hot baths were indulged in (once). Hair was combed and styled. Makeup and perfumes tried and refined. Ancient books were studied in the Great Library. Gaming tournaments were played on the Count's favorite chess set, and an imported backgammon board, and with dice, draughts, and cards (Gillette slyly introducing them to Pharo, an addictive betting game that promised to rob everybody of their valuables if they played it seriously, though Isabeau swore she knew a system to defeat it). Delicious meals were prepared by the General's cooks, and feasted on in the sumptuously done up *l'entrée grande* before a roaring fire. Margeta was even allowed to hijack a lower priest from St. Grigori to observe proper daily services in a side-room, as long as they held their noise down to that of a monastic order devoted to silence; everyone but Aria attended, even the non-Catholics.

The amusements kept the princesses at bay, as the Count sorted through them at his will. There was a bit of backwards obversation as well: while they really couldn't complain to Amalina that they weren't seeing enough of the Count, as they'd come at her invite, not his, and only Gillette had openly declared she was there to assess her uncle's suitability for marriage, in time they probed and raised questions about him. Obliquely. *What's the story of these strange soldiers he keeps in his castle? Why, if ever he visits us, does he only visit us at night? Why, for being such a pleasant soul,* does *he spurn the church with such seeming antagonism and aggression?*

There was another question, too, that arose, and was lofted unanimously:

Anyone with unrestricted access to a massive library of books—as the princesses now had—and possessed an imagination—as the princesses most certainly did—and had grown just a little bored—as princesses often do— went hunting for something a touch piquant; to speed the heart, jangle the soul and excite the nerves. In the age of the printing press, the promise of a little zestiness—a lurid word, saucy passage, or detailed wood-cut depiction—lurked behind every staid leather cover onto which a princess set her gaze. Robine, Isabeau and Pia hunted privately, each in her own furtive way; always with similar sly looks; nobody else aware. Aria and Gillette, twinned with keen hearts for adventure, went into the rummage together, a low husky laugh and titter of misbehavior between them. Only Margeta did so publicly, with the help of her butler, on the pretext of determining that the Great Library was free of salacious smut and ungodly material 'meant only to provoke restlessness of spririt, and to inflame carnal desires in the bosom'. And though for a moment there was a stir of excitement, until it was determined that they were looking at an illustrated manual on armed and unarmed combat, in the end Margeta and her butler seemed dismayed to the point of dripping when they reported the Library was, after an exhaustive search, indeed without a shred of saltier things.

The entire group registered their disappointment to Amalina, when they finally realized they had not turned up so much as a gentle and tasteful love story. This, in the library of a worldly bachelor? "No romances?" they complained to Amalina. "Not even a book of love poems?"

They all wondered: What does this say about the Count?

Amalina had been over this before with Lisbet Spaarvierlet, she recalled, but the matter had never been resolved, and she still didn't know what to tell them. And at the time, even she didn't yet know what new, dark, romantic idea had taken root in his ancient head.

. . .

"Romance?" the Count had said, strangely picking at his teeth, when Amalina came to him in his study, to report the complaints from her companions: his Great Library was not so great. It was, in fact, deficient in the one subject that most pleased his guests. "Haven't we been through this before?"

"Um, yes," said Amalina, stepping further into the room, sheepishly, under the glare of General Marosh. Marosh was standing at attention next to the Count, who was seated at his desk, a litter of tiny messages creating a pile next to several sheets of paper and the unrolled map of Ardeel. "I know you said before you thought they were silly, or frivolous or something ..." Marosh's teeth gnashed loudly. "But if you are busy ..."

"Nothing takes precedence to the happiness of my lady princesses, Mouse," he said, sounding sarcastic. "Do come closer and add yet another log onto this blaze of discontent I find myself in ... after returning from what I had thought was a refreshing night."

Amalina recognized now: the Count was pulling hairs from his lips. There were little spots of blood on his shirt. He was wearing his hunting cloak. Even on his teeth, there were traces of red, and a sticky crimson bubble here and there. And his eyes bulged like eggs with red, ropy veins filling in the whites. Engorged with blood.

"Now, what's that look?" the Count sneered at Amalina as she boiled in rage.

"Have you killed another?" Amalina said angrily.

"Another what?"

"Another princess." But she was thinking something else: his Murder Service.

"Never," he said, amused. "I've no intention. Ragalande, or whatever her name was ... she brought it on herself. She forced my hand. But never mind *this*," he said, tossing away what was the last of his victim's hairs.

But Amalina could not *never mind*. He'd gone out and killed. Killed again. And though it shouldn't have been a surprise, while surrounded by her friends and the ordinariness of their days his filthier habit had passed out of her regular thoughts. And now this reminder. And worse, she wondered if what he'd gotten up to wasn't even something more sinister. Had he gone out in service of that evil, vile man? Had he received an update on some victim by pigeon post, and killed an innocent girl in cold blood?

Of course she couldn't challenge him on this subject, and had to pretend it was something else.

"You think this is going to change?" the Count said irritably, wiping at the wet spots. "Is that it?"

"Not for the princesses ...?"

"Not for you, not for the princesses, not for anyone. I am who I am."

"Yes, sir."

"I haven't forgotten your little suggestions," he said derisively. "Haven't forgotten them at all. No."

"Suggestions?" said General Marosh, jealously trying to get into the conversation.

"Yes, *yessss*." He explained in a scolding tone: "Our mouse had some idea of converting me to a new religion."

"When, sir?" she objected.

Marosh shook with anger and stamped on the floor in Amalina's direction, upset by what the Count had told him. Or for her objection, she wasn't sure.

The Count warned her with a look: to interrupt again would be impolite. He tilted his head back to Marosh, and said in a humorous tone: "She thought that for my own benefit, and to please the people of Ardeel, I might conduct my life as some kind of leech. A slinking, scurrying, petrified pusillanimous parasite. Sipping here, sipping there. Never going in for the kill. Instead of what I am: A man of the hunt. A beast of prey."

"The King of the Hunt, Your Magnificence."

"Yes, *yesss*. At least you understand, General. At least I have *your* confidence. But my little mouse, here ..."

"Begone!" Marosh stamped again, his wild hair like a thundercloud rising out of his head, ready to shoot thunderbolts.

"No," countered the Count. "I will speak with her."

"What about the—?"

"We aren't moving."

"Master. Your Excellency. My Highest Lord of Lords, you can't ignore what is happening. Each message is a new catastrophe." He pointed at the little scrolls heaped on the desk. "These are your strongholds. You are—you *must* be—being targeted. It's best to remain elusive until we've identified—"

"The Mouse does not instruct me on matters she little understands. You won't either."

The red X on Marosh's head turned white as his whole face flushed at being compared to Amalina. He glanced at her with fury and terror in his eyes. He possessed an army, which he'd led across the country to serve at the will of the Count. What did *she* possess?

Amalina stared at the floor and wished she hadn't come.

"We're staying here for now, General. We leave only when I see a good reason." He dismissed his general, who got down on his knees and backed out of the room, his hair shaking and rustling.

When the door shut, the Count lifted a finger to keep Amalina from talking.

"I have lived a long enough time and have made a study," he said. "Centuries, my dear, I've observed the time and consequence of all that walks and slinks in my territory." He pointed to the blood on his shirt and collar, gestured to the hair on the floor. "You think I prey on the most innocent: Women. Ladies. Females. The weaker sex. Yes, the *innocent*. That is what upsets you so, isn't it, Ms. Dalca?"

He waited until she nodded. He might have waited all night if she didn't.

"You think they are innocent, only because they are the same sex as yourself. But this is a mistake, Ms. Dalca. A grave mistake. As I have just said, I have lived a very long time. You have not. And I tell you, these women ... The feminine ... They are not innocent, as you would have it. They are the worst of creatures. These are the conclusions of a scientific mind, over centuries of keen observation. No, let me tell you, Ms. Dalca. I have made my choice for justice. I attack only the most *deserving* of earthly creatures." He was working himself up. "Manifest terrors, I can tell you ... "

And with a dripping mouth, he proceeded to do just that.

• • •

"... How cross I grow at the appearance of discontent on their faces," he said, somewhere to the middle of his diatribe "The restless body when they are suddenly impatient or bored. As if life need invent a new entertainment for them on the hour. Tap and tap and tap with the foot. Pouty, pouty. Entitled beyond contempt!

"Men kill men for survival," he fell into a new rut. "Women, well ... Don't you know that women—who are spared from the battlefield for their weakness—women kill women (or men, or children, or house pets, for that matter) just for spite, or other reasons in their heads which are heated to a boil and then quickly forgotten. Forgotten! And then they complain they wish they hadn't done it. Oh, how they regret it! Poor them! Pouty, pouty. Don't *they* feel bad now that someone else has suffered at their hand. And shouldn't people pity *them* for their mistake ...

"And oh, how they can lie if they don't want their mistakes known. From little to tall, should they do something they would rather they'd not done, after they have already gone and done it, they lie and say it *wasn't* done. Deny it. Even to themselves ... until even *they* believe they didn't do it. Can you imagine! Though, now ... here is something else: Denied and forgotten, watch them revel and glory in the remembrance of this thing forgotten, this thing denied, in the darkest hours, when they think no one's watching ... thefts, affairs, murders, oh, ho, ho!

"Lucentius was most wrong," declared the Count, coming upon another point an hour later, "when he had the upright women of his opera complain *men* are 'never constant in one interest, much less love'. Unless he was simply illustrating that sex's capacity to shift blame. Men are constant. Women are bored easily. Men may stray from time to time as lusts rise, but are content to lay at their chosen mates' side all the same. Until the grave eats them. The women, well ... *They* remain virtuous partners, demanding their mate's undivided attention and promises of mutual passions *forever*; until they themselves have drawn enough out, their interest wanes, and they discard their *'eternal joy'* with so little concern. If that lover should be found burning in a fire before them, they couldn't feel a twitch in their black hearts. See how many men dote on their stricken wives for years, with dalliance in the flesh, perhaps, but with infinite love and patience for their lover. Yet consider all the men abandoned by their suddenly bored wives should he become lame in head or body ... "

Though the Count's eyes were huge and demanded her attention, Amalina turned hers—constantly—to the pile of pigeon messages on his desk. After a while she tried to tune him out.

The messages on the desk made her, once again, consider the ones in the book devoted to his murder service. His enraged harangue (which she was trying to ignore) made her think of the considerable heat of his comments written beside the latest pasted-in note. He had shown anger in those marginal notes—... *a selfish errand for you! ... be patient, or leave me alone! ... before this service of murder becomes tiresome! Even to me! ... Keep the money!!!*— where otherwise, in other places, he would put in a dull comment. At most a wry observation. It was, this service—it had always been—a game to him; which he observed from a safe height. Never personal. The only reason for him to show agitation of any kind was if he'd been touched. The loss of payment hadn't bothered him, of course. What set him off was that he would be unable to live up to a promise—even to someone as vile as the wrinkled man—his word being something of a currency which he prided himself on (so long as he had intended to honor it). But this time he was forced to violate his word. And why? Because of his interest in the princesses. They were, after all, something important to him.

They were important to him! These women!

"Count how many bachelors there are and then spinsters," he was saying, when she broke from her thoughts and realized he was still listing the deficits of a woman's character, "and when you've determined that there are more than twice as many spinsters, then tell me which gender is content to live alone for its own selfish pleasure ..." He was tireless, and the bile inexhaustible.

• • •

Eventually the sun rose. On the following evening, the beast's only remark towards the past night's discourse on the perfidy of women was to lament that if he had not followed his second wife's 'infernal instincts' to stay put in Ardeel, he would not have been trapped here—encumbered by his affliction, unable to escape its rocky ambit. However, he was 'willing to forgive her' because she couldn't know his being 'eternally imprisoned in the middle of nowhere' would be the result. And he figured, charitably, she probably wouldn't have wished the fate on him. It was an amendment that took back none of the charges.

If Amalina was insulted by what he'd said about her sex, she didn't feel it. He was no longer a man but a creature. A monster. This was, as it follows, a monster's opinion. But she would spend some time picking apart the venomous thoughts he'd laid out plainly before her, to try to understand what troubled him. So she might be able to use it against him in some manner; if the need arose.

"I detest women, you see," he had mused in consclusion on that following night, when he'd cornered Amalina privately; apparently to provide for her some measure of explanation for why he'd bothered inviting the princesses to his castle considering how he regarded the entire female population. "Still, my loathing for them aside, understand me, I cannot deny myself the pleasures of their charm, their beauty. The question is," he posed himself in a philosophical aspect, "whether to set one up forever in that position."

20

The Rite

The Count smiled. It was bright and warm, if a little impish.

"Sir?"

"What did you ask me, Ms. Dalca?"

He had been so intent to get to the princess. To transform her before the night was out. But now he spun on Amalina with great interest. "Tell me what you said just now. I had said that you knew just how *thorough* had been my vetting of the princesses. And then you had some objection and said ..."

"I said: 'For a man who doesn't even own one book—*not one book!*—on the subject of romance, how can you claim to know love?'"

"You called me a man," he said boastfully, if still a little impish. "Not creature. Not monster. Not thing. A man."

Amalina was surprised when she reached up her hand and found her mouth wasn't actually hanging open.

"Isn't that the most important ingredient to marriage?" she forged on, redirecting him to her point. "Love? It sounded before like you only *hate*—"

"Oh, Ms. Dalca. Only a mind warped by the hallucinogenic dew of sickly sweet songs and the palpitating literature of sodden poets would say, much less believe, a sentiment such as love being any part of marriage."

"*You* used the words, sir," Amalina defended herself. "'Beloved', 'Darling'. I didn't put those words in your mouth. And what you plan to do ..."

"What?" he said after a silence.

"Remember the Woman of the Falls, sir. What you plan to do now, it is permanent. Very permanent."

"Let's just get it right."

"That's what I mean. Don't rush into it."

"I mean, what we are about to do, Mouse. Let's not make a mistake."

"That's what *I* mean," she said more emphatically. "This could be another mistake. And you don't have another wheel to stick the princess on if you've made an error of the heart."

"There are two sides on that wheel," he said nastily.

"You've already made one or two errors before in marriage. And think how quickly you hurried your love of Lisbet—a third *affair d'acouer*—and now you don't even think of her."

"We weren't *married*, that Antwerpian darling and I. And didn't we *both* tell you to grow up about these things?"

"I have. But that doesn't change my point."

His look grew fouler still, but then, with a sudden patient smile: "Now, Ms. Dalca, I need you to concentrate. I am a very deliberate man, and choices are always difficult. Oh, how choices are difficult—" Amalina thought of a customer who frequently said 'oh, choosing is difficult' as she sorted through a basket of twenty identical rolls to find the perfect one "—but I know what choice I am making. You must trust me on this as you have trusted me on so many other occasions."

"This one you can't take back."

"On which occasion have I made a decision I could take back?" This settled Amalina for a second. He turned and ushered her. "Time moves forward. And we are wasting it with idle chatter. Now, here we are at the entrance."

There didn't seem to be an entrance. Just a stone wall. He must mean he would make a hole in it quickly. She tried to remember what room lay on the other side. It must be the one that looked like a bathing room. With a tub. And large jars all around. She imagined it was probably laid out with tall candlestands, and stuck on them rows of burning candles. A confused and waiting princess sitting somewhere in it all.

"You are to say nothing. She is expecting the both of us, but I want to do all the talking."

"I can't imagine what I would say."

"Don't imagine saying anything," he said helpfully. He handed her the cup. "Here, you will hold this and find the nearest corner. You will stand there and look lovely and smile for your friend on her greatest day."

"I won't be looking at her."

"Maybe a wink. And a nod."

"I'm keeping my eyes closed."

"Not when you walk in," he snapped cheerfully. "Come now, Mouse. I'm not going to pounce as soon as we enter. We find our places. She looks expectantly at me, not knowing what to expect, but looking forward to the miracle. I say some words that will get her heart pumping. She is taking a bath. A warm bath. Yes. Yesss. Her blood will be flowing nicely. Her skin soft and penetrable. I will speak to her, and she will be calmed, and open, and accepting of the moment." He stood there with his large eyes focusing on the scene that he'd just described. His tongue tracing his lips and the bottom edge of his mustache. "And *then* I will pounce. You will have had plenty of time to get into position, Ms. Dalca."

Amalina stared at him, feeling the cup getting heavier in her hands.

He added with one of his strange looks: "But you can watch if you want to. I won't mind if you peek."

"I won't."

"We can talk about it later if you do."

"I won't." Then she said, onto another subject: "You don't really mean you're going to pounce on her."

"I will do as it is done."

"Not jump on her then."

"Jump at her. Leap."

"Attack?"

"It is only *slightly* predatory," he allowed. "But that is how it is done. It's how it is always done. Even in that stranger's book—which you so helpfully smuggled into my home—tells of how it was done to him, and it began with an attack. And as I said, it will be a *gentle* attack."

"To you it happened differently."

"I don't know how it happened to me."

"You said Bario did it slowly. Over the course of time. So that you didn't know what was happening to you. And he used the cup to feed you."

"Is this another one of your obstinate delays, Mouse? I won't have it."

"I'm saying that if you just out and attack her you will scare her."

"Better if it is done this way. Much quicker. We haven't the time."

"But so violent and bloody? When he did it to you, you didn't even see what was happening. Wouldn't that be better? Really?"

"Faster is better."

"It's bloodier."

"You won't be looking."

"And scarier. For her."

"I'm the one who had it done the slow way, and I'm telling you I would have preferred it quicker. Anything that can be done fast shouldn't be done slowly. Better to get it out of the way and have her gift delivered by night's end. Which is fast approaching, I remind you, Ms. Dalca."

"The way I see it," said Amalina, feeling the growing tension as his body shifted and seemed to rise higher, as if inflating; his attempt to intimidate her, "you are rushing into this … this marriage—but really it's just turning a princess into one of your kind—just to get it done. Just to see that you can do it. You're just rushing it. And now you're rushing the event itself, though it can be done more gently and kindly."

"It's very simple, Ms. Dalca. You stand in the corner, eyes closed. I will say what I have to say to please my darling—what have you—and make her relax. As is the way you'd like it to be. Then I will do what I *must* do. And it is the way it will be done as I say it should be done: quickly. Which just *feels* right. And she will not feel the loss of her blood, but it will merge with the warm water of the drum. I shall cut my own wrist and let the blood flow into the cup. I will not tell you, but you will feel the added weight, I am sure. When her body has given up its last drop, I will ask you for the cup. You will hold it out, like so, so that I can have it at the proper time. I will take it from you and feed my beloved with my own essence—a divine spirit handed down through the ages—so that it will fill her, and merge with her flesh, and join with her soul. And she will be one with me."

Amalina stared at him.

"Do you understand?"

She cleared her throat. She nodded.

"I see. I hope you won't let this affect your relationship."

"What's that?"

"I expect all this delaying and fretting and carrying on about love and romance and moving too quickly is really about your own fears, Ms. Dalca. Isn't it? You are losing someone you considered a friend. She will be with me, and one with me. Your positions will be quite altered, and you weren't prepared for it."

"I'd think more about her parents' reaction than my own."

His eyes closed and lips pursed in a tut-tutting way. "Don't lie to yourself. Face the reality. Never mind any pretend squeamishness—where was this cowardice on the night we met? It didn't exist—and be serious for a moment. Now: Even though she was once your friend, are you accepting that she will, from this night on, exist in this mortal plane at a new and greater height?"

Amalina furrowed her brow and shrugged. "As long as she doesn't care. As long as she wants to."

"You aren't thinking this through," said the Count. "Think this through for me, Ms. Dalca: Will you be able to serve her? And obey her? And show her your most supreme loyalty, as you have for me these many years? Will you be able to call *her* Master?"

"I've never called *you* 'Master'."

The Count laughed softly like she'd told him a joke. "Will you be able to look upon her as my equal?"

Will you? wondered Amalina. An unexpected thought. Then she wondered again who he'd selected. *Aria, Margeta, Gillette, Robine, Isabeau, or Pia?* She supposed she must have nodded, because suddenly the Count straightened, became serious again. All business.

"Turn up your collar a little, my little mouse. Both sides. That dress looks magnificent and will please her to see it."

Amalina rolled her eyes and then did as instructed. Then she held the cup with both hands.

"Are you ready?"

Amalina nodded.

In the quietest whisper she'd ever heard him say, he said: "You *can* watch, you know, if you decide to."

Then he waved his hands and became a black blur. He put out the lights in this room. Then he opened the wall.

"Look, here she is," he said as they entered. Amalina wasn't sure if he was talking to her or the princess.

The room was warm and hazy with moisture, candlestands all around just as Amalina had imagined, with the candles looking like vague, floating, fat yellow balloons in the mist. The air was thick and close. It took a few seconds to find the tub, and then to see the princess sitting there in the tub.

When Amalina recognized who it was, she thought: Of course she's the one.

. . .

The blood was so thick and thorough, Amalina's dress looked like it was made of red metal. Amalina stepped gently, on tiptoe, as if she'd just emerged from a bathtub. Her left hand was covered and glued to the now crimson cup. Her right hand wiped her eyes—though her lashes remained clumped together and drooped heavily—and opened a hole for her mouth.

"That didn't go well," the Count said as he shut the wall, closing off the flow of blood and horror."

"Sir," her voice echoed in the empty room, sounding low and husky. "What happened?"

"I did only what came naturally," he said, dismayed and trying not to sound defensive. "But it seems I've had too much practice with what comes naturally ... And then to try to interrupt that natural process ..."

They were both mumbling, almost incoherently, as they stumbled along, seeming without direction.

"What are you going to do?" she asked.

"Do you think anyone heard her scream?" he said.

"Her people will be ... they'll be so ..."

"That's one down that I can never get back ..."

"So much blood, I can't believe it ..."

"... can say nothing, of course ..."

"... so sad ..."

"... unexpected ..."

"... and horrible ..."

"... Perhaps, after all, Mouse, doing it slowly *is* the right way."

Ha, Ha, Ha

Sir Hak Vogoneyevic's army began its northward march. Hak sat ramrod straight in the saddle, looking like the young, glorious commander Attila had dreamt. His men thrust out their chests and beat their feet to the martial time of the drummer to rise to meet their general's esteem. This was the start of Ardeel's liberation after a centuries' long tyranny.

"A clear shot all the way to Marosh?" asked Hak, needlessly. Attila assumed with his standard dull gaze that his champion was trying to get further into the spirit of his new role.

"The governor will not challenge us, if that is what you mean, Sir Hak," said Attila. "Zsolt hasn't returned his forces to post and refuses entreaties to do so. *Someone* has to meet him."

"Me," said Hak.

"But you won't be charging into battle the way you did at Krom's tournament. This time you will reserve yourself. Leave it to your men to blast into that shameful traitor. Make him regret his decision to side against us. And maybe force him to consider returning his loyalty to the people's cause. Even if he doesn't, the battle will be the distraction. We need to keep as many of our forces—"

Hak pulled something out of his saddlebag. He put that something into his mouth and bit a good hunk out of it. "Want something to eat, Mr. Bronk?"

"As I was saying … "

"You say that a lot," said Hak, his mouth full. "'As I was saying.' Don't really need to say it, the way I understand. You are always saying things. Might as well just continue on and say it. Everybody will know what you were already saying, if they were paying attention."

"Were *you* paying attention, Sir Hak? Or were you paying attention to your saddlebag's treats?"

Hak laughed. "I understand what you're saying. You don't want me charging in at the castle, 'cause I need to save myself for that creature fella."

Attila nodded. "It will be the greatest challenge of all of our lives. Your ancestors and the souls of all those innocents the villain has claimed will be watching."

"Now you say that a lot, too, Mr. Bronk."

"I don't believe I've said that more than once."

"You kept telling me Gug and Man were watching me as I was training." At this he looked shrewdly at Attila and took an annoyingly large bite out of the jerked meat.

"I did say that."

"But are you fibbing me now, Mr. Bronk, like you were fibbing then?"

Attila looked like he was about to fall asleep. He didn't answer.

"I know what you were up to there, Mr. Bronk. Telling me all that. You were afraid I was fallin' down on the job. You didn't like the drinking and the relaxing I was havin'."

"Relaxing."

"Being a hero is hard work, Mr. Bronk. You just sit there whispering from the shadows. Just like you fired that rifle behind me at the tournament, 'cause you didn't trust me."

Attila glanced his heavy-lidded eyes at his snapping and chomping champion. Hak Vogoneyevic had never looked so full of himself.

"Think I didn't feel that bee-bullet buzz past me, Mr. Bronk? Think I didn't see you down there under that stand? But I'll have you know that them cabbages came down because of me. Just like I took every other event, I did that one in all fairness. Took everything I had not to bust out laughing when I saw you hiding under there with that rifle, though I was mad enough to bust later. You not trusting me like that. And could have killed me. Why, it was hard enough hitting those darn cabbages without worrying your shot was going to go foul and take out a second one. Make Krom think I was some kind of cheat."

"My shot hit the cabbages."

"Not even," said Hak, taking another big bite.

"You are a fair shot. But at that distance … yours went into the dirt. Mine hit dead on."

"You can think what you like, but as *I* was saying: You talked a lot about Gug and the children watching me. And I'll swear that it helped me, yessir. But you don't need to say that kind of stuff no more, Mr. Bronk. I've been trained up into a proper Vogoneyevic."

"Yes?"

"Ask anyone and they'll tell you. Even papa would have said so."

"I don't doubt. That is why I'm by your side."

"But you do doubt. That's why you keep reminding me about somebody or another watching. Well, I'm telling you, I'm satisfied with my own watching. I think I've done pretty well and smart. Look at this jacket. And, I say, you just stand back and watch me do what I'm going to do. You sold me on the plan, Mr. Bronk. And I come to believe you are right," he shook a ropey end of the jerky at Attila. "I am meant for something. Or none of this wouldn't have happened. And now I will go up to that castle—reserving myself for the real fight, as you say—and I will turn that creature into the dust he ought to have been for hundreds of years now."

"I'm glad to hear you talk that way."

"Then I'm going to bring Gug and Man and Lija to the castle. See if they won't like to live up there."

"To return the creature to the ground, as you say," said Attila, "it will require all your strength and concentration. But it will also require impeccable strategy and tactics. One-on-one he is invulnerable. We need overwhelming force—which means twenty to fifty men at least—fresh and ready with their rifles. Bayonets on. Swords at hand. Cannon, too, if we can manage it safely and speedily enough—which will be a challenge in itself with winter setting in, which will be worse in the mountains. But such unusual timing, to strike when armies normally rest, will be to our advantage. Throw Marosh and the monster off their game by not playing to expectations. Above all, we need to trick the creature and play with him like a chess piece, and maneuver him without him knowing it to the position we want him. Then descend on him *en masse*."

"He won't know what hit him," Hak bellowed with another annoying mouthful, holding the jerky up in their air like it was the sword of victory. Then he tried to send up a whoop of victory. Instead he coughed. Then he gagged. Then he doubled over and then he fell off his horse.

Attila dismounted and ran to Hak. The nut-brown tan skin was turning dangerously red, and Attila tried to get a grip on Hak, to pound on his back and send out the jerky.

But Hak fought Attila's hands away like a frightened animal. His eyes bulged and looked panicked in all directions.

They had somehow rode ahead of the marching column. The cavalry was in the rear. It had been Hak's desire to lead from the front, and now, unknown to Hak's army, Attila and Hak were wrestling with each other, falling into the forest, their leader desperate to catch a breath.

Hak slapped Attila's hands away and ran through the cold, wet, fall-thickened underbrush, clutching at his throat. The veins were popping out all over the exposed parts of his body. He sprang and leaped and would not hold still until he tripped and fell headfirst into a large flowing stream.

The water was clear, but Attila couldn't see him. He jumped into the water and avoided the stupid impulse to call out Hak's name. The man was underwater. Attila thrashed this way and that in the water, and felt the current pulling him, trying to take him down. Someone called out for Sir Vogoneyevic. They were happy and curious voices. They wondered why the Champion and his right hand man had vacated their horses. Suspecting they'd gone off to relieve themselves.

Attila was aware time was passing. He glanced upstream, and then stared downstream. For a hand. A leg. Something to place where Hak was. A bridge was just a few yards away. A couple heads shown there.

"Sir Vogoneyevic!" Attila shouted, though he looked utterly bored. This confused the men for a second. Then they caught on. "Search for him! Hurry! We must find him!"

"Sir Vogoneyevic! Sir Vogoneyevic!"

"Hak! Hak!"

Attila found Hak Vogoneyevic one hundred yards downstream. He was washed up onto a small, curved, shallow bank, his lower legs stuck in the sand, the rest of him still shifting at the tug of the current. But his brown face was no longer brown. Below the surface of the water his eyes, still looking soft and kind and a little tired, as Attila'd first seen the man, were also unfocused and surrounded by discolored blue skin, his tongue almost looking purple and sticking out of his mouth.

Attila stared down at the dead body, looking as unmoved as ever.

Then there was a twitch at the corner of Attila's mouth.

The twitch was followed by another, stronger tremor that moved up the side of his face.

His right eye opened wide, then closed, then opened again.

He convulsed with a laugh that almost came out. But then it did. Followed by hysteria.

22

Night Moves

The princesses' personal servants were aware something was amiss. By the afternoon the princesses, prodded by their servants into curiosity, began to ask the question: "Where is Robine?"

Pils delivered the formal answer: "Robine has returned home."

Amalina felt ill. It was the expected explanation, but knowing what carnage lay behind the innocent statement—because Robine's staff would have also been silenced, of course—was still enough to make her grow pale and push away any attempts to put food in front of her.

"But why?" asked Aria, incuriously. Her cool smirk making plain she was pleased a competitor was gone.

"She hated it here," said Margeta. "Your company is enough to drive anyone away."

"Am I really all that bad, Margeta? You're still here."

"But in winter?" said Pia. "She couldn't wait?"

"I thought she liked the castle, and adored Uncle Tepsji," said Gillette. "That's what she told everyone."

"Shows what you know," said Isabeau. "You don't know anything. I was her closest friend here."

"And?" asked Gillette.

"She came to me last night. Before she left. She told me everything." Isabeau eyed everyone knowingly.

Amalina felt a new sickness sit on top of the old. It was like one giant pot of gas in her stomach. She couldn't get her mouth to work, but stared at Isabeau, who was delighted sitting at the center of attention. Amalina could only think of how her skin still hurt at scraping off Robine's blood, still tasting the coppery taste in her mouth, and wondering if Isabeau was about to reveal enough to spoil Count Tepsji's plans and expose Amalina as an accessory to their friend's death.

"Well?" said Gillette, annoyed. "Out with it if you know something different."

Isabeau milked the suspense for another minute, feigning the need to have a bite of buttered bread, then to chew it, then to have a sip of beer to clear her mouth to speak. Each princess waited in her own way: Aria hoping she'd been the one to drive the French girl away; Margeta hoping there was a triumph for her, if the news was true; Pia and Gillette both bit on their lips, with some degree of private concern Amalina could not guess at, and couldn't be bothered to. And given more time, Amalina now worried beyond her own incrimination: that Isabeau was about to say something that might launch a mass exodus from the castle. A terrified stampede out the gates. Which would only seal the bloody fate of five more princesses and their hapless servants.

"She missed her home," said Isabeau. "It is as simple as that. This is not her home. The Count was no match for her lover. Oh! You all *knew* she had a man back home, didn't you? Or perhaps that was another of her secrets she trusted to me *alone*. Her longing for his love was too much to bear. She came to me in tears, asking what she should do. I told her to trust her heart, as any good woman should do. Why waste her time here in the mountains, when she knew what she wanted in her life. This was not idle temptation. God would not have put the desire she had in her for another man if he didn't want her to obey it. She thanked me, and kissed me tenderly, with tears on her cheeks, and thanked me for being her good friend, and that I should write her as soon as I return home."

It sounded so convincing, it took Amalina a moment, blinking several times, to understand this was a wholly manufactured story. Its falsity was exposed by the simple fact (never mind all the other disparities) that Robine had never *had* a lover at home, a sad truth reinforced by her clear desperation to achieve on this trip some level of intimate companionship—a close, meaningful, confidential relationship—with Amalina or the Count, no less; and *not* Isabeau. It had been Robine's tragic loneliness which made it so easy for Amalina to understand, when she saw Robine in the Count's chamber waiting to be transformed, that *of course* Robine would be the one out of all of them who would willingly grasp at such a terrible offer—to lose one's humanity—just to be accepted. Isabeau knew nothing of *that*.

Isabeau's selfish lie disgusted Amalina. Amazing how the character of someone could change so dramatically, and one's perception and opinion of them, no matter how hard set they might be, when that particular personality is placed in the company of another. Isabeau, who amalina had once esteemed as a generous and knowledgeable soul, had become a petty liar now in proximity to Amalina's guests. Why? Had Isabeau, in a calculated way, manufactured this tale of Robine's far-away lover to encourage Gillette—with her own man, Samuel, waiting offstage—to follow suit? Why would Isabeau say such a thing, really? It seemed like such a cold thing to do. *Maybe if she knew what really happened to Robine and her people, she wouldn't have made up such a story*, thought Amalina—in a last minute bit of charity.

"Wasn't Marosh then?" muttered Aria, darkly. Some of them made little gasps at that. Aria shrugged. "That seems more realistic. He'd be good enough excuse to drive anyone from this place. Even in winter."

Amalina excused herself, put on her heavy coat, and went down to the carriage house. Robine's carriages were gone. The other princesses' carriages were expertly boxed in by the general's carts, wagons, carriages and sleighs. Nobody would be getting out fast.

Amalina walked a wavering line through the courtyard. At the sound of wind wailing along the crags in the mountainside she looked up. A bird circled restlessly above. Jing, jing, jing. Amalina felt a small throb in her chest. A sensation almost lost in the horrible memory of the night before. She followed her impulse to go to the aviary and let it in.

. . .

Marosh was quicker. He was removing the small letter from its leather case when Amalina entered. He looked back at her, dark, puffy circles under his eyes.

"What do you want?" he asked.

"Came to let in the bird."

"It's none of your business, girl."

"Who says it isn't?"

"Go away, *Princess*."

"Lady Princess Robine Beaujeulle went away in the night."

Marosh stared at her.

"Left the castle. With all her servants, everything."

Marosh continued to stare, his face as hard as a block of wood.

"Don't think I don't know what happened," said Amalina. "I'm not stupid."

"No, you're a clever girl. His Excellency warned me. And I shouldn't have to warn you not to go gossiping about what you think you know."

"I *know*, General. I don't just *think* I know."

"You've something to say to me about it?"

"You helped the Count. Got rid of Robine's carriages, her horses. All her luggage. Her people. Cleared her out."

"As far as anyone knows, she and her servants did all that. Cleared themselves out."

"But that isn't the truth."

"The truth is as our Master wishes it to be." He leaned his head so that his eyes were glaring through his big brows with hirsute menace. "And you aren't to question him."

He turned and opened the small letter.

"You were probably clever, how you got rid of it all—and them—so quickly," Amalina said. "But if they left in the middle of the night, there would be tracks in yesterday's snow on the road." The general's head shifted. He was listening. "You should have had some of your men drive her carriages down the mountain, if her servants weren't around anymore. That way you would have gotten rid of what you needed to, and left some believable tracks for the princesses to see. The princesses aren't as dumb as you think, General."

"Thank you, girl," he said softly with a nod as he read the new letter. Then, finishing the letter, he growled unhappily and stared thoughfully out the window.

· · ·

A crisis had slowly and quietly built over the months. Kept a private matter between the General and the Count. Only witnessed here and there by Amalina, or Pils or Anka. It now came to a head.

Pigeons—the sleek ones, with the bells on their legs—had been arriving all the while with emergency notice: the Count's castles suffering catastrophic fires, landslides, and collapses. One by one, they had been falling.

"You can no longer ignore this, Great High One," said General Marosh through gritted teeth, gripping the latest notice as if he wanted to crush it. "Something must be done. And we must leave this castle."

"Which one this time?" the Count said irritably, perhaps still demolished by his evening's failure.

"Crecu."

The Count's eyelids lowered in thought. He muttered, "All still in the south it seems to me."

"Moving north, Master."

"There's nowhere else to go, is there? What game is being played?"

"This is no game, my liege. It is a coursework. A plot. A stratagem. While we sit still and let it continue. With no plan of our own, and no answers."

"I've heard of a rogue agent stirring common sentiment against me down there. And he's brought a Vogoneyevic into his plans. They were raising an army of some kind. But that doesn't seem like their style. And from what I know, that tide is petering more than cresting considering the season we've entered. Still, I see you could be right, it could be some strategy at work there."

Marosh fell to his knees and struck his forehead. "We must leave this castle, Master."

"No. If it is a test or judgement from Heaven, it will fall on me wherever I stand. If it is an active rebellion against me, it matters not where I am. It will either continue to avoid me, as it has so far, striking like a cowardly thief, or it will come to meet me. Here is as good a place as any."

"No, it is not, Master. This castle is not a good castle, it is not a proper castle."

"And what do you mean by that?"

"There's no moat. Its courtyard is small and cramped and can't hold all my men. We need somewhere that will not only withstand a siege, but discourages the enemy from beginning one."

The Count nodded. "I suppose you brought the Mouse with you to gang up on me?"

Marosh shook his massive head, the beard over his square jaw trembling. "She followed me here. She was there when the pigeon came. When I read it, I saw no harm in her knowing. If someone is going to explain what's happening to the princesses, it would have to be her."

"A good excuse," the Count agreed with some lingering suspicion. "Mouse, come forward. You will tell Aria and Margeta and Pia and Gillette and Isabeau we will be leaving this castle on an expedition. No need to get them agitated like Marosh, here. That's his role. You will make them understand that it is a voluntary movement on our part. Something fun and exciting."

"In the middle of winter?"

"What could be more fun and exciting? It will be a sport in itself, no? Come, they must like the idea of getting out into the fresh air for a while. And it isn't 'in the middle of winter', so don't be that way."

"Where are we going?" she asked.

"Where would you suggest, General Marosh?"

The Count pulled out his map and studied it, using his fancy, long-feathered quill to strike out the castle icon outside Crecu while he did so. "Hm, hm, hm. The Black Castle is excellent for a direct siege. But I don't like the idea of fighting within sight of Tsobl."

The General and the Count went over the positives and negatives of a few more castles, none of them fitting entirely what one or the other felt would be best.

"What about the hidden castle?" Amalina suggested, reaching a finger out to point at it. In a stinging blur, the Count swatted her hand away. It felt like a bone snapped somewhere inside her skin.

"Hidden castle?" asked the general, his eyebrows rising. His eyes squinting at the map.

The Count chose to ignore the question. The general glanced hotly at Amalina, but then dropped his eyes back to the map.

It didn't take much longer for the Count and his general to decide on the perfect one. It came as quite a surprise, though. Even to them.

• • •

The Princesses and their staff all delighted at the idea of a journey through the snow. To have some new distraction. They begged Amalina to describe their destination. Since she'd never seen the place before, she told them it would be a surprise.

"But I'm astonished you're all so game for this," said Amalina, wondering if it was because they wouldn't openly contradict the Count's wishes. Though Aria, if nobody else, would tell her the truth.

"You don't want to go?" asked the always perceptive Pia. "It seems like you don't."

"With the library and the gallery and the good food and scenery, and with Netz at our feet, I thought we were comfortable here."

Pia made a face of someone who is too shy to hurt her friend's feelings.

"But I was evidently wrong," said Amalina.

"It's all very pleasant, dear Kat-Kat. But something new wouldn't hurt."

"Princess Spaarvierlet could spend several months in the gallery alone," said Amalina. "She said it seemed Uncle had captured everything in the world and put it there"

"Everything in the world?" said Gillette. "Where was she from?"

"Certainly he captured everything," pronounced Aria. "And trapped it! Bottled it! Gutted and stuffed it into a bunch of lifeless dust gatherers! Really, Amalina."

"Well, we'll see how you feel when we get to where we're going."

"I'm sure it will be fantastic," said Pia.

"When are we leaving?" said Aria, a bit of desperation in her voice.

"It's too bad Robine left so quick, eh, Isabeau?" Gillette said. "She won't know what she missed."

. . .

"Where?" said Genadie, blinking greasily as he sat up from his bed, coming out of his torpor like a newborn fawn rising from the slimy puddle of its birth. He blinked quickly. "Oh dear Olympus! It is the middle of winter—"

"—That's what I said!—"

"—Has the world gone completely mad?"

"Everyone's going," Amalina told him, not wanting to pet him the way she usually did, on account of how gelatinous he was looking. "Aren't you coming too?"

"Why should I? Nobody told me. I'm unwanted."

"I told you."

"But Master didn't."

"He didn't tell anyone anything. Except Marosh and I. Marosh is telling his people. I was to tell Pils, Anka and the princesses."

"So he didn't mention to tell me by name?"

Amalina smirked and shook her head. "Well, we're going to be in Netz for a week or so while the General takes care of things. He's taking all his people out. If you don't want to be alone, you should come along. The princesses have all been nice and have been asking where you've gotten to."

He heaved a sigh and ran a hand over his face. Then he got a contemplative look. "It's winter. *Winter.* Snows have fallen. Oh dear Olympus! I'm needed. I'm needed, and he isn't even willing to ask." Then, turning from his self-pity, he grinned at a thrilling fancy. "It is a test. Another test."

"I think it has to do with the rebellion in the south," Amalina remarked.

"Master wants to see if I will come through for him." Genadie straightened his crooked body with a show of resolve. "And I will. I will!"

But Marosh disagreed.

"You can't have those horses," the General said, towering over Genadie. "Quit messing up the order here."

"You'll need my help," he insisted. "You've only heard of that castle. You've never seen it in winter. You'll never make this work without my—"

"It's taken care of, rat," said Marosh. "You can tend to this castle if you feel like doing something. Or go to hell, for all I care. But you won't be having the horses."

Marosh took the reins from Genadie and threw them into the hands of one of his hooded soldiers. Then he glanced back, but more at Amalina than Genadie.

"You can still come to Netz with us," said Amalina. "While we wait."

"No. Let him have his horses. I don't need them. But Master'll need me. Master will need me, just you see."

"I don't see why you care whether he needs you or not, Genadie. Not after what he did to you."

"They will see what I'm worth. That's all that matters in this world, Ms. Dalca. And I shall prove my value."

Genadie fetched his small flute and went out of the castle. At the edge of the forest he sounded it, running his fingers over its holes in a frantic but meaningful way, though Amalina heard nothing but air. The horses came from the woods, looking dead-eyed and compliant. Solid workhorses suited for a purpose.

"Where do they come from?" Amalina asked.

"Better to do at night," he said, not answering her question. "The position of Orion, I think."

These horses he brought into the castle and then began to harness to his ingenious winter contraption: the low sledge with the massive angled blade in front, and with the heavy rollers attached to the back. She'd never seen anything like this vehicular contrivance until she came to the high castle. Genadie used it to cut into deep and heavy snow, shove it aside, and crunch it down to make passing over it even with regular wheels an option.

"The dumbbell Marosh doesn't know a thing," Genadie was muttering to Amalina as she helped fasten the harnesses. "Master needs me. He can't do without me; moving to that castle in the middle of winter. And away from his Olympus. Such a thing. But one should not question …"

"Genadie, you—" Amalina said, but then hesitated.

"I, what?"

"You still believe he is Zeus?"

Genadie shrugged.

"You shouldn't care so much, Genadie. Really. If he is Zeus, he doesn't really need you, you know. He could just wave his hand and make all the snow disappear."

"Well, he hasn't has he?" Genadie challenged. "That's just what he'd do if he had a mind to do it. But since he hasn't, he leaves it there for a purpose. A purpose to hinder? Or a purpose to test? And I will rise to the occasion. I will pass his test."

Amalina decided to leave him to his delusion.

· · ·

Amalina enjoyed Netz, possibly for the last time, not showing her concern over the true reason for the move. The trouble in the south feeling like an ambiguous assembling of clouds, perhaps a low rumble that might be thunder, but no real evidence of danger. She laughed lightly at all the party's jokes, gossiped, attended multiple services at the cathedral, treated her friends to numerous three- and five-course meals all through the village's inns and restaurants (wondering if the anonymous letter writer would finally make an appearance—it was now or never). And they all laughed (Amalina sheepishly joining them, only to feel cruel and ashamed later) when Genadie paraded by with his pitiful looking horses, seated on the strange looking sledge. On his way to the new castle to prove himself to Zeus.

It was then she noticed Marosh had been standing at a distance the whole time. Watching. And when they left the inn and returned to the block of apartments reserved for the princesses, he followed after. There was no asking to stay in anyone's rooms, everyone was nervous about the coming trip and attending to their staffs, who were preparing for the actual voyage ahead. She would be expected to do the same. General Marosh, eyes unwavering, massive bearded jaw set in a grimace, followed Amalina into her own house, and up the stairs. She heard his heavy footfalls behind her. She tried to hurry but he put on speed as well. He eclipsed her before she could close her door. He pushed her inside.

Amalina's eyes flicked around the room for private items she might have left in the open. But Anka had cleaned in preparation for the move, if not because there was nothing better to do. The room was clean. Even the maid wasn't there.

Marosh touched Amalina's arm, she was thrown toward the bed.

"What are you doing?" she asked.

"You're going to tell me what I want to know," he growled. He lurched at the bed. He spread out a wide page he pulled from his pocket. He stabbed his finger at it. "Show me where the hidden castle is."

The map was smaller than the Count's, and was highly detailed and modern. There were some handwritten icons added in places, Amalina didn't know their purpose. She couldn't help but turn her eyes on the city where the hidden castle was, but her back was to the general. He hadn't seen.

"Where is it? Show me."

"Why should I, sir?"

He gripped her arm and shook her. "You will show me, little girl, and you will show it to me *now*."

"If your Master wanted you to know, he would have told you. I don't know why he hasn't, but he obviously doesn't wish to."

"Why do *you* know? Why does he share with you such information?"

"I don't know."

"It's my business to protect him. It's what my life is sworn to. How can I do my job if I don't have all the information I need? It's impossible."

"Maybe he's testing you."

Marosh took out his hunting knife. He was so tall that holding it (threateningly) beside his belt was level with Amalina's throat. The blade was so big it was probably wider than her neck. She stared at it while, with the fingers on his free hand, he rang notes off its razor-sharp edge.

"What if I were to kill you if you don't tell me, girl? If you don't tell me right this moment where that Hidden Castle is?"

"The Count wouldn't be very happy with you," she said, hoping it was a good enough answer. Unable to think of anything beyond the blade.

He plinked more notes and stared at her neck; her chest; her head. Ideas were burning behind his eyes.

"I'll give you one last chance, girl. You point on this map where it is, or you die."

Amalina couldn't believe he would really kill her. Not from the way he fell to his knees before the Count. Not with that giant red X carved into his forehead. He wouldn't dare. Would he?

"I'm not going to warn you any more. Use that finger. Point. That's all you have to do. Or you'll never see your father again."

It was a threat that she had heard once too often. From the Count. From Kralov. And now her reaction was quite the opposite of what the general would have expected.

"Get out of my room," she said. "You get out of my room right now. And you'd better pray I don't tell him what you've tried here, with me."

"I am devoted to His Excellency," Marosh purred dangerously. "He would understand."

"If you think he'll understand, then get to work. Or you go away, and never say such a thing to me again." For added measure she took his map and tore it to pieces. "Now what are you going to do? You can't find anything."

Marosh's voluminous hair rose from his head and his skin turned red.

"Now, girl. That was *my* map."

She threw the scraps at him. "Get out!"

"You don't believe in him," he snarled with disbelief. "But he *trusts* in you."

Amalina began to shake, starting with a temble in her knees. She hoped Marosh would leave the room before her body collapsed. Avoiding the blade, she pushed him. But he was as heavy as a four post bed.

"What else do you know, I wonder?" He sheathed the hunting knife with a casual movement, as if they were just finishing a friendly conversation. Then he shook his finger at her.

"Leave," said Amalina.

"Mountain Goat," he said.

"What? No. Nevermind. Out with you."

He stood there looking. Unafraid of her, and yet she appearing unafraid of him, too. "I could have killed you," he said.

"Then why don't you?"

He said nothing. But something in his expression spoke: *I misjudged you. You're more than I thought you were, little girl.*

Or at least that's what Amalina thought Marosh was thinking. Before he walked quietly out the door.

PART THREE
MONSTER

23

Kyrgil Castle

Kyrgil Castle stood right atop a promontory piece of mountain. It looked as if the mountain's crest had been blown away and flattened and the castle stuck into it. And then, over the centuries, the castle had fused with it. It stared intimidatingly down an almost sheer cliff face to the village of Kyrgil below. Connecting the village to its synonymous castle was a thin trail of switchbacks that was exhausting to consider when gazing up at it, exhausting and terrifying when climbing, and absolutely impossible to ascend or descend in winter when the frequent snows buried the ladderlike trails into one long white grade that avalanched frequently. It was this last part which had spoiled the primary allure in putting a castle there—so high out of reach, and without any good approach for an invading army—rendering it into an aborted project when the builders were shut out (or frozen in) for months on end; innumerable workers died and materials were lost in tumbles and drifts and slips in the rain; and the drawbacks for any monarch trying to rule his kingdom so remotely were reluctantly realized.

Kyrgil Castle was purchased by, and became the haunt of, an eccentric and wealthy powerbroker who craved isolation, who worshipped privacy, and who loved the view. When he died as a very old man (mere months ago), the property was taken up by his oldest and dearest—and only—friend in the world: Count Tepsji. Who now sent to it all his forces and servants and guests from his high castle outside of Netz, to perhaps protect them from a suspected rebel force advancing methodically north.

As a defensive position, the Kyrgil Castle was without equal. Its 'moat'—which all respectable castles sported—was its more than thousand foot drop just outside its walls. Its sight advantage over any enemy was its more than thousand foot drop just outside its walls. Its strategic and tactical domination of the battlefield—for raining hell on the opposition while keeping themselves out of that oppostion's effective reach—was its more than thousand foot drop just outside its walls. The problem, at the moment, was that to get themselves into that enviously-situated, well-defensible castle meant their climbing that very unenviable, more than thousand foot face. And it was wintertime, which meant the route was clogged; buried under ghastly depths of snow. General Marosh was keen to ignore and deny all obstacles, considering his men were willing to do anything, and sacrifice anything, for him and their ultimate master, the Count. But reality would impose a heavy loss of men and equipment if they were to reach the castle by week's end (which was Marosh's timeline). *Unless*, as Genadie so rightly imagined, *he* were to put his *own* life at risk, and use his special sledge and rollers, and his experience at clearing snow from mountain roads, putting them all to the *ultimate test!*

However, Genadie's heroic moment was not to be.

There was a sudden heatwave, as if heaven sent, like it was summer, that melted away the snow. Easing the princesses' journey to Kyrgil and then up to its castle. The princesses—and everyone involved in the trip—were overjoyed. Except Genadie, who was sent spiraling into a depression—as if plunging over a thousand foot drop himself.

"He's forsaken me," wailed Genadie, kicking his dripping sledge. "This wasn't a test at all. He wanted to show his contempt for this pathetic wretch of a servant."

"I don't see why you *care*," said Amalina, patting his shoulder, knowing she was repeating herself. "*After what he did to you and your lovely family?*" This didn't help. She scrounged for something else to say. "And, anyway," she said with an upward lilt, "maybe he was just being nice and saved you some grueling work." Genadie glanced at her with a pathetic hope. "After all, you did come all this way to Kyrgil with your wagon and the horses. You intended to do it. What more could he want?"

Genadie was obviously warming to the idea, his lips were wriggling. Amalina regretted mentioning it.

• • •

The village of Kyrgil was not prepared to be overrun by an Ardeelian Count, a famous general and his attached army (with cannons), much less accept and host six worldly foreign princesses. The village turned out in force, goggling and smiling and waving, but then night came and everything was shut up and boarded.

"My God, Katty," said Gillette, "What is it with your country? Everything closes at sundown. I've never seen such a thing. I thought it was that way in Netz because of St. Grigori and that boring cardinal. But this is absolute. I tried to take a walk just now and the lady of the house almost hit me for trying to open the door."

They are afraid of the Count, Amalina thought to explain. But it would open too many questions. And in reality the people here didn't know it was Count Tepsji lurking behind their hardened rules and superstitions. And besides, it would also paint her uncle in a bad light, which he wouldn't appreciate.

It was only several nights of boredom. And then came the terror of the ascent. Near vertical angles in a carriage, on a sharp-turning, crumbly trail that seemed half a carriage wide, and pitched toward the village below.

"Oh, my. Don't look down," said Amalina, staring out the window and feeling like she was already falling.

"But it's thrilling!" said Aria with a solid grin, who was either immune to fear or a devilish bluffer.

"Give me a handkerchief, oh my, I think I'm going to be sick," said Pia, turning slightly green.

"Just don't look down and you'll be fine," assured Isabeau, gripping the side board and turning her face into Margeta's unwelcoming shoulder.

"They look like ants on ice cream down there," enthused Gillette, always the excited sport, looking like she was ready to open the door latch for a better vantage. "Here, look, look."

But after another hour of shaking and halting and jolting and sliding, all of them settled into the rear bench, the view getting all the more worse, even the heartier ones began to pick up Pia's color. Except Margeta, who had transformed herself into one of the carriage's fixtures; inanimate.

"I thought I heard your uncle, on several occasions, I believe, refer to the *first* castle as the *high* castle," Margeta said through unmoving lips, sounding incensed by the innacuracy.

"Obviously this is the *higher* castle," Isabeau intoned smartly into Margeta's armpit.

• • •

As unsatisfying as the village had been, once the princesses got over being handled up the treacherous trail, the Kyrgil Castle presented a much worse disappointment. The castle's interiors had never been completed. There were no doors, the rooms were separated by hung drapes—and in some places, carpets! Even darker and draftier than the Netz castle, it seemed setting bonfires in the fireplaces couldn't warm it. The old man who used to own the place had been pleasant and gentle, but frugal to the end. There was a very modest library, and barely any works of art. The ladies' entertainment, apparently, was to fall to whatever they'd brought with them, or whatever they might convince Amalina or the Count to retrieve from the once high castle, which would take almost a week, round trip. Not even a good band of players could be managed from the village below.

It was Isabeau's moment to shine.

"Well, this is interesting," said Isabeau, rounding the girls into her court. "Did you know Kyrgil was not the first name of this town? It was *Ceopercsparti.* Which means 'Broken Hoof', or 'Broken Hooves'. Because, you see, people traveling through these mountains, wanting to get somewhere else, you see, generally at this point would be stopped here because their horse's hoof would break. On account of the rocks."

"Oh," said Gillette, sounding interested. This encouraged Isabeau.

"Oh, yes. That's why the village is here in the first place: everyone's horses breaking down. Now what is *really* interesting is that Tsobl—you know, the capital of Ardeel, which they are now thinking to rename Sobelburg—"

"What?" said Amalina, startled.

"But you see," Isabeau continued on, "Tsobl was also called Ceopercsparti. And for the exact same reason, you see. And that caused a bit of a row between these people. Only one could have the name, but there were two. And one tried to claim that their town was named first, while the other said they were the larger town, so it would be better theirs remain unchanged as to avoid confusion. But then someone said one was originally named 'Twenty broken hooves', and it had to do with the old evil sultan sending a saboteur to break one hoof on every horse in the cavalry to prevent them participating in a coming battle. But they rode the horses anyway, and the sultan was defeated. But nobody could remember which place it was where the battle happened. So they both agreed to change the names to Kyrgil and Tsobl. Well, really, Tsobilisi and Kyrgiskulj, or something like that."

"How do you know all this?" Amalina challenged, wondering how Isabeau could keep so many things in her head—true or false.

"Your uncle, of course. He's very smart and knows a lot about history. And I like history. Well, I like knowing things in general. But history's one of my favorites. There's so much to know."

"Besides history," fumed Aria, "Maybe you can find out why he brought us here." Though she continued to talk to Isabeau, her eyes glanced directly at Amalina. "That Palace of Pleasures was charming enough, if not all I'd hoped. But why here? There's *nothing*."

"What more do you want?" chided Margeta. "This world wasn't built for your gratification. For anyone's pleasure. Maybe at home you sit too close to the pretty sea, but this world is built for pain and suffering."

Aria laughed.

"Maybe he hopes we'll come to appreciate the other castle better, visiting this one," said Gillette, also glancing at Amalina. "You see what I mean?"

"*Do* you know why?" asked Pia, flexing the arm she had wrapped around Amalina. "He must have some reason."

Because he thinks we are going to be attacked, Amalina thought but did not say. This would also shed a bad light on her uncle, one he would not appreciate.

"Like I said, I've never been here before," said Amalina. "My uncle is a strange one, sometimes. I've learned it's best not to ask too many questions. He has his reasons."

They stared at her.

"I will ask," she said, freeing herself from Pia. "If I can find him."

. . .

Amalina found the Count in the evening. She just had to listen carefully for his voice—his all-penetrating voice—and wind her way through the various rooms, pushing past drape after carpet. She paused outside a heavy drape, when through an opening she caught sight of General Marosh's back.

"I know there's a delay," said the Count. "But I still want my birds. I can't help they're trained for the high castle. I won't go around and collect them all and retrain them, when you can just relay whatever messages might still be received there to here. And bring along whatever bird it is, so I can reset it for Kyrgil. But, oh, I hope we aren't too long here that I should need to."

"It can be done, My Liege," answered Marosh. "But we won't know how long—"

Amalina nearly yelped when her arm was grasped. Anka was there, putting a finger to her lips and trying to pull Amalina away.

"You mustn't," whispered Anka. "Doesn't pay to snoop around. Especially here. He'll know you're standing there listening. Why, that's what started the whole mess."

"What mess?"

"With Pils and I," said Anka, sadly.

"Well, I wasn't standing around listening. I'd just paused because I didn't want to interrupt. But seeing we're making such a racket—"

"What are you two doing there?" said Marosh through a parting he made.

"Coming in," said Amalina, pushing past him.

"Going away," said Anka, spinning in the other direction.

"Mouse," said the Count when she entered. "How are my lovely, lovely ladies?"

"The lovely ladies still left?" she said tartly. "Wondering why you brought them here."

Marosh grunted humorlessly, "To save their skin."

"I don't think they know that," said the Count, with gentle charity. "But I'm sure, Ms. Dalca, you will see that they adjust to the new accommodations. I was just telling our General that I hope it isn't for too much longer."

"But there isn't any way to know how long, Your Excellency," said Marosh. "Is there? They've blown the castles pretty regularly, but it does take time. They're coming from the south, and there're still many more castles between them and us. While we're hiding out, Master, it could take a while for them to finish hunting you down."

"I was thinking about that," said the Count. "I believe I have taken care of that problem."

Marosh's head tilted. "What do you mean, Master?"

"I've had the word spread around the south that I am in the Kyrgil Castle."

"What, Master? No! Why, Master?"

"I don't plan to hide in my own land," said the Count, with a sniff that left one nostril hoisted into a sneer. He stared meaningfully at his general. "I will meet any force with force, but I don't plan to wait around like a mole as whoever-they-are continue to demolish my property. We've identified the proper castle for defense and here we are. Better to have them come now."

"But, Master."

"Or what, general? Risk them trampling *all* my holdings? Hazard losing my high castle in Netz? No. No, I say. Better to signal where I am. And have them come at me so they can be identified and destroyed."

"But ..." Amalina stopped, wishing she hadn't started.

"But, what?" said the Count, now lifting his nostril at her.

"If you plan to have a war, why would you bring the princesses here?"

"Where else would they go?" said the Count.

"Send them home."

"No, no, no. No, no, no. It's winter. This is *our* time. There is no going home."

"Then into town. Away from the castle.

"They are my guests. They are safest with me."

"When did you start this dissemination of information, Your Excellency?" said Marosh, evenly. "Who knows where you are?"

"My agents, everywhere. And it began as soon as we arrived here."

"But not all of the defenses are in place. The cannons are still being moved."

"Yes, yes," said the Count, testily. "It will take time for the word to filter down. And then time for this rebellion to get word and make a decision. It's all just like these princesses. There will be a delay, then a decision made, and then they will act. Your men will be in place, and so will the cannons. You think I don't know about these things and don't consider them?"

"Of course, My Sovereign King," groveled Marosh on the floor.

"You act as if you have all the burden. It will be much more difficult to put all the rest of *my* forces in position than yours, but they will be in place when the time comes."

"Uh ... the *rest* of your forces, Master?"

"Yes."

From the floor, Marosh turned his head and stared at Amalina.

And later, he was in her room, the drape barely making a noise as it was pushed aside.

"Do you know what forces Master is talking about?" Marosh asked Amalina. His voice was deep and commanding, his body tense and threatening. But it still felt like he was begging in some way.

Amalina shook her head.

Marosh stepped forward, hand reflexively seeking the hilt of his sword. He was looking down on Amalina like an enemy. "I always believed my life had a purpose. But I began to lose hope when I saw my life squandered away in endless, meaningless hunts. Only when that curious traitor came to my home and opened his mouth did I realize my destiny was truly something much greater than what it seemed. If I only dared," said General Marosh with a gleam in his eye. "How can I now fulfill my mission if I do not have all weapons and intelligence at my command?"

"I really don't know what he was talking about," she answered.

24

The Angry Peasant and her Axe

The small farm in Baibey Valley looked much different in early winter. Attila had seen it once during the spring, with everything green and flowing with the winter runoff. Now it was as if the cumulus-like bundles of leaves and flowers—roiling with powerful emerald-greens, with bits of white and purple—which had existed ten feet above their heads, had changed to a yellow-brown color and lowered to ankle level, then spread out in every direction. Then the first snow had come, then melted, leaving a thick, dank, pungent carpet.

Attila dragged his body to the small, dilapidated, poorly constructed home, but saw he need not enter. Gug was outside chopping wood. The children were circling each other, tossing some kind of rag between them that the dog snapped at.

When the children saw Attila they grew big smiles and ran toward him.

"Papa, Papa," Lija shouted.

Attila felt a pulse inside him that made him want to collapse in tears. Constitutionally, it wouldn't happen. Feeling the impulse was just about enough.

The children, acute readers of expression, now understood their father had not come back with Mr. Bronk. They looked at each other, at their mother, then sheepishly returned to the game they were playing, unsure of whether to approach the stranger that their mother never liked. But maybe she might pull a knife on him, which was always entertaining.

"What do you want, Mr. Bronk?" asked Gug. She planted the ax in the tree stump. She'd already chopped a good deal of lumber. There was an accumulated stack of quartered logs half the size of the barn. She was panting. She'd be tired. Not as much a threat, then. "I told you none of us are going to visit him. Let Hak finish and come home. When he's ready. There's nothing else to say. And I made that clear."

"I've something to tell you."

. . .

Gug didn't cry. She nodded. Her features tightened, and she pulled a lock of her stringy blond hair out of her eyes, as if to see Attila better. "Looks like it's hurt you," she said. "You've changed."

Attila nodded, his lips slightly downturned.

"I told you what you were risking. What his loss would cost us."

"Yes, of course. I don't know if he understood fully how brave he was; how much I felt that to be so. I never told him enough of my own private thoughts. I never found the time ... But the loss to *you* ... There's nothing that can be done about that. But I promised you payment from the coffers, and I keep my promises."

"You promised he would return to us."

"Return a hero—"

"Return to me and the children is all I wanted. He was a hero to us, without any of your fool quests."

"Of course. But, well ... I can only keep the promises within my control. You will receive payment."

"So the money survived and so did you. At least that's something."

"I can't tell you how sorry I am."

"And I wouldn't care," she said. "How awful. Did he suffer?"

"No."

"That was fast. They coming after us?"

Attila didn't understand. She gently explained how some of her great uncles had been tracked down after the war and executed. And some of their wives and children, her relatives, of course, were killed or jailed or indentured. When he explained that Hak hadn't died in a battle, Gug was suddenly incensed.

"These things happen," said Attila. "It is the will of Heaven. He was still a hero. He was prepared to put his life on the line. But this was not to be."

"What do you mean this was not to be?" Gug objected. "He built an army. Did they all die?"

"No."

"Then what are you doing here, Mr. Bronk? Why are you talking to me? Why are you not out there throwing your army at the enemy? You said he must be destroyed! Why are you not destroying him?"

"Madam, Sir Vogoneyevic is dead."

"That's one man. One good man, but *one* man; out of an army."

"The army is disbanded."

"And why would that be?"

"It's winter ... "

"It will reconstitute in the spring."

"No."

"Why not?"

"Well ..."

"Well, what?"

"Of course, as I said ... Sir Vogoneyevic is dead."

"Shut your mouth, you ..." She hissed and spit. "My God I should have killed you when I had the chance! You take my Hak away—take him away from his children, his farm ... his dreams. You give him a purpose and an army and then, *just because he died* ... ? Mr. Bronk, I don't believe I heard this from you—you so full of grand ideas and purposes! My God, My God you are going to take that army back up, and you are going to do with it what it was supposed to. If they all have to die to do it you are going to see it through, Mr. Bronk. But you are not going to come back here until you can look me in my face and tell me you did all you could."

"If I only could ..."

"Why can't you?"

"He's d—"

With a one-handed whisk Gug wrenched the axe and swung it at Attila.

"You're dead if you don't," she said.

"But how—?"

"You can see everything, but you can't see *that*? Use your twisted brains in that twisted head of yours."

"Without him—"

"You have him! You have his family! You have his first born son! You have his memory!"

"What you ask, madam!"

"I'm not asking." She swiped at him again. "I will hunt you down. I will abandon these children just make sure you have joined Hak's side."

"That's a thing to say!"

"... Before you think of quitting on him!"

Now tears were raining off her cheeks. Man and Gug were worried and somehow hadn't picked up on the meaning of the conversation, but were certain this time the violence was not fun at all.

"You will take my husband's army and you will send them against the enemy," she ordered.

"Not all will follow, now that—"

"*You will send my husband's army against the enemy.*"

"I would if I could. But he's the one they—"

"Resurrect him! Give him his own Easter! Convince *them* like you convinced Hak, that it's the right thing to do. And you will use them as you used him, and you will do that thing that was so important!"

"If you'd stop swinging that axe ..."

"Pay attention, Mr. Bronk! This is what will happen, and you will die making it happen. Or you will die as meaninglessly as you'd let Hak die. Only, for you it will be at the hands of an angry peasant and her axe! How's that for noble, eh? No more monster for your great enemy. Just a simple widowed farm girl; nobody knew her name. Well, you have your choice now, don't you? And how's that for a good end to you! Chopped like firewood. I'm starting to like the sound of it."

Attila did not like the sound of it. Not at all. And he could not bear the whoosh of the axe as its sharp, heavy blade sliced down on him.

Think, he told his weary brains. *You got me into this, you get me out of this!*
Whup! Whup! Whup! went the axe.

25

Enter the Monster

A few days later some gypsies were dragged up to the mountain, as well as some curious members of Kyrgil who'd always wanted to see the inside of the castle. They were all dressed gaily, for a festival of a different season, but with heavy jackets thrown over. They lost the jackets quickly enough when the music played, the wine was distributed, singing and dancing was had, and everyone began to forget they were perched on the top of some foreboding mountain.

Amalina watched from the corner, noting the main room had been arranged to an approximation of the high castle's *l'entrée grande*. A long table was arranged there—though now pushed aside for dancing. And some of the old tapestries from the high castle were hung on the walls. There, beside the fireplace, also transplanted from the high castle's *l'entrée grande*, was the suit of ancient armor, and on the otherside: the pedestal with the plain gray cup. The cup opened a pit in Amalina's stomach. Was this just for show? she wondered. Or was the Count seriously plotting to try that whole fiasco again? Robine's blood had been cleaned from it, she saw, before looking away.

A figure entered the room. A man. He was directed by Pils to Amalina. He was young and was dressed in a fur jacket whose tufts were so large they met with the fringes of his fur hat. He looked exhausted, but smiled when he was pointed to Amalina, and strode quickly to her.

"Sorry for any importunity on my part, Countess," said the young man, dropping to his knee. "But I was told to deliver the message directly to you, and to trust it to no one else."

"What's the message?" Amalina asked, her heart beginning to thud.

The man produced a small square of paper which she took. Opening it, she was shocked what she saw. Again, in the same perfect penmanship, was a very familiar note:

> Pretty Princess Katarina Tepsji, niece of Count Tepsji, please, if you will, come down from the castle to the village of Kyrgil. There order a five course meal at the fine inn, Bene Ceop. I will meet you.

Amalina was speechless. She felt some vertigo, and wondered where she was; if she wasn't back in the high castle after all. She looked around the room to the princesses—though not to Margeta, who'd excused herself and retired for the night—and at their servants, and at the visitors to the castle, who were enjoying themselves.

"Who is this message from?"

"I don't know," said the courier. "Just a young boy. I never saw him before. He told me his master wished for this message to be delivered to the Countess up in the castle, and I would be paid double if I delivered it directly to her hand. Which I have done, would you say, milady?"

"You mean to tell me, you came all the way up the trail, in winter, at night?"

"The snow is still," he shrugged, *"light*. And there isn't ice to speak of. And I'm assured his master will pay well, milady. Thank you." He bowed low and backed up, trying to get out as quickly as he could.

"Couldn't you find out who it is?" she said, coming after him. "As a favor to me. I can see that you are paid well, too. Just find out who that master is, so I can know."

"Yes, milady. I will try, milady. Of course, milady." He was all smiles now. He would do what she asked. But, she realized after he left, she'd still have to go all the way back down the side of that dizzying cliff to get her information. She hadn't told him to come back with it.

• • •

Still the night wasn't done, and was just winding up when the last surprise came. As the wine flowed, and the rules were relaxed, everyone mixed and reveled without distinction to their proper strata—the servants vastly outnumbering the guests, and the princesses allowing a shocking degree of casual association. But it was winter, and that dim castle needed all the warmth and comeraderie the bodies inside could generate. Otherwise it would just be a cold rock.

From within the waltzing figures, Amalina noticed someone walking around the periphery. His knees bounced in time with the gay music, and there was a big smile on his face, and a glimmer in his eye like he'd had too much to drink. He looked from one face to another, and shook his head as if he couldn't believe so many people were having such a great time. And Amalina at first thought it was the Count—for some reason—but then recognized immediately she was wrong. He didn't look a thing like the Count. He had the sturdiness and confident movement of a soldier, but it wasn't one of Marosh's men, of course. He looked so familiar, and she thought it was because of the wine that she couldn't place him exactly. One of the Kyrgil people? One of the princesses' footmen or liverymen she hadn't learned the name of? She tried to keep track of where he was as she danced this way, then turned that way, then spun this way around, as he continued his circumnavigation of the room and envied all he saw.

Then with a very cold thrust into her chest, so that she was immediately sober, she knew *exactly* who it was.

She did not go to him right away. But he knew she'd seen him, and recognized him. He politely kept up his wandering among them, nobody quite taking notice. He could have been anybody to the other princesses. So he courteously mingled, without saying a word.

Until the party began to break off. People staggered away, or fell asleep in corners, or otherwise found other places to be. For some reason Marosh was gone. Maybe he was in his room, or manning the walls in a vigil against the coming enemy.

"Amazing, amazing," said the Strange Man, coming up to Amalina now. "It's all true. All of it. I wouldn't believe it if I didn't see it. But you … you've transformed into some kind of … royalty?"

Amalina gulped, and wished Genadie were there beside her, to share in some of the guilty feelings and the adrenaline rushing through her.

The Strange Man smiled, bent his head, shyly played with a lock of his brown curls, and said: "Yes, I believe I will speak to your master now. Go get him."

• • •

Half an hour passed while Amalina, Anka and Pils tried, and failed, to locate the Count. Amalina was elected to see if Marosh knew where he was. She whispered to the angry bulk of hair: the Count was needed, the Strange Man is in the castle.

"Who?" asked Marosh.

"The *man*. The man of the diary. You *know*."

"I don't know who you're talking about," growled Marosh, his features twisting resentfully at the fact: *yet another secret he wasn't in on.* When he asked Amalina where the man was—instead of just *who* he was—and she told him, he shoved past her and stomped purposely for the great hall, his hand gripping the hilt of his sword.

"Wait, wait," Amalina continued to whisper. "You have to get the Count." She grabbed his arm to hold him back, which resulted in her dragging along the floor. "Stop, wait, you have to be careful. You don't know what you're doing. He's just like the Count."

This stopped Marosh.

"What?" He spun at her and panted. "What did you say? What do you *mean*?"

Amalina explained as best she could in a quick whisper, knowing the man could still—probably—hear her every word. She said nothing disparaging, limiting herself to the sheerest facts: here was another person with the same powers and abilities as Count Tepsji, who she and Genadie had met in their western travels. "Summon the Count."

General Marosh looked in the direction of the hall as if he could see through the drapes and carpets. "What does this man want?"

"Bring the Count here immediately."

Marosh shoved past Amalina again, only heading back in the direction he'd come. Amalina didn't want to return to the great hall alone. But who knew what mischief the Strange Man might be getting up to. She took small steps, and thought and thought, and tried to delay for as long as she could. A bell began to sound. It was the heavy bell Genadie used to ring in case of emergencies when the Count was away.

Soldiers in full armor, pistols and sabers in belts, rifles at the ready, began to file into the outer room, gathering in ranks, and then pressed toward the hall. This pushed Amalina forward to get ahead of them. They stopped a few feet short of the wide curtain. The first rank raised the barrels of their rifles.

· · ·

As he patiently waited for his audience with the Count, the Strange Man slowly paced the length of the room, looking at this detail or that, stopping to study the armor and the cup and the many tapestries, a gentle smile and a placid look in his eyes. He alternately put his hands on his hips, or clasped his hands behind his back, swinging his legs around jauntily as he moved. Quite relaxed and amused. He nodded at Amalina to acknowledge she'd returned.

At first she thought everyone in the hall was dead. They lay here and there on the floor, or across tables. On a second glance, they were sleeping.

"The Count is being ... found," she told the man.

He nodded again, slowly, deeply, exaggerated, looking unconcerned. "Tepsji is what he calls himself? Interesting. Where is the gentleman you were traveling with, hm? He is still alive, I hope? Or have circumstances changed in the *accord* of your relationship?"

She didn't know what he meant. "He's here. Of course."

"You like him?"

"He's all right."

"He's your father. No? A relation of some kind. No? Your lover. No?" The man shook his head with a smile of admiration. "Go. Bring him here. I want to see him."

Amalina hesitated, unsure it felt right to obey the Strange Man's commands. Then she realized doing so got her out of the room. She worried he would follow her.

He didn't.

A shiver pulsed through the front rank of soldiers as Amalina slipped through the curtain. She gasped and ducked the bayonets. The men stood there, hauntingly still and silent, peering through the holes in their masks and down their barrels. Some adjusted their grips.

"Genadie, Genadie," she shook him in his bed of hay. He curled into himself, just a shadow in an unlit run in the barn. His black horses did not stir, but were visible as darker shapes in the blackness. "Genadie, get up! Don't you hear the bell?"

"It rings for Master, not me."

"But it rings! There's an emergency!"

"What is it? Is the castle burning?" Genadie shifted but didn't sit up. "That's my bell. That was my bell once ..." She told him the emergency. Genadie shot up, crying: "Olympus! Olympus! Olympus!"

"We aren't in Olympus, Genadie. Wake up. We're in Kyrgil castle."

"I know where I am!"

He'd only been cursing.

. . .

The Strange Man gave Amalina and Genadie a curious look when they entered. He was now sitting on a chair, legs crossed, looking utterly comfortable.

"So it is true," he said, shaking his head again.

"What do you want, sir?" asked Genadie, trying to stand straight despite his natural downward curves and slumps.

"Your *Master*."

On the left, a curtain moved as if a wind had blown on it. The Count pushed it aside. He was followed in by Marosh. Marosh had his head tilted backward and his body puffed to an impressive size. But there was a regrettable dull luster in his eyes—an alloy of anger and fear—that cheapened the overall effect. The Count's head was hidden inside his black hood, but Amalina could see the blood on his lips, dribbling down his chin. His face would be bloated, his eyes bulging with red, ropy veins over their white surfaces. When the Count saw the only ones awake were Amalina, Genadie and the Stranger, he pulled the hood back. And his face shook—in an odd way—when he looked fully upon the Stange Man.

The Strange Man stood and bowed.

They stared at each other.

Genadie said: "Master, this man ..."

The Count nodded, not taking his eyes off the Stranger.

"It is true," said the Strange Man, shaking his head with disbelief and admiration. "I knew it was true." He shook his head more positively now. "But you. I don't know you, do I? You look familiar, but ..."

"I don't know you either," said the Count, putting a finger beside his mouth and discreetly wiping at the blood.

"Well, you'll have to forgive my forwardness, Count Tepsji," he said with a small bow. "I know I wasn't invited. But in some ways, I feel I was."

"You asked to see me," said the Count.

"Oh, yes," he nodded. "I had to see. To make certain it was true."

"What was true?"

The Strange Man smiled a smile that said it should be obvious.

"I met your ... Well, now I don't know what to call them. These two. Your niece, is she? But no, not really. And her man here."

"He isn't my man," said Amalina, not believing she was entering the conversation. The Count's cutting glance warned her not to do so again. She took a step back.

"They *both* serve you," he said, looking straight at the Count. "Equally. Separately. And all these people ... All these people ..."

"What is your name?"

"It doesn't matter. Or, that is, I have none. Like anything else in this world, time has worn it away to nothing. And only I remain."

"Where are you from?" asked the Count, his fingers creeping up his cheek to stroke at his mustache.

The man laughed lightly. "As I said, I met Princess Tepsji and Genadie along the road. Or, I should say, they met me. And helped me. And to repay them I lent them a book. My biography. Did they show my book to you?"

The Count nodded. When asked if he'd read it, the Count paused before he said: "It was a touch melodramatic. After a while I couldn't decide if it was a fiction."

"Well, it is very true, *Count*. And if you read it, you know my story. No sense wasting time about it."

"How did you know about me?"

"That depends on what you mean. But be assured, these two said nothing to give you away. They tried their very best to deny the obvious. Their only mistake was not killing me. That is, if they wished to keep your existence a secret."

"I see. And what did you mean your explanation depended on what I meant?"

"Oh, well, I knew *about* you in *that* sense. That you were alive and here. But in another sense, I knew nothing about you at all, did I?"

"Why did you come here?"

"These two've had enough time to read my memoir," he said, off-handedly. "I came to reclaim it. And perhaps meet the man they served. A baron of some kind, they told me. In a different kingdom. A falsehood and diversion that I will not fault them for. They were serving you and wanted to throw me off the track."

"How did you find me?"

The Strange Man shrugged. "You invited me, didn't you?"

"Not that I recall."

"Let's not be coy. When I found no baron—as the two had described you—and knew I had been lied to, and had lost their trail in the meantime, I headed north and began to search. And when I came across the logical places, with all the signs of being the haunt of a certain kind of person—the kind of person I was looking for—I knew I was on the right track. It was only a matter of time before I found you. And them." He paused. "I hate wasting time, though. I knew it would be much faster if I destroyed the castles and—"

"You were the one."

"Because if you were crafty, and clever, and a hiding sort, you'd be forced to come out. It took longer than I expected, but after I'd burnt and broke enough, I began to hear stories passing among the people—circulated at your behest, of course?—of the great old Count who owned what I'd torn down. He resided primarily in Kyrgil Castle."

"You destroyed what was not yours."

"So they *were* yours? Some said the owner was, instead, an old Voivod."

The Count rubbed his mustache. "Properties legally transferred to my accounts. They've been mine for over two centuries."

"But still the castles *were* empty, yes? A few had caretakers. They knew nothing on this subject of a Voivod, or who you were. I suspect a good number of them were squatters. No, they won't be missed, really, will they? The castles, I mean. You live here now. And, well, for what it is worth, you have my apologies for my actions. But you understand my reasoning."

The Count shrugged as if it were no matter after all. "You had my General worried there was a rebel army on the march."

"*Your general*," said the Strange Man. "Yes, isn't that interesting, too? You understand, I came for my book, but I also came to see if it was all true. And it is: Servants. A general. An army. A court. It is quite amazing. It is. I've met several of our kind in my life—"

"That wasn't in your book."

"Perhaps there will be further volumes. Hopefully published. But what I find so remarkable is that ... Well, *how did you do it?* For me I find it impossible to have more than one servant at any one time. No?"

The Count shook his head.

"If there is more than one," continued the Strange Man, "and if they know just what I am, there is no living with them. The bickering and the fighting make everything impossible to bear. I tried all I could think of, but it always ended with one left alive, the rest dead. No variation. Until I had to simply come to accept it. But you ... And all of *them*." He gestured to include the sleeping bodies. "Servants, generals, armies, a full castle."

"I can't tell you what I did different than you. In your book you didn't mention your methods, either."

"I didn't think much on the subject. Until I met these two."

"Well, nameless," said the Count, as if summing up, "you've seen them again. You have met me. And I will have your book returned to you. However, it is growing late. Is there anything else you want before you leave?"

"I still don't know who you are," said the Strange Man. "You're from Ardeel. I thought I would recognize you if I saw you. Who was it who created you?"

"You don't know who created you, do you?"

"I do. I found out. But he wasn't the one who created you. No, that was long before your time, wasn't it? And I killed that one."

The Count's fingers paused midstroke on his mustache.

"You killed him?"

"I could never forgive him, could I? And it was in his nature to create more. I couldn't have that. Quite wrong. But now ... Now that I think of it, I believe I do remember someone. Yes. It must have been around that time. You are still young, I see. And it would be ... Yes. Perhaps I know who it was. But still, *we've* never met." The Strange Man shook his head slowly. Now it was with the deliberateness and coldness of a snake before its meal. "No. I am sure we did not."

"Until now."

"And we return to the point: I don't *know* you. I am from this land, but I've never heard of you or the name Tepsji. So how did you come by your name? Manufactured, or ...?"

The Count mumbled it being some variant on his ancient family name of Teppes, a famous name which he'd dropped to stay incognito.

"Are you telling me," said the Strange Man, looking amused but dubious, "that you are one of the Teppes? No. No, that can't be. You don't have the look, really. Are you serious? So then you weren't a Count you mean? To lay claim to all these fortifications and castles, you must be ... but it couldn't be. King? The Voivod Teppes, even?"

The Count did not answer but continued to stroke his mustache, looking somewhat put out and not knowing what do with this person before him. *Believe me or don't if you like*, his look said. *But leave.*

"Well, it's incredible. Way after my time, as I've said. But to think the Voivod of Ardeel should become an element of the night. What a change. What a transformation. It very much surprises me, a man of much humbler origins."

"The hour *is* growing very late, nameless. Is there anything else you want before you go?"

He was still shaking his head, his eyes fixed on the Count.

"You have some place to stay?" said the Count, hopefully. "You'll be leaving Ardeel? Perhaps a return to the west?"

The shaking did not stop. The Count remained still, but Amalina could hear Marosh's fists clench. "I will be leaving, yes."

"And I trust you've come to the end of your ransacking, and will leave the rest of my various properties in peace."

"Oh, of course," said the Strange Man, now with a return of his gentle smile. "If I'd known where to find you, if your people had not been so naughty to me, I wouldn't have touched a single one … "

"It is no matter. It's enough to say, from now on, we leave each other in peace."

"… Especially since I know that it was a bit of a mistake on my part."

"Think not on it. I will not, either."

"Because I should have liked to have kept them whole for myself."

The Count stared coldly.

"At least one castle. You can't need them all. One you can spare. Yes, I'm very sure you can spare at least one, from so many."

"You raze my castles, wantonly. And now you ask me to give you one?"

"Oh. No, no, no, no, no, don't be mistaken, Count or King. I'm completely out of practice on *that* subject. Asking? Do *you* ask for things? I can't imagine it. To *Ask*. Why, I haven't asked for anything in centuries. No, no, Tepsji, I'm not *asking* you at all."

26

Deadly Serious

The troubled air the Strange Man left in the castle was very thin: The soldiers had not understood what was happening when it was happening, and didn't understand it any better when it was over. When dismissed to barracks they followed their orders, hung up their weapons, and returned to losing money at cards. The princesses had already gone to their rooms for the night, for various purposes, and knew nothing. The princesses' servants, the gypsies, and the villagers who'd remained in the hall had been drunk, entirely asleep, or both when the confrontation began. It was only Amalina, Genadie, the Count and General Marosh, who'd met the Strange Man, and the only ones to feel the tension. And react.

"He will have the Black Castle," said the Count in a dull tone, after dismissing everyone but his anxious general. As an afterthought he added with a cynical murmur: "Of course he will have it. It is close to Tsobl; all that *life* stirring at his feet."

"You should have conceded nothing," Marosh raged, then caught himself and added: "*Master*. Not one rock, not one blade of grass, Your Excellency. Not to *him* ... If only you had *allowed* my men to *fire*."

"Worthless."

"He walked out of this castle alive and emboldened."

"And holding something he thinks I care an inkling for. General, how can I reassure you? At the very least I drew him away from the high castle in Netz. My purpose. That is all that matters. Yes, I think that is well and good."

Marosh looked like he had something to say about that. He turned crimson instead.

"I just wish I had thought of this possibility," said the Count.

"Thought that there were others like you?" said Marosh with shocking presumption. The Strange Man, on so many levels, had rattled the general's nerves. "Did you know, Master?"

"Who said he is *like me*? He is nothing *like me* at all. Who controls this vital land? And who's controlled it since I was born?—for centuries!"

Marosh fell to his knees, tears ran down his cheeks. "My King, of course! Of course, My King! Ardeel is yours forever!"

Still, there was an awkward pause. This fact didn't erase the present situation.

"We should throw him out," said Marosh, his teeth gritted. "Before he can cause trouble. I can take my men and the cannons—"

"Useless," said the Count. "Yes, *yesss*. It would be a waste. And cause bad blood between us, just when we reached an amicable accord. I just wish— as I was saying—I had considered this as a possibility. I might have moved my remaining forces quicker. As it is now, they are late, and might still take a couple more days for all to be in position. So slow, you regular folk."

"Great Crowned Father," Marosh said softly, and slowly. He was being careful. "What other forces do you speak of?"

"Ones more effective than some toy soldiers and their stage weapons."

"Master, I assure you my men are the best army in Ardeel. Perhaps the continent."

"There is no doubt, General Marosh, or I wouldn't have humored your presence in my home. And now is the time for you to shine."

"Oh! Yes, Master!"

"You will send a detachment to pick up my mail. I don't plan to leave this castle as often as before, and the more mundane things still need to be done while I entertain my beautiful guests."

"Mail, Master?"

"And you are some keen hunters, I understand."

"Legendary."

"Oh, I like a good boast here and there, General. I like to hear your enthusiasm! You will be on the look out for birds."

"Your pigeons, Master?" Marosh sounded like he was expecting to be disappointed with this other assignment, too.

"Any bird. Any bird seen flying about the castle, harry it or kill it. Put your best marksmen and trappers on this. I am deadly serious. I don't want to hear the flutter of wings within this structure."

"My Highest Sovereign, your will will be done." Marosh looked horror stricken, as if the Count had gone mad.

"Go now and see to it," the Count dismissed him impatiently.

Zsolt Marosh's eyes goggled when he turned his back to his beloved Master. The ends of his beard wiggled as he strained to keep composure as he left the room.

Amalina waited to see what the Count would do next. But, with nobody left in the room, he sat as still as a statue. Amalina knew this could carry on forever. She was already chilled to the bone. She tip-toed back to her room, slipping through the drapes and curtains like an odd breeze. She quickly spit the bone onto her bed and got into her clothes.

Just as she popped her head through the neck-hole on her shirt, the carpet covering her doorway shoved aside.

"General," said Amalina, trying to sound annoyed. She also tried not to glance guiltily over at the bone on the mattress cover.

Zsolt Marosh's mouth was a wide rectangle of teeth behind his beard. His eyes were squinted with anguish, a trail of dried tears below them. He almost charged her.

"General!"

His breath was fast and hot on her face as he came to an inch before her nose and whispered: "You knew that there were other beings on this planet like our Master?"

"Of course."

"You knew about this man?"

Amalina nodded.

"You said nothing to me."

"It was between your Master and I. But I thought you knew—"

"By keeping secrets from me, we are now faced with the most dreadful of situations, girl. Something in Ardeel on the same level as our Master? How dire!"

"Is it *so* dire, general?" Amalina tried to back away, to put some distance between them. Her bed pressed at her back, kept her in place.

"That man who came here tonight, he will attack very soon."

"He seemed reasonable enough, and satisfied with the Black Castle the Count gave him."

"He's not satisfied," said Marosh. "He won't be until he has everything."

"How do you know?"

"Is he a creature just the same as Master is? Are they the same kind, hm? Are you sure?" When Amalina nodded in reply he said: "Then you have your answer."

"But they came to an agreement."

"Opening ploy, stupid girl. He's established himself. Now he comes for the rest."

"If the Count can keep an agreement with the people of Ardeel, why can't this man keep one with the Count?"

"The Count does whatever he likes," said Marosh. "There is no deal between him and us."

"I've seen it."

"The ancient contract? The capitulation to the Knight of Ardeel? Is that what you mean? You've seen meaningless paper and splotches of ink."

"I don't understand," said Amalina. "It still doesn't make sense. You won't do anything ... anything on your own to anger that man against the Count and bring him back here ... will you?"

"I'm telling you, girl: I need do nothing. He will be here soon. And so what I need is—"

"But *how* do you know? How do you know he won't be satisfied with the Black Castle?"

"Was our Master satisfied with possessing the Black Castle alone? Or was he not satisfied until he took all the castles in Ardeel? You know a lot, girl, but you seem to understand nothing. Nothing about power."

"Please leave my room, General Marosh."

"Tell me: What is this secondary force Master possesses?"

"I don't know what you're talking about."

He leaned over her and it felt he was about to crush her with his giant head. His hair blocked the light and she could only see the whites of his eyes in the general gloom. In an odd thought, she wondered if she would see him better if she were wearing Pia's glasses.

"Girl, I *need* to know! I need to know everything if I am to protect the Count."

"But I've already told you, I have no idea what he's talking about. He never tells anyone anything unless he has to."

"You knew Master—these creatures—can turn good Christians into their kind?"

"Yes, sir."

"*How* do they do it?"

"You're making me uncomfortable. Do you, uh, do you really believe that strange man will return here?"

"Only a matter of time, girl. Now tell me how it's done."

• • •

When Amalina entered the Count's private quarters for the second time—visible now, the bone stashed in her pocket; Marosh's worries echoing in her head accompanied by images of the Strange Man's smirky leer; and she thoughtfully clearing her throat at the heavy drape before pushing through—the Count was still in the same position she'd left him.

"Sir," said Amalina.

He clicked his giant brown eyes toward her. "Mouse?"

"Will we now be returning to the high castle?"

He tapped his fingers on his lips.

"I can bring the princesses there," she offered.

"Better they remain under my supervision."

"You're going to stay *here*, sir? You *want* to stay here, sir?"

He tapped his lips again.

"You want *them* to stay here, sir?"

He tapped his fingers on his lips once more.

"Now that he knows," she said. "We could … I mean, we don't have to … I mean, well, we probably should … you know …"

"What are you trying to say, Ms. Dalca?"

"Well, the General thinks he might return here. That he *will* come here. Soon."

"So what if my general thinks that?"

"Well?"

"The General also thought I should have had his men fire on that dwarf. Worthless, I say. He's not always right, and I know more than him on these matters."

"Yes, but, if *he* knows *you're* here … then if he *did* want to … I don't know … with you … that is … a fight of some kind … well, you see then … moving back to Netz—"

"No, Ms. Dalca. I've decided. I'm against drawing that upstart gypsy's attention to the high castle. Or any of my remaining castles, really. Relocating anywhere would paint a bulls-eye for him, wouldn't it? Yes, I think so." He then whispered, with eyes growing narrow and glancing at the curtains: "Better he thinks I favor this one best."

"Well, yes, sir. Of course, sir. I see what you mean. Then again, *you* don't have to come with us. It can be just the princesses and I."

"Didn't I just tell you that *my* wish is that *my* guests should remain under *my* direct supervision?"

"Yes, sir. Or maybe then, they could just … return home?"

"Home?"

"Because the man."

"The man?"

"You know the—"

"That little black squirrel? The Buffoon?"

"If we're thinking of my friends' well-being, sir, against whatever he might do, if he should return … well, they may well be safer here under your protection, that's true. But wouldn't their lives be better *guaranteed*, don't you think, if they weren't here at all?"

The Count shook his head dubiously. "Ms. Dalca, it isn't even spring."

"But, sir …"

The Count became a blur and reconstituted along a wall. He held up a spider in his fingers and frowned. As its legs wheeled around, searching for the wall it had been running on just a second before, the Count made motions with his lips and tongue and turned the spider in different directions. Looking dissatisfied, he crushed the spider.

"Think of the roads," he said, glancing curiously around the room. "The dangers there. No, I won't have it. They will remain here, with me, and we will enjoy our time together."

"But the man—"

"Never mind the man." The Count patted a drape and watched for skittering pests.

"*You're* minding him."

"Ms. Dalca, these princesses know nothing of this bumpkin. It is my wish that you mention not a word of him to anyone. And especially not to one of *them*. Do you understand? If you frighten away one of my ladies before I am done with them … Well, I won't bother reestablishing, at this moment, for your benefit, what is already well-known: what a mistake violating one of my wishes would be. For you *and* your family. Yes, you know the consequences well enough."

"Yes, sir. But, um … When do you think you will be 'done', uh, with the princesses?"

"I haven't decided," he said, sounding petulant.

"But what if they would like to leave?"

"They won't."

"How do you know?"

"Leave that to me."

"Sir, you aren't planning to …" Amalina swallowed on a very dry throat. "Sir, you aren't planning to, um … to attempt what you did to Robine—on someone else, are you, sir? … are you?"

27

Defectors

"**W**here are we going?"

Amalina knew she was coming off a little panicked. She tried to cover it with a smile. As she began to explain to her friends for the second time, she appeared alarmingly giddy. "Down to Kyrgil—"

"What's the matter with you, Katarina Tepsji?" grumbled Aria. "The party went very, very late. Or didn't you notice? My heavens, we've only just gotten up."

"But it's a beautiful day," said Amalina. "Look outside."

"Call me when it's night." Aria closed her eyes and rubbed them to relieve some pain. "Have some respect for your uncle and close that window."

"But you wouldn't want to go down that trail at night. This morning's perfect, and—"

"Then you should have told us yesterday you had plans, shouldn't you?"

"Who is going?" asked Gillette, looking tired but sly.

"I'm going," said Pia, wrapping an arm through Amalina's.

"Where's Margeta?" asked Aria. "Is she going?"

"She's already having her luggage put in the carriage."

"Luggage?" said Aria. "How long are we—?"

"Well, if she's going, I'm not going," said Gillette.

"Why not?"

"She's going to spoil any fun. I suppose she's going there to find us another bore of a priest."

Aria laughed silkily at this.

"Oh, but you *have* to leave with me. You must!"

"Must we?"

"*I'm* going, if nobody else," Pia reminded Amalina with a squeeze.

"But I need everyone."

"Now you *need* us?"

"Yes, Aria, need. Need, need, need."

"*I* don't feel a need," said Gillette with a yawn. "Does anyone else?"

Amalina, wildly frustrated, growled.

"Such a little girl," said Aria.

Amalina growled again. *How am I going to get them to listen? How am I going to get them to leave before the Strange Man returns—or the Count tries his transformation on another?* It felt hopeless and that a tragedy for the princesses was inevitable.

"Look, look, look," started Amalina, tamping the air with her hands to settle them down, or rather herself. "Okay, I'll be honest with you. I'll be completely candid. There is a need, it is true. Very true. And I will admit to you: There are two *very* good reasons why we are leaving this castle and going down to Kyrgil. And why we're leaving in the morning and *right now*."

"Two reasons!" marveled Aria.

"Well?" asked Gillette.

Pia leaned into Amalina, prodding her to begin. Amalina bit her lip, then nodded.

"Do any of you recall my receiving a courier from the village last night? Well, here it is." Amalina had stashed the note in the waist of her skirt, she took it out and opened it for them, thrusting it in their hands. It felt strange to have their eyes reading what had been so private a subject. "Read it for yourself: An invitation."

"Such an elegant hand," said Pia.

"I don't believe it," snickered Gillette. "This is why we were making shameful gluttons of ourselves all through Netz, isn't it? You were getting letters there, too, weren't you, Kat?"

"Perhaps our Kat *isn't* such the little girl I'd thought," said Aria, grinning sharply. "Keeping your admirer from us?"

"Seems more like he's keeping away from Kat," said Gillette. "He's never come for you, has he?"

"Yes, there's mystery, but then there's arrogance." Aria shook her finger and made a tsking sound.

"I was ready to give up," said Amalina, truthfully. "But now comes a letter from the same person right here in Kyrgil. He must have followed me. He must be serious!"

"But who is it, and what could he want of you?" asked Gillette.

"And why doesn't the coward show himself?" added Aria.

"Who says it has to be a man?" said Pia. "It could be anyone."

Amalina told them the story every courier gave her: An anonymous man (presumably wealthy), sends a pageboy to the courier with a promise of considerable payment should he deliver the message directly to the Countess' hand. The pageboy refuses to identify his master.

"All this trouble, and the aficionado doesn't reveal himself," sniffed Aria.

"I think," said Amalina, with a clever thrust of her lip, "it's because I've always dined with others. Not alone. You know I could never eat so much on my own without looking piggish. But I hadn't thought that was what was intended. He must really want our association to be kept private."

"It could be a team of kidnappers, you know," Isabeau guessed.

This sent Pia's arm clenching Amalina's protectively. Pia said: "Oh, Kat, I hadn't thought of that!"

"But it couldn't be," said Amalina. "Who would dare kidnap the niece of Count Tepsji? And why have me eat publicly—and so many lavish meals—if the point was to commit a piece of abduction? If nothing else, I'd be that much heavier to haul away."

"They have pistols for motivation," said Isabeau with authority. "And the meal would be a method to put you to sleep with all the heavy food."

"You have some mind, Isabeau," said Aria with admiration.

"But still," said Gillette, "if the problem is that you were eating with us, and that frightened this tomcat away, why do you need *us* to come with you?"

"Because you are my friends and you will keep a watch on me. We will rent apartments near to the inn, and you will observe from a distance."

"Does Margeta know about all this?" asked Gillette.

"I've only told you four. She just wanted to visit Kyrgil and get out of the castle for a while. She thinks it's too cold up here. Says she's afraid we're going to run out of firewood."

"Does have a point," said Gillette.

"But still, you only need *one* of us to keep an eye on you," said Isabeau. "Why do you ask all of us?"

"Because why not?"

Aria shrugged but widened her sharp smile. "You said there was a second reason?"

"Because if you looked outside, you will notice the clouds coming from the north. By noon it may begin snowing. And then, if it should snow, we might be trapped up in this castle for weeks before we can get down to Kyrgil, and I don't want to miss my friend with the expert penmanship."

This began a rush to ready their belongings and carriages. Aria was already halfway to the door when she said, "Honestly, you could have stopped at 'trapped for weeks.' In this castle?"

"I will have my drivers and valet bring their best pistols and rifles, of course," whispered Pia, waiting to detach from Amalina once the others were out of the room. "Just in case Isabeau is right and it *is* a gang of kidnappers."

• • •

In a foul mood after the restless night, Marosh had retired to his quarters with instructions not to be bothered—unless the Count requested his presence, or (unlikely) the Strange Man should return. His order was to be obeyed at point of flogging with irons, or death.

As a consequence, he belatedly learned of the princesses' defection from the castle. Near nightfall, when he emerged from isolation in an unimproved state. He had no one else to blame for losing his master's guests, so he went back to his quarters and loudly cursed. Then he called for his favorite horse to be saddled.

28

The Offer

The snows returned immediately upon the princesses' descent, covering the trails and turning the scenery white. The severe peaks of the mountains surrounding Kyrgil looked like gray wolf's teeth emerging from a foamy froth.

Genadie was delighted at the return of winter. He set immediately to the death-defying work of clearing the trail with his apparatus, only to find he had to begin again, in reverse order, when he was done, as the snow continued to fall in wagonloads the whole time.

Isabeau spotted him first from her apartment window. Then they all kept track of him when they were moving through the snow-jammed streets, the servants beating paths to the doors of wherever they wished to visit. Though, as they already knew, the prime offerings for princesses on the make in Kyrgil were slim.

. . .

At the Bene Ceop Inn a five course meal (which leaned heavily on soups to fill in the unprecedented, nearly grotesque winter extravagance) failed to produce Amalina's wealthy admirer. But nightfall brought the Count right into Amalina's private suite.

"What have you done with my princesses, Ms. Dalca?" the Count looked in a murderous disposition, but the skin was withered and loose. Not as intimidating as he could have been. Still, Amalina was nervous enough to feel her knees quiver, even as she dredged courage up from the bottom of her stockings.

"They're my friends, sir. They came here to visit me and they wanted to come down to the village, so what was I to say to them as a good host?"

"Anything to keep them inside the castle."

"They would have seen through any excuse."

"You're pretty convincing when you want to be," he said, running a white finger along the seam of his cloak.

"What does that mean?"

"It means you should have tried, little mouse. However, you did not."

"But, sir, what if I hadn't done it quite right? They might have suspected something was wrong. Maybe they would have gotten scared and wanted more than just a holiday in town, and instead wanted to return home."

"You see," said the Count humorlessly, "you *are* very good with excuses. Yes. Yesss you are. But I told you I wanted my guests near me. And you led them away. Took them from me right when I lay down to rest. You knew that, and that's why you timed it so. Get them away so I could do nothing about it. *Yesss*. Now, I don't like that at all, Ms. Dalca. The naughty Mouse is one thing. Active disobedience is something entirely another. Especially under the circumstances."

"They are safer down here, sir."

"That is my decision to make. And I made it. And now I want them back in that castle immediately."

"Well, what are you going to do? Fly them back up there? Reveal what you are, to them, their servants, and everyone?"

"Now, Ms. Dalca," he growled so low she felt the vibrations through her dress, "what a thing to say to me. I have lived a very, very long time, and I have seen some things. And I have seen mice take up friendships with cats. And I've seen lambs take up friendships with wolves. And sometimes those friendships last. But I have seen the weaker ones grow complacent and unmindful. I've seen the friendly duck devoured by the friendly fox, after such a long comfortable friendship. With such a surprise on her silly little duck face."

"I'm sorry, sir."

"Now, what shall I do with you?" He took her wrist and ground the bones in it.

"Sir," she coughed and winced. "I was only looking out for your interests."

"Or what shall I do with that old baker in Korr, father of an unmindful, disrespectful little girl?"

"Really, sir," she moaned through her teeth, and the pain. "Listen to me: If the man comes back, he'll be aiming for the castle, not the village. Right? So if they are down here ... it's the same way you kept him from finding the high castle—"

The Count was suddenly behind her, his hand hard over her mouth. It took an extra second for the pain to come pulsing through her lips, teeth and jaw; in that moment she just inhaled his musky, mildly rodent-like scent. Then the pain hit, and Amalina almost screamed. But his hand was in the way, even if she tried. Pressing and sealing her mouth.

"Yes. *Yesss*," he hissed softly into her ear. "Just as I distracted him from places *I did not want known*—and, you understand, I expect their names *never to be spoken aloud* by anyone I have not given permission, especially not here. I do take your point, Ms. Dalca. But you don't know everything, do you? You have no idea what he is capable of, what measures are at my disposal, and where the princesses are safest. Your fear for their well-being might just have cost them their lives. You don't have to agree with me. You don't have to believe me. But do you *understand* me?"

Amalina nodded.

"I expect to see our smiling cherubs back in Kyrgil Castle by tomorrow night."

. . .

Amalina reminded him coolly, once his hand was removed, of the snow, which had turned the castle's trail into a white sloping edge that stopped near the village bridge. Genadie had exhausted himself and the horses. And the equipment was now essentially buried. Everyone was now trapped in Kyrgil until the weather broke, or unless he chose to whisk who he wished up to the castle on his own, revealing his unnatural abilities to them. Always a quick grasp of the situation, the Count congratulated Amalina on her small victory. He would return to the castle then, alone, to stand guard against the Strange Man. Promising to slip down each night at various hours to keep 'his ladies' company. A promise which gave Amalina the shivers.

Now she would be watchful: whoever the Count favored, he might target next for transformation. And maybe she could convince that special one— or all of them, if she was clever enough—to shy away from his attentions. But that was if she couldn't be wilier still and persuade them, altogether, to escape Ardeel for good.

The princesses grew rapidly bored with the winter shut in (some of their servants catching the worst of it, with reprimands and beatings by their frustrated mistresses), but understood being locked up in the village was preferable to the isolation of the Kyrgil Castle. Somehow the Count was making it down—he wouldn't reveal his method of transport 'even to my beloved niece,' he said, but the princesses supposed there was a secret staircase; which they had no interest in climbing—and his presence livened things up at night, at least, as they all waited for when the storms lifted and they could finally be free to move about.

The Count quickly reconsidered his strategy against the Strange Man, abandoning his night vigil in the castle—"Oh, Marosh won't miss me, he is as content as a baby, formulating new plans and running emergency drills"— in order to spend more time with his pretty distractions, giving up and returning to his protective rock only when they fell asleep, or the horizon turned pink. Secretly, the Count served as the princesses' protection at night (in a role of host, where he continued to endear himself). The sun and its burning light—even when screened behind a snowcloud—barred a potential daytime assault by the Strange Man. And when a week passed, and the daily routines became lazy and comfortable, the threat of an attack shrunk away. Marosh's concerns about a nemesis coming to call seemed to be unfounded after all.

The princesses, of course, remained unaware of any underlying threat to their lives, whether in its coming or going. Only for Margeta was there a persistent watchfulness against the world's abounding unholy dangers. Gillette seemed to be flagging in an unhealthy way, growing sore, secretive, and reclusive, though it was supposed more from the strain of night-and-day living than any awareness of outside menace. In a positive reaction, Pia did sense a relaxation in Amalina's arm, which she often had entwined with her own. A relaxation in her favorite companion she took as a warming relationship. The Count's irritation at Amalina's close and constant presence to Pia—and any other girl he preferred on a night, with Amalina's eruptions into dull chatter icing his preternaturally confident wooing labors—grew notable: a lift of his thick right eyebrow; a smile which wasn't quite a smile below his staccato mustache plucking.

"Perhaps you should go visit your parents, little mouse," he suggested at one point.

"You'd allow that?"

"I'm only your uncle," he said (in case a princess could hear). "What kind of monster would I be to keep you here? I can tend to the ladies' needs while you are away. Confident you will return soon enough." He added: "Though not too soon." Then added onto that: "But not too long, either. You'd be missed."

"I could go with you, Kat-Kat," Pia offered, having overheard. "I'd like to meet your parents."

"No, you stay here," purred the Count. "My brother and sister aren't the most agreeable people. But their little mouse could go there herself, and maybe she could convince them to come visit us? What do you think, Mouse? Will you *go*?"

"It's too bad about the weather," said Amalina, causing him to pluck his mustache hairs harder.

But it wasn't only Amalina's interest in monitoring the Count which kept her from fully appreciating the fact that she had just been offered—and she refused!—an unheard of moment of freedom—no matter if she couldn't take advantage of it. Many outrageously decadent meals were bought and consumed (in the winter, no less!) to entice her admirer out of hiding, to the point it began to noticeably disgust the villagers, and add weight to Amalina. But still, no matter how she fattened herself, the admirer did not show. This became a preoccupation for her, till the princesses all expressed openly that Amalina should give up on him. Or at least let them dine with her, and not spy with growling stomachs from afar.

. . .

Finally, and for the second time, the odd winter relented and warmed to where everyone was walking about without coats, and the sleighs and wagons were freed from drifts and blocks of ice for real use. Taking advantage of this window, the Count told Amalina he was going to reconnoiter his castles, just as he had done a couple of years ago. Since the Count couldn't risk himself being caught by the rising sun in a location which could no longer hide him, his damaged and razed castles in the south would be inspected by minions, to see if they could be repaired. The rest he would personally assess by sight. And he'd take care of other outstanding bits of business as well, which he had neglected for so many days in favor of courting the princesses. At the suggestion of outstanding business Amalina pictured the evil man with his wrinkles and his pigeons and his nefarious desires.

The Strange Man was not discussed directly, but he was still there in the background of Amalina and the Count's conversation: The Count *preferred* that his ladies return to the castle once Genadie opened the trail. But he would leave the ultimate decision to Amalina. If he returned to Kyrgil to find they had stayed down in the village—*despite his wishes*—and had come to harm in any way, Amalina would suffer beyond the tortures of a sainted martyr. But, to be reasonable, if they defied him and had stayed down in the village but were found all intact on his return, it would be the same as if they *had* obeyed him and gone to the castle as he had politely suggested. The Count would be satisfied. *But it was all up to her.*

"And when I return in a week," he told Amalina in a pleased and disturbing whisper, "I will make my selection—for I am over decision's edge—and we will perform the rite anew."

29

Admirer

For the second time in so many days Genadie cleared the trail. This time a soldier came down with him. He presented to Amalina a paper square that opened into a familiar looking letter. The paper was different, but the calligraphy was unmistakable: Amalina's secretive correspondent.

> I regret I could not meet with you sweet Katarina Tepsji at our arranged rendezvous. I decided to go to the castle myself, only to find you had gone down, and I was stuck here.

> Here I linger, peering down at the village and longing to spot the beautiful princess moving about. I will wait for you here.

Amalina asked the soldier who had given him the note. Again, as the answer always went, it was some nameless young page. But, as the next question demanded: had some new guest arrived at the castle? a man of some means? The soldier shook his masked head and managed an apology from behind it. "None that I saw."

"So then who was this page?"

"I don't know. I've never seen him before."

"He came with someone. Who does he belong to?"

"I don't know."

"When did he arrive?"

"I didn't see."

Genadie was no help, either, when she went questioning him at the foot of the mountain and found him cleaning ice from the sledge's runners. "I didn't see him," he said, looking exhausted enough for three bodies, but with a prideful happiness that removed some of the years. He continued after munching on some millet. "I've been clearing. Just clearing. As you can see, Ms. Dalca. Quite a bit of work. Don't know much about anything but clearing. All I see is white, I can tell you."

Thinking about it from the opposite end, Amalina hadn't seen anyone coming up the trail when they were heading down to Kyrgil. But their paths should have crossed. The trail hadn't been open since then.

Amalina asked Genadie: "Nobody came down with you just now but the soldier?"

"That's true. I think." He threw a glance over his shoulder.

"Then this person who wrote the note is still up at the castle, waiting for me?"

"He must be. Want a ride?"

Amalina looked to genadie's sledge. Amalina noticed four thick ropes trailing behind it. Two were lashed around the sledge's rear legs while the two others fed into the rear cargo area. The ropes' length ran off into the distance, then turned, then seemed to hang straight up the side of the mountain.

"I'm attempting a new system," Genadie explained, a bit hesitant but obviously pleased with himself. "It's too much work and much too dangerous clearing the trail starting at the bottom and working up. All the snow above you just crashes down on your head as you push along, and ruins the trail just cleared. Oh, how many times have I cut my way up only to look back down and see my work erased? Which means having to do it all again. So I've devised a system, Ms. Dalca, to winch the machine back to the top. Clever, eh?"

All three of them leaned backward and looked at the Castle above, and tried to find the point where the ropes met with the lip of the mountain.

"Does it work?" Amalina asked.

"It should."

"You haven't tried it before?"

"This is the first test."

"Can't you drive me up the mountain now and test it later?"

Genadie looked wounded. "No, I don't think so. As it is, they are waiting for me to give them the signal."

"What happens when you give the signal?"

"They begin the winch and the cart runs on its rails, along this slope to the side here, next to the roadway. Best to test it now while we have good weather and can see where improvements can be had."

"And you're going up with it?" said Amalina, amazed. "*In* it?"

"Me, yes. And Marosh's man here." The man looked stunned, even behind the mask. He gulped. "Nothing to worry about. We tie ourselves into the hold and up we go. The cart and everything."

"Even the horses?"

Genadie's face fell. He stared blankly at his sledge, and then he eyed the nearby horses as if they'd betrayed him somehow.

Amalina went back into town, paid for a fast looking horse at a local concession, and charged it quickly past Genadie, the soldier and the sledge and horses, and made for the trailhead.

· · ·

The body stepped from behind a tree and into the road. As she tried to make sense of who he was, of what she was looking at—and she could not, no matter how fast her thoughts churned—anxiety knotted her stomach. The head was too large. The eyes circular and unreal. The skin a strange yellow/orange. Is there a nose and mouth? Does he have hair? What is the matter with the body that it bulges in different and odd directions? Matters didn't improve as Amalina rode closer.

Positioning to intercept her before she met the trailhead, the body moved slowly, deliberately, and reached a black gloved hand in the air, signaling for her to stop. It wore a heavy cloak with the hood thrown back around its neck (or where a neck should be), the front parted. The head looked like an enormous gourd, with black holes as wide as eggs for eyes. The arms, torso and legs were in a thick, lumpy one piece outfit of blue. She'd seen many unsettling masks and costumes during Venice's Carnivale, but this was almost monstrous, something out of the plague-times. "Countess Tepsji," said the voice cordially, though muffled within the smooth yellow/orange shell. As muffled as the words were, they drummed inside her chest.

"Is that you?" Amalina asked, already understanding that it was the Strange Man. Out in pure daylight, no clouds to screen the burning sun. But he was encased by so many layers of cloth, buried essentially inside a protective suit. "Can you see me? How does this suit work?"

"You recognize me?"

"Your voice."

The gourd shifted. "Returning to the castle, girl?"

"Yes." On a thought: "Are you the one who sent the letters?" But on another thought, she wished she hadn't asked. She'd seen his handwriting in the diary. It didn't match the perfect penmanship of the letters. It couldn't be him.

"What letters?"

"To the restaurants. The rendezvous."

He stood motionless. No, he was not the letter writer.

"Nevermind, sir. Your costume is a brilliant idea," she said. "Did you come up with it yourself?"

He nodded more at the shoulders, and patted his chest and hips gingerly. "I should have been wearing it the day of the accident, you know. But it is so uncomfortable and restricting. I'd taken my helmet and some layers off when ..." His gourd tilted. "Well, no matter. I'm here ... It is good to see you."

"I'm pleased to see you are doing well, sir. I thought you were in Tsobl. Or going that way, anyway."

"Perhaps eventually. Right now I have to deal with your Master."

Amalina kept quiet. The knot in her stomach twisted tight again.

"Has he spoken of me? Of course he has. What did he say about me?"

"Well, sir, it's hard to tell."

"Why?"

"You should have given yourself a name, I think. So it's hard to say, you know. When he's talking about 'you know who' and 'that person'. He knows a lot of people and is very busy with this-or-that. I can't always be sure."

"I see."

"I know he's talking about you when he says things like 'brown curls' and 'shorty', and 'small stuff', but then he isn't really saying anything but being mean because he's pretty mad about giving you his *favorite* castle."

"If the Tsobl castle is his favorite, why's he here?"

Amalina felt her cheeks go red. "Well, of course, this is where he likes to stay ... when he's entertaining guests, which he does often. Because of the view."

"Entertaining guests ..." the gourd mumbled moodily.

"But if he had his *choice*, he would be in the Black Castle. It's very big. And right outside the capitol. 'So much life stirring around in Tsobl', I've heard him say on occasion. I can tell you that is *my* favorite, too. It's the best."

"He has learned something which I have failed to do in my time," the Strange Man continued. "I was so surprised when I realized ... realized there were two of you. It was impossible ..."

"Sir?"

" ... I could have threatened you two, I could have tortured you ... but if you *were* his servants, and loyal to the core, there is no guarantee either one would have cracked and informed on him before succumbing mortally to my techniques. No, I had to bide my time, and be truthful, and generous— something I am *very* unused to being—in order to have my answer. I wouldn't have been able to live with myself if I didn't have an answer." The Strange Man talked just like the Count: to himself and about himself; round and round, with Amalina as his hapless audience. "And I came here, I found you out, and I found my answer, what answer I had surmised was true: you *were* both servants to one of my kind. Servants acting together without quarrel, free of the incessant rivalry. Comfortably. No perverse jealousy needing to remove the other, in order to gain your master's favor alone."

There was a long pause. The gourd made it impossible to read what he was thinking.

"I hope you and he will be able to get along," said Amalina. "Being so close to each other, that is. If that's what you mean."

"I don't see how it's possible," he said conversationally.

"I don't see why not," she said, troubled.

"He permits you to speak with him as an equal? Is that it? I don't know if I can allow it so easily. But I *might* try. Will you have no trouble serving me, the way you have served him, if I give it a try?"

"But I *am* working for him, still."

"I don't think for much longer, though. And I would like you to serve me the way you have served him. Even if you find, in the end, I am a little *less* lenient. We can't all be the way one would like."

"Not much longer, you said?"

"Oh, yes. I will defeat him. I will take all that he has. Including you and Genadie. I would very much like that."

"Defeat him?"

"Will you come work for me, child? I do hope so."

"If I worked for you and he found out, he'd say that I betrayed him … he'd kill the people I care most about."

"He said that to you, did he?"

Amalina nodded.

"I could do the same," he said in a pleasant sing-song voice. "If you won't."

"But must you? Defeat him, I mean. I don't see why, sir."

"I always wanted to return. I never really felt at home in the west. This is *my* land, *my* place. And what better time, now that everything had been put into proper order. All it would take is to topple an unworthy opponent."

"Unworthy, sir?"

"How did he come by that name?" continued the Strange Man, not necessarily answering her rather than just carrying on. "Tepsji? I mean really. That's no real Ardeelian name, really. Much less one carrying the stink of nobility. Or could he seriously mean he is Teppes? I've known them all. Believe me, he has no royal blood in him. Or I would tell you. And so what does that make him? Nothing but a commoner. A commoner."

"But I don't see why that would make a difference, sir."

"No, I don't like being spoken to like that at all," the Strange Man said to his audience, as a way of warning to Amalina. "Even her. No. I don't like insubordination, and that sounds like insubordination. He is weak, and that is how she gets away with it. Well, I will destroy him," he said, pointing up towards the castle. "And I will take all that is his. Even this breezy open-window of a castle, I will take. Because he doesn't know what he is doing, and he permits too much," he said. "*And* he is a liar. *And* a cheat." His body pivoted and he pointed at Amalina. "And wouldn't you rather be alongside the one who is stronger, and smarter?"

"Those are good qualities," said Amalina soothingly, after swallowing the lump in her throat. "But fairness is also good."

"You mean to assert 'good' as a virtue? Well, virtues are worthless," he opined. "You consider him fair?"

"Mostly."

"He's a liar. He's lied to you. Is that fair?"

"How has he lied to me?"

"He never told you the entire truth about himself, did he? He witheld the facts about who he is, hidden for fear you might exploit them. Tell me he didn't and I'll call you a liar, too. He deals in half-truths and obfuscation. So how could you trust someone like that? How could you find it in your true heart an honor to serve someone like that? Didn't I give you my book? Didn't I give you the gift of the bone?"

Amalina nodded shyly.

"Have you used the bone?"

"Haven't had the chance, really."

"You know it *works*," he said, peevishly.

She nodded. She decided not to tell him it was a disappointment, on account of not being able to wear clothes while using it. She wondered if she should ask how long its power would last.

"And what has he given you?" demanded the Strange Man. "Anything other than the threats you've mentioned? So what binds you to him? Can't you see that you are needlessly attaching yourself to one who is most undeserving? Two hundred years at his disposal and he hides under stones. Would he dare walk about in the sunlight as I do? I am much better than him. Much smarter, much braver, much stronger. You will see when I make good my promises: I make mine his castles. I cull half of this country's population to make myself comfortable."

What? Amalina choked.

"Like an overgrown garden it is," he complained, like a prospective owner eyeing a property. "Because the gardener is timid and overly fond of his mindless plants. I will impress you, child, with my incredible power. You will be overwhelmed with admiration."

. . .

Plans changed immediately for Amalina. There was so little time. It was good fortune that she had been on her way to the castle when she met the Strange Man, she thought while galloping as fast as she safely could up the thin, snow-and-ice trail; where, most amazingly, almost providentially, he'd confided to her his outrageous grand design. She now required items that she'd left behind weeks earlier in her rush to get to Kyrgil.

When she reached the top of the mountain she heard the loud wood squeak of the series of wheels at the edge. The winch had been engaged and the thick ropes were moving slowly, somewhat jerkily, as it pulled the sledge. Genadie must have solved what to do with the horses. Amalina didn't dare look back over the side. It would frighten her and she didn't have the time to be falling over in a fit.

Inside the small castle courtyard the ropes were working overhead and angled down to an unseen area where presumably a winch and a power source were noisily yanking Genadie and his sledge upward. The groans and creaks of wood were loudest here and echoed throughout the castle.

Someone was shouting: "Keep going, keep going. Careful, another knot coming. Another hundred to go. Keep going!"

Amalina kept going. She was already halfway up the stairs when she realized she'd forgotten what she'd originally come for. Amalina's mystery letter writer hadn't been in the outer waiting area. If he had, maybe she might have stopped. Now she hoped she would not meet him at all. There was too little time. No time at all. Already she was thinking what she planned was impossible. But to attempt it beginning at nightfall would be madness.

Pushing through the red patterned curtain into her room, she was startled by a quick movement. A small black blur out of the corner of her eye. But there was nothing there when her eyes settled. Was it the Count? Had the Strange Man followed her into the castle? Her heart thudded hard.

"Hello?" she said. "Who's there?"

A head popped up from behind her bed. A small head. Then came a small body. Dressed in shabby clothes. Amalina thought of the many children who used to run around the high castle, Georg's nephews and nieces. He did look familiar. But this one had a rug of blond hair, and strangely flat blue eyes that looked like blueberries.

"Princess Katty?"

"Aklan?"

Princess Spaarvierlet's young brother, Aklan Spaarvierlet. Who'd arrived as a stowaway on her carriage, and who'd survived the rebel attack on the high castle, only to leave as an unwilling stowaway aboard his departing sister's carriage, she never having known he'd come with her, and was now secretly returning home with her. But ...

"How?" Amalina asked. "How are you here?"

For a moment Amalina thought Lisbet Spaarvierlet had come back, too. But Amalina would have seen, would have known.

"Came here, of course," said Aklan proudly, as he charged from behind the bed and nearly tackled her with a hug. "Oh, I'm so relieved."

"But how? How?" She pushed him back to arm's length to see if she wasn't hallucinating. He had grown since she last saw him. No longer a carefree rambunctious child, and with more of his childish fat burned off, his lines had strengthened and hardened. Until the young man he would eventually become could be detected in his small face.

"You've changed," said Aklan, studying her right back. "So much bigger. You look almost like a real princess now."

"What does that mean?" she said, offended but smiling.

"You were just a bitty girl."

"You were just a silly little boy," she said. "Out to hunt down barbarians. How did you get back here?"

"You don't know, Princess Katty?" said Aklan, somewhat surprised. "I never left. I've been trying to meet with you for so long. For so long, Princess."

She suddenly understood. There was never a secret admirer. "You've been writing the letters."

"Yes!"

Of course: The impeccable handwriting was the well-tutored calligraphy of a prince.

"I got out of that trunk the first chance I had. Sealed it up so Carila wouldn't know. I thought I would be able to go right back to your castle. But I didn't know where it was or really which way to go, because I'd been inside of boxes coming and going. And then I didn't speak the language too well, did I? So I was stranded. And then I saw your carriage riding out and that was that. I thought I was done for. But then I decided to get to the castle anyway, and wait for you.

"And I did, too, Princess! When they came into town to get supplies, I hitched a ride and pretended to be one of their kids. There were so many, they didn't know no difference, you see. And so I just hid where I could, ate when I could, and tried to pick up the language as best I could. Which wasn't too hard after all. They had a little school for the kids, which I got myself in on."

"That's clever, Aklan," she said. "But why'd you leave the castle after that if you were already inside? Why didn't you stay on for me until I came back?"

"Didn't you notice anything wrong with the castle when you returned?"

"What should I have noticed? I thought they'd repaired it very nicely."

"Repaired? They were all gone!"

Amalina gulped and felt like a callous fool. Of course she had noticed. It had come as quite a shock when Georg, Abraxa and Georg's whole family line were suddenly disappeared. But there was so much landing on top of Amalina's head, that singular mystery was something she had forgotten.

"Yes, I noticed *that*," she said matter-of-factly, not knowing if this was something to lie about or not, but doing so just in case. "I suppose I meant them, too, when I was asking. Why did you all leave?" Then she supposed: "Was it because of General Marosh?"

And here Aklan shivered. And he told her what had really happened. How Georg's people had begun to fight among themselves, over things he hadn't understood. But in less than a month, and during the most beautiful spring he had ever seen, he witnessed some of the greatest horrors of his young life. And as a prince he'd seen pieces of war, and the crushing of rebellions, and the torture and executions of outlaws and heretics. But those grisly events made sense. Here, family turned on each other over the seeming least offense. They acted jealous over every little detail. Who did what. Who served who. Who ranked higher. Even Georg and Abraxa grew angry and cold to each other, and argued more often than not. Before long Georg's nephew's body was found hanging. Then another was murdered with a knife. Abraxa took up with another man and they plotted to have Georg executed, only to have it revealed that this was a ruse against her, and she was stabbed and drowned. But the carnage did not stop, even as General Marosh and his men tried to hold together order. That family killed each other, bloodily and viciously by the handful, until the courtyard was filled with blood, and the soldiers had to wade in to do some killing of their own. Even the children were targets for the family feud. It just helped that Aklan couldn't be recognized as being from one side or another—as the sides shifted—because he didn't look like any of them, so he could duck and escape when a would-be killer hesitated or outright spared him. But, in the end, the whole lot was done in. And Aklan slipped himself out of the castle and back to Netz before he could be held accountable.

"What did the Count do during all this?" asked Amalina.

"I don't think he was there. I never really saw him, anyway. You know how your uncle is, Princess."

Amalina didn't comment on that. "Why didn't you go home, Aklan?"

"Because I want to be here with you!" he shouted. "This is the most exciting land I've ever known!"

"My gosh, how your parents must be worried sick. I'm surprised they haven't sent anyone to look for you. Not even a letter."

"They didn't know I was here, remember? Only Carila. And what was she going to say? That she knew what I'd done? And then she lost me on the trip back?" He got a remorseful look on his face. "Well, maybe *she's* worried sick and upset. But she was pretty mean to me always. You saw that, Princess. You couldn't want me to have to deal with her for the rest of my life."

She would have to ship Aklan home wrapped in chains, she figured. But now wasn't the time.

"And so you just thought I'd take you in when I got back?"

"Won't you?"

"Why didn't you identify yourself in your letters to me? Why the big mystery?"

"I didn't want anyone to know who it was, or that I'd already been to the castle. I mean, there was no way I was showing my face there unprotected. I thought it'd be safer to meet with you, alone, outside the castle, so we could plan what to do. My, oh, my, it was such a long wait for you Princess Katty. It was difficult to survive on my own, let me tell you. I almost starved and was bullied and they almost caught me stealing so many times. Thank God they didn't kill me. And because I had to be so careful not to get caught, and I'd be stuck outside town or hiding somewhere, then I'd miss you when you came in to Netz. I'd only hear about it later, after I'd got free and you'd already left. Then you switched castles altogether! I thought I was a goner."

"Those scares are nothing you'd have had to deal with if you had just gone home."

"Aw, Princess Katty! This is much more fun!"

Amalina wanted to strangle him. She swatted his head. "Could have gotten yourself killed. You should have just come up to the castle. Or just said who you were in the letter."

"Ouch! Maybe. But I wasn't sure. And I figured I'd be safer pretending I was someone important's page, than a kid all by himself with no money. It was hard enough finding people I could send up to the castle who hadn't already heard of the other guys being stiffed for their service." Aklan's grin grew huge, and his blueberry eyes wide with delight. "That was clever, wasn't it? Tell them they won't get paid until after they returned and could prove they'd delivered the letter directly to the princess? I just rattled a bag of metal filings at them and they thought they'd be rich. Then they never found me again."

"Yes, that was very clever," said Amalina, starting to feel restless and realizing she needed to get on with what she was there for. Aklan would just have to be dealt with, or folded in. "Of all the things, why was the rendezvous always some restaurant and why did I have to order a multi-course meal? Was that some kind of code?"

"No. I was hungry."

· · ·

Genadie's sledge was only halfway up the mountain when Amalina headed back down to Kyrgil. She could see in the sledge his knees and feet (and the soldier's) hanging out the bed in the back. It must have been terrifying. And by now the sun was beginning to set. The cold would be awful, if not deadly.

She went to tell the princesses her new plans and found them in Isabeau's apartment watching the sledge get hoisted. It seemed word had gotten around about Genadie's crazy plan and the whole village was preoccupied with the entertainment. There was no southern-facing window space that wasn't jammed with faces. When Amalina told them what she had to say, it only partially distracted them.

"Maybe you don't need to stay on here," said Amalina. "Not if you don't want to. Don't let me keep you here in Ardeel, if I take too long to return."

Their silence and guilty looks said: *You know, you are* not *the only reason we are here.*

"There's no telling when the Count will return," Amalina said to this.

"He said a week. Maybe less," chimed Isabeau.

"Well, if that's too long, I'm just saying I would understand why you might *want* to leave. To return to your home and families."

"In this weather?" said Aria. "Rather here than wind up in a ditch."

"Princess Tepsji might have a point," said Margeta, with an imperative hum. "About going home. If you think about it."

"I can keep you company," Pia said to Amalina, trying to get close enough to wind her in her arms.

"No, I have to do this alone, I'm afraid," said Amalina. "You'd be bored, anyway. I won't have time to see to you. Oh, I do have to get going, I'm late as it is and I can't spare another minute."

"You *will* come back to us?" said Pia.

"Uh, of course, of course," answered Amalina, her face turning red. "I just can't say exactly when. The weather, you know. And, well, I just wanted to thank you all for coming, in case you wanted to leave early."

Nobody did. Though Margeta assured Amalina she would, for the others' benefit, "try to make them see reason."

When Amalina went downstairs she was surprised to see the soldier who had delivered her letter earlier that morning, now standing next to the hitching post, staring up at the mountaintop. She was sure it was him. But they did all look alike.

"Did you give me the letter this morning?" she asked him.

He only glanced down at her briefly, then looked around to see if there would be anyone present who would require him to bow. He returned to regarding the mountain and the perilous lift. "Lady Katarina. Yes."

"Aren't you supposed to be up there with Genadie?"

He made a low cough. "Uh, no. I needed to be down here to take care of the horses."

"Who is up there with him?"

"Nobody."

"But I saw someone else inside the cart."

The soldier came up on his toes as if that would telescope his vision into the cart. "Did you? I don't know. There wasn't anyone—"

Someone screamed. It sounded like Gillette. The soldier gasped. Amalina's heart sank into her stomach.

Up on the mountain, Amalina saw just as the sledge plummeted below the line of sight.

"Mother of God!" Margeta groaned in Italian and she crossed herself in the window. "The ape has seen to his own death. Fool."

The rest of the princesses and their servants piled out onto the street, the villagers joining from their homes. It became a crush, all eyes fixed on the mountain, rushing up the street to the site of the crash.

"Surely you aren't leaving now," Pia said to Amalina, who had also joined the anxious throng.

Miraculously, Genadie and his sledge (and all the equipment) had survived completely unharmed. They only had to be dug out from under several cubic yards of snow. Bystanders stood in a ring around the rescue operation.

"My, my," Aria's maid clucked as the villagers, and the more daring of the princesses' footmen, cleared away the drift. "I can't imagine living in this every year."

"It seems there's more snow here than I've ever seen in my life," said Pia.

"That's very true, even for natives of Ardeel," said Isabeau, knowingly. "Because of the mountains' configuration, Kyrgil gets this territory's deepest snowfall. It's one of the reasons they gave up on building the highway to Tsobl through this area. Which is also one of the reasons why Kyrgil never really became as big as it could have, considering how much open land they have." Isabeau paused. But it was just because she needed to catch her breath in the thin air. "Someone might suppose the lesser snowfall is the reason why Netz, which is in a greater distance from the actual highway than Kyrgil, is actually much, much larger. But that isn't true at all. And it isn't even because St. Grigori and the cardinal are there. It's because Netz has almost all the mining operations, which necessitates a larger and complex population base and expanded economy."

The princesses looked to Amalina for verification. Amalina stared at them blank-eyed.

"Where do you get this stuff?" asked Gillette with amazement.

"Yes, where do you get this stuff?" Aria demanded with annoyance.

Once Genadie was freed, the soldier leaned into Amalina. "You see, Princess, he was all by himself."

"Are you all right, Genadie?" asked Amalina as some townfolk tried to apply warm blankets to him while others tried to wipe handfuls of snow on his face.

"Yes, Ms. Dalca. A good thing you didn't come with."

Amalina wanted to ask him if there were someone else they should be looking for in the drift, but so many other voices were commanding him to get into the blanket or to accept the snow on his face.

"What happened?"

"Those knots are going to be a problem," someone else said. "But I told you that. Who ever heard of a rope miles long? Impossible!"

Amalina leaned in close and patted Genadie. "Maybe you shouldn't do this anymore."

He rounded his eyes at her, as if she'd just swore at him.

"Take a rest, anyway, while the weather is good."

"Have to repair the ropes."

"Well, I have to go," she told Genadie, speaking directly into his ear. "If I don't leave now I might be stuck here for another night. You be careful and take care of yourself. Watch out for you-know-who."

"Who? Wait a moment, where are you going?"

• • •

As Amalina rode away on a sleigh built for deep snow, with Aklan, dressed in one of Genadie's footmen outfits, seated next to her on the bench, Pia cried at their backs: "I wish I could come with you. Do come back quickly. I'll be waiting." And Margeta nodded with narrowed eyes and tight smile, promising silently: *I will reason with them, Katarina.*

And later, as the lanterns played on the ambiguous contours of the highway, and Amalina wondered if the Strange Man would appear in the sleigh that night, or even the Count, she had a thought. Maybe it was the Strange Man she'd seen with Genadie in the sledge. Would the rat hide such a thing from her if it were true?

Finally, after deciding it would be impossible to tell if Genadie had lied to her, she changed topics. She giggled at the funny expression on the little rat's face when she had said upon leaving him: "By the way, Genadie, I borrowed a couple of your spare outfits. They're ones you don't wear anyway. And tell the Count when he returns, I took him up on his generous offer: I'll be visiting my father in Korr."

30

The Secret Visitor

"**M**y God," cried the Cardinal as he fell back from the doorway, crossing himself against the shadow-figure he saw in his room hunched low in his high backed chair. "Who are you? What are you doing there?"

The figure roused and pulled back its hood, but the face remained hidden in darkness. "My apologies, Cardinal. I did not wish to be seen by your underlings. Not until I saw you first. No sense having you warned. Or my being interfered with."

"And who exactly are you? And how did you get into my—?" as the figure leaned into the candlelight, the Cardinal's mouth twitched at the corners.

"You can relax. I'm no assassin."

"Yes," said the Cardinal, entering more confidently into his chamber. "I recognize you now. You are … You are one little dangerous man."

"Couldn't be too dangerous," said Attila, his eyes looking sleepy. "I've never killed anyone in my life. Unlike you."

• • •

Unlike *you*?

The Cardinal had never assumed the low constable—that is, the *former* low constable—capable of theatrics. He was unsettling enough with his deadpan calculations. The last time they had met—which was also the first and only time they had met—he'd breezed in as the representative of Tsobl's law enforcement. A low man in their ranks who presented himself as not *overtly* sharp. He eyed everything as if half asleep, but ran an exceptionally animated internal thought process which gathered all the little bits and pieces that fell within his view and assembled them into a fantastic narrative. A narrative he then pronounced to his audience, no matter how fantastic, with a listless, humdrum voice, as if it were all so matter-of-fact, almost yawning as he did so, as if floating above it all. The man was immune to emotion, a hollowed-out soul. A bare wood signpost unlikely to point out someone's positive guilt with even the slightest enlivening note.

But now: "I've never killed anyone … unlike *you*"? At the end there … the final word. Was that a ringing tone of accusation? the Cardinal wondered. Or did I just mishear?

Because the Cardinal hung on every word in a conversation the way a spider's leg caresses the fine threads of a web, feeling for tell-tale vibrations of threats or victims, awaiting his alert to retreat or to pounce, and this visitor with his inscrutable face and monotone delivery was so damned difficult to assess, the Cardinal's spidery nerves were winding in on themselves, reverberating, causing him to sense for menace in every syllable. So damned distracting. But was it there? Had the former low constable invaded his sanctum in order to cause him some harm, then? To put an end to him? Or his career? But how could he?

The ambiguously muted indictment had the Cardinal scrambling for a side-table, convinced the former low constable *was* a direct danger now, since he had (possibly just) abandoned his once stubborn mask of neutrality. The Cardinal made it look like he was rearranging items he didn't want Attila to see, while he worked feverishly (but with extreme caution) at a certain jar. "You've never killed anyone *directly*, former low constable," he muttered defensively. "But you've done some damage from what I've heard. With that *beast* of yours."

"Sir Vogoneyevic a beast?" Attila frowned slightly.

The Cardinal's thin, angular brow lifted at Attila's frown, remarking privately: an *actual* physical expression of some *emotion* from the wood post?

"Well, that got a reaction out of you," the Cardinal noted agreeably—though suspected this was still an ill portent. Better to keep him distracted and to draw his purpose out. Keep talking, then. Begin the dance: "But you're smart enough to know not everyone venerates a disinherited malcontent like Vogoneyevic. One who, in cold blood, murders twenty council soldiers. single-handedly I will add. Or laude such a force of destruction as a saint. Instead, they would consider him for what he is: a dangerous animal."

"So you maintain he is a dangerous animal?" said Attila, sitting forward and directing his dull eyes at him, almost as if trying to see through the Cardinal's back to discover what he was up to. "Have I mistook you, sir? I thought *you*, of all people, could be counted on as an Ardeelian nationalist. I mean, haven't you been clearing the churches of their Tsobl loyalists? I'd heard the last Tsobl cleric—Bishop Brandt, whose sympathies were soundly with the governor and council—died shortly after meeting with you. As countless others have. Are you really now taking the side—and willfully echoing—the government's propaganda?"

"God forbid," said the Cardinal, seeming to recover himself. It appeared to him, in any case, that by the former low constable's reaction he had not rejoined with the government. But it only *appeared* so. The Cardinal finished whatever he was doing at the side table. He held his right hand out in front, supported by his left, his glittering rings outthrust. He continued the dance: "But I was letting you know that rumors and sympathies get muddled very easily, and you aren't as clean as you think you are, and perhaps I'm not as criminal as you've come to believe ... laying dead bodies at my feet, as you have, you dare impugn me to my face? Call me out as some kind of murderer, while sitting in my chair, in my chambers, in my cathedral?"

"Fair enough," said Attila, as if to release the heightening tension. "However it stands, you've nothing to fear from me."

"Nor you from me," said the Cardinal with a crooked smile. "Though it's a little hard to believe I'm not in for some nasty surprise, the way you've snuck in."

"I have reason to. Nobody should know I'm here."

"Ah." The Cardinal pulled a cord along the wall. "However, Rosczy will know. If you don't mind."

Rosczy entered, looked surprised, and then was ordered to arrange food and drinks. He was also given instruction not to tell anyone that St. Grigori had a secret visitor. Rosczy bowed, and returned some time later with food and several bottles of wine.

The Cardinal placed a smaller chair in front of the larger one in which Attila sat. He pointed to it. "You may sit here."

Attila nodded and changed positions. The Cardinal stood over Attila, imperiously holding out his right hand until Attila accepted the challenge and kissed what was offered. Though everything was not yet settled to the Cardinal's satisfaction, upon Attila's kiss—which definitely settled *one* point: the former low constable was a dead man—the Cardinal's posture now loosened, and he made himself comfortable in his taller, highbacked chair.

"Now, tell me ..."

. . .

"The reason for your previous visit was very clear," said the Cardinal. "You were an agent of the government, dispatched here, by them, at my request. But since, at this moment, you're notorious, some kind of traitor, or rabble-rouser, you seem to have no obvious purpose here in St. Grigori Cathedral. Unless it is ... sanctuary?"

"No."

"No, you didn't look it. Then why exactly have you come?"

"Sir Vogoneyevic died. You could say I have caught his quest."

"Oh? Would you like something to drink? Or something to eat?"

"Yes, please," said Attila. "It was a long trip. And the cold makes me hungry."

The Cardinal was happy to hear this and had Rosczy set a small table nearby, with a platter of food and a jeweled goblet on it. Attila dug in hungrily.

"Young Vogoneyevic dead," said the Cardinal above the chewing noises. "That's troubling. How did it happen?"

Attila told him of a tragic accident though he rounded away from its details.

"As you were there when this tragedy struck," said the Cardinal, with refreshed mistrust, "you must forgive a little suspicion on my part; when a man comes to me, speaking seditiously of the Tsobl government, and even in his opening words links me to similar illegal nationalism—or *Ardeelianism*—yet it turns out that, while he just so happened to be the right-hand man to a rising Ardeel-blooded national, this great champion of yours just happens to end up dead in some vague accident. You have an active mind in these sort of intrigues, former low constable, so you must understand how problematic it looks. Um, try the wine."

Attila gulped it down. "I had no part in Sir Hak's death. As I stated before, I'm no assassin."

"And you aren't here to recruit me to your uprising? or convince me to support this movement of Vogonyevic's in some way?"

"*Would* you join with me in the liberation of your people, Cardinal?" asked Attila, dubiously, then munched on a roll. "I'm not an agent for Tsobl, sent here to poke around for revolutionaries or their supporters, if that's what you think. Well, I will tell you what I have to say, and then you can make up your mind. But, in fact, we *are* on the same side, sir. And the reason I am here ... well, as it happens, it *does* concern my last visit."

"Oh? You're no longer the low constable. And you signed off on your conclusion of the evidence at the time. There should be nothing more to it."

"No. But last time I was here at St. Grigori, if you recall, as a side note to my duties I'd found your graveyard attendant, Neku Jonker, had been playing unfairly with the bodies in his charge—"

"That was *your* determination. Unofficial. Unreported."

Attila stared dully ovesr the half-eaten roll. "I'm not here to waste either of our time, Cardinal. Neku Jonker was digging up the bodies and playing the puppeteer. Only, at it turns out, one of his victims belonged to someone very powerful, who knew what he was up to and was not pleased."

"Please, try the chicken."

Attila ate the chicken to please the Cardinal and spoke around it. "As I was saying, this powerful man, he knew about Neku, and he took matters into his own hands."

"A powerful man, you say. Why didn't you tell me about this before?"

"I felt I first needed to consult with the higher body in Tsobl, my superiors. I had not yet come to my senses."

"And this powerful person you speak of? Who is it?"

"You know, of course, Cardinal. It is the Knight of Ardeel."

The skin on the Cardinal's head seemed to inch downward.

"You're speaking of something you've learned about through ... ?"

"No need to challenge me. I've read the secret accounts of the sheriff of Tsobl, and seen the agreements signed by men who should have had stronger spines against this monster. I know how through cowardice and humiliating capitulation, Ardeel was turned into a tranquil field for the Knight; for him to pluck the flowers he liked, without any recourse to the law."

"The law. Now you speak like you're still an entrusted officer of our government, former low constable."

"I will always be an officer, securing the eternal laws of justice; enforcing the principles of right and wrong."

"And you say we are on the same side?"

"Aren't we?"

"Have some more wine. Tell me how you know all this, Neku's death and the involvement of this long-ago Knight."

"Simple enough. One of Neku's victims, who was taken from her mausoleum within the graveyard here, was once the Count's wife."

"I'm sorry? Count ...?"

"Knight, Count; this one has gone by many names ... to have lived so long. For centuries. And he changes names to obscure his identity. He is known as Count now, but he was once Voivod, king of Ardeel. And he has—"

"Voivod, you say? That's amazing. Have some cheese there. It was a gift from Rome. The flavor is sharp and excellent."

"You don't want any?"

"I already ate. And my stomach these days can't handle too much. You understand. But now ... His wife, you say?"

"Her family tomb is here. She was installed over two hundred years ago. And our enemy has probably watched over her this whole time. Living up above in the high castle of Netz."

"Count Tepsji lives there now."

"Yes, and when this Count Tepsji found out what was happening to his wife, he entered the graveyard and killed Neku Jonker."

"Well, it's been years since you were here, no? Our new attendant hasn't uncovered any evidence of a murder. And alive or dead, Neku has never been found. It seems more likely to me the cretin was not killed by anyone, much less a man of high title, but rather he ran off—"

"If you look in the mausoleum of the Count's wife, you will find Neku Jonker's body. It is hidden inside her sarcophagus. His corpse will be mummified because it was drained of every drop of blood."

"Rosczy." The Cardinal's fingers danced a signal to his lackey. Rosczy left the room. He cleared his throat and spoke in a lower voice, one that promised he would now give some admission. "The Voivod's wife—not the Count's wife, but a once feared Voivod's wife, his Queen ... Her mausoleum *is* here—allowed to be here—because of private agreements between my predecessors and certain parties. Permissions I would never have agreed to, but I had to respect by my oaths. The best I could do was to remove all decorations and allow the weeds to grow. And try my best to forget she was here. The ignoramus who tended the graveyard did his own kind of meddling. I should have paid more attention, certainly. But what you claim to have happened is wildy fantastic and …"

"As I said, let's not waste time, Cardinal. You've just sent your man to check the crypt because you know it could be true; everything I have said."

"I wasn't denying *everything*."

"You've been denying the basic factor in it all: The Knight of Ardeel, who is the Count. And this Count, who *was* once the Knight of Ardeel, was also once upon a time—you know just *who* he was once upon a time—the very Voivod—"

"There is no saying who he is or was, former low constable—er, I'm not even sure *how* I'm to refer to you, as you are now. But given all you have purported … let us allow everything you've laid out is true so far, what does this have to do with *why* you are here, again?"

"So then let's come to it: You've been playing games with that entity, whatever his name. *I* do not play games. Sir Vogoneyevic's army was raised as a counterforce to Zsolt Marosh's. Which, as you must know, now serves as protection for the high castle."

"Ah. Very good. A counterforce to Zsolt Marosh. As a defense against an incursion by him in the south, do you mean? Or, no. This is an active army against him, heading north, for some kind of siege."

"Cardinal," said Attila, flatly but with force, "the game you've been playing with the Count is at its end."

"If you think I'm playing a game with him, you don't really know him."

"A game of utility. How I understand it, the Tsobl government appeases the creature in order to hold him as a curb on your power and to repress the native Ardeelian population. You soothe this creature to keep him as a check on the Tsobl council, and as a potential ally against the council once you've accumulated enough power to overthrow it. It's the only logical explanation that follows all the deaths—the influential personalities who have died, or disappeared—and the constant political maneuvering. The Count has been propped and positioned, and serves as a fulcrum in the balance of power within this country, *and at the expense of the people themselves*. I've heard straight from the mouths of two governors, mind you, that, though they know the Count can now be credibly challenged, they wish to continue this farce. It's half the reason why Marosh has been empowered to stay where he is."

The Cardinal's tight lips smirked, knowingly. "Ah. And so you've come here to see if I, unlike the Tsobl government, will take your side and approve your attack against the Count. But has it occurred to you, besides impeding my rise by the Count's continued existence, that there is a bit of self-preservation in the council's decision to deny you and your lofty plans? If they should approve an attack on the Count, and that venture fail, it would have been their outright vote for suicide."

Attila drained the rest of his cup.

"I wonder if you really understand everything the way you think you do," said the Cardinal, eyeing the cup. "Or if it is just hubris on your part."

"So far, what have I gotten wrong?" challenged Attila. "Nothing?"

At this point, almost magically, Rosczy returned to the room ashen-faced but for a cherry-red blush on both cheeks. He confirmed Neku's wrenched and twisted body was in the tomb.

"And so Vogoneyevic is dead," said the Cardinal. "And you've taken on his quest. What more can you ask from me? Other than my blessing, which will be quite impossible."

"No blessings, Cardinal. I need information, and a small piece of assistance on your part."

"Assistance that won't—and cannot—be traced back to me? Assistance which manages to hold my own safety against the Count absolutely inviolable? Because *my* safety is vital, despite your noble crusade."

"I won't appeal to your religion," said Attila, levelly. "Though you should look to it if you truly believe. But you should understand, I meant what I said. This Count has exploited everyone's mutual need for a balancing power to pit us against each other, and continue his reign of terror and his general slaughter of innocents. This shameful state of affairs will be put to an end. You both—you and the government—fear the loss of your block against the other. Well, now think what will happen when it is gone: Zsolt Marosh has taken the central force and moved it up here to the north. Hak mobilized the most superior army in the south west. By these defections, Tsobl and the Germanian king's hold on this country will have been reduced to a paltry few arms. And after the Count falls, Zsolt's forces will be incorporated into our own ranks. So anyone who stands at the head of this renewed national force ... will become the savior of Ardeel. That will be the history of this nation."

"How do you expect to run an army against the Count and have it survive intact?"

"I am not running the army against the Count. Not anymore. The Count will be conquered from within. The army will take the credit, but it will survive quite 'intact.'"

"And you will be the savior," pronounced the Cardinal, cynically.

"The position is open for anyone who wants it."

This gave the Cardinal pause. He could not believe where the conversation was heading. "You don't want it, former low constable? Then where do *you* fit into this?"

"As I said: I'm the active force managing it and seeing it through. I am the party who wants justice to finally prevail, after centuries without.

Anything after that can belong to someone else." Attila nodded toward the Cardinal, meaningfully.

"You've no qualms about offering me the position?" He was genuinely surprised. "Because that is what you are doing, isn't it? Despite all your suspicions and rotten accusations?"

"I would have preferred Hak to be the one. But he who needs to be on top of this army is a person who knows how to wield power and has, in his heart, the true interest of the Ardeelian people. If you make the right decision now, you've proven me your worth, and you will have my loyalty."

. . .

It was a stunning reverse from what the Cardinal had expected when entering his room and finding the former low constable there inside, hunched and waiting. The Cardinal studied Attila for a full minute, feeling repentant for having poisoned him. Then his fingers danced. Rosczy moved behind Attila.

"More wine, Attila Bronk? Let us both drink, in celebration. A choice bottle from my reserve."

Attila accepted the newest cup, and waited until the Cardinal held a cup, too.

"Are you attempting to poison me for a second time, Cardinal? Or did your man just pour an antidote into my drink?"

The Cardinal was astonished.

"Well?"

"I don't know what you're talking about," said the Cardinal, without shame. "However, I *suggest* you drink this wine, for your own health."

"No need." Attila set down the cup. "I never kissed your ring. That is where the poison was all along, wasn't it? Rosczy delivered the antidote."

The Cardinal didn't answer but gave his ring a furtive glance. "Attila Bronk ..."

"It was rather obvious," said Attila. "By all the accounts, those who died after meeting with you did so at varying lengths of time—which, of course, made it easier for you to deny your responsibility. I had assumed the food, which you entertained your guests with, was where a poison was introduced. But then I learned by several anecdotes: the more a person ate the longer they survived. Which went against my theory. The food fortified them against the poison, somehow. It was a guess then, but the only common point of interaction with you was the kissing of the glove or the ring. Today I saw you use the old magician's trick of forcing the ring at me. There was a peculiar lustre to the main stone after you went to your sideboard. That is where you applied the poison, after you discovered me in your chair."

"What makes you think Rosczy put anything into your cup, Attila?"

"I saw him pour a powder into the wine and mix it ... in the reflection on that upright platter behind you."

The Cardinal didn't react beyond his fingers dancing angrily. Rosczy left the room.

"You kissed my ring."

"I pretended. And by pressing the band with my thumb it made you 'feel' the pressure of my kiss. My thumb has a thick enough callous. I was safe. You hadn't poisoned me after all."

"You want information and assistance," said the Cardinal, moving off the current subject before its repetition made him feel as much the low criminal he must be.

"Assistance is this: Marosh is a ferocious paranoid in service of the Count. You will provide a reference for me to get inside the high castle without undo suspicion. The Count and Marosh trust you well enough. If I fail in my mission, you can always claim you were duped into my confidence."

"What kind of reference are you looking for?"

"That will be determined later, after I've studied the comings and goings of the castle itself. But it will be a plausible one and I'll make sure to leave a false trail that would sustain any inquiry. You won't be suspected."

"That's all?"

"The information is this: For centuries your church had to power to repel this vermin. Now it does not—"

"And how did you arrive at this?" asked the Cardinal, with a pointy arch of his brow.

"The sacred grounds of the church have been inviolate since the beginning of the accord. And it is said the male blood descendants of the original signatories are untouchable. The Count breached both of these bounds by his murder of Neku Jonker in your cemetery. Proving his power is strengthening. Or your wards are weakening. Or both."

"I see," said the Cardinal. "So you've read the accord and the secret histories of the Tsobl sheriff. However ... However, each village has its own history, and its own accord. And not all of them are entirely accurate, beyond the signatures. And even some of those are forged. Or removed."

"You mean ...?" But Attila was surprised and dismayed by his error.

"He made agreements here and there with different peoples, and so made some promises to some people that he did not make to others. He doesn't seem to be pleased to enter a holy house, it is true, but he is not forbidden it. And he can kill anyone he likes. And worse."

Attila's eyes hooded, as if he might doze off.

"Here's where you are right, Attila Bronk," said the Cardinal, happy to have something the former low constable didn't know, and could not detect with his eyes. "This particular Cathedral does defy him physically. How he managed to kill Neku and put him in the mausoleum, I leave to you to figure out. But he cannot enter these grounds. Not easily, anyway. Because he is not invulnerable. He has many weaknesses that can be exploited if someone was daring enough to try. And St. Grigori and its grounds takes advantage of one most effectively. Would you like to know our secret?"

Attila said yes.

"Well, I will tell you. And I trust with your agile mind you will probably be able to fashion some kind of absolute weapon against our Count. But, I will vouchsafe this secret to you, as long as I have your word you will not betray me, and you will back any moves I make against Tsobl in the afterward."

"Of course you have my absolute, fervent agreement." Attila's eyes rounded and looked, for a moment, a little greedy. Some primary emotion bubbled there.

"But first I'll let you know that you are quite wrong on another matter," said the Cardinal, proud to deliver another blow. "The Count isn't in the high castle at all. But, don't worry, I'll point you in the right direction. And then you will have my blessing in your most dangerous and most righteous quest. Now where shall I begin?"

Attila sat forward to listen.

31

The Boy Who Paid With Gold

Covered with snow, the village of Korr looked quaint and slumbering, and much smaller than Amalina remembered. But she knew heading in that even with the weird weather fluctuations moderating the white swell to a manageable depth, business in her father's bakery would be reduced to just about nothing. Winter was a time to hole up in the home and venture out only when necessary. Dragomir Dalca was thoughtful enough to fashion his seasonal loaves bigger and hardier, so that they would hold for a week or two; one form of his artisan's charity. So after Amalina drove the sleigh to a neutral street, so that she (and it) would not be associated with Dragomir, and then secretly wound her way around the smaller streets and alleys to the bakery, she then entered wearing her disguise, but confident she would meet nobody other than her father and maybe Jenna. The disguise was in case there was a customer, but more in case the Widow Lidsz happened to be around, mooning over her father.

"Hello?" said her father, in a jovial tone, though sounding somewhat surprised as he looked up from a book in his lap. He was sitting on a small bench by the sideboard.

Wiping away the fog on her glasses, Amalina saw his apron wasn't dirty. He hadn't been baking. Jenna was also there, a few feet behind him. She was idly working needlepoint, and also looked up to see who'd entered. They did not recognize the dimunitive figure before them. This man was so heavily wrapped in cloak and hat, and his whiskers and misted glasses hid all but his oddly colored, oddly textured nose.

"Some bread for you? We have a few loaves in the oven. You're welcome to wait. Where are you from?"

Amalina wiped Pia's gift glasses again as she stepped closer. Maybe she had never seen her father so clearly before. The gray hairs in his beard were scattered fibers in a thick and lustrous coat of wild black shag. His eyes—with crow's feet finely etched on either side—were warm and welcoming; even if he didn't know her from a stranger. She didn't want to say anything. She wanted to throw her arms around him. She wanted to leave the store. She stood there.

"Have we met?" said Dragomir, making another attempt at conversation with the oddly behavioured man. "Are you new to Korr? Did someone recommend us?"

"Papa," said Amalina. She pulled off the hat, the glasses (whereupon the nose clattered to the floor) and the false beard (and there was nothing to be done about the touch of actor's grease). Still she couldn't bring herself to take the forward step that would allow her to hug him.

Dragomir's eyes popped open. He gasped and choked, and threw his book carelessly onto the sideboard. With a whoop, and tears of joy falling, he grabbed his daughter around the waist so hard she thought she might break.

. . .

"You've been set free, my beloved daughter? He set you free!"

"No, papa."

"Then how are you—? You've escaped him. That's why you're disguised."

Amalina shook her head. Jenna stood behind Dragomir, peering over his giant shoulder at her. She said nothing. There was almost something of fear in her eyes.

"I almost didn't recognize you, my daughter," he said, squeezing her again. "You've grown up! My little girl has grown so tall, and so strong. Well, look at you. Look at you!"

"I'm so happy to see you, Papa," she said, feeling something weird inside. As if her words were unreal. As if the moment weren't really happening, but being played out on the stage; or something she was reading in a book. "I've missed you so much. The home. Everything."

"Even baking?" said Dragomir, beaming proudly.

Amalina nodded. Then she went to the door and barred it.

"I need to speak to you, Papa. This is very important. He allowed me here and I don't know when I will get this chance again. There is something I must tell you."

"Yes? I as well. Much has changed since you've been gone."

"I see Jenna's taken my place."

Dragomir didn't hear the bitter note, so happy he was that she was there. "And she's doing such a wonderful job. Who would have known, eh? She's a very quick learner. Aren't you, Jenna? Eh? Don't be bashful, girl, come out from over there—" she had retreated behind the counter "—and say hello to your cousin. Give her a hug, eh? Isn't it wonderful to see Amalina, safe and sound?"

"Hello, Amalina," said Jenna, tipping forward to hug her. Jenna wasn't as tall as she used to be. Something had changed in her. Her eyes had softened. She looked almost bashful. She nearly curtsied and then backed away as if Amalina was contagious. "That's a funny thing you're wearing. You're dressed up like a man. And is that makeup you're wearing?"

"So I won't be recognized," said Amalina. "I thought it best—"

"Yes, very smart of you," said Dragomir pulling on his beard, eyes twinkling. "Always the smart one. What a clever girl you are. Sent me the message in that book. Did you get my message?"

Amalina nodded shyly again. How mad she had been when she'd read his message. A secret correspondence carried out inside a book lent from Tepsji's castle then returned. Dragomir's hidden message: 'i love you too we miss you very much stay safe and come home when you can'. *Stay safe and come home when you can?* As if she were boarding away in some Tsobl college. As if he were perfectly happy that she was locked away in a monster's castle. That while she was enduring unknown terrors, he was content—very much content—and still enjoying life. The image of him holding hands with the Widow Lidsz, which she had spied on last year's secret trip to Korr, came again to mind, tearing a little bit of the pleasure of the reunion.

"I thought you would write again. I was hoping. It would have been a perfect way to speak to each other. And when no more books came, I worried we'd been caught."

"No, we weren't caught," said Amalina. "I just never had another chance. I've been—it's been busy."

"Several royal daughters rode through here. Do they have something to do with it?"

Amalina nodded. "But really, I have news that I must tell you—"

"And so do I. But first, let me ask you, beloved daughter. Have you been in Korr before now? There was a rumor going round last year."

"A rumor?"

"The minister's wife, Sadra. You remember her. She put it around that she'd seen you in our streets. Yes, last fall, or the spring before, I think it was. Wasn't it, Jenna?"

"Yes, I think so."

"But was it you? Did you come? There've been many mysterious things going on here, and I wondered if if could have been true? Well, Amalina, tell me if Sadra was right."

Amalina turned red and felt her heart pump, but she shrugged the coat about her shoulders so that the collar blocked some of her face again. "No."

"And there have been other rumors, too. Incredible ones I couldn't believe. But you must be careful, Amalina," he said. "To come here and be seen."

"The Count has given me permission. I told you."

"Well, it's not only *that*, daughter. It is, well ... It's just not that, is it?"

"What is it?"

Dragomir scratched his beard. He ordered Jenna to check the ovens.

"Listen Amalina," he said when they were alone. And he told her the story he had given to their customers, neighbors and friends: Amalina had gone out of the country, to somewhere in Germania to take care of a fictitious relation who needed comfort in her sickness. It would have been very awkward if Amalina had shown herself without Dragomir's knowledge, and without her prepared with the cover story. It was going to be difficult enough now, trying to explain to Jenna what had actually happened, or a better lie, after all she'd just heard.

"But why did you tell them that, Papa? Why didn't you tell them the truth?"

"I couldn't."

"Maybe not everyone. But most everyone. Please, Papa, I've read that treaty with the Count. I know how many here in Korr have signed it. Almost everyone knows about him. Even the minister—even Sadra."

Dragomir looked taken aback. But then became stern, as if she had been caught reading something she shouldn't. "You know about this?"

"I've lived with the Count for three years now, haven't I? You think I wouldn't know?"

Dragomir hugged her. Hugged her tight. "It seems impossible. But it is true."

How can it seem impossible? Amalina thought angrily. But she said, pushing away, "So why didn't you tell them? Were you embarrassed?"

Dragomir looked shy. But then he nodded softly. "Well, of course."

"Yes, of course," said Amalina. "It must be very embarrassing for you."

"Yes. Yes. Well, you understand, don't you? To have your daughter run away with the Count—"

"Run away!" Amalina shouted.

"Well, what else would they think? You opened your window, daughter. You made yourself known to him. What would everyone think if you then joined him in his castle? It would bring down such an embarrassment on this family's name."

"Embarrassment?!" she exclaimed. "You sent me to him!"

"I ..." Dragomir looked bewildered. "No. He took you away. He stole you from me, my daughter. I did not—"

"How can you lie to me, Papa? I saw it! I saw your letter."

"What letter?"

"The instructions you wrote telling me to leave with Genadie. You said you didn't want to even see me until I was free! You are going to tell me you don't remember writing those very words, which sentenced me to an endless punishment with that horrible beast and broke my heart? How mad I was at you! I will never forget, Papa! To send me away like that. And now you think you can lie to me and I would forget it?"

Amalina was panting. All the pain of the treachery welling up. Yes, this man was her father. But he had betrayed her so coldly. And now, to act like it was *her* fault.

"But I don't know what you're talking about, my daughter. I never gave you away. He took you. I did my best to protect you. But that creature sent his people and he took you."

"I'm telling you, I saw the letter. You *wrote* it to me."

"I never wrote such a thing, Amalina. You went to the well, when it was daylight and I thought you were safe. Then you didn't return ... and I found the buckets ... and I knew ..."

Tears were in his eyes. A new kind of water. Nothing to do with joy.

Somehow Jenna had slipped back into the room without them knowing—maybe she'd been listening the whole time—and was looking on this scene with an open mouth. Shocked, unaware of any of this. She probably didn't even know who the Count was, or the creature. What were these two talking about? she was wondering.

"Amalina," said Dragomir. "I *never* wrote a letter. You were tricked!"

• • •

Adding new crimes to the Count's villainy had become a tedious exercise. One was always surprised, and appalled. But it was like discovering a new loop of body on the snake that was constricting you, or yet another hairy leg on the spider that was stinging you, another wolf in the pack that was chewing on you: it was upsetting, but in the end, you already knew it was trying to kill you, so what was the difference?

And yet, this new revelation, as hot as it was, enough to make Amalina's blood boil, became a confusion for her, because it lifted a burden that had been sitting on her for so many years: the thought that her father had simply handed her over to the creature. She could not believe he could be so cowardly. And now he wasn't. He was back to being her father, Dragomir Dalca, the upstanding and popular baker of Korr. Who everyone counted for the best loaves of bread (and the best gossip). The man with the large shoulders and who could always be trusted. He was that again.

"You fought for me?" Amalina asked him.

"Oh, yes, Amalina, my precious daughter. I tried to protect you. But once he had you ... I was devastated beyond all imagining. Even more than when your mother died."

Again, the image of Dragomir hand in hand with the Widow Lildsz rose to spoil the moment.

"Are those your glasses?" Jenna asked. "Do you wear glasses?"

"It's a disguise," explained Amalina, hiding away the spectacles. "Very hard to see through."

"Oh."

"But you came here to tell us something important," said Dragomir. "What could it be? Or can I go first?"

"I think I can already guess what you have to say."

"Can you?" he was genuinely surprised.

"But that doesn't matter right now, Papa. This is much more important than anything else. Something is happening in Ardeel. It is about to become very dangerous to be here."

"The creature?" Dragomir gasped. "He's up to something? *He plans to break the treaty?*"

"There's another one of them, Papa. He's come to challenge the Count. He's already torn down some castles. But he plans to kill half the country."

"What!" Dragomir gulped heavily. Jenna looked at him, confused but understanding that this meant something. The two weren't talking idle nonsense. "A second one."

"Papa, you have to leave here. You have to leave quickly."

"When did he say he was going to do this?"

"There really isn't much time."

"But when?"

"I don't know. It doesn't matter. If you're here, you might all be killed."

"And you? Are you leaving?"

"I'm safe."

Dragomir began to laugh. Then he nodded his head. "Amalina, my daughter dear. My, you are a brave one. Please don't worry yourself. You mustn't worry yourself over this, or over your old papa, Dragomir. I am just as brave as I made you."

"No, but there's no need to be brave. Just leave Ardeel."

"And create a panic?"

"You don't have to say anything. Or close the store, tell them you are visiting me and the relatives in Germania. But go. The highway will take you to safety."

Dragomir shook his head now, sobering. "I can't do that. No. I would never leave, Amalina. This is my home."

"But if you stay, you will die."

"Haven't I survived here this long?"

"But this is different."

"Every time it is different, Amalina. Every war is different. Every plague is different. So now there is a new creature. It is going to scare me away, when nothing has before? No, I stay. I fight for what is mine. If God wants me to die, I will; and I will know his wisdom in Heaven. But I will not become a coward now. No. Not ever."

This chilled Amalina. She could already picture the Strange Man tearing him apart like a rag toy. "You don't know their power."

"This is my country. This is my province. This is my village. This is my business. You are my daughter. I am giving up nothing. I will die having never done something so low, no matter the odds. Always willing to fight."

Why did I come here? She wondered. "You're being stupid! I came here to warn you!"

He brought her into his arms. "But I wanted to see you again. I had prayed I would see you safe. And talk to you. And tell you all the wonderful things that have happened while you were away."

"Like what?" spit Amalina. "Like that ugly Widow Lidsz?"

"What was that?" It was a soft voice. Not uttered by Dragomir or Jenna. They both turned to look further back into the store, embarrassment on their faces. "What is everyone shouting about? Who is that there?"

Widow Lidsz emerged from the oven room. She was wearing a heavily dusted apron, and wore flour on her wrinkled cheeks like a novice baker. There was even streaks of dried dough on her headcap.

"Amalina, I wanted to tell you. This is your new mother."

. . .

How life repeats itself, Amalina remarked, as she ran crying through the streets, just as she had last year. Last year it had been because she'd discovered that she'd been replaced so easily by Jenna. Now it was because her dead mother, who Dragomir had paid so much depressing lip service to on so many depressing nights, had been so easily replaced by another. And by who? Widow Lidsz? That small-eyed prune!

And just like last time, Amalina was wearing a disguise, with false nose and men's clothing, and trying to impossibly escape herself, hopping through alleys and sidestreets. But now the village was pressed down with snow, with very few people about. Her tracks the only ones in some streets. Last time she seemed to be tripping over everyone she didn't want to meet. Here, she could fall over into a snowbank and freeze, and nobody would know until spring.

It was funny, when she stopped to think about it. As Dragomir had announced—proudly so—his new wife, Amalina could not look at her, and her eyes had cut across to Jenna, who had made such a face. Such a sad face. Such a disatisfied face. Not her cousin's old, immature pout. It was a mature look of disappointment. Jenna was just as unhappy with the situation as Amalina. It was obvious. This perked Amalina up.

Amalina slowed and felt the anger flying off her. When she'd been so mad last time she had eventually cooled down. And now it was like that previous experience had been practice for this one. Perhaps a growing maturity. Or maybe it was the cold winter's air prying away at the layers of heat to get at her heart.

Before she could don her beard and false nose, which would protect her face from the biting wind as well as her identity, Amalina came round a corner and stopped short. Two black figures broke off from each other and headed in opposite directions, both with hurried and nervous steps, one up the street, the other down a side alley. Amalina knew instantly who the first one was, her heart skipped a beat, but she fumbled and put on her glasses just to be certain.

The evil man with the black clothes, long hat, and green winkles sped along the street, not even looking back. The other body disappeared down the alley.

Amalina allowed a safe distance between her and the evil man, then began to trudge after him, thinking: It's true. He lives here in the village. How did I never see him before? Well, we'll find out where he's going. Oh! Be careful! He might hear your footsteps. It would be just perfect to be caught. Where is he going? Put on your disguise, quick, before he sees you.

Amalina hid herself in doorways, behind lampposts and corners, and popped into alleys as she followed, her fidgeting hands trying to pry apart the beard, which had sealed itself together in her pocket. When she slipped into the next alley, she heard a small burbling cry. Amalina saw at the opposite end a figure bunched up in the snow.

The gray-green-skinned fig was continuing on, and was about to turn along an angle in the street. He would disappear if she did not keep up. But the crying brought out a natural sympathy in Amalina, and though growling in frustration at knowing this meant the secrets of the evil man would be abandoned here, put off for another time and opportunity, she stepped back into the alley.

"A ... Ama-Amalina?"

The figure in the snow was looking up at Amalina—and it was nobody else but Cristine! The last Amalina had seen of her, she was still under assault by the larger and more viscious girls of the village. The way Cristine looked now, nothing had changed.

Only *something* had. As they came together, once best friends, and gripped each other's arms, and kissed each other's cheeks and looked into each other's eyes, it was obvious to both that time had taken hold of them. Just as Aklan had grown an inch or two and had his lines become defined, Cristine had filled out. Her slender jaw was still angular, but a bit softer, not like a boy's. She looked almost like the older princesses Amalina courted in the west. A firm set to her expression, but womanly so. A solid bearing, but somehow feminine. She still had the perfect nose, and perfect teeth, and perfect skin, but they'd adjusted to more perfect positions to the symmetry of her face. All dominated by her razor-sharp, icy blue eyes.

"Cristine, Cristine!" Amalina cried, hardly able to control herself. It had been years. So many years since they'd spoken. She wanted to cry. "Are you all right? What's happened?"

"Amalina," Cristine cried, too. Somewhat tearlessly. "You're back! It's true!"

Suddenly Amalina felt shy and looked around to make sure they weren't being observed. She pulled them further into the alley.

"What is it?" said Cristine.

"I—I just shouldn't be seen. Not here. I'm not supposed to be here."

"But why not? What's on your face? Is that paint?"

"Make up. I can't be here yet, but I can't tell you why."

"Why not? I haven't seen you in years. Look what you're wearing! A man's overcoat and hat. What are you up to? Some adventure?"

"Why were you crying just now?"

"It's nothing. Never mind."

"You're still being picked on?"

"Let's not talk about that, Amalina! That's old news, isn't it? You need to tell me what has happened to you. You disappear without a word to me. I find out you went away to Germania, and you never wrote me one letter!"

"I wanted to."

"So why didn't you?"

"I wasn't allowed."

"Well why not! I wrote you at least one hundred letters."

"You did?"

"Yes. And your father posted them for me. And when I complained to him you never write back, he said you were too busy and didn't have stationery. And I left plenty of room on the back of my letters for you to write back, but still no word."

Amalina's lower lip quivered. To think of it!

"But I never got them," said Amalina. "Not one."

"What could have happened?" Cristine said. "Your father swore he sent them to you."

"I don't know."

"And then," Cristine sulked, "I not only hear nothing from you, the only word I get is that you'd gone off to France."

"Who told you that?"

"Is it true?" Cristine's eyes pinned Amalina.

"Who told you that?"

"I'm not saying until you tell me. Now that I think of it, it may be childish, but we swore an oath together. Don't you remember? Swore it in blood. We are blood sisters and bound to tell each other the truth and everything we know. Now, if we are still friends, and you want to please me, you tell me you've been to France!"

"Look," said Amalina, "I'd like to tell you everything. I really would. We are still blood sisters. But there are greater dangers out there than you even know."

Amalina stopped. She looked at Cristine with a critical eye. Not many people would be out on a winter's day. And yet she'd run into the evil man and an associate of his, and then she'd come across Cristine, crying in an alleyway. Could the evil man or his associate have been the cause? Did her friend perhaps know of some dangers of her own …?

"Amalina, you've been to France. It's true. I can see it in your eye. There's no reason to lie now."

Amalina nodded. "But you can't tell anyone. Not that I was here, and not that I was there."

Cristine pinched Amalina painfully on the ear.

"Ow! What was that for?"

"I can't believe it!" cried Cristine. "You *were* in France. So it's true. And you saw the Vokent boy."

Amalina was shocked and her legs buckled. "What! How did you know?"

"He came through here months ago looking for you—wearing a fantastically handsome soldier's uniform! But I don't have to tell you *that*, do I? Well, he didn't tell anyone exactly what I just said. But he spoke with a couple girls he thought were friends of yours, and your cousin, and they told him to talk to me. And of course he isn't the brightest young man, no matter how good looking, and I got it out of him he'd met you in Paris. He wanted to know if I knew where you were, since you weren't here. I told him I was sure I wouldn't know anything about it." Cristine's crystal eyes became daggers. "He loves you, Amalina! Of all the girls, you conquered Ivanti's heart!"

Cristine made to pinch Amalina again, but she held the jealous girl off.

"Is it true?" asked Amalina, with naked excitement. "He was here? He came for me?"

"Well, he isn't here any more," snipped Cristine with a nasty grin. "You showed up way too late. He'd only come through on leave but he had to return. I told my mother I thought he made like he had to return only because you weren't here after all."

"But he did come for me!"

Cristine angled her head to pierce Amalina with another look. "So is that why you're here? A lover's rendezvous? No wonder you never wrote back. What's to tell that wouldn't drive me mad with jealousy? Of all the girls, of all the girls!"

The remembrance of Lt. Vokent's—darling Ivanti's—warm embrace was easy to turn away when staring at the open wound of Cristine's envy. Which led Amalina to another thought entirely.

"Look, Cristine, I haven't much time. I have to leave immediately."

"Why?"

Amalina swore it would take too long to tell. That her friend would just have to trust and believe. But she'd come there out of love and friendship and to fulfill their blood oath—a lie that was surprisingly easy to fall off Amalina's lips. Cristine waited in anticipation.

"I don't know if this is possible," began Amalina, with a heavy and serious voice. "But you must see if you can convince your father to leave the country. If only for a little while."

"To Paris?" Cristine panted with excitement.

"It's as good as any," said Amalina, trying to impart how serious this was. "Whatever he can arrange. Even if your whole family can't. If he can send you away from here, manage that at least, Cristine. My dear sister."

"What's happening?"

"Even if I told you, you wouldn't understand or believe it. It's too incredible. Nobody would believe me, but it's all true!"

"Tell me, sister! Tell me!"

"Who is that there?" came a voice that made both girls jump.

"Sadra!" both girls shouted.

Sadra, the tall, thin, angular minister's wife, with gloved hands on her hips, towered above the two girls the way she managed to tower over anyone and everyone else in the village when they were up to something. She wasn't in a coat proper, just a dress of thicker black fabric and several undergarments. Her eyes blazed down at the girls, trying to burn to a crisp whatever wrongdoing she'd stumbled upon. "Cristine and ..." Sadra's jaw worked soundlessly. Then her eyebrows went up. Then they came down. Then they lowered even further over her hardening, narrowing eyes. The thin-lipped mouth became set as a rectangular box around her teeth, and she said, very definitely: "*Amalina ...*"

The terror of tyrranical Sadra was a force so elemental that, upon sight of her, it triggered masses of nerves deep in a child's cortex. Amalina and Christine were already running before Sadra had finished speaking. Before even they knew they were running, and found themselves out of the alley and half up the next block. These innate reflexes caused a curious series of reactions in the body, starting with flight, and was followed immediately by wild, naughty laughter, and pangs of guilt. This Amalina and Cristine succumbed to as they continued to run, half caught in each other's arms, trading looks. But as they exchanged looks, they both saw in the other's eye that they each knew they were a little old to be doing this.

"I—I have to go," said Amalina, trying to break away. "She's after us. But she can't know it was me. Go back and tell her it was someone else."

"Yes, okay. Anything Amalina."

As they cut down another crooked alley:

"But get your family away as soon as you can. As soon as you can, I swear. I tried to warn my father and Jenna, but they won't listen. If anyone I love is going to survive, you must do this."

"Why won't you tell me what's happening? A plague? A war? What can I tell Father?"

"Think of something. Anything. Don't scare him, just convince him."

"We'll meet in Paris?"

"I'm staying. I have to. It'll be over soon enough, I think. I hope."

"You must write me!" said Cristine.

"I don't know where you'll be! You must leave! Please!"

"Where can I write you?"

"Send letters to, uh," Amalina almost stumbled. "Send mail to the High Castle by Netz. Address it to Katarina Tepsji. They will get to me somehow, I promise. Tell me where you've gone to and I'll let you know when it's safe to return."

"Katarina Tepsji?"

"Amalina! Amalina Dalca!" Somehow Sadra was catching up. She'd never seen the woman run, much less run in snow. But she had to be, to be coming on them so fast.

Amalina broke their embrace and pointed her towards Sadra's voice. "Please, Cristine. Stop her. Then get away. Far away."

Cristine stopped, nodded and turned to intercept the minister's wife. She said quickly: "So you *are* a princess now?"

Amalina didn't answer but fled around the next corner, then the next, then the next, switching directions like a fish between the rocks in a stream, avoiding the closing paws and teeth of a bear.

. . .

By the time Amalina returned to the sleigh, she had the disguise back in place. She found Aklan inside the general store trying to make himself as low a profile as a small boy wearing the livery of a royal servant could get. Pagra and Vusjcu, the owners, well-acquainted with Amalina but not recognizing her, stared at the two novelties in their store. They were wondering if these weren't more of the eccentric nobility pouring over the border. It was a little late in the season.

Amalina grabbed him out of there, and Gulgas the hunter, also very familiar with Amalina but not recognizing her, helped attach her horse to the sleigh, and break the ice that had formed on the runners.

Before she could climb under the blankets on the riding bench, another acquaintance appeared. And this one looked quite shocked as he recognized Amalina.

"You," said Bistl the Chemist. "It's you! The silver!"

Amalina's eyes goggled behind her glasses. "Away," she hissed at Aklan, slapping his thigh discreetly. "Away! Now!"

Bistl the Chemist chased after the sleigh, waving his hand in the air, as the sleigh sent up sparks when its runners, cutting through the snow, sawed down into stones.

"Who's that?" shouted Aklan.

And as the sleigh slowed to a steady shushing rythmn on the highway out of Korr, and Aklan nibbled on the corner of a fat sausage and tried to get comfortable under the thick blankets, and Amalina tried to light the lamps with already freezing fingers, and as the conversations that would feed the next day's gossip commenced: Widow Lidsz wondering aloud what sort of catastrophe Amalina had been talking about, and could the girl be taken seriously; Cristine confiding to her father that she had seen Amalina in town, and her best friend was now engaged to be married to the marvelous Ivanti Ion Vokent, and this former baker's daughter was now a princess in Paris, France, and she herself should be sent to visit her dearest best friend at once, but all correspondence to be sent via the High Castle in Netz (which raised her father's eyebrows); and Sadra swearing to her husband, the minister, that for the third time in two years she absolutely, *positively* saw Amalina Dalca on the streets of Korr (*it just had to be her*), even though Dragomir the Baker continues to swear up and down that she attends to a sick relative in Germania; and for the second time in a year, Bistl the Chemist whispering to his friend that the strange boy with the make up and false nose (and now with added glasses and whiskers), who last year had brought him gold and a link of forbidden silver, was in the village *again*, and this time joined with *another young boy(!)* who paid for food and care of a horse with *yet another* gold coin—which Bistl was called in to assess—and who rode into the night on some expensive sleigh (every article of which raised the eyebrows of the friend); and the evil man with the gray-green skin and wrinkles being informed that he was followed that day by some oddly blemished young girl wearing a grown man's coat and hat (which raised the evil man's eyebrows as high as his bunching wrinkles allowed) ... while all that happened, Amalina's thoughts were a confusing mash: Forgiveness toward her father after blaming him for the Count imprisoning her; anger at his betraying her and her mother by marrying (*marrying!*) the Widow Lidsz (*without even consulting me!*); granting grudging admiration to Jenna who had avoided her inevitable death sentence of being a 'Bad Girl' by taking Amalina's place in the bakery and doing a good job of it (that Jenna also didn't like Widow Lidsz was a mitigating factor in her favor); and writhing in frustration that she hadn't accomplished what she'd come for, and so what was the point in trying? So Amalina settled it all by considering Lt. Ivanti Ion Vokent, attache to a general in the grand army, who had come all the way to Korr to seek her out. A pleasing thought to warm the miles ahead.

32

Sledding Day

"**B**ut I told you not to use the gold ones," Amalina said angrily, as she and Aklan warmed themselves in argument on the neverending highway. "There was every kind of coin in the bag."

"It was the easiest one to find," said Aklan with a carefree smile.

"The gold was at the bottom."

"But they're the largest. And shiniest. And I have no idea how much the other ones are worth."

"But a gold coin? Just one is worth one hundred times the rest of the others in the bag."

"So you see, that made it easy to spend," he said.

"You think it wouldn't draw attention to us? You saw how I paid for everything else with regular bits. And you know I told you not to even take the gold out of the bag."

"Then why have them in there in the first place?' he asked with innocent logic.

"Because you never know when one will be needed. But it certainly wasn't needed to feed the horse and get us food."

"Are you mad because I overpaid? or because the gold made us look suspicious?"

"Yes! And because you didn't do what I told you!"

"But I never spent a gold coin before, Princess. Not personally. That was fun."

"Made me so mad that I forgot to send you back home."

"Too late now," he crowed merrily. "You *know* I'm not going back. Never."

Suddenly they were back in Kyrgil. It seemed like a month had passed. It was only a week.

On her return, Amalina was dismayed to find that everyone was still there. "I tried to reason with them," said Margeta solemnly. But Margeta hadn't returned home either, had she? And all the princesses were in a good mood it seemed, even Margeta, for their own personal reasons.

. . .

"Isn't this the greatest fun?" said Gillette, bursting with energy at the top of one of her good moods, as they hauled themselves up the steep incline of the mountain. Behind them the servants and villagers attended the princesses nervously, waiting to catch one if they should slip, while others struggled to pull the several large sleighs up the incline without slipping themselves. "Do hurry up. Katty hasn't had any fun yet."

Aria was grim-faced against the cold, but the eagerness and pleasure shone from her eyes. She pointed to the right.

"What is it, Aria?" said Gillette.

"I agree," said Isabeau. "Let's try over there, where we haven't made any tracks yet."

Gillette nodded and directed everyone to the right, and a fan of bodies spread in that direction; the sleighs giving trouble in making the sharp turn to follow.

"No, no, *cretins*," said Gillette. "First to the top, then over. *Mon Dieu*, you're trampling all over the virgin snow!"

"Just wait till you try," Pia told Amalina enthusiastically, as she suctioned Amalina up the hill in her tight grip.

While Amalina was away the princesses had overcome their boredom in many ways. The latest diversion had been devised the night before, and Amalina had arrived just in time for it. Inspired by Genadie's fall down the side of the mountain, the villagers recalled some of their own pasttimes to the princesses' servants, which then filtered upwards and entertained their imaginations for several days, before they decided to try Genadie's plunge themselves, on safer slopes and riding more reliable sleighs.

"Whee!" shouted Gillette and Aria as the two took the first ride down the untried slope. "Watch out for the bump!" (there was no steering the sleighs) "Wow! Yie! Whee!"

Somewhere near the bottom of the hill, where it straightened out and fed into the back of Kyrgil, a makeshift anchor was deployed. The bodies flung forward awkwardly and the sleigh dragged to a halt.

"Much better," said Isabeau, appraisingly. She informed Amalina: "We absolutely destroyed the first one. It crunched into that house over there. You see? Then we destroyed the second when we used the wrong anchoring device. Much too heavy, and with a hook on the end. Stopped the sleigh cold, broke off the back of the sleigh, and the runners, and then it flipped over."

"It was still fun," said Pia. "Only D'Antoigne, my butler, was hurt. Oh, I do hope he's all right. But let's get in this next one. All three of us can ride down together. Then we'll do all five of us next."

The experience wasn't any different than the past week for Amalina, riding on runners as fast as possible over a blinding field of snow. Though it was disconcerting here because there wasn't a horse in front to keep the sleigh in control, and two princesses were on either side screaming in ecstacy. After a while, Amalina felt a slight headache coming on.

Pia kept hugging close to Amalina, and forcing Amalina's arms around her, and would kiss her before, during, and at the end. And the kisses became passionate.

"Why do we keep kissing?" Amalina asked, remarking that she'd never kissed anyone so much. Even with her friend Cristine (who, admittedly, had a cooler mind on public displays of affection).

The sledding party was a great success. Sleighs of all sizes and shapes—and then after a while it was tables (overturned), benches, and pieces of wood—traveled up the side of the mountain under the power of servants and princesses (and eventually the whole of Kyrgil), like a disorganized troupe of termites making off with the village. And they shot down with glee, abandon, and chaos. With shouts, and cries, and laughter. One over the other, over the other, over the other. Until the entire open patch in the western slope was flattened, cut with meandering, ribbony patterns, littered at the bottom with broken wood. Decorated in a couple places with a small spatter of blood. Only nightfall put an end to it. It was a day that would be talked about and relived for years. Everyone retired to their homes with a strange sense of victory.

• • •

When they were stuffed inside Isabeau's apartment, drying off and warming up, Amalina realized what she took as happiness all around for the princesses, was not exactly so. The sledding had been a distraction. The return of Amalina had been a novelty. They were trained princesses, expert in the art of turning a smile in the most adverse of situations, especially if competition was nearby. And Amalina had been on the road for so long, with just the company of a little boy, a horse, and several confused and morose Ardeelian families that put them up for the night, she'd lost proper calibration on genuine joy.

The smiles in the room were surface. The eyes were dull and wandering. Amalina caught sighs and shrugs and vacant playing at dresses and hair. Are they unhappy with me? she wondered. But then understood it had nothing to do with her at all. They were unhappy for their own personal reasons.

"You eat like a snake, with writhing lips and rolling gullet," said Gillette to Aria observationally, looking weary again, as Lady Princess Aria Ecci chewed langorously on a piece of jerked fish.

"Well, you eat like a cow," Aria returned, with a polite smile.

"How do I eat?" asked Isabeau, curious, taking a bite of sausage.

"You eat like a monkey."

"Well, I'm sure I eat like a bird," said Pia from the couch, looking embarrassed at their behavior. "What of it? We're Katarina's little menagerie, aren't we?"

"What animal does Katty resemble when she eats?" asked Aria.

"Certainly not some animal," said Pia.

"She's like a Mouse, as her uncle calls her," suggested Isabeau.

"I'm sure I don't spend my valuable time studying the lower species of this planet to suppose one way or another, about any of you," Margeta intoned from her satellite corner of the table.

"Is everything all right?" Amalina whispered to Pia, since the red head was wrapped around her on the couch.

"Oh, I think so," said Pia, rousing from her own funk and twirling a lock of Amalina's hair. "Who is that boy? You have a servant now?"

"I suppose so. His name's Aklan. My parents gave him to me."

"But I saw you leave here with him."

"Yes, they sent him to fetch me."

"Ah." Pia's thoughts retreated deep behind her eyes. Her kiss was slow, automatic and absent.

"Everyone seems so unhappy," said Amalina. "Even you."

"I felt so alone without you, Katty dear."

"Well, I'm here now. Why do you keep kissing me?"

"Don't you like it?"

"It's unusual."

"I feel close to you. Don't you feel close to me?"

"Maybe the others are upset that I'm neglecting them so."

"I doubt that. Don't let it bother you. Here, hold me closer. They don't care. They don't even know you're here."

"What's the matter with Aria?"

"She's just bored. I don't think she likes women very much. Not as much as men."

"And Margeta?"

"She doesn't like anyone. She tried to convince us all to leave while you were gone. She's sore it didn't work."

"And Isabeau?" said Amalina, spotting the girl reading a book now with a small pout across the room.

Pia made a discreet laugh in the nape of Amalina's neck (which felt good). She eyed her rival and summed her up, too. "We're all tired of listening to her. She resents us all for telling her to shut up. And remember her fool-proof system to defeat Gillette's Pharo game? Well, what can I tell you, but wasn't that a lesson for her in tranferring to Gillette all her sapphire and ruby rings, bracelets and necklaces?"

"All her jewelry?"

"Do you see her wearing anything?"

"So then, if Gillette won all the jewelry in her game, what's the matter with *her*?"

"Hm," said Pia, pausing to think. "I don't know. Can we try kissing on the lips?"

"What are you talking about?"

"I think I need practice."

"Practice for what?"

"We don't have to if you don't want to. But it never hurts to be good at kissing, don't you think? When the time comes?"

No matter how heavy the gloom was that had fallen over the princesses, it lifted like a bird at a shot when, after sunset, the Count entered the apartment.

• • •

Like a handful of cats, the princesses prowled and preened and vied for the Count's undivided attention, which had him pulling at both sides of his mustache and basking in half-lidded glory. But even he had something stirring behind his eyes that denied his full contentment with the scene. The girls groaned when he told them—as he commonly did—that he had to leave them for business. But they looked on with curiosity when he said he would speak to Amalina alone for a minute, and they saw the glower he gave her.

"And so you return to me, my little mouse," said the Count to Amalina in her private room. "Who is the boy?"

"My new servant. He's young enough, he shouldn't bother General Marosh's sensibilities."

"I don't know him. I don't recognize him. But he looks … *familiar*." This seemed to bother him. "Get out of this room."

Aklan, with wide eyes—surprised as a prince was to be commanded so—and still terrified by the menacing Count Tepsji (who, he knew, had bested a rebel invasion, and was associated in some way with the madness and bloodbath of his former servants), bowed and scurried from the room.

"Something very familiar about him, yes. *Yesss.*" The Count stared at the door as if he could see through it. Maybe he could.

"When did you get back, sir?" asked Amalina, feeling a stir of heat inside her. Because, after all, didn't she have something important to say to *him*? "How are the castles?"

"You left our lady princesses alone for nearly a week, little mouse," he rumbled. His large eyes turned to her, he frowned.

"You said I could visit my father."

"A willfully obtuse reading of my offer, *Ms. Dalca*. No, I don't think for one second you did not understand my meaning of—my intention for—the offer at all."

Amalina didn't deny it. She turned red.

"But you got what you wanted, little mouse."

"Yes, I did, sir. Thank you, sir. It had been so long, sir, since I was able to speak with my papa. So much has changed."

"Yes, I'm sure it has. Though not much does, you'll realize—if you live long enough. Not much in the scheme of things."

"Yes, it was very good to talk to my papa. I learned some things, too. Do you want to know what I learned?"

He smiled at her, touching his mustache, and looked intrigued by the welling of something in the girl before him.

"Genadie showed me a letter the day I was taken from my village, taken away from my father. He showed me a letter written in my father's own hand that said I was to go with Genadie and to serve you. And all this time I had thought he'd asked me to serve you, sir. All these years. And now I find out, it was a fake. It was a lie. He didn't want me to leave home at all. I was tricked! I was kidnapped! And isn't that why you never wanted me to see him, to talk to him, to write letters? You knew I'd find out! Well, I have now! I was tricked and kidnapped!"

Amalina panted. She was flushed. She was sweating. She stared all the anger she could muster at his stone-like expression. How was he going to react? Let him try to deny it! Let him try to make excuses!

He stood up slowly and patted lint off his breeches before shifting his heavy cloak forward on his shoulders.

"Welcome back," he said, unperturbed. Then, on his way to the door: "I don't believe the village is a suitable place to perform the rite. Nooo, I think not. So you ladies will return to the castle." He winked his large brown eye. "While you were away, Ms. Dalca, I made my choice. I hope you are quite refreshed and ready to assist."

33

The Choice

"What's wrong?" asked Amalina.

The princess shifted uncomfortably under Amalina's close watch, but did not pull her hand out of Amalina's. Instead, she placed her other hand on top of their soft, knotted ball of flesh, knuckles and rings, and she sighed and squeezed. She tried to look out the window, but that was a mistake.

"What a drop," said Gillette, looking sick. They were close to the top of the trail, and this was where it narrowed, and the drop to the village below looked disastrous, and inevitable. The point at which, the first time up, game and adventurous Gillette had finally lost her daring and developed a shake in her knees.

"I can see something's wrong," said Amalina. "Please don't hide from me. We're friends."

"Why did you ride with me?" said Gillette, sounding a little stronger. "I'm sure Pia is jealous. You shouldn't have insisted the way you did. You might have given her a complex."

"Let's not avoid the question, Gilly. I've asked it. Please answer."

Gillette looked hopelessly at Amalina. Then she uttered a pathetic laugh and shook her head, closed her eyes. "You're still such a little girl. I don't know ..."

Once they were inside the castle, there would be no ready excuse to be alone. Amalina needed to know what was bothering Gillette. If she did, maybe she would know if this princess was the Count's choice. There was little time left. Gillette must be the one, mustn't she? When Amalina had tried to make idle chatter, to sound out the ladies and guess who it was, by an expression here, or a word there, they had all been unhelpful. "How do you find my Uncle? ... Did he entertain you well while I was away? ... What do you think of him, really? ... Has he won your heart?" Only Margeta was honest in her answer: "Really, Princess Tepsji, he is so old and ugly, why would I want to be with him in any romantic way? If that is your rude implication." For Aria, he was to be admired as "a clever old boy." Isabeau deemed him "smart" and "deep" and "philosophical" and "wise" and "learned" and "capable of understanding me, and really listening to what I have to say." Even Pia admitted with a blush that he was "sweet, if a little timid and shy."

"Really, Pia, who the hell are you talking about?" said Aria.

"It's like you don't even know him at all," Margeta had chimed in.

Only Gillette had kept quiet, and looked like she wanted to disappear from the conversation altogether. Just as she was now in the carriage, even when alone with Amalina.

"Please," said Amalina.

"This is serious business." Gillette's eyes roamed across the side of the mountain.

"It seems so."

"It requires discretion."

"I am quite capable, if you'll only trust me."

"I'm pregnant."

All of Amalina's training at controlling expression could not hold back her surprise. Her whole body spasmed, she almost fell into Gillette's lap.

"Say nothing! Say nothing, Katty! I beg you. You promised!"

"Of course!" Amalina assured. "But why would you think such a thing?"

"Why would you think?" Gillette returned brittlely. "Why would you *think*?"

"I mean, how do you know?"

"Well, of course, I haven't had my period."

"That's all?" said Amalina, somewhat relieved.

"It's been so long," said Gillette, still irritable, confused by Amalina's breeziness. "There couldn't be any other explanation."

"There's a very good one," said Amalina, now squeezing Gillette's hand. "A *very* good one. This is a very common thing, my dear princess. I don't know if it is our water, or the air, or the altitudes, but ladies from the west who come to Ardeel often—very often—find themselves relieved of the burden."

"The burden?"

"Well ..."

"The altitude you say?"

"It could be ... well, anything. I don't know ... You've been eating the sweet round candies, have you?"

"Oh, Katty, do you constantly have to bring those up?"

"I just meant ... maybe it is the mountain air, or maybe a dietary issue."

"You can't be serious."

"It even happened to Princess Spaarvierlet last year," Amalina insisted with a gay smile. "She wasn't too upset. She said it freed her to do more of the things she enjoyed."

"It's a horrible thing," said Gillette. "Who would want to stop something so natural and necessary? How ridiculous it all is, Countess. No, I've never heard such a thing, and I've lived in mountains and eaten all kinds of sweets ... You people are so superstitious: tell me, is it some kind of curse you put on outsiders to punish them?—Oh, I'm sorry, I didn't mean to say it that way ..." Gillette returned to their two-handed grip and shook it. "But if it was a curse, I'd ask you'd lift it. I … I've never so wanted it to happen in my life, Katty. It would be a relief."

"A relief?" she said, not catching on.

"Because it would mean …"

Then Amalina caught on. Because, of course, her problem would just be a symptom of something else. Not her fault.

"But then you've done something …" Amalina didn't know how to proceed. She proceeded: "Someone here? Not your beau back home. Samuel, was it?"

Gillette shook her head. Not with shame but a general embarrassment.

"No, it's been too long for that, hasn't it?" said Amalina. "But, who?"

"Oh, dear Katty, please shut up," said Gillette, with a shaky, tearful smile. "It's too late."

They had arrived in the castle. Gillette broke free and fled to her room. Her servants stared at Amalina.

• • •

Pia's evaluation of the princesses had been spot-on: Aria didn't care for anyone's company. Neither did Margeta, for her own judgemental reasons. Isabeau was disappointed in everyone's universal annoyance and rejection of her (and was still more than a little miffed at losing all her jewelry). And Pia herself craved Amalina to the point of obsession; with Amalina's remoteness vexing her more.

The only mystery had been Gillette's upset. And to a degree it was now solved. But even knowing she had been intimate with the Count, this did not settle whether she was the one the Count had chosen. It was only a detail. There was no way to tell.

After dinner, the Count excused himself for the night. When he didn't pull Amalina aside, and more importantly, he didn't make away with any of the other princesses, Amalina followed his lead. She complained of headache and fatigue, fought off Pia's ministrations, and retired to her own room. Allowing enough time to pass, she took off her clothes, and clamped the bone in her mouth.

Amalina shivered as she moved from room to room, pushing gently against a curtain or a rug, making just enough room for her to pass through, and swerving to toast herself by the fireplaces. She wasn't certain where to visit first.

She came upon Anka and Pils who were mending fabric on a bench.

"So they are back," said Anka sullenly. "Kind of livens up the place again."

"Don't kid me, old goose," said Pils. "You don't like it. You enjoyed the quiet we were having."

"Well, that peace and calm does remind one of how it used to be, when it was just us and Master, doesn't it?"

"Not with this eerie army hanging around everywhere one turns."

"Well, never mind *them*," said Anka. "They're quiet enough."

"Not when they're drilling. And are you forgetting about all the others we used to have around? Poor Gavril, and Atrensil, and Reika, and Jeno?"

"Oh, how I wish I could forget; what that dragon made of them. Oh, why did you bring them up? What a pity. And we scrubbed the walls and floors for days. It makes my heart break. So never mind. I was just talking."

"Right. Never mind. But why did *he* spare *us*, eh? Out of everyone. That's what I can't understand."

"You're alive, so get over it. I can't imagine what calculations wind through that evil, wyrmish brain of brimstone, sulphur and dry chalk. I just meant, Pils, that with that foul creature out of the house, it had almost felt like *home* again. Didn't it? Don't ruin it for me. But, didn't it?"

Pils nodded. "And here you'd almost returned to your old self, my goose. Thinking too much on everything, as you always do, you've been a mess for moons. Unpleasant company, you must know. I was glad to see you back, so please don't let matters spoil you once more. But, tell me, what would our poor old departed master think of it, do you think—a good old fellow, he was—if he knew who was living here now?"

"He'd be partial to the princesses," Anka said with a winking tone.

"That he would," laughed Pils, rocking back on the bench. "Say, did you feel a breeze just now? Did a drape come loose again?"

Amalina moved out the opposite end of the room while Pils tried to locate the source of the draft.

• • •

Aria's servants were collected in the outer chamber of her suite. They were playing Scapone and making faces and flirting with each other, in a carefree way. Amalina brushed past them and wound from one room to the next, until she found Aria and the Count laid out naked on her bed.

The two lovers were looking deep into each other's eyes, breaking contact to glance down at one part of a body or another, to place a hand or a kiss or a nibble. They were both growling like animals. The Count was fitting into her in an agreeable way.

"They don't know a damned thing, do they?" Aria smiled a wicked smile.

"Not a whit, you naughty little cat," his mischievous grin wider than hers.

Amalina had felt a little detached having stumbled on them without warning, but the rhythm and intoxicating passion tempted one to stay to the conclusion. The two moved in interesting ways. Amalina left the room, all the same. Their lovemaking meant nothing toward marriage, or whether the Count had chosen her for transformation. Hadn't Amalina seen him do just the same with Lisbet Spaarvierlet? And that had not even resulted in a tepid correspondence by mail. And apparently Gillette had been with him, too.

Gillette might be surprised to find out about this dalliance, Amalina thought with snappy indignation. Amalina then reflected in a worldly way: *But she couldn't—and* shouldn't—*be too surprised.* She decided not to include her French friend in her discovery, but began to wonder if the Count hadn't managed to seduce them all.

• • •

Margeta had one fist balled against her cheek, while the other hand worked loudly through the beads of her rosary. She glared at the man kneeling before her.

"I did all I could, your highness," said the man.

"If you did all you could, then how do you explain her presence in this castle?"

The man didn't look up, but curled his head closer to the ground.

"Are you telling me God wanted her to be here? To challenge me? What? What was that sound you made just now? What did that mean?"

"Nothing, your highness."

"Tell me at once or I will have you whipped."

"I meant to say: It isn't just *her* anymore, your highness. There are three others, aren't there?"

"I didn't know about them before I left. And neither did you. So they have nothing to do with this conversation. The point is you were to stop the one I *did* know about from getting here."

"Yes, your highness. I did all I could."

"So you say."

"From the very beginning. I sabotaged her carriages and her horses. I stole valuables and money. I misled them and spread false rumors. Your highness, I did deeds I fear my soul must pay for, all in order to keep Princess Pia Lampeda from reaching her destination."

"Everything? You say everything?"

"Yes, your highness. Everything, your highness."

"Why do you think I summoned you here to this miserable rock of a country?"

"To aid you, your ladyship. As always. It was difficult to locate you, but I have come, your dutiful servant. Ever willing."

"Then you might consider doing the one thing you did not."

"Which is?"

"There is one crime you did not undertake."

"Your highness," he said with a tremble.

"And now," said Margeta, clacking through her beads even faster, "three more have been added to your duties: Aria Ecci, Gillette Arronde, and Isabeau DePense."

"Your highness."

As calm as if she were praying, Margeta concluded: "It is not my fault they lacked the good sense to leave when they had the chance. Count Tepsji will be mine. And if you think your job is cruel or difficult, perhaps you can find inspiration in that *my* reward will be to receive willfully the slime of an old man, all for the treacherous and life-risking purpose of breeding a brood of mongrels for him. And, of course, an interminable lifetime of choking down the bland, tiresome cuisine of these mountain folk."

He had nothing to say to that, but kept his head down. Amalina circled the scene but could not get a good look at his face. Margeta's assassin was dressed in the clothes of a footman and had a bald spot. It was difficult to picture a man with such a bald spot murdering someone.

What an evil woman, Amalina thought on the way out.

• • •

Isabeau was practicing whistling with a bored maid. "Mine just doesn't sound right," said Isabeau. "It's a matter of the lips," said the maid. "I can never do it right, no matter how hard I try," said Isabeau, "how do you do it, Grandine?" Isabeau studied the shape of the maid's lips as she whistled, and tried to get hers to look the same. "Oh, it makes no sense," fumed Isabeau. "Birds don't have lips. But perhaps one could infer they have a set of lips further back in their beaks, or in the throat. We must consult an *ornithologist*—who is an expert on birds, as you know. Oh, frustration! If I still can't whistle." "You might also be blowing too hard, milady," said the maid, patiently.

• • •

Pia was sewing a dress while sitting on her bed. She hummed and sang a pretty Italian song, the words not perfectly clear. Amalina could only watch and wait for a minute before she grew tired and moved on. Just as she was trying to fit herself through the curtains without fluttering them, Pia shot forward in a violent movement. She had tackled a large, well-packed goose-feather pillow. She assaulted it with kisses, wrapping her arms and legs around it. She kissed and kissed and kissed as she practiced, making yummy sounds.

Her two maids in the corner laughed.

"Why couldn't we have brought Gege with us?" sighed Pia, in a frustrated non sequitur, detaching herself from the pillow. Gege was one of her family's dogs.

• • •

Princess Gillette's servants were removed from her inner quarters, just as Aria's had been. But they didn't seem as carefree as Aria's. They wore uneasy looks, even if, as if to cheer them, one maid played a lackluster flute. Whether this was their natural attitude was impossible to tell. Gillette was a difficult princess and might oppress them, even in her off-hours and they left to their own devices. But the similarity of their physical arrangements to that of Aria's caused Amalina to immediately suspect that the Count had somehow concluded his affair with Aria, and hurried straight to Gillette.

The expansive naked back inside Gillette's bedroom confirmed Amalina's suspicions. Until her own body registered a new surprise; a visceral surprise before the truth was fully understood: Gillette was retreating toward the bed, her eyes troubled, her lips slack with worry. The towering body that advanced slowly, confidently on her, had a more fleshy pinkish skin; and emanated an animal, musky smell; and was capped by thick, wiry black hair which stood like a great dark cloud over its head.

Marosh!

Amalina made a noise of surprise in the back of her throat.

They both turned to the empty doorway.

"What was that?"

"Nevermind. Just the wind," said Zsolt Marosh, closing on her again.

"I'm not sure," said Gillette. "I really don't think—"

"I don't know what you're saying," said Marosh, his giant hands coming up to her shoulders.

"No," she said, finding the right language. Her French accent made the words sound incongruously sweet: "This is wrong. I don't want it anymore. I'm already in trouble and everyone will find out."

"Let them find out," said Marosh. "You are beautiful, and I love you. And there is nothing wrong with that. I was once a great baron. My family line had kings. But I love you."

"I don't think that is so."

"From the moment I saw you, my blossom ..."

"Please no. Not until I know—"

"There's never enough time for us!" he snarled. "I won't be denied. Not even by you!"

Gillette had brought her arms up across her chest, her hands protectively at her neck, but Zsolt Marosh tore her dress open with an ease that suggested practice. The top came down and the sleeves trapped her arms at her elbows. His massive right paw was already at her breast.

Amalina cried out, the bone coming loose in her mouth. Her body fluttered into visibility. Marosh took the cry as Gillette's and violently covered the lower half of her face with his other hand.

Amalina couldn't get her mind together. Outrage and fear broke this way and that, and she found herself grasping toward the curtains. She had to get out of the room. But because there was no door—just the damned curtains!—with no solidity or handle, and with her invisible hands giving her no spatial relationship, she pawed and scrambled at the fabric, managing to catch and twist herself in it. And she fell back into the room. She raised herself onto her feet, breathing heavy, feeling another cry of frustration, her lips pulling back, her jaw working back and forth, grinding and rolling the bone between her teeth. The bone fell out of her mouth.

Marosh had turned his head at the sound of the pummeled curtains. Now he saw Amalina, half crouched, completely nude, staring at him.

"What?"

The bone was back between her teeth. She jumped from the doorway as he fully faced the phantom image. His eyes were wide with confusion. Gillette stifled a cry of pain, teeth biting her lower lip, as he gripped her wrist to keep her with him. He scanned the room, this way and that, in a sudden fever, as his other hand went for the hilt of his sword.

"The mountain goat?"

Amalina wished she hadn't left the doorway. She could have just pushed her way through. *You idiot!* she told herself. But then she spotted something on his belt, as he half-drew his sword, which became her new focus.

"What is it?" Gillette cried.

"The mountain goat. No."

"What's the matter?"

"Nothing! Get in the bed." He threw her onto the mattress, which blew out the sides of the heavy fur blankets when she landed. Seeing her vulnerable there, he could not help but bring a knee onto the bed, and lean his great body over her. "Keep quiet."

Amalina darted at his back. She grabbed the handle of the large bell hung on his belt, and pulled it free from the hook. Her other hand yanked out the wad of cloth that held down the clapper. She shook the bell hard and fast.

. . .

A thunderclap and the Count was in the room, the curtains torn inward as if they were made of light tissue. Amalina hadn't yet gotten to the third shake of the bell. Perhaps the Count's speed was because the threat of the Strange Man had him vigilant and ready to respond. He was not prepared for the scene he found himself in. Amalina let the bell fall.

"Master! Master!" Marosh wailed as he threw himself on the ground.

The Count's eyes clicked back and forth between Marosh and Gillette, who was in the bed with the front of her dress torn wide open. She didn't cover herself, but just stared at the Count with a slack jaw. Then tears appeared. Then the tears began to fall down her cheeks. Still, she did not move.

It took Amalina a second to remember that she was invisible. She stepped back into the corner of the room, trying to hold her breath, champing down on the bone as hard as she could.

"What are you doing to my guest?" the Count said acidly, only a corner of his mouth registering some amusement. His fingers hesitated at stroking his mustache. "What are you up to, General Marosh?"

"I am in love, your highness," he wailed again. "I could not help—"

"Be quiet. Of course you could. Well, well. And here I thought what you did to your men was to show respect for me, when it was to cut down your own competition."

"No!"

"No?"

"No, sir! No, my master!" Marosh pounded the floor with his great fists. He pulled a knife and whittled some more X's on his forehead, sending down a flurry of blood.

"There's no need for that," said the Count.

"It was love, oh Great King."

"Love ... No love for *me*."

Marosh whittled again.

"I said to stop that. You will frighten my guest." But Gillette was well forgotten. Her face was a puddle overrunning to her breasts. But she made no sound. At least none that exceeded the noise of Marosh. "These ladies were *my* guests, you will remember."

"I ask you to forgive me, Master. Have pity on me, High Lord. Show me mercy, Knight of Knights," groveled Marosh. "It was weakness, of course. But also love. True love."

"Aren't you a little old for her?" said the Count, with a glimmer of curiosity.

"Mercy, my liege. Mercy, Emperor of the World."

"Why did you do this to me?"

"Love alone. Unconquerable love. I swear, Master."

"And you thought I wouldn't notice what you were up to? You thought I would not care?"

"I thought ..."

"What did you think, General?"

"I didn't think you could possibly have all of them for yourself."

This brought on a fit of indecent giggles. The Count covered his mouth. His eyes were alight with anger and mischief and delight. The fire Amalina had seen in them on occasion had ignited.

"Please, my Highest of High," began Marosh, more humbly now. "I delivered my army and munitions to your service. I have always cherished no one but you. I have sacrificed everything for you."

"And I think one more sacrifice is in order. Don't you, General?"

"But I command the men, Master. They came here at my will. If you kill me, I do not know what will happen to you."

"Are you joking?"

"They've served me, Zsolt Marosh, and the Marosh family, their whole lives ... I ... Without me ... I just don't know. They might leave."

"And what do I care?"

"These men and I, we keep you safe. And alive."

"Nothing is safe or alive without my allowing it," said the Count, flippantly.

"You say this, even while that *Man* remains a threat to you."

"And what do you and your army think you can do about him?" the Count sneered over the General. "Protect *me*? You think much too much of yourselves. It's as if you don't understand one thing about us."

Marosh sat up on his knees and looked back toward Gillette. Then he looked around the room, as if searching for something. Amalina swallowed hard when his eyes traced through her. Then he saw Gillette's servants crowded in the doorway looking shocked and upset and entirely helpless.

He jumped to his feet. He pumped up his great hairy chest toward the Count, then grabbed Gillette's ankle. The Count stood there silently, watchful and amused.

"Out!" Marosh roared. "Out! Get out! Leave this room! Go away! Out, Princess! Go! All of you! Take your princess away! Go, before I cut off your heads!"

His face was bloody and horrific, and he bowled the princess right through the door and into her servants. They grabbed her and retreated, their faces masks of fright and terror. "Leave!"

• • •

"Now you're sending my guests away?" asked the Count, amused but puzzled.

Zsolt Marosh rounded on his Master, standing full up to him, his beard dripping blood as it shook. He punched a finger at the Count. "Tell me," he said, his voice hoarse. "Tell me about you two. Tell me something about your power. I came to you a willing servant, a loyal general, and you have told me *nothing*."

The Count twiddled his mustache. "You came to me. I did not come to you. As I consider it, General, I owe you no explanations." He grinned, mockingly. "What do you wish to know?"

"There are more like you. You have the power to turn the living into entities such as you are. To give us your power."

"Who told you? Well, I suppose it's no matter. So it is. If I wanted to do such a thing."

"I have sworn my life to protect you. I, Zsolt Marosh, the greatest warrior and hunter this land has ever seen. Yet you sneer at me because I am nothing before your greatest enemy. Because I and my army could not match him. But, my king, you can give me the power to match him."

The Count twirled the end of his mustache, his smile frozen, then curdling.

"If you were to transform me, you would have nothing to fear from that man, or any enemy ever again. And I could transfer that power to this army of mine. So that we could lay waste to any army. The world would never have witnessed a king such as yourself, atop an army such as my own."

"Yes," said the Count, dully. "Yessss, they are still *your* army, aren't they?"

Marosh blinked. But he saw what the Count was getting at. He hurried out: "There could be another round of tests. To prove positive their absolute loyalty."

"Sounds a little rich to me, coming from you."

"Or, or, or," stammered Marosh, as he blinked some more. "It doesn't have to be the whole army. Just me. You can trust me, after all. The Marosh devotion to Ardeel is legendary—"

"That's at a bit of an end, I think."

"No, Master. Grant me this boon, and with all my power I will guarantee their service and keep them in line. And I will ensure your peace of mind against all future threats, as well as the current threat we stand under. I swear I would sacrifice myself for your continuance, if it should come to it, if you elevate me now."

Zsolt Marosh was massive and powerfully built for a man even half his age. But somehow the air around him seemed to be shrinking, and he, too, was shrinking. He was no longer panting. The blood was no longer pouring, but had solidified into a glistening red crust on his face. His eyes looked like egg-sized white holes in the red, with blue and desperate little dots floating inside them.

"I should give *you* my power, General?" the Count laughed, but his smile was venomous. "When you've already set my hand to wipe your name from history?"

Marosh looked around the room again. "Wait, Master. That girl. Amalina."

"Not her, too, General."

"Wait. There's something *about* her ..."

"I find that's true of Ms. Dalca almost every day," said the Count. Then Marosh did not have a head.

34

The Loyal Man

The following day was so tumultuous and eventful that, come the night, Amalina was dumbstruck when the Count came to wake her. "Get up. It's time. Can you guess who it is?"

I hope not, she thought dismally. *Oh, please, I hope not.*

But as he handed her her gold dress, and then when she was in it and they went to retrieve the dull gray cup (he had forgotten to bring it to her room), Amalina's confidence that she knew *exactly* who it was lent each new step an extra pound of dread. *Don't let it be* her.

But how could it not be? The tumult and events had already shown who it was.

. . .

The chaos following Marosh's death—or, more exactly, following Gillette and her servant's flight from her bedroom, which caused a minor uproar requiring containment—had occupied the Count long enough for Amalina to escape and return to her own room, spit out the bone, embarrass Aklan, and then dress before the Count came for her.

She saw the flecks of Marosh's blood on her arm and wiped them on the back of her skirt. The Count stared at her.

"Who is this?" he asked, pointing to Aklan.

"My new servant, remember?"

"Yes. Leave."

Aklan left.

"What do you know of Marosh and the princesses?"

"Marosh?" Amalina asked innocently.

"Already you are blushing and your heart is beating like a drum. Tell me."

"Gillette."

"You knew?"

Amalina thrust out her jaw. "I just found out tonight. She didn't tell me, sir. But I figured it out. She intimated she thought she was pregnant. And I saw the General near her rooms."

"Yes, *yesss*, I see."

"And you've found out? Did she tell you, sir?"

"Did the hypocritical cad touch any of my other guests?"

"Not that I know of."

His eyes narrowed. He was trying to read her, but she was telling the truth. There was nothing to worry about unless she started lying again.

"Nobody has said anything."

"You?" the Count asked.

"Me, what?"

"Did he?"

"Never, sir."

"He told me there was something about you."

"What about me?"

"I thought you might know what he was talking about."

"I can't figure, sir. Really."

"You're not exactly telling me the truth now. Are you?"

"You're worrying me, sir. That's all, never mind. What *could* he mean?"

"Well, now we'll never know," said the Count, turning to leave the room.

"Has something happened, sir?"

"Go to little Lady Gillette. Tell her she is not pregnant. Tell her she is in no trouble with me or anyone else. Tell her that I am a discreet man from a discreet family, and she need not fear that I will inform her parents, or that I have forsaken her. And then see to the rest of the ladies after that. Find out if they've enjoyed the sheets with my general. While I recruit his replacement."

. . .

Besides Gillette and her people, nobody in the castle knew what had happened in the night. And even Gillette and her people did not know what ultimately befell Marosh in the confrontation, though an understanding of chivalric honor dictated the results. Gillette was assigned a new room and the other ladies were told that she wasn't feeling well—perhaps an illness caught from her maid Coterie-Ann—and she was imposing on herself a kind of quarantine; to which she submitted gladly. She didn't talk much to Amalina, but did take comfort in Amalina's assuring her again that she was free of child. "Poor Samuel," sighed Princess Gillette, "the charm of Ardeel and my amorous nature proved too great."

Amalina didn't bother to investigate the others regarding Zsolt Marosh, assuming the general had been telling the truth about his love for Gillette. Instead she made her way through them trying to determine which one the Count had settled on while she had been away. They probably wondered why Amalina had suddenly become chatty again, but she excused herself by saying she wanted to make up for lost time, having gone to visit her parents.

An excuse which, in the end, seemed too wordy and rustled up more suspicious looks.

Amalina was also on watch for Margeta's minion with the bald patch.

"I heard you received a visitor yesterday, Princess Margeta," said Amalina.

"A visitor? No."

"Someone came to the gates and identified themselves as one of your house."

Margeta put on a frown. "Not a visitor. A servant. Nothing more."

When Amalina continued to ask questions, Margeta rankled. "I don't see why it is so interesting to you, Princess Katarina. He was a personal servant who was too ill to travel when I came here. Then came when he could."

"Such a devoted servant."

"But it is staffing business and you shouldn't waste your time on it. Do your people always inform you on everyone's little comings and goings? I'd think it was a tremendous waste of my spirit."

"Why are you getting so touchy?" asked Aria with a look, sensing a nerve had been struck.

"It's their job to look after these things, but not for our dear friend Princess Katarina."

"What was your man sick from?" Isabeau wondered. "I hope it isn't what's going around. First Coterie-Ann, then Gillette."

Amalina saw the opening: "Yes, maybe he should be isolated. Just for safety's sake. Until we know he is fully recovered. Wouldn't want you getting sick, Princess Margeta."

"Oh, no, we wouldn't want that," said Aria sarcastically.

"Just to be sure," insisted Amalina.

Margeta studied them all irritably. With a sniff she said: "Already has. Couldn't get any more isolated from us. I sent him away, of course. A weak man, in body and spirit. Couldn't control himself to come running after me. Dismissed him from our family service, and good riddance."

Amalina didn't bother to embarrass Margeta by telling her nobody has left the castle since last night. The man was still inside, and planning to act against Margeta's rivals. But Amalina sensed if she became too inquisitive, too intrusive into the lady's affairs, she might also be targeted.

• • •

The assassin wasn't among Margeta's servants. The ones Amalina could find. She toured the castle and enlisted the aid of Pils and Anka to look for a man with dark hair and a large bald spot on the back of his head. Any other specifics, like features, build, height, mustaches or beard, etc., Amalina could not say, but it was someone who had newly arrived, so having features they had not seen before. Glad for the diversion, they spread out and combed through the other lady princesses' servants and Marosh's support staff. Besides two near misses—men who had black hair and were wearing hats, which Pils then tricked them into removing—the bald man eluded them.

"The only thing left to search are soldiers," said Anka. "And I'm not asking them to take off nothing. Not enough curiosity in the world for that."

Of course, thought Amalina, *the soldiers!*

. . .

Amalina found the Count in his room staring at a wall.

"Too soon, Mouse," he said. "It will be tonight, when I am at my strongest. Don't worry, just a few hours to go. Still can't believe that surprise about Marosh ..."

Amalina told him about Margeta and her assassin. His eyes immediately lit up and he sat forward, pulling on his mustache. "How do you know this?"

"I overheard them talking."

"How?"

"I was wandering around last night. These carpets really don't keep things private, sir."

"If I planned to live here my whole life, I'd have them replaced," he said. "But for now they have allowed us to learn something quite intriguing. Old Pious Margeta out to kill. Hm-hmmmm. Yessss. Very interesting indeed."

"You ... You don't care?"

"Haven't I just expressed my interest and enchantment?"

"'Interest and enchantment?'"

"Is something wrong, Ms. Dalca?"

"She has a cutthroat in this castle, with orders to kill the other princesses. How are you not upset about this?"

"Upset about what?"

"She intends to have your bride murdered." *Unless Margeta was the one he has chosen*, it occurred to Amalina.

"But that won't happen," he said, looking irritated that his reverie was inconsiderately interrupted. "Because I am here and I would never allow such a thing."

"You can't be everywhere at once, sir. While we're talking, he could already be at work. We have to find him and stop him."

"But you must admire her," said the Count. "I always suspect everyone, but hadn't seen it in Margeta. Such bloodthirstiness is a prime attribute for a noblewoman. She is a realist, where I thought Isabeau was the only one with open eyes. You must admit that, Ms. Dalca."

Does he favor Isabeau, then? she wondered.

"I can't find him anywhere," said Amalina. "He hasn't left the castle. He could be hiding among Marosh's soldiers. They wear their masks and hoods and it would be very easy."

"I should have gone to sleep," groused the Count. "You're making the day very long."

"I'm sorry, sir."

He settled his chin in his hand and closed his eyes.

"Sir?"

"Of course," he said, opening his big eyes all the way, a smile exposing all his teeth. "Yes. *Yesss.* Ms. Dalca, you've given me a solution. Very good. There *is* something about you, isn't there? I might have acted prematurely, but you have given me the perfect final test."

. . .

Suddenly there was a reviewing stand in the great hall. On a small dais was the modest thronal chair. Flanking that were dinner chairs and benches fanning out on either side. With a grave look which struck Amalina as overly theatrical, the Count insisted all the Lady Princesses were to come and sit in review. They chose their dinner chairs and sat. Aria slumped into hers, though her eyes looked about the room with interest. Margeta, annoyed, flipped through her beads. Isabeau read a Russian primer while waiting for things to start. And Gillette sat at the very end, a veil over her head and a maidservant holding her hand, looking as if she'd really rather lie down.

Pia held Amalina's hand and they sat closest the throne.

The Count marched or stood as straight and tall as a statue, alternately, as fitted the moment. "My dear guests and Lady Princesses. So lovely you are, sitting there. But I must now reveal a darker side of life in Ardeel. For it is just that I do so. I would never hide anything from you, but have you understand it as the remarkable—and formidable—women you are. Well, let me tell you: I, as a nobleman of Ardeel, have many enemies. You might have heard of a small incident last year, which frightened away another friend of Mouse—um, er—Lady Katarina. Well, these dangers arise from time to time. And that is life, is it not, my ladies?

"At this moment I find I must deal with the latest threat. An assassin has been introduced into this castle. My spies assure me this is true. And far from hiding this fact from you, I will now show you something a bit strong—but it is true Ardeelian justice. You will witness how well I hold in my hands your safety, and how much I control the populace. Would you like to witness an execution?"

The ladies became very eager. Execution was a popular entertainment of the day, even if, in the end, they couldn't bear to look. And they stuffed fingers in their ears. And they might have nightmares that evening. It was *still* a popular entertainment. Even now, Gillette folded her feet back onto her chair, as if to recoil. And Pia gripped Amalina's hand to breaking. And Margeta, of course, did not break her placid glower, but a sweat began to build on her upper lip. Only Aria rubbed her hands and narrowed her eyes in keen excitement.

"Nobody is afraid of a little bloodletting? A little carnage? Very good. This is a tough but fair land, let it be known. Let it be said." The Count withdrew to his chair. Before he sat down, he said: "On the orders of my steady right hand man, General Marosh, who can not be here at the moment, every party in this castle has been taken into custody. This assassin, who has infiltrated the castle and would have himself invisible, will now be exposed and dealt with. First, the exposure."

To the gasps of the princesses, the various servants of the lady princesses who were not already attending their charge were marched into the hall. Some looked fearful, half-bent, while others stood very plainly, just another act of humiliation in their mistress' service.

"Why, Jean-Jean," said Isabeau, confused, "what are you doing there?"

"This must be a thorough examination, I am afraid," said the Count. "Do accept my apology, as far as it goes."

Margeta's upper lip was drenched, so that it looked shiny and as if her nose might be running. "What are you doing, Count Tepsji? These are our people."

"Of course," he smiled, looking at her keenly. "But, as I said, it is to be a thorough examination. Now, all of you ladies, look upon your servants. Are they all present? Is there anyone you don't recognize, or does one not belong?"

Margeta fanned her face, her eyes looked dead. She glanced once at Amalina, but it was more of guilt than of accusation.

The servants were all present and accounted for, with no extras. The Count saw with a discreet sidelong glance that Amalina did not signal the assassin was among them. The servants were excused from the room.

The next group belonged to Marosh. They looked more upset than frightened. They were used to seeing their own master—General Marosh—every day. Since they hadn't seen him in hours, this made them anxious and grumpy. They stared blankly back at the petty little princesses, some with contemptuous smirks. But the assassin wasn't hiding among them.

"You might have learned of the severity of General Marosh, and what he demanded of those who served him—the many soldiers of this army that protect you and this castle. I will confirm now that the rumors are true. And you will witness the intense loyalty and will of the Ardeelian man, when we now move to my own personnel. As Marosh commands, begin!"

In groups of twenty, soldiers (stripped of weapons) marched in lockstep into the hall, turned to the reviewing stand, and then, upon the word, removed their helmets and hoods. The princesses said nothing, but took in the scar-etched faces, some looking decorated, but most sadly disfigured. Some still had eyebrows. Some had lost an eye, or the end of a nose, or a lip or two. Some still tried to grow a mustache or beard. Many had little tufts and patches of whiskers between raw and unhealing or scarred-over flesh.

The Count's face was unusually neutral as his eyes flicked over everyone in the room. But Amalina assumed he was gathering, for later use, practical information. And some entertainment.

They went through several rounds this way. Until, the hoods coming off, one stark white blemishless face was revealed in the menagerie of horror.

"What is this!" The Count said, coming up in his chair.

The man dropped to his knee, and in a high voice declared that he'd taken "the third option."

"What is the third option?"

The man explained, to the princesses' distraction.

"You outdid Marosh, I should think," said the Count, looking suspiciously at the immaculate soldier. "Drastic step. What is your name?"

"Vezel."

"Ah, yes. Vezel Umalasju."

Vezel's eyes grew large and he faltered.

"Your parents should be proud, though I fear there will be some disappointment considering lineage and descendants. Stand aside. Let us continue."

Two more rounds. Then when the last group came to ranks, and removed their hoods, another white face. This one with a thin mustache. Amalina couldn't help but look to Margeta. Margeta's expression had hardened to wood, but the color ran out.

"You there, explain yourself," said the Count. "The third option?"

The man understood he was being addressed, but he didn't seem to know what was being said. He probably didn't dare try to speak—if he even could speak the language—and give away his accent. His eyes found Margeta. Then he took in all the burned faces surrounding him. When he saw the only other clear face dressed in armor—Vezel—he pointed to him, and then at himself. He was strangely overlooking that Vezel's head had the gouged X on his forehead. A difference which he was slowly processing as his eyes clicked back and forth.

"Yes. *Yesss*, the third option." The Count nodded. "Prove it."

Margeta's assassin flung himself flat-out toward the dais. A long blade was in his hand, and it was directed at Pia Lampeda. She screamed, but the Count was already there and cracked the knife out of his hand with a chop. The Count had moved with the speed of a black blur, which astonished those who weren't ready for it. They blinked and shook their head, as if their own minds and senses were at fault for what they'd missed. The Count picked up on this and hung back. He kicked the assassin a great blow at the hip, sending him skittering across the hall.

The assassin did not hesistate again. Using the momentum as he slid, he walked his feet up onto the floor and then jumped headlong toward the nearest exit. The other soldiers lunged for him. He struggled with the curtain and could not find its parting. Amalina sympathized, though she saw the incriminating bald spot from across the room. Three soldiers took hold of him.

"All right, I believe we have found our man," said the Count. At swordpoint the assassin was kept kneeling at the back of the room, next to Vezel, as the rest of the army revealed their tragic faces.

Then the assassin was brought forward to the center of the room. Margeta began to rumble with belches, she clicked her beads harder. The Count walked next to her, then turned his back on her as if to screen her from everyone else.

"This assassin was here to kill me," said the Count, ignoring the bold facts of minutes before, where the knife had been aimed at Pia. "Sent here by enemies far away, too cowardly to come face me on their own. But, as always, their attempt has failed—*they* have failed. It is always the way. And now you will see how treachery in my home is dealt with. And know, by this what you are witness to is my commitment to your safety and health while in my trust."

The Count stepped forward and took a sword in hand.

"Oh, no," said Pia, hugging herself to Amalina and shutting her eyes.

"You cannot watch?" said the Count, inquisitively.

"I feel sorry," said Pia.

"There is nothing to feel sorry for. In a minute he will be paying an eternal penance for what he hoped to accomplish here. It is just."

Pia nodded.

"You are bothered by the sight of blood?" he now said, turning fully upon Margeta. "I see your hands shake as you loudly rattle your beads."

"I pray for his everlasting soul, however the judgement placed upon him."

He lingered over her. She stared up into his eyes, then. Almost defying him. He nodded and went to the bowed assassin. With one last address to them he said: "I do this for you, my brave princesses, who have come to show your friendship to my niece, and your adventurous nature to visit this great, if untamed land—"

"Oh, no," said Pia again, bringing up a hand to shield her eye. The Count noted this again.

"… and your *courage* in the face of a common enemy."

The Count chopped the man with a blow that severed him in half, starting at the left side of his head and traveling all the way down to his groin. The armor parted like it was an illusion. Blood and organs and entrails blasted onto the floor.

. . .

"Now L.P. Margeta la Brichese knows the consequences," said the Count to Amalina later, after the ladies begged, one after the other, to return to their private rooms to rest following such an excitement. "Won't happen again."

"You aren't going to punish her?"

"I will reward her," said the Count. "But I have to be subtle, so as not to encourage the others. But our Margeta is a *daring* one. That she is."

"I don't believe it," said Amalina, then stuck on: "Sir."

"Ah! And who else to reward but the extraordinary Vezel Umalasju. Somewhat inferior stock, but he has shown nicely. I will reward his family by replacing Marosh's name with theirs in the history books. His line will become magnificent."

"I don't think he will have much of a line," said Amalina.

"I'll see to it," said the Count, vaguely. Then he called for Vezel. "Vezel, lad, by the path you've chosen, you have shown yourself above all the others. General Marosh wishes to reward you personally. Come."

The two walked to an inner chamber of the Count's apartments. Vezel's face was taut with some kind of nervousness. Since Amalina couldn't tell which kind, and she was intrigued by his bright young face, she followed along with the two.

Marosh's body sat up in a chair with a bloody stump in place of his head. Vezel Umalasju drew back reflexively, defensively, but then checked that action and stared.

"He is giving you his command, Vezel," said the Count. "The General's great big head made a very interesting decision, considering the raw consequences. I hope you aren't one to snatch crumbs from your master's table without asking first."

"And I should never ask for them," Vezel said through lips that barely moved. "I would never think to."

The Count stroked his mustache. "I am curious to see how you disappoint me."

"Never, sir."

"Don't you want to bow to me or something?"

Vezel dropped to his knee and bowed his head.

"You military types are interesting."

. . .

Returning to her room, Amalina found Pia and Aklan inside. Pia's white skin was looking rather greenish, and she had the bottom of her face cupped over with her hands. Aklan was swinging his arms this way and that, as if he was holding a sword.

Pia flew to Amalina and wrapped her in her arms.

"It was terrible," Pia shook, "and magnificent."

"Magnificent?"

"One blow!" cried Aklan. "I've never seen such a thing. Our headsman sometimes takes five chops to get through the neck. Your uncle took him apart like a chicken with *one blow!*"

"You saw?"

"The whole thing! Moves like lightning, strikes like the sword of Heaven."

"He has the power of Heaven, it is so," Pia swooned. "He is ..." she struggled for the right word. "... *Magnificent.*"

"All right, that's enough," said Amalina. She felt herself shaking. A delayed reaction to the execution perhaps, or an immediate response to the sycophantic rejoicing to the butchery. "That's just enough."

Pia pulled away and Aklan stopped in mid whack at an invisible assassin.

"You both are acting like a couple of fools," she said, "because he cut a man in two."

"I've never seen it done," said Aklan, defensively.

"He was protecting us."

"That may be true," Amalina admitted. "But is it a reason to fall in love with that thing?"

"That thing?"

"Are you in love with him, Pia? Has he seduced you?"

"I ... I ... No." She hid her face. "What do you mean? I love *you*, Katarina."

"You're being seduced. All of you are being seduced. And I keep telling you you have to leave. You have to go home. Get as far away from this place as you can."

"But why, Katty? I love you."

Amalina pushed her hands aside.

"That's just great, dear Pia. I can visit you in Rome. But leave. Because you are in danger. Every one of you are in danger. And maybe *Uncle* can protect you from assassins, but that's the least of your worries. Let me tell you, Count Tepsji is *not* what you think he is. He is no man at all. You saw what he did. You saw how fast he moved—"

"Yes," both said.

"—Well is that something a human could possibly do? No. No, that man is no man but a creature. An awful hideous creature."

"But he's your uncle."

Amalina swore and then told them everything. What monstrous being he was, and the sacrifices he requires to sustain his power; his two-century rule over the land of Ardeel, and his desire to spread out over the rest of the world; how he conscripted her into his service; and how he intends to convert the princess of his choice into a being just like him.

"Are you all right?" asked Pia, trying to encircle Amalina with a comforting embrace. "I think the execution was too much for you."

"You don't believe me! You don't believe what you saw with your eyes?"

"He's just powerful," said Aklan.

"It's impossible," Pia joined in, but finding a different subject: "I can't believe you are not a Countess, as you've sworn to me."

"Let's not think of that now!" Amalina pulled the bone out of her pocket. "How about this? What if I told you that this was given to me by one of these creatures? And it gives me the power to turn invisible. Does that sound impossible to you?"

They both nodded.

"Good." Amalina bit down on the bone.

"*Mon Dieu!*"

Amalina paraded around a bit, flinging unseen arms and legs in the air as her empty dress pirhouetted around the room between them. Then she spit the bone into her hand.

"You ... you used that thing before," said Aklan. "I thought you had just snuck back into the room and I didn't see. But why doesn't it work on the dress?"

"The point is: what I said about this bone, you thought it was impossible." She bit on the bone again, then took it out, then put it in, then took it out. "But I was telling you the truth. And everything I've told you about Count Tepsji is also true. Will you believe me now?"

Their expressions were remarkable.

For the lady princess, it was as if her world were a gorgeous cake and someone had turned it upside down, set it on a table, and shook it hard.

For Aklan it was as if someone had just confirmed that the world is *just* the way he wanted it to be.

"But is he really as *bad* as you say?" said Pia, after awhile.

Oh, no, thought Amalina.

• • •

"Right this way," said the Count. "Just through here, Mouse. Now we've gone over everything. You know what to do. You don't even have to open your eyes if you don't want to. Although, you *can* if you want. But you know how I feel on the subject. Let's just get it right this time, so we don't have to do this again."

Please don't be who I think it is, thought Amalina. *Please don't be who I think it is. Please don't be who I think it is.*

"I had better not have to do this again," he grumbled lightly. "I have taken everything into consideration. Not just what the lady from the falls told me, but every detail. Because one must be scientific and systematic about these things. Not just the methods alone, and the hour of the day alone, and the phase of the moon alone, and the astrological positions and signs alone, but altogether. Discounting nothing that is absolutely crucial; including the makeup of the woman."

It can't be her, thought Amalina. *It don't want it to be her. Please, no.*

"Have you guessed who it is yet?" said the Count. "I don't want to say. And please don't tell me. But let's get to it. I just have to open this ... Where is the parting in this curtain? ... What a pain these drapes are ... I am coming to you, my love, here we come ..."

Please don't let it be Pia. Please don't let it be Pia. Please don't let it be Pia.

She tried to close her eyes.

"Oh!"

35

A Dreadful Thing

The room was a solid gray haze, but Pia Lampeda's red hair was visible through the mist, cut off only at the rim of what would turn out to be an ornate tub. Someone had lugged the heavy, intricately carved marble tub from the high castle. Or perhaps the former owner of the Kyrgil castle shared the Count's taste in bath materials and steamy ambience.

"Hello, Katty," said Pia.

"Nevermind her," said the Count. "She's just here to attend; and only *perhaps* observe—if she's feeling adventurous."

"Does she know?" said Amalina.

"Your eyes are *open*," observed the Count with approval, slyly winking at Amalina.

"Pia, do you know what is happening here?" she asked the princess directly.

"Let's not spoil the mood, Mouse."

"I ..." began Pia, sitting up in the tub. "Of course I do. Don't I?"

"Yes, you do, Princess Lampeda," the Count assured her. "I have explained it all. Quite at length. And I believe you were very excited to receive this gift."

"Yes."

"So go to the corner, Ms. Dalc—uh, er—Mouse. As we've rehearsed. There you are."

"I just want to make sure she understands *everything*."

"She is a grown woman," said the Count.

"Yes," said Pia, sounding wounded by Amalina's doubt.

"She knows through experience ... what happens to one ... when the body changes," said the Count, soothingly. Almost a chanting rhythm. "Yes. When the body goes through its unceasing changes. Yes. *Yesss*. And when the body alters against your will, isn't that dreadful? Isn't it appalling? Unbearable? Wouldn't you want to prevent it?"

"Yes," said Pia, her hand moving as if it were washing her hair. Tendrils of steam rose from the water; caressed her arms and body; up over her eyes. "Better to resist."

"And this is the way to resist the impulsions of the body," answered the Count. "To punish it for its misbehavior. To gain dominion over its willful and unruly organs, to wrest stubborn limbs and harness disobedient cells; to unleash the power inside."

"Yessss."

"*Yesssssss.*"

"Yessssssssssssssss."

They sounded like snakes. Amalina watched as the Count's black shape moved through the gray, a bubble in fresh milk, slipping from one side of the tub to the other.

"This is the beginning of new life. This is the transition to superior being. This is the summiting of existence."

The Count was suddenly at Amalina's side, his cloak and shirt off. He had opened a slit in his wrist which he held over the dull gray cup. A black-red fluid fell out of him. Amalina thought it would be heavy—just as she had last time—and tried to resist the imagined weight. Her arms, encountering the insubstantial, shoved upward, flinging the first gout up into the Count's face and over his chest. He took her hand and crushed it against the side of the cup, and centered it under the flow. "There!" he hissed quietly to Amalina, "you incompetent! Use your eyes, damn you. Would it hurt you so much?"

"They *are* open."

"Wha...?" said Pia groggily.

While the Count filled the cup, he extended himself toward Pia, holding out his other hand to stroke her cheek. "Together we ascend the highest tower, and surpass the pinnacle set by nature."

"Yes."

"*Yessss.*"

"Yessssssss."

"Aren't you supposed to bleed her first?" whispered Amalina.

"Already done," the Count mouthed, eyes flashing.

Amalina leaned forward on her toes and saw that the surface of the water had gone from gray-silver to crimson-black. Pia's head was laid back against the rim of the tub, facing the ceiling. The wounds must have been below the waterline. How he'd done it, Amalina couldn't guess. Now out of his jacket and shirt, the Count was a creamy white smoothness that matched the marble surrounding Pia, holding her blood.

"You did it too soon," Amalina whispered, lifting up the cup, imagining it clotting all too quickly before she was ready.

"Better than too late or too fast," he whispered.

"Katty, are you there?" said Pia.

"Together we vault above the clouds," intoned the Count. "Together we swim with the stars and merge with the elements of the universe to make them our playthings."

Pia sighed, "Yes."

"*Yessss.*"

"Yesssssss."

The Count moved behind her and encircled her with his arms. "This is the end of tears."

"Oh, yesssssssss."

Then he slipped like a snake over her shoulder and into the water, sliding in soundlessly. He was under for half a minute. Pia's body turned, not as if she were moving but as if being manipulated from below, at the waist, until her lower torso, then shoulder, then neck, then head turned and flopped over. And then she slid into the tub, just as the Count rose noiselessly but dripping and glistening from the end where her feet should have been. As he rose, Amalina saw a shapely pale leg in one of his hands. When he stood to his full height, and still grew ever taller, he pulled Pia out of the water, dangling her by her ankle. Blood still seeped from a number of slashes in her skin, the slick of blood and water painting her skin red.

Pia's left leg stuck out awkwardly from her center, falling forward and outward, spreading herself open mindlessly. The Count shook her up and down, and pressed her body to him with his free arm, squeezing her. He retrieved her wild leg and let go of the other and repeated the massaging action. It began to sound sticky and plicky as he manipulated her, with the tinkling of the dripping water lessening as time continued. Though the haze cleared some, the room was still gray; interrupted only by the dull white tub, the count's pallid skin smeared here and there with swipes of crimson, and Pia's red-sheathed form, ending in the fiery red mop of hair that flowed back into the water. Gray, white, red. Amalina closed her eyes.

A shake. A movement. A spasmodic splash. Pia's body began to shake and wobble sickly.

"Here, here," hissed the Count. "Here, here."

Amalina ran forward with the cup, slipped on the wet floor and banged into the edge of the tub. The contents of the cup spilled into the water.

"Fool! Watch where you're going. Open your eyes!"

"They *are* open. I slipped."

The Count sat down in the tub and was guiding Pia's convulsing body into the water. Her face was glossy red, with only pieces of white—part of her forehead; the top of her ear; the inside of her eyelid; an open eye; the corner of her lip; a row of her teeth. Her green eyes were unfocused and rolled up to the right. Her teeth clattered together.

"How much did you spill?"

"I told you you did it too soon."

"How much is left, damn it all?"

"Here, have it. Is she dead?"

"Quiet. Quiet. Let me feel her. Here, into her mouth. Let it flow."

"She's shaking too much."

"*You're* shaking too much. It isn't that heavy. Come closer and don't handle it like a cup of acid. You're throwing it. Pour."

"Is she dead?"

"She needs more."

"Hold her steady. She's thrashing too much. Is she in pain?"

"Be quiet and hold the cup while I fill the cup again."

"Oh, no, it's going to take too long. She's dying, sir. Another one, dying again."

"If you'd have moved faster and not spilled. And hold still, Ms. Dalca. How many times do I have to say it?"

His blood splashed heavily into the cup this time, the force meeting the urgency, as Pia's body began to subside in a surrendering to her death, to the loss of her most vital element.

"It's too late."

"Stay still and let me fill it."

"But it's too late."

"I'll hold her mouth open and you pour it. Come right here and pour it in. Don't worry about shattering her teeth, just get it in. All of it. While I massage her neck to get it down. That's it my princess, swallow. Swallow it."

"She isn't swallowing she's dead."

"Let her drink it all."

"She isn't drinking, sir,"

"It's going down, just be careful not to keep spilling. You keep spilling."

"You keep moving."

"You keep moving. Oh, don't start in on your blubbering. You're such a child."

"I'm not. Forget the cup, just put your wrist to her mouth!"

"Quiet. But there's an idea ... If *you* can hold her."

"Is she even alive?"

36

Blood Foe

The Strange Man came in the morning. He was dressed in his peculiar suit and wrapped around by a heavy cape. He lifted his head toward the top of the gate, and pointed his finger at the soldiers there. But he spoke to—and through—the whole castle with a calm, yet body penetrating, bone-jangling, nerve-shivering voice. Like heavy vibrations through loosely packed sand.

"I am here for my castle," he said. "Open the doors and let me in."

He didn't expect it to work, but he let his words settle for a moment and watched the reaction of the soldiers above.

Inside the castle, late risers were thrown out of bed. Early risers steadied themselves and wondered if they were still asleep and dreaming. "What was that?" "What's happening?" "Who said that?" echoed everywhere.

Amalina recognized the voice and pulled on her jacket. "Stay inside," she told Aklan. "Go to the princesses and make sure they are okay."

"Another rebel raid?" he cried. "Again?"

"Worse," said Amalina. "Keep them to the back of the castle until I know what's happening."

• • •

Amalina came to the wall just as the Strange Man was winding up for more.

"Everyone in this castle is a trespasser," he declared, but in a lower voice, just booming enough to carry into the courtyard. "I want you to open these doors and vacate the premises."

The soldiers stared down at the odd figure. They were silent. Some flexed their arms, weapons in hand, but out of sight of the challenger below.

"Is he serious?" one asked another.

"Mad," said a third.

"Is there anyone behind him on the path? Does he have anyone else?"

"Nobody."

"Where's the General? He needs to see this. Someone send for him."

Amalina pulled back enough so that she could watch the Strange Man, but hoped she wouldn't be noticed. She felt helpless and didn't know what to do. The princesses were trapped in the castle with nowhere to run. How would this be handled? How *could* this be handled?

"I will repeat myself," said the Strange Man. "Open the doors and let me in."

"And what if we don't?" called one of the soldiers.

"I am giving you the opportunity to do what is right for your new master. Your rightful master. To do as I command. To prove your loyalty to me. Now, open these doors."

"Why don't you come do it yourself?"

"Because I don't want to damage my property prematurely," he answered. "And I am waiting for you to demonstrate your loyalty."

"Won't happen."

"And I am waiting until noon, when the man you have chosen to serve is at his weakest. And I have given you those hours to look inside yourself and come to the proper decision, to abandon that one and choose me. There will be no hard feelings."

"And if that don't happen?"

"I will try my best not to damage my property as I kill everyone inside, including that fraud you call your master."

"That I'd like to see."

"I mark you," said the Strange Man to the heckling soldier. "I will give you a treat. *You* will have the king's viewing chair."

"What's happening here?" growled Vezel, charging up to the post, a sword in each hand.

"Vezel, what are you doing? You're too good to wear the hood now?"

"I'm in charge here."

"You don't have the watch."

"I didn't say I have the watch. I said I'm in charge. I'm in charge now."

"Says who?"

"The General."

"Where is he?" said the soldier, skewering Vezel with a pinched look. "Is that his armor you're wearing?"

"The order is not to engage with the Master's blood foe."

"I know."

"Who was speaking with him?"

"That man down there, you mean? I did."

"Why have you violated the order?"

"I was waiting for the General to come. Got bored with waiting."

"You disobeyed a direct command."

"Let's see you stand here, Vezel, and not respond to that little madman. He isn't a blood foe. He is a lunatic who thinks he's going to invade us on his own."

"You're looking at a Mountain Goat," said Vezel, meaningfully.

The soldier paused, and gave the figure below a serious reassessment.

"That's no mountain goat," he grunted. "It's someone's idiot. Look how he's dressed."

"Mountain Goat."

"You're wrong. The General's armor is too heavy for you and you're wearing out your brains. He's a fool and nothing more, Vezel. And so if I feel like having a little fun with him, I will."

"Retire to barracks."

"Who are you to tell me?"

"I'm in charge."

"Let's have the General come say so. I don't believe you. I don't like you. And I won't serve under your command if it's true."

"You won't serve under me?"

"I won't repeat myself," the soldier said, presenting his back. "You retire to barracks yourself, Vezel. And when you come back here again, you better not be wearing the General's armor, you scum."

. . .

The soldier fell off the wall and onto the small lip of the mountain where the Strange Man was standing. Nobody saw how he managed to land safely, as they were all faced inwards watching Vezel toss him. But they saw him cradled in the Strange Man's arms and then he was set on the ground.

"Who are you?" said the Strange Man.

"I'm not speaking to you," he said, struggling to his feet, wondering how he'd managed to not die and only feel like half his bones were jarred or broken.

"I believe you just were speaking to me, weren't you?" persisted the Strange Man. "You were the man with the funny words. You said you'd like to see me try. You were the one I promised a treat."

The Strange Man reached out as if to hug the soldier. In four sharp twists he turned the man's arms and legs into knots. As the soldier screeched, the Strange Man muzzled him with a kerchief. Then he set the man against a stone marking the top of the trail, so that he faced the front of the castle.

"You will see me try," said the Strange Man to the soldier. "You will see everything now."

. . .

"Did you see what he just did?" The second soldier turned with a blanched face to his friends and Vezel. "What is that thing?"

"Mountain Goat. The Master's blood foe. Don't speak to him. Don't listen to him. Just let me know what he is up to. If he makes any direct moves against us."

"Listen to me," came the Strange Man's voice from below. "What this man—your brother of metal helmets and nicely patterned tunics—failed to understand is that I keep my promises. Now, crucial to yourselves, I have promised that at midday I will enter that castle and kill all that have not renounced their loyalty to this pretender and pledged their lives to me. I will do this because I am a man of my word.

"The one inside that castle who calls himself Count Tepsji, the one you have mistakenly pledged yourselves to, he is a creature of lies, deception and fraud. He is no Count. He is no Knight. He is not a man of royal lineage or blood. It is a game he is playing with you. He is nothing more than a poor gypsy's son, who was given the power by a stray creature. Left him behind to have fun with the true nobility of this land. The poor gypsy's son was meant to be a curse to Ardeel. A living curse! And this gypsy's son *was* a curse. And after a time he thought himself clever. And he imagined himself in the clothes of the rightful heirs to the throne. And he stole the clothes, and he stole the titles, and he stole the land and the castles. He stole names he never possessed, the jealous little gypsy, and he spread his lies until you all believed.

"Tepsji, Tepsji! Who has heard of such a name? Listen here: This Count Tepsji can't even bring himself to rob Teppes outright of his honored name, for fear your old genuine Voivod will reach out of his grave to chastise him for his insolence. So in his timidity, this sneaky worm relies on suggestion and allusion to that great family, and slimy excuses for his cheap counterfeit name. Tepsji! What is that? *Who* is that? He is the embodiment of a timidity of such an offensive nature, if the dead Voivod cannot punish … then I will. I *will*. Unless someone else should rise to do what is right; you within this castle. Do you wish to serve the son of a lowly pauper and nomad? Would you really follow after a King of Lies to where he is leading you, instead of the True King of Ardeel? Think upon this, men, before I come and make good my word."

"Did you hear that?" said the second soldier.

"I told you not to listen to him," said Vezel.

"You were standing there listening, too."

"I was watching him. And if you disobey me and listen to him again, you can have your limbs turned to screws." Vezel stormed off.

"Why did he call him the Mountain Goat?" Amalina asked the soldier.

"Because he thinks he is one. And I'd say he's right. So would our poor sergeant down there, I think."

"But what does it mean? Mountain goat. The General called me that."

The soldier met Amalina with a strange, cautious look. "He did, did he? Well …"

"What does it mean?"

"Why don't you go ask him what it means," the soldier said, now peering over the side. "And while you're at it, ask the General why he's lent his armor and command to that ball-less freak."

"Sh!" said another soldier. "He's still talking."

"And you aren't supposed to be listening."

"I'm not," came his reply, laden with guilt. "Just keep it down."

"Why do you think he does not meet me now?" the Strange Man continued on. "He is afraid! He is scared! Of course! You would never see him dare to come out under the sun, as I do. Because he is weak, as I have proven to you. He is nothing more than a frightened gypsy's son with a fraying mask. He hides now, eh? He sleeps somewhere in the castle. If you wish to show your fealty to me, you will go to him now. Any of you. All of you. Go to him now. Find him out. Surround him. His power is at its ebb. Surround him. Stab him through his heart. Cut off his head. Drag him out into the sun. Watch him die. Watch him burn and shrivel to dust. See what power *you* possess. Go do this thing that I ask. I will reward you beyond anything you could ever dream."

Amalina turned from the wall and entered the castle.

• • •

"Did you hear him?" asked Amalina.

Genadie nodded and gave a shrewd look as he munched on some millet. It was the same aspect he presented when Commander Kralov had come to invade the high castle with his rebels. This was wartime Genadie, with knife and pistol stuck in the loop of his leather belt, looking calm and determined.

"Well, what do you think?"

"What could you mean, Ms. Dalca? You don't mean I'd go following that man's orders and hunt down our Master."

"No. I mean, do you think he's telling the truth? Is the Count really just a poor little gypsy boy?"

"I don't see what difference it makes," said Genadie with another munch of millet, small pellets leaking out of the corner of his mouth.

"Well, he's been lying to us. He was never a count."

"Come, Ms. Dalca. Even if that's the way he started out, he's the King of the World now. It's what he made himself to be."

"The King of Ardeel you mean," said Amalina. "Afraid to step out of his castle in the daytime. Afraid to ride in carriages in the daytime. Afraid to leave this country."

"Ms. Dalca, you've been listening to that imposter. And he has you questioning our master. That isn't a good thing."

"What isn't good is that you aren't thinking properly. Why stick up for one of these creatures now that there are two of them? Here you've gone and sworn your life to the one who destroyed your loved ones. That's all he's ever done: gone around and destroyed and killed innocent people. The Count kidnapped me and threatened my family. Now is that any reason for me to treat him like some kind of friend? When he tears people apart and kills my friends right before my eyes?"

Amalina began to cry.

"I told you he wasn't responsible for that girl," said Genadie, thinking Amalina was returning to her usual complaint of having seen the Count murder Lucinda Skeldar.

"Not responsible. I know all about that, Genadie. All about the little service he runs for the evil people of this country."

"It's not evil," said Genadie. "Master passes no judgements."

"But I was speaking of Robine!" Amalina punched Genadie in the arm. "I was speaking of Ragonde! I was speaking of Pia! I was speaking of *you!*" Amalina grabbed him by the shoulders and shook him.

"Me?" he said with surprise and embarrassment. He laughed. "Me, really?"

Amalina didn't continue the list for him: Erik Kosche, Odetta, Kralov, Piotr. That would only have invited suspicion. But she remembered *them*, too. All the previous victims she'd known personally.

"How many times have I thought you dead, all because of him?" she said.

"Only twice."

"We need to begin thinking for ourselves, Genadie. We aren't *them*. We need to stick together as our own kind."

"That sounds like treason, Ms. Dalca," scolded Genadie.

"You mean it sounds dangerous. And that scares you."

"I suppose it does. But what are you thinking, eh? What exactly do you propose?"

"We have no idea what's about to happen. That thing is going to blow in here, and we have no idea if the Count can fight him off or not. And I don't think there is anything we can do, one way or another to stop what's to come. Do you?"

"And still, what are you proposing?"

Amalina cleared her throat. "I have no idea. I hoped you and I might come up with a plan, so I could see my father again. It wasn't fair what you did, to trick me to come here, was it? Showing me that note."

Genadie had been so happily taken by Amalina's warm, heartfelt admission of friendship, that this sudden turn—a cold reminder of his criminality and treachery against her—made him twitch as if he'd been slapped in the face. Tears sprung out of his eyes. He turned away.

"Did he come to you, Genadie?"

"Who?"

"*Him*. The stranger. I thought I saw him in the cart with you."

"When, Ms. Dalca? No, never."

"When you were being carried up the mountain. Before the crash."

"I was alone. Why?"

Amalina remembered the Strange Man standing in the road, frightening her with tales of tearing apart the country, and then blandly asking her for assistance. "*… Genadie and that General, too,*" he'd said enthusiastically. "*Also* *servants, whoever they might be. I'd like that, yes. Ask around. See if they would serve me as they have him. You'll ask them, won't you?"*

"If he'd come to you earlier, and asked for you to serve him—if the Count were to be defeated, and this Strange Man had beaten him. Would you serve him as you have the Count?"

"Oh, Ms. Dalca," Genadie moaned. "Oh, Ms. Dalca. What are you saying?"

"What are you doing here?" said Anka, bustling up to Amalina. "You mean you aren't down there?"

"Down where?"

"He's a devious one, that Count," said Anka, looking caught between awe and loathing. "He told the princesses that you were down the crevice with Pia and the General."

"That I was dead?"

"What? Heavens! Down the crevice." Anka quickly explained how the previous owner had once found a split in the mountain rock. He had a stairwell cut in with the intention of creating an internal stairway to the village below, to allow safer passage to Kyrgil during the winter. But the construction was halted when some wandering caves were discovered, and it wasn't clear if any further digging would harm the very structure of this outcropping which the castle sat on. "So he told the ladies that early this morning you'd taken Pia to go exploring, then sent Marosh in when you hadn't returned. Then suggested they all go after you, in case you were in trouble. And with some food in case they found you all well and make an interesting lunch of it."

"What a strange lie," said Amalina. "Everyone believed it? Even Gillette?"

"When that voice rang out this morning, shaking us good, Pils told them that was someone blowing the emergency horn from the caverns. They believed it. Though they were curious when your 'Uncle' insisted they take along all their servants. Not everyone wanted to go, but they sure did when he encouraged them."

"And what's the purpose? Just to get them out of the way?"

"Protect them. Once they get down past the stairwell and into the cavern that tricky Count of yours is going to seal them in. Until he's dealt with the real emergency."

"Why didn't you go down with them?"

"Pils is friendly with tight spaces. I can't stomach it. But I'm surprised you aren't down there. That you didn't know a thing about it."

"I didn't," said Amalina. "That was very tricky of him. What is the Count doing now?"

"Eating Marosh's head," replied Anka, "for alls I know. Best you two find some shelter, or get down into the crevice before he seals it up. With two of these creatures at it … oh, Master, why did you leave without us? Left me and Pils to the ever doubling nightmares and madness. And here I thought it would be a good thing, us coming back to your blessed Kyrgil. Soldiers catching mice and spiders, have you ever? Whatever will I do with myself …?"

She wandered away, shaking her head.

"Well that was clever of him," said Amalina. "Covers Pia and Marosh, and gets the princesses out of the way."

"You see, Ms. Dalca," said Genadie with a renewed spirit, "he *is* looking out for us."

"If he were looking out for *us* he would've had us go down with them."

"Well, maybe he has something better planned. We *are* his favorites."

"You've got an incredible mind," said Amalina, derisively. "Well, I hope Aklan made it down there, anyway."

"No, I'm right here," said Aklan cheerily, with a laugh, peeking around a corner. "Been right behind you the whole time, Pretty Princess. Didn't you notice? And not a magic bone to it!"

"Who is that?" asked Genadie.

"Someone else I have to look out for," she sighed.

• • •

"I know I have friends inside," boasted the Strange Man confidently. "I know there are hearts which feel my words and who know I am right. I speak to you, my friends, and stir your hand to action against our common enemy: the fraud who has placed on his frail breast the costume of a royal. Who has gained your confidence by deceit, and should be punished as any criminal is justly punished by the rule of law. By my power, I deputize you to seize him. By my authority, I commission you prosecute him. I have done all I can. And I will do all that I have promised. But it is *your* turn to act, my friends. So *act*."

Vezel stood at the entrance to the main building of the castle, watching his soldiers in the courtyard with a jealous eye. He shook the pistols in his hand, his swords now stuck in his belt.

Some of the soldiers were formed up in proper ranks, while others were bent over with clubs in their hands walking steadily along the walls. Because their faces were covered again, you couldn't tell what they were thinking.

"What are they doing?" Amalina asked, watching the men with the clubs.

"Going after rats and vermin," Aklan explained. That's what Anka had said, hadn't she?

"Why?"

"I don't know."

"Why are they doing that?" Amalina asked Vezel. Vezel stared down at her and said nothing. "Um, *General*."

Vezel continued to stare.

"Um, sorry to bother you, General." She became unnerved. But it seemed rude to repeat herself, yet also rude not to find some thing to say under his watchful eyes. "One of the men told me I should ask the General— um, *you*—what you mean by calling someone a mountain goat."

"The General's first hunt," said Vezel in his soprano voice, somewhat reverently, if rather automatically. "When he was a child. He and his cousins went to hunt a goat that was bothering shepherds on his land. They found it up in the mountain, and the goat killed them all but him, and he almost did not survive. And the goat got away. A mountain goat looks like a goat, and acts like a goat, but it is not a goat. It is tricky, has power, and speed, and knows how to move on the rocks in ways we do not. It should not be taken lightly. It should be respected, if not feared."

"Oh."

"Why did you want to know?"

"Well, I heard you say it about the … uh … Well, thank you for telling me."

"One of the men said General Marosh called you this."

"Oh. Oh? Well yes."

"Do you know why?"

"I don't think so. No. I can't think of a reason. He was probably joking, or something."

"Joking? General Zsolt Marosh?"

Now Vezel's stare *really* grew uncomfortable.

"Where is the Count?" Her attempt at a brave voice sounded light and tinkly in the cold air.

"Where is the Count, you ask?" boomed the Strange Man on the other side of the wall. "Where is the false Count Tepsji? He hides. He shrinks away. He sleeps in dark corners while men stand tall in the sun, as I do. We are coming to the hour, and still you haven't delivered him to me. It will be hard to overlook your unfaithfulness to me. I understand you have good hearts, and you feel you have an oath you may not break. But an oath sworn to a scoundrel means nothing. And that is what he is. Wrapping himself in your useless flesh, in the hopes to preserve himself when he knows it is futile. You will sacrifice yourselves to someone such as this? I think not."

. . .

On and on, the Strange Man implored the humanity of the castle to his side, while berating the master of it; until some of the soldiers shuffled nervously and it was obvious they were beginning to have their thoughts turned. "Where is General Marosh?" they muttered, not believing the excuses given. "Where *is* the Count?" they whispered, eyes darting suspiciously. "Have they fled?" grew the hum. "Have they left us to die?" they worried almost in unison.

"The hour draws to a close," shouted the inexhaustible Strange Man. "Where is this coward, Count Tepsji? Where is your hero, who you have not dragged before me, but follow needlessly to the grave? He is a sheep bleating in the mountains. He is a sniveling mole, dug into the ground with only his ass in the air for you to kiss it. He sends you to meet me. He leaves you to meet me, alone. Unwilling and unable to face me under the sun himself."

"Have the men cleared the castle?" the Count asked Vezel, his voice ringing through a metal visor. The full suit of armor clumped with a nonchalance next to his new General.

Amalina did not recognize at first what she was looking at, but it was the suit of ancient armor that had always hung out in *l'entrée grande*, and then in the Kyrgil Castle's great hall, next to the gray cup. This was, and had always been, the Count's armor. Its openings and joints were covered in shirts, pants and sleeves of herringbone chainmail, and under that, a sheath of some material that looked and sounded like tar-rubber. With all this his motions were pretty effortless, and it was the material that sqeaked and squawked in protest of its handling. If he limited his motions, it was to keep the integrity of the suit whole.

"They are doing as you commanded, Great King," said Vezel, in his high voice. "I advise we call them off and bring them to full ranks to meet this foe."

"What's the point of that?" said the Count. "Better they are doing something useful."

Vezel bowed, "I am a man of military expertise, Master. I cannot understand your ways."

"What's not to understand? Every mouse, rat, shrew, mole, cat, dog, rabbit, spider, mosquito, bird … Well, anything that creeps, crawls or flies: they must be removed from this castle. They are spies."

"Spies?" Vezel tried not to look skeptical, but simply naïve for his Master.

"No such creature would have any business here at this altitude and in this cold. And I didn't order them here. So they are enemy agents. Kill them all. Even now I see a falcon that one of your sharpshooters should be dealing with."

"Oh, yes, Master! His words are interfering."

"Worthless," said the Count. He snatched the pistol away from Vezel and shot the wheeling bird. The soldiers in the courtyard spun and gaped at the armor with the smoking gun in its glove. Then they cheered.

"You'll pay for that," boomed the voice from the other side of the wall.

"Can you see, Master?" asked Vezel.

"I can hear better than see," said the Count. The visor slits looked utterly black, as if the black rubber encased his head. But that wasn't the case.

"Smoked glass," he touched a glove gently near the eyes. "Very thick. Is that one of your men I saw sitting on the ground next to the dwarf?"

"Not sitting. Had his limbs plucked like a spider's."

"Why that one?"

Vezel explained how he'd knocked the soldier over the side when he disobeyed a direct order. Since the soldier had been teasing the Strange Man, as the explanation went (Vezel, as always, calling the Strange Man 'the foe', or 'your blood foe'—and never 'Mountain Goat' before the Count), the Strange man was keeping him alive to witness his planned assault.

The Count chuckled at the clever cruelty. "And I will do the same with you," he said to Vezel.

Vezel jerked his head at the Count, his eyes wide.

"But I'd do no harm to you, like that upstart dwarf. You see how I do not engage in wanton brutality, as *that* one does. I do not relish in pain and torture the way the lowborn do. You understand."

"Yes, Master," he replied, requisitely.

"But you are no doubt wondering what I meant. And what I meant was this. I will place you above in the main building, so you witness what I tried many times to hammer into Zsolt Marosh's head: A human army is useless against one such as I. An utter waste of flesh, blood, resources and time to engage in such foolishness. Go above and ready yourself. But first order these men into the ranks you so wished to see them in. A handful accompany the lady princesses, and they will be the ones you are left with. If *you* manage to survive, that is. Try not to let him see you. Perhaps send twenty inside with me."

Vezel did as ordered. The soldiers, seeing their knight suited up so impressively, were breathing heavy with pride and confidence and faced the doors.

"What about us, Master?" Genadie dared to ask.

The suit of armor turned and bent to look Genadie and Amalina (and Aklan) up and down. "Try not to get yourselves killed."

37

The Count vs. The Strange Man

The great doors of Kyrgil Castle opened. The Strange Man was presented with a courtyard of five rows of fully armored soldiers, staggered and at various heights (some kneeling, others standing), pointing rifles at him. Behind these rows, inside the main building's elevated doorway, was the Count in his armor. All along the wall's parapet was another row of muskets at the ready.

"Ah," said the Strange Man, in a cordial tone. "Count Tepsji."

"You are violating our peace without reason."

"Now, men of the castle, are you delivering this confounded son of a gypsy whore to me, as I have requested? I will have your answer. Yes? Or no?"

The soldiers stared down their barrels at the blood foe.

"By your silence, by your not casting his lifeless form at my feet, I must unfortunately assume that you have chosen to throw your lot in with him. If this is not true, speak up now."

"You are engaging in an action that cannot be undone," said the Count, calmly.

The Strange Man raised his gloved finger then trotted to the pruned soldier. He unwrapped the man's limbs and then tied them about his shoulders and waist, so that the man was carried on the Stange Man's back (and screaming wildly behind the gag), with his head lolling above the shoulder. If he stayed conscious, he had a perfect view of what was to happen.

"You've made your choice, so be it," said the Strange Man, crouching with one leg stuck forward as if he was about to run.

The Count turned and walked back into the castle.

"Show me your back, you coward? You'll regret that!"

A master-at-arms in the courtyard, without looking out at the Count's foe, let his arm drop and shouted: "Fi—"

The five rows thick of soldiers fell almost in unison. There was just enough separation in time, following the blur of black cloth, which lent the spill of bodies a subtle, wave-like effect. As the heads came down like a heavy, shiny rain of helmets, the men along the parapet toppled over, headless as well. The bodies howled from their necks, jerked mindlessly, fluttering in the forming lake of blood. The Strange Man seemed to disappear for just a second. The remaining helmets from above splashed down into the rising scarlet tide, just as the Strange Man reappeared in the spot he'd been in, and realized his mistake as he heard behind him the man-at-arms lifting a fallen musket.

The hammer and flint came down, but the powder was drenched and did not ignite.

The Strange Man tossed him out the door and over the ledge.

He slapped the face of the man hung over his shoulders. "Don't tell me you missed everything."

He took the gag out of the man's mouth and slapped him a couple more times. The man screamed. The Strange Man threw him out the door and over the ledge, too. Then he swiped the blood off his legs and tested the flexibility of his clothes. Then he hustled into the main building.

• • •

The Count stood in the anteroom to the great hall his arms held casually at his side.

The Strange Man had already pushed through several curtains, his gourd head turning this way and that, making him look wary of some kind of trap. He stopped in the entrance to the anteroom, not moving past the threshold. The black eyes of the gourd sized up the suit of armor and its many openings.

"You won't come out of there?" said the Strange Man.

The Count shifted his weight, the armor chanked.

"You're afraid we'll be outside," the Strange Man continued. "One of us will, I promise. And that man won't be wearing a silly steel suit. You aren't going to say anything? I've been talking all day, and you've nothing more to say to me?" Chank, clank. "Guess I'll shut up now."

The Strange Man charged. The two bodies met with a deafening crunch and they fell and tilted on the floor in a whirring ball of cloth and metal. It was too fast to see, but if one could, one would see that wherever the Strange Man set his hands to the armor, it cracked and bent inward as if the metal were soft putty.

Suddenly the armor collapsed. The Strange Man stumbled forward. He saw the curtain to the right flapping wildly. He looked to the empty suit.

"Overconfident," called the Strange Man. "There are still hours of daylight left. And I will catch you, and drag you into it."

• • •

If one could see what happened next, if one could follow the movements—human eyes could barely capture but a black blur, and the ears a throbbing hum, and the skin a breeze and a charge of electricity—the Strange Man pursued the Count through the castle, blowing through the curtained and draped doorways, always his fingertips just shy of the Count's white ankle. Though the Strange Man had studied the layout of the castle by his own reconnaissance and the assistance of his tiny spies, he was not familiar with it. He was forced to hesitate at corners and new rooms, unsure if a trap waited for him. So the Count kept ahead. Always ahead. Maddeningly ahead. The Strange Man growled in frustration.

With the halting but somewhat rhythmic nature of the pursuit, the Strange Man had time to think. He felt he understood the Count's strategy: To wear him down. And the only thing he could do to put an end to things was to not think but to trust all his energy to a final shove, an unthinking leap at his quarry. He would have him. Tackle him. Bind with him so that the Count could not become ethereal. And he would drag the poor fellow out of the main building and into the burning daylight.

The curtain to his right billowed. The Strange Man chased there. The curtain billowed on his left. The Strange Man chased there. The curtain billowed to the right again. The Strange Man chased there and ran straight into a stone wall. The gourd shattered with a hundred cracks (but held together). It sounded like his skull cracked as well. He staggered backward with a surprised groan. And saw the blur of the Count blow off through the curtain where he'd just come from. His enemy had pulled a cheap trick, and now he was doubling back because he had run out of rooms. But he wasn't fast enough, he'd lost a fraction of a second. The Strange Man leapt through the drape.

But the drape did not end. It seemed to open to another, and then another, until he was screened in as the curtain before him narrowed. And it was above him and below him and still, as he pressed forward with his hands, and as the resistance in front of him increased, there was cloth behind him that closed in.

• • •

The Count fell on the curtain: the long, extended, reinforced, heavy, carpet-like cloth that was already twisted into a kind of tunnel, cinched at one end. Having hold of the other end now, he spun the way alligators do with their prey, and whirled and wrung the curtain from this side. Which closed, constricted and constrained the Strange Man into an ever decreasing space within the cloth tube. It would take a moment for the enemy to hesitate. Confused, but still cautious, he wouldn't move before he considered all his options, and all the possibilities of what might be happening. That's why the soldiers stepped forward, as their Master had commanded them, when the foe was wound into a ball, and fired their muskets into the pouch. And even before they could withdraw, the burning oil was thrown on top of it. Some of the men screamed and caught fire, but the bag was immediately soaked and burning. The next wave of men fired into the burning carpet, and then the next. Until the suit of armor appeared where their Master had been a second ago, gathering both ends of the elongated curtain.

As soon as the Count appeared inside his armor, the coverings were pulled down from all the doorways leading to the courtyard. The Count was so fast, he almost blew through the last several sets of drapes *and* the soldiers opening them.

His feet clanked down into the center of the courtyard. And then with a shallow bounce he was through the great doors. The burning bag trailed behind him, looking like he'd caught the tail of a meteor. He spun once awkwardly at the lip of the mountain, and, with a muffled sound of protest from inside the cloth, threw the bag as hard as he could.

The bag, with the Strange Man in it, now flew high into the sky and then arced down, falling somewhere beyond the far edge of Kyrgil. Onto one of the surrounding mountains' rocky haunches. It left behind it a sparking cloud—in time, more a grimy rainbow—which the wind blew slowly out of position.

38

The Fear

The bag in Amalina's lap felt heavy. This added to her sense that what she was about to do was much too dangerous. The three soldiers below her, at her feet, were packed in shoulder-to-shoulder, fully suited in armor and loaded with weapons. They were very heavy, which multiplied Amalina's apprehension. And what did not help to ease her knotting stomach and her clenching jaw was the carefree excitement of the boy sitting next to her, who kicked his legs out and sang excitedly.

"Be still," said Amalina.

"Why? What's the matter? We haven't even started yet."

Genadie's head came into view over the rail of the sled. "Are you ready—uh—Princess Katarina?"

Amalina wanted to bark a sarcastic 'no', but Aklan beat her: "Let's go! What are we waiting for?"

Vezel's face also came into the scene, next to Genadie's and said: "Go. Now."

The two heads above them disappeared and then the sledge began to move. The crunch of snow was heard. And it was felt along their backs as they lay on the floor of the sledge. Then the world began to adjust angles, weight shifted, and the sky that was in front of them moved above their heads. They now sat completely upright, with nothing but miles of open air between them and the next mountain summit. Below them—far below them—at their feet—was Kyrgil. Sickeningly, the rope to the castle above let out slack, and they dropped a foot and halted with a jolt. The rope creaked threateningly.

All the extra weight inside the sledge became real, and grave, for Amalina. The rope had snapped when only Genadie had been riding in it. Now here was Amalina, a bag of gold pressing into her lap, three large, heavily armed soldiers, and a child who seemed to want to turn the lowering sledge into a swing. *Don't think about it, don't think about it, don't think about it.*

"Stop it!" said Amalina, swatting Aklan and then holding onto his hand for safety.

"What's the matter?"

"We *are* moving now."

"Isn't this the funnest thing ever? Would never see anything like it in Antwerp. Reingart would be so jealous."

"Be quiet."

"Talking isn't going to hurt anything."

"You're moving around, and talking so much, because you are scared."

"That's a lie!"

"Well then sit still and be quiet and prove me wrong."

Aklan laughed, but knew he was bound up by Amalina's squirrely logic. "All right," he said. "But for the record, you're the one who's scared, Pretty Princess. Not me."

Amalina sighed, closed her eyes, and reminded herself the reason they were there was very logical and reasonable. Besides tearing through most of Marosh's army in two snaps of the fingers, it turned out the Strange Man had gone through the entire courtyard and decimated anything living: the servants (who hadn't gone inside or ventured in the caverns), and the livestock, including all the horses. Everyone's horses.

"We need to get down there and make sure he's dead," Vezel had said, looking stern and ignoring the lake of blood spilling out of the courtyard onto the lip of the mountain.

"Now you see what I was talking about," said the Count, drawing his attention to the beheaded army. Vezel dutifully ignored this and repeated what he'd just said, to which the suit of armor replied, "There's little point. When the cloth burns off, he will burn. Or, if he's alive, we'll know soon enough. Especially when sun sets."

"Can't you send a bird or something, Master?"

"I've killed them all. The rest of my forces are in place and will prevent a direct ground approach. I need them here, and not risk having them turned or killed by him on a scouting run. I need all my pieces on the board, General. You can play with yours."

There would be no getting down to Kyrgil and out to the site where the Strange Man had landed before nightfall if his men marched down. Amalina, at the same time, had realized what a panic would go through the princesses when they saw what had happened while they were away. They might not notice the missing soldiers, but they would certainly notice the missing horses. So she had suggested going down to Kyrgil to buy up all the horses she could and bring them up as replacements. The switch would be noticed, of course, but not immediately. And the princesses would have the confidence that they were still mobile, even with a different set of animals.

So the decision was quickly settled. Amalina would go down to Kyrgil with money and a scouting party. She would buy up as many horses as she could, the soldiers would take two of the mounts and race to check on the body, while she made her way back to the castle. When it was pointed out that it would take much too long to walk down the mountain before the sun set, Genadie was pleased to point out that his sledge contraption could lower them five times faster than descending on foot. At this, Aklan excitedly volunteered to chaperone his mistress.

"Where's that whistle of yours," said Amalina to Genadie. "Give it to me." She spotted it hanging around his neck and pulled it off.

"That's a flute, my dear. What do you plan to do with it?"

"How do you work it? How do you call the horses I always see you doing?"

"Really, you just blow into it, Ms. Dal—uh," he looked around to make sure nobody could hear them. "Ms. Dalca. But … no, no, wait. You can't use it here."

"I don't want to hang off the side of the mountain in that sledge. I'll just call up a pack of horses—"

"No, no, it won't work! That's what I'm telling you."

"Why not?"

He looked at her like she was being ridiculous. "Because we're at the top of a mountain. You need a woods nearby. Some tall shrubs, at least."

"Why?"

"I don't know," he'd said. "It just doesn't work that way. You've seen me. You can't do it in the open air like that. Has something to do with the natural elements and line of sight or something. It just won't work here."

"You mean I have to ride that thing down? Why don't *you* go?"

"You don't know how to work the lift—er, the lowering device. And you have much better experience using the sleigh as a sled. You were doing it all afternoon a couple days ago, weren't you? And having some fun."

"What do you mean?"

"To get you down faster, when you reach the slope General Vezel intends to cut the line."

"What are you talking about?" she exclaimed in horror.

"You were all smiles about it a couple days ago."

"There are trees at the bottom. There are houses and buildings."

"The blade's a good brake, and I'm sure the drift that's still there at the bottom will catch you before the village. Or the creek."

"Now I'm not going. Absolutely not."

"It's already been decided, Ms. Dalca. But take the flute anyway. If you can't buy enough horses, just get near the forest all the way down there and keep blowing. No saying how many, but I'm sure you'll get at least one, you're a good girl. A pleasant song if you can, that brings them out better. Though, I have to say, the best ones come at night. But we can't be greedy."

So it was down the side of the mountain, winds tearing at them and the sledge, until they reached the top of the drift. Then they'd be cut loose and sled to the safety of Kyrgil, where they would buy their horses and climb back up. With the boy's kicking around in the pendulous sledge, Amalina secretly determined that she would sneak to the forest and use the flute to bring out at least one horse—those ferociously inhuman horses that rode without stopping until there was nothing left—and lash Aklan to it and send him back to Antwerp.

"I know you didn't want me to say anything, Pretty Princess," he said, presently. "But I think there's something strange."

"What is it?" said Amalina with pressed lips. She knew from experience how it felt to plunge from a height, and how her head would ring for days after—if she didn't die outright. Every disturbance was the start of the fateful drop.

"Going to have to open your eyes."

"Are we there?"

"We just started, Princess."

"Then what is it?"

"Open your eyes and have a look."

Amalina opened her eyes. Aklan pointed down at Kyrgil, which shot up at them, and paused, and shot up, and paused. She closed her eyes again. "I didn't see anything. What is it?"

"I don't see anyone."

"We're too high up."

"They usually look like little ants. There's nothing moving."

Amalina opened her eyes. "There's smoke from the chimneys."

"You'd think we'd see somebody," said Aklan.

She heard the voices of the soldiers. She looked down and saw a hand pointing—and then witnessed the sheer drop below the sledge at just the same moment the sledge took another lurch downward. Amalina gulped and felt a cold sweat, which the frigid wind turned to a sheet of ice on her skin.

"What are they talking about down there?" Amalina asked. "I can't hear."

"Look over there," he said. "There's black smoke rising from behind that mountain."

"That should make him easy to find."

"Can I go with them?"

"You're helping me with the horses."

Aklan protested and Amalina pinched him and told him to be quiet.

Whether it was a knot giving way, or Vezel had swung the axe, the rope broke and down they went. Amalina screamed as she felt them tip in the wrong direction.

• • •

It sounded like the sledge broke on impact, but one of the soldiers began uncoiling a length of rope and then ran up to meet the chopped end still being lowered from above. He would tie them and Genadie would lift the sledge—or whatever of the sledge remained together—out of the drift and back up to the castle. The two other soldiers secured their weapons, patted the snow off each other, and then they, Amalina and Aklan went into Kyrgil; Aklan excitedly recalling for them the fall they'd just had, how exciting it had been, and that Reingart would have been *really* jealous if he knew about it.

The people of Kyrgil were not happy to see Amalina or any of the Count's party.

"You've brought a sadness with you," said the mayor, who met them with his deputy and a village elder Amalina could not identify. They were guided into the nearest home, where the homeowners also made faces at them.

"What do you mean?" asked Amalina politely, setting the heavy bag of gold coins onto a table.

"Since you and this Count have come to our simple village, many good times have been enjoyed, it is true. But we cannot ignore any longer the darker truth. We have lost many good people now. Young and beautiful. Our daughters and granddaughters. Disappeared or killed. Massacred."

"No."

"It is like the old days," said the deputy. "We have enjoyed many years of safety from the evil that used to plague our valley. Only with the arrival of the Count and his guests, it has been loss after loss. Murder after murder."

"Since when?" asked Amalina.

"Since *you* came here," said the unidentified man. He had a long gray beard and pinned her with a look from under bushy white eyebrows.

"Some believe it might not be the Count," said the mayor, holding a cautioning hand in front of bushy brows. "That because of the certain members of our community we have lost, it might be the foul deeds of a jealous princess. Or two."

"We don't have time for this," said one of the soldiers. "We need some horses, right now."

The mayor scowled at the soldier. "Masked like criminals."

The first soldier obliged the mayor by removing his helmet and lifting his black hood. When they gasped and crossed themselves he said: "For your own benefit. But these scars mark our fidelity to our Master, and our duty to the peace of this country. We've had no hand in whatever might be happening here. But we do have orders that must be obeyed. Now, sell us some horses or we will be taking them from you."

Some of the villagers looked saddened by his demand, some put on a smug smile. "I was speaking of the tragedies fallen on this town," said the mayor. "You didn't let me finish—"

"You're finished now," said the soldier beginning to walk for the door.

"You'll find no horses," called the mayor. "You see, it pays to listen. All our horses, all our donkeys and mules, all our oxen and cows, all our sheep, all our goats, all our pigs, all our chickens—every living beast were killed last night. Slaughtered to a one."

The soldiers exchanged looks. They hefted their rifles, patted their swords, and clattered out of the house.

"No horses at all?" asked Amalina.

"We saw the omen an hour ago," said the mayor. "The comet falling over the crown of the castle. It is too much. We can't have you here any longer. We can't accept you into this city."

"That wasn't a comet," said Amalina.

"As soon as the bridge is rebuilt, we ask that you leave here. If you don't, we will petition the governor to force you out."

"We will have the Cardinal of Netz drive you out," said the man with the beard and brows. "The forces of all of Heaven will be brought against you."

Amalina caught the impulse to sneer before it reached her nose. What a horrible reaction that would have been, she thought. Instead, her face became slack, she unable to decide how to react. It was true, the horror had come to their village. Twin terrors. The Strange Man must have gone through their livestock for some reason, just as he had the castle's. Whether as a curious punishment, or to prevent them from being used against him, or maybe as a way, before he attacked the castle, to fortify himself—

At that thought, Amalina gasped and put a hand over her mouth.

But the door flew open at just the same moment.

"Haralamb," said an anxious man with a bald head. He held his frayed hat in his hands as he spoke to the mayor. "Haralamb, they said you were here. You have to come."

The man noticed who else was in the room, his eyes goggled at Amalina.

"Get back to the bridge," said the mayor. "Let the soldiers do as they will."

The bald man looked confused. He shook his head and pointed to the far wall. "Haralamb, something is happening. A fog is coming from the north. Gedik came from his farm, he said he heard screams from the Borszovaras. Terrible screams—"

The esteemed men of the village glanced to Amalina. The mayor straightened himself.

"The comet," he said to the others. They nodded. "What do you know of it, Tepsji?"

At first Amalina didn't realize he was talking to her.

. . .

The fog was white and as thick as smoke. It moved with a wedgepoint at shoulder level, with tendrils here and there that seemed to be reaching out. Behind it was its thick wall that ended just below the top of the highest buildings. They watched as it rolled around the curve of the valley and enter the town. The bald man was right, screaming could be heard somewhere inside it.

The deputy was the first to break his concerned stare away and look back in the opposite direction. His mouth fell open and he pointed toward the castle. A cascade of snow was falling so thick that behind its white sheet it was almost impossible to see the gray rock of the mountain, much less the castle above—though the blacker hint of the sledge climbing up its face looked like a spider ascending its thread. But even the sledge was lost in the next blast. It was as if the storm was racing down its payload of snow to match the progress of the fog. A howling of wolves began from the storm-battered mountain.

"Wolves," said Mayor Haralamb.

"In the daytime," the deputy put in. "What in St. Grigori's name is happening?"

Haralamb nodded soberly. "Screams of death from the front, the yowl of death from the back. We're trapped."

As he said this, the fog surged forward with impossible speed up the street. A voice spoke ominously from somewhere in the whiteness: "Pop says Gedik says he saw something drag itself out of the river!"

"Weapons, take up weapons," Haralamb said with resignation. "Defend yourselves, defend your homes, whatever comes."

"Damn this scourge of the Tepsjis," said the old man with the eyebrows, not even looking at Amalina.

"What do we do?" said Aklan, beginning to look worried. "I only brought one pistol. Not much powder. Maybe three balls."

He began inspecting his pockets. The fog rolled in around them.

A rifleshot sounded in the distance and echoed down the street.

"Maybe we should take the girl as a hostage," eyebrows suggested.

Amalina grabbed the pistol from Aklan, then took his arm and ran back towards the castle, away from the thickening fog. On a second thought, she turned right.

"Where are we going?" said Aklan.

• • •

Amalina had to punch holes with her feet in the heavier drifts and yanked Aklan over them. She didn't stop until they were inside the woods. The fog was so thick, as she leaned against a tree to catch her breath, she could only see a tree ten feet away, and the one behind that was dim shadow.

"Do you hear the screams?" said Aklan.

"Shut up," warned Amalina. *He might hear you*, she didn't say.

"Aren't you scared?" he whispered.

"I'm trying to think."

"Why here?"

"Sounds like the screams are coming from in the village," said Amalina. "So maybe stay out of it."

"We should go back to the castle," said Aklan, his eyes and lips set like an expert strategist's. "Now, before it gets worse. Can barely see a thing. And night's coming, too. We shouldn't just wait here."

Amalina pulled the flute from her coat and looked at it. She put it to her lips.

"What are you doing!" cried Aklan, knocking it down.

"Testing it."

"You just told me to shut up, and now you're going to start playing?"

"Do you know the way to the castle from here?"

Aklan nodded. She handed him his pistol. "Stay out of the village, but make for the trail. Then get up to the castle."

You're coming with, his look said.

"I'm keeping you alive so your parents can see you again," said Amalina, with a reprimanding tone. "So nevermind me. I'm going to play this flute. You get going. With any luck, I'll see you soon enough. Now go!"

Aklan took off, saying: "Just follow this creek bed when you come, Pretty Princess. It'll take you to the road." As he became a shadow, and then vaporized entirely, he said: "Don't get lost."

Amalina walked in the other direction and began puffing breaths into the flute. It sounded too loud. Aklan was right, it might bring whatever was attacking the village—the Strange Man, of course, it must be. But it was going to be evening soon, and they had to get back to the castle. If there was any hope for protection, it was with the Count. Amalina would let Aklan get ahead on his own, then she would catch up to him on the horse and take him up the trail. She only had to get the horse.

She blew into the flute. She blew harder. It was tuneless. Nothing in the way Genadie played it. She imagined the best she would bring out was a lame sheep. She stopped and listened for hoof falls in the snow. With the fog so thick, she might have already produced a herd and she just couldn't see them.

There was a scream. Far off. At the far end of the village. Another rifleshot.

Amalina tried the flute again, using her fingers on the holes spasmodically, without tune or charm. Still she kept it up. Then she stopped walking, figuring maybe for it to work she had to stay in one place. She found some familiar notes by putting her fingers on certain holes, and pieced the notes together roughly to attempt a song she liked. That felt right. She tried again. Then she tried again. And she blew harder and more accurately as the minutes passed, her fingers landing in the right places—and in time, to her relief. But still there was no response from the forest. And the screams kept biting into the melody, making her heart pang. Then she remembered that most times when Genadie did it she couldn't hear the sound of the flute. She blew lighter, then changed and blew stronger, so that the air was passing so fast there was no sound to be heard.

After a while she started stamping her feet, and thinking she should give up and go after Aklan, and felt the beginnings of a headache as she blew harder and harder, and worked her fingers faster.

It looked like a piece of the fog detached itself, leaving a dark hole behind. The freed piece was in the shape of a horse. As it moved it collected more and more of the white vapor until it worked itself into a solid form: a giant white charger trotting toward her, the tubular black space in its wake filling in slowly. As the horse reached Amalina, she couldn't believe her eyes.

Amalina petted the horse as she walked around it, inspecting it with incredulity. Though it had those frightful eyes of Genadie's beasts, it could be no other horse: White Snow. The horse she had lost in the wolf attack last year. How brave it had been. Yes, as she saw now, the only difference between the two horses was a series of red marks (like patches of blood) on its rump. Just where the wolves had struck.

"Incredible," she whispered, patting his neck. Genadie's horses were always night black. Here, on her first try, was the snow-white charger she had lost. "You've come back to me. Oh, I'm so sorry what happened to you. I didn't mean for it. I didn't know. But now we have some business to do. You don't mind helping me again, do you? White Snow?" She put her cheek to the horse's cheek and ignored that it was as cold as ice. She cooed and encouraged: "No, not White Snow. You're somebody new. I will call you White Mist. What do you think of that? Will you help me, White Mist? Will you be my horse again? I swear I won't treat you like Genadie does his. And I will feed you the best hay. What do you think, White Mist? Eh, White Mist?"

White Mist knelt down and lowered its head. Just like something out of a fairytale. Amalina wanted to shout with delight.

A scream came from closer within the village. It sounded like a man's scream.

Amalina hopped onto White Mist with a hop and grabbed hold of his mane, then sent him galloping for the castle's trailhead.

39

The Wolf, pt. 3

Aklan's tracks were difficult to follow. The fog was thickening or the sun was setting, it was impossible to distinguish. At some point along the frozen stream, Aklan had crossed over to the other bank. But as she reached the foot of the mountain, the swirling gusts of snow covered the tracks, and she could only suppose the boy had found the road, then the trailhead, and then began the climb; fighting against the blizzard, with its hard wind and needle-like snowflakes.

"Aklan," Amalina shouted into the wind. "Aklan!"

Amalina found the trailhead. The snow was piled thick, any tracks erased. But she would have passed Aklan along the way, so he must be further up. Up she went.

Up. And up.

White Mist climbed the narrow trail, rounding from one switchback to the other, his hooves slipping more and more as the incline grew severe. How odd it was that, while looking straight ahead, it seemed the worst snowstorm she had ever been in, it threatened to make her snowblind. But if she looked to the village—on her right now—aside from some sheets of snow, the air was clear. The sun had not fully set, and the sky was a pretty pink along the mountaintops that darkened to a marvelously rich purple. The fog was just a white liquid poured into the streets of Kyrgil, with the roofs showing above it. She couldn't hear screams, only the howl of the storm.

Howls.

They sounded closeby.

Amalina looked around from head to tail as White Mist pushed forward. Then she saw, at the end of the coming switchback, at its turn, in the snowbank, were several curious depressions. As she drew closer to them, they were holes. Large round holes, each resembling the mouth of a snow cave. And once upon them, looking down into them, in each one was the burning eyes and snarling, snapping teeth of a wolf.

White Mist reared.

Only the slipping backward of his rear hooves kept White Mist upright. Amalina didn't think it was possible, but the horse spun itself back around the way a fish can double-back on itself. But then it ran right into the bite of the wolf that had quietly materialized behind them.

Amalina screamed. The wolf who bit White Mist's snout had a giant, black, misshapen head, with eyes lit by pure hate. When Amalina and the wolf's eyes met, they recognized each other. She could see its shock. It fell back, letting go White Mist.

As the horse wheeled his front feet in the air, he was hit from behind by the wolves that had been hiding in the holes. Skin and hair tore away with squirts of blood. White Mist huffed and snuffed angrily.

Amalina could not hold on, and realizing she was coming off, steered herself to the side that wasn't a hundred foot drop to the next switch back. She regretted it. White Mist was wheeling and kicking frantically, and she was now trapped between his flailing bulk and the mountain. And on either side, the wolves looked for an opening to leap at her. If it wasn't for the narrow passage between the stamping hooves, Amalina might have tried to take the drop after all, hoping the snow on the trail below might keep her from immediately snapping something vital.

Amalina knew she was in trouble when the wolf behind her bowed its head and pulled back. In front of her, the black-headed monster—the pack's inhumanly undying leader—was coming.

. . .

Twice before she had looked into those eyes and seen her death in them. Twice she had felt its fangs drive into her skin, its paws and claws tearing through her clothes, searching for her heart. Only by the luck of a stray spark and a torch had she survived the first attack; and had thought she might have mortally wounded that black-haired beast as he ran away. The second time it was luck again, finding cover which shielded her and provided escape routes, as she dashed through the forest to get away from the hunting pack, given space to run by the sacrifice of White Snow. She should have been torn to bits, she should have died. Instead she lived, wearing scars for a few months, because she had been able to squeeze through a hole that the black wolf couldn't. And then she'd bashed its head to a bloody pulp. She thought she'd gotten to its brains. Was sure she had killed it.

Now its malformed, scarred head—just as large and terrifying no matter how deformed, perhaps even worse for it—with rows of finger-length, bent-out-of-place fangs, was looking straight at her and thinking the same thing: How was this girl still alive? How had it not feasted on her tasty flesh? *Why is she here again before me ... if not for me to—finally—make a meal of her?* He warned off his gang. They would take care of the horse (*again*). And now he came for Amalina. No torches to save her. Nowhere to dodge or hide unfairly on a slippery, slight trail, with a wall of rock on one side, and a plummeting death on the other.

She's had it now, he licked his chops hungrily, with a final growl.

Then he came for her.

. . .

Amalina twisted, threw out her arm. Then she pulled it back quick, hoping his bite would find only her thick coat. It did. But as the wolf withdrew, he dragged Amalina along. Something fell out of her coat. She couldn't believe her eyes. The pistol. Somehow Aklan had slipped the pistol into one of her pockets. As she reached for it, she was yanked away.

White Mist bucked and hit one of the wolves in the chest. It flew off the ledge with a high yelp of surprise. Still, his back end was being shredded. His heavy shoulder crashed both the black wolf and Amalina into the rock wall. She staggered back, dizzy, holding her head.

Off with the coat, she thought.

She pulled off the coat. When the black wolf lunged, she fed the coat into his mouth. Then she lunged for the pistol. She took it out of a pistol shaped hole in the snow. She spun just in time to see her coat lob high over the neck of White Mist and cartwheel down to Kyrgil.

Another yelp. Another wolf joined its brother over the side. The black wolf took an angry bite out of White Mist's snout.

Amalina cocked the pistol and pointed it at the black wolf. Point blank. She pulled the trigger as its eye looked up the barrel.

Ssst. A small sound. The spark, hitting the little dry powder, did not combust. The pistol was worthless. She tried again. The second time there wasn't even a sound.

A flake of snow went into Amalina's eye. She winced. The pistol was ripped out of her hand and she felt the hot, foamy drool on her knuckles. She let go or she would have gone with it. But she watched as the pistol went into the air, then fall on the opposite side of the berserk White Mist.

Yelp, Yelp. Two more wolves gone. Only two left: the one snapping at White Mist's haunch, and the black wolf bowing down and preparing to leap on Amalina.

Amalina blew into the flute. This did nothing but confuse the black wolf for a moment. Then he leapt. She threw the flute at him as he was in the air and she rolled underneath the horse's dancing hooves.

The black wolf couldn't believe she'd done it, but was ready to brave getting trampled to get at her. Then, in a clever move, he leapt up and ran his shoulder into White Mist's flank. The shove was enough to send White Mist tumbling. The horse slid to the edge, and then went over, taking the last wolf of the pack with him. White Mist didn't make a sound. His kicking hoof caught Amalina in the arm. It went numb and she thought it broke.

The black wolf straightened up as she lay in the deep snow. He paced back and forth before her, studying her, his eyes crammed with murderous intent as drool fell in gobs from his mouth. He growled.

"Leave me alone," she said, still holding her arm, wincing at the painful throbs. She felt the snow soaking her dress, sapping her heat and strength. "Go away."

He leapt at her lengthwise body, any delectable part of her open to his choosing. He bit into her stomach, claws coming down on one thigh and her other shoulder. All of them scored where they landed and she screamed. The thickness of her dress prevented his teeth from biting out a good chunk. Instead his teeth locked in, and he reflexively tried to pull away, dragging her again. She scratched at his eyes and punched his snout. Finally he flicked his head and the fabric tore.

His head fell backward as his teeth came loose. She grabbed his head and kicked it, wishing she could gouge her fingernails through the thick fur, into his skin. She wanted to tear open one of its scars. But the fangs were in front of her, dripping blood. Her blood. Mingling with the ropes of saliva. He licked his lips loudly and looked on her gleefully, knowing she wasn't going anywhere. There was no escape.

She scrambled a hand into her pocket, then she bit down on the bone.

The black wolf fell back with a growl. It looked up and down. There was the dress, with fresh stains of blood. But the victim inside was gone. He pranced around in confusion. Then, seeing the dress still moving, and the wider bell of the bottom of her dress too ambiguous, he went headlong for her midsection again.

Amalina spun herself so that his chin slid along the fabric. Unable to see her arms, she was able to rake his eyes with her fingernails. He felt her even if he couldn't see her and so snapped at the invisible limbs, trying to get a hold of one. Raked his claws at her. His fangs tore at her skin. One paw came down on her stomach to hold her in place.

A hoof smashed into his head, knocking him sideways with a squeal.

Amalina swam through the snow. She saw the groove White Mist had cut through the snow as he'd dragged himself up the trail. He must have landed on the ledge below and then come right back for her. White Mist did not present a mysterious target. The black wolf charged at him with fangs and claws and the fury he wished he could express on Amalina.

Amalina tore off her dress, underclothes, stockings and boots while trying to run back down the trail. She made it several yards away.

The black wolf sensed the movement and hopped away from White Mist. He stopped and stared at the dress again. It was flatter now. Laid out on the snow, not pressed into it. Bits of steam rose from the boots. The white stockings were invisible in the snow, but he could probably smell them. The wolf shook his head to clear away the falling snow and get a better look.

Amalina saw her tracks in the snow leading away from the dress. So did the wolf. She saw the puffs of her breath. So did the wolf.

Amalina leapt into White Mist's prints. The icy cold snow nipped at the skin on her feet and the sides of her legs as she ran. She saw the pistol-shaped hole in the snow, and dove her hands in after it. It took a second to locate it and pull it out. All the while she tried not to breath. When she did, she blew out the breath with a wide hissing shake of her head, to diffuse the puffs into the falling snow.

Now the wolf saw a stick of wood and metal, reeking of gunpowder, floating above the ground. He shook his head, and growled angrily. As the snow continued to fall, a vague empty shape formed within the flurry. The wolf charged for the shape, centering on the stick, but Amalina dodged at the last second. His head hammered against the stone wall. Amalina charged back to the dress. She held it up and made it dance. The black wolf didn't need the incentive. He had already turned and was coming back, snarling with rage. He bit into the dress with such savagery, Amalina cried out. She let the wolf have the dress.

She dropped the metal butt of the pistol onto his head like a club. The pistol's ramrod was already sticking out her other fist. She slammed the thin narrow rod right into his eye. The black wolf shrieked. She landed another blow from the pistol, then another, his great head bobbing in confusion under the onslaught, swiveling on the neck to find his attacker with his good eye, while yelping in frustration more than pain and trying to understand.

She knocked him with her shoulder into the wall, then pummeled his head again relentlessly. She sidestepped easily as he leapt blindly for her. She shouldered him off the trail.

He hung at the edge, with his powerful forearms and claws. But the claws could only hold so well on the snow and ice. They began to carve grooves as the weight of his body pulled him down.

Amalina crunched down in the snow, and with both hands on the barrel of the pistol, cudgeled his head. He squealed, the horrific fire in his eye changed to an aspect of terror, and on the final blow howled as he pushed himself away from the edge to escape the attack. The black wolf fell into the soft white air below.

. . .

Amalina did not let go of the pistol. She did not take the bone from her mouth until she had the dress in her hand again and went to White Mist.

The horse was swallowing breaths of the cold air and blowing out steaming clouds. He stared up at Amalina.

"Come on, White Mist, one more ride if you can."

He rolled onto his shredded belly and she climbed onto him.

. . .

"What a remarkable horse," said the Count, still dressed in his suit of armor, as she arrived at the top of the trail.

"He's dying," she coughed. She felt fozen. Her limbs ached as she slid clumsily off White Mist's back. Her numb hand was still locked onto his mane.

"He's already dead," said the Count. He patted White Mist's side.

Amalina saw how the soldiers, holding torches outside the gate, were staring. The Count, too.

"Why are you naked and bleeding, Ms. Dalca? Where are the horses you were bringing to me and my guests?"

"Did Aklan make it back?"

"Who?"

Amalina turned and stared down towards Kyrgil. The storm had lessened, leaving the trail buried. The city was still shot through with the fog, the creamy, almost luminescent vapor more visible than the buildings, as the last of daylight petered out. In the sky, stars were already shining, the moon was tucked behind a cloud.

Somewhere below, she'd lost Aklan.

"I think he's still alive," said Amalina. "The man."

"Yes, I think so," said the Count. "Right there."

In that instant, a ball of flame rocketed from the far end of Kyrgil. Another joined it. Then another. Then another. The village erupted into a massive bonfire, with all buildings ablaze, not one spared. The surrounding mountains faded to pitch black as the flames at their center intensified. The neighboring forest started to catch. Smoke burst from the evergreens. Somewhere Aklan was down in it.

"Oh, no," said Amalina.

"Here is your city," boomed the Strange Man's voice. As the village burned in the greatest conflagration Amalina had ever seen, and she felt the heat of it press against her skin, a black form rose from it. At first a shadowy cloud within the smoke. Then it stood out: a torso that grew two—then three—then four times the size of the city. The silhouette of something like a bull, with ragged, gaping holes for eyes, nose and mouth. The mouth moved. "Your city is destroyed. This is the price you pay for defying me, you son of a poor shepherding family. Son of wanderers. Lying usurper and coward. Nothing shall survive the night. Not even you."

"And now he comes," said the Count calmly.

The smoky shadow grew and grew so that it was as large as the mountain behind it, and it leaned over slowly, drifting with purpose, toward them. The Count strode to the castle.

"He will crush this castle in a single blow," a soldier marveled.

"No," said the Count conversationally. "He needs to know I am inside first. That I haven't tricked him somehow. He has to get his hands on me.

Ms. Dalca, dress if you want, but do put the horse away before you come in."

40

Battle's End

The smoky silhouette reached out an arm as long and wide as the valley itself. It arced down to touch its finger to the edge of the mountain, just outside the castle's open gate. The smoke retracted to the finger, and there stood the Strange Man in the archway. He was dressed in a light linen shirt and purple breeches with silk stockings. He looked bloated, his eyes bulging and red. But the folds of the skin suggested there was an effort to keep himself bound together, an internal strain and a tiredness. But there was also his incredible resolve. He tensed and untensed his shoulders, rolling them back and forth. He shook his head at the neck like a prize fighter. With one more careful look around, he proceeded inside.

He could not strike fast as he'd done before. That had been a mistake. He was on enemy ground. Everything was suspect. Move too fast and the defender can spring a trap. Better to be deliberate. He could haunt this castle for a century waiting for his opponent to come into the open.

It did not take more than five minutes.

The Strange Man avoided the curtains, the drapes and the carpets. Many of the doorways had been cleared of them. An excess of torches in each room suggested his opponent wished to frighten him with fire, to make him nervous, to create blind spots. The Strange Man shrugged it off.

In the anteroom before the great hall, just as before, the count stood there in his full armor, with all the dents put into it hammered out. Scattered on the floor around him were small lengths of fuse cords, lit and sparking and hissing like little snakes.

He's trying to confuse me, thought the Strange Man. To distract me. He doesn't know what he's doing. He's an amateur. He has never faced one of his own. He doesn't know what to do.

What to do?

I can zap right through his neck, take his head right off, and never touch a foot to the floor.

He's counting on that. He has reinforced the gorget, the armor's neck, most likely. Better to understand what he's wearing and take advantage of it. Didn't the fool know there's no reason to wear clothes at night, even armor?

The impossible fool!

Watch this.

The linen shirt and breeches and silk stockings and shoes dissolved to nothing. He was naked except for the luxurious rings of hair that covered his body, matching the thick locks on his head. Here and there his pale olive skin shown through, and where his sex stuck out between his legs.

With a grin he entered the anteroom, gently kicking aside the hissing lengths of cord as he made a straight line for the Count. He picked up one of the cords from the ground and held its burning end up near his eyes. He twirled this cord and stuck it behind his ear. He put another behind his other ear, now looking like he had burning horns. For the next bit, he took two cords at once and put them under his upper lip, with the burning ends at the bottom, below his chin. Sparking fangs. The Strange Man smiled. He was not afraid of fire at all.

He picked up two more, held them in his fists and planted himself before the armor. He took the two hissing pieces, pointed their flaming ends just outside the eyeholes of the visor, and slowly pushed them in.

The twin explosions were felt throughout the castle. Behind the curtains on either side of the anteroom sat two of Marosh's cannons, their barrels aimed directly in line to the spot where the Strange Man stood. When he had stopped before the Count's armor, fixated on his enemy, the wicks were lit, their sound muted by the hanging carpets and masked by the dozens of already burning cords.

Before the Strange Man had time to think, two cannonballs were colliding inside his lower ribs. He cried out and fell to the ground.

The suit of armor was blown back, but then jumped forward, pistol in one hand, thick knife in the other.

Four soldiers jumped through the tattered drapes and fired their rifles into the Strange Man's body.

The suit of armor fired into the Strange Man's head, then plunged the knife towards the Strange Man's heart.

The Strange Man's leg became something entirely different, and knifed into the back of the armor's neck. The helmet popped off. Meanwhile, the Strange Man loped like a rabbit out of the room, leaving behind him a wake of red-black blood and piteous wails.

• • •

"What happened?" said Amalina in a distant corridor.

"He's not dead," whispered a soldier, his eyes wide with fear. "But he must be dying. Listen. He is wounded. Must be. If we can get to him ..."

Amalina looked to the soldier, who kept one arm out in front of her as if to shield her. Whether it was for physical protection or to preserve her modesty, it seemed a dumb thing to do. But then, having run inside the castle had probably been the dumbest decision she had ever made. Or so she felt now. She had wanted to go to her room for clothes, but was suddenly being taken by soldiers, for her immediate safety, through rooms and corridors. Away from the blood foe, she was told.

And now she was left cowering at a dead end corridor, holding a small shred of curtain in front of her, the bone clenched in her other fist. Protected by a trembling soldier holding a rifle—mounted with a bayonet—with only one hand. There was a ghastly sound from somewhere nearby in the castle: scuffling, wheezing, and a liquid sound. The soldier took his hand away from Amalina, not to firm up his aim, but to tear away his black hood.

"What are you doing?" she asked.

He grasped his rifle with both hands now, and turned his head so she could see the side of his scarred face. In its youthfulness, his handsome features—strong cheek bones, contoured eyebrows, straight nose, and ravishing lip—could be detected beneath the waxy red and yellow devastation. "I want him to see me before I kill him."

There was a sound up the corridor. From around the bend. Men were running, their silhouettes could be seen on the wall. Then their limbs and heads bowled into the open.

The soldier lifted his rifle, the bobbing bayonet affixed to the front betrayed how his arms were shaking.

A shadow appeared on the wall from the approaching hall. It was inhuman, with a head as big and wide as a wheel of cheese. And arms distended, bent in the wrong places.

Amalina dropped the worthless shred of curtain and plopped the bone into her mouth, and prepared to run again. The Strange Man had said he could see her when she used the bone. It was *his* magic, after all. But she couldn't know for sure, and it was her only hope at the moment. She was cornered unless she wanted to leave the castle through the window to her left. But if he couldn't see her, she might be able to sprint past him.

What peeked around the corner was not a man. It was green as a blade of grass, with a solid triangular head and milky green patches at the high corners that seemed to peer out from inside glass there. Its arms were in three segments, each half the length of a body, and as sharp as a sword's blade. A praying mantis twice the size of a man.

The soldier was transfixed.

"Fire," she whispered past the bone. "Fire for heaven's sake."

The praying mantis crept closer, its head twitching this way and that. It seemed only interested in the soldier. Maybe he couldn't see her after all. Thank heavens.

Amalina wanted to run, but the mantis took up so much of the close corridor, and the rifle's barrel was pointed right at its face.

She stuck her finger through the trigger guard and shoved the soldier's finger. The flint dropped. But the barrel tipped, the shot went wide.

One arm fired out of from the mantis and took the soldiers head.

"Give me your blood," it hissed sadly.

Amalina hurried up the corridor, sidling along the mammoth twitching insect, unsure where to go, where she could hide. But hurrying, because when he was done with this soldier he would be hunting again. There weren't that many more people in the castle. Where was the Count?

"Don't be frightened," the Count laughed. "He is dressing in costumes to scare you. But he is wounded. He is dying. Fall on him."

She looked back. The mantis shook its head and made eating noises. Its rear legs were motionless, as if paralyzed.

"Fall on him before he can take your blood and renew himself," instructed the Count. "He will resort to all means. Even the most distasteful."

"Coward," the mantis chuckled feebly. "Prissy weakling. How fragile and squeamish."

The Strange Man was gaining strength even now. His rear legs spasmed to life. Amalina ran. Only to be pushed back at the mammoth monster by two soldiers charging with bayonets. They both fired, but tripped over her as she tried to get out of their way. The mantis skittered back-end-first toward the soldiers (it could not turn around in the narrow passage), and speared one soldier and then the other with its forearms. It ripped off a head and began nibbling at the fountaining neck.

"Remove this shield of men flesh and come face me, sneaky pauper's boy. How many could be left? I hear seven hearts at most. Wait, what is this? Two have just silenced, and not at my hand. Listen you faithful men, your Master is eating you for sustenance."

"Not true."

"Lies! He will consume your power as nourishment for his," the mantis chortled between bites.

There was something utterly repellent at seeing a giant insect feasting on the body of a man, but also to hear a man's voice coming from inside the insect. Amalina shook and wanted to back out of the corridor. Its renewing legs were extended behind her now, and moving slowly, the way she'd seen insects stretch lazily and test their limbs fresh out of a cocoon.

"A disgusting thing I would never do," answered the Count.

"Fear for your lives if you see him," crowed the Strange Man with his dripping, penetrating voice. "He is coming for you. He will kill you without hesitation because he fears me so. Fire on him if he approaches."

Amalina saw the small hole in the side of the mantis' green body. A dribble of dark green goo around the breach. One of the shots had hit their mark. The thick carapace could be penetrated. She saw the blank ecstacy in the mantis' eyes, with the soldier's blood creating thick red veins inside its semi-opaque body. Amalina had hesitated before at the thought of stabbing the Count. But here was a giant, abominable, man-eating bug. She'd killed plenty of pests and vermin, and felt a thrill of satisfaction sometimes. And she knew she would feel it this time, too. She saw the rifle on the ground, with its bayonet pointing just two feet from the mantis' chest.

"Trying to turn my men against me, you mongrel interloper?" said the Count. "Who fears who?"

The mantis answered contentedly, and with a challenge: "Come to me and fight fair. But you won't. Because you know I would defeat you. As I so easily did the one who made you. Yes, I know who the scoundrel must have been now. Bario. Yes, it was Bario. Amusing himself with children in the Ardeel. You must have thought he was so strong and powerful, didn't you? Yet tremble when I tell you, when I caught that meaningless dog ranging my territories, humbling nobles by larking as night haunts and will-o-wisps in the fens of Cesena. With one blow I slew him. Tremble, yes, tremble at your master's humiliation and despair your own fate. But do, come and stand yourself before me for judgement. I am waiting."

Amalina seized the rifle and with all her strength sent the bayonet into the green body. On contact, the sharp metal point bumped and slid along the mantis' armor at an angle, but then caught at an arm joint and shoved through. The feeling tingled her arms and she dropped the weapon.

The mantis bellowed in pain, then looked down in disbelief at the weapon, and the body of the soldier on the ground and chopped away his head with a swipe that almost caught Amalina. The mantis froze and turned its head, its light green pupils swimming sickeningly toward her direction. The antennae on its head twitched at if tasting her, and its queer geometric mouth chewed and spat human gore like a machine. A rifle shot came through the window. The mantis flicked its arm through and there was a scream outside. Amalina tried to back away, tripping on the boots of the fallen soldier. As the mantis pulled up to stare in her direction again, Amalina was blown down into the soldier's body. Stamped there. She cried out, but wasn't noticed. The Count was on the mantis in a blur.

Amalina clamped down on the bone to hold in the pain. It felt like several muscles had torn where the count's foot had landed on her. But she stood and ran as fast as she could, her left leg catching painfully until it became a limp.

Outside? No.

As the Count and the Strange Man's shouts filled the air and shook the castle's walls, Amalina went where she'd first intended to go. She went to her room. She found a thick robe and a heavy fur coat. These went on. She'd lost her boots, and she didn't want to deal with stockings or tight shoes if she had to suddenly remove them. She put on her slippers. She didn't let go the bone, but held it firmly in her fist. She went to the desk and looked for anything important. The only thing she added to her pockets was Pia's gift glasses.

Now what to do?

The castle seemed to be shifting on its foundations. Rocks creaked and pebbles fell off the walls and ceiling. She thought of climbing into bed and throwing the covers over her head. Whoever won, they couldn't fault her for that.

"Where've you been?" shouted Genadie angrily. He was dressed in his heavy green winter coat with a black cloak thrown over it. His face was red with patches of white as if he'd been out in the storm the whole afternoon. His lips were dry and split. "What are you doing there, Ms. Dalca? Come on, we have to leave."

He surprised her with his strength as he grabbed her arms and hauled her out of the room. It sounded like the fight was happening in front and in back of them. She felt the air humming on a strange breeze. Torches were fluttering or were out. A cyclone was building within. The whole castle was jolting and shuddering by titanic blows. "They're going to bring the whole thing down," said Genadie. Without looking back, he grabbed a torch off a ring and took them out.

• • •

The snowstorm was over. The sky was clear. At the edge of the mountain, where Genadie led Amalina, the village was still burning, but its heat no longer reached them.

"We have to get off this mountain," said Genadie.

"And where do we go?" said Amalina. "The trail's buried."

"I'd suggest the sleigh, but we can't go back inside. No." He stared at the shaking castle. Fumes were lifting from it. "Where's your horse?"

"Inside," said Amalina with a smirk. "But I'm pretty sure he's in no shape to take us."

"We could try sliding down."

The castle shook. The outer wall broke as something like a whirring cannonball flew out and plowed into the snow. The snow hissed and turned to steam instantly, causing the ball to cry out and leap from the hole. It was the Count, his skin blackened and shriveled in places. He held a cannon in his hands. The castle roof tore open as the mantis grew to a great height, laughing victoriously. The Count slammed one hand on the end of the cannon where the wick normally fed in. The cannon boomed and a ball took off a portion of the mantis' chest. That part of the Strange Man shriveled, as he shrieked in pain and blindly struck out with an expanding arm.

"Down!" Genadie cried, slamming them both over the side and onto the trail. They gasped and tried to not inhale the snow as they pulled themselves out of the deep drift. Genadie spat out a mouthful and said, desperately, "We have to get away from the mountain. It's coming down. It's all coming down."

"Princess!"

Both turned. Aklan was staggering with exhaustion up the incline and through the snow.

"Aklan!" They raced to him.

"You made it, Princess," he said. "I thought you were dead for certain. I came up … and saw what's happened to the city."

"Where were you?" cried Amalina. "I got the horse. I was looking for you."

"I climbed the tunnel," he said, pointing back over his shoulder. "I knew it might take a while, but I wouldn't have to worry about the storm. And I figured the fog wouldn't know where I was."

"What tunnel?" asked Genadie.

Aklan, out of breath, pointed again. Toward the end of the switchback below. Amalina didn't need to see the entrance. She knew it was there. One of the holes the wolves had lain in wait.

Genadie looked sober. "It's a tunnel down the mountain?"

Aklan nodded.

"All the way down?"

"I'm telling you, that's how I got up here."

"Pretty steep?"

"Very. Of course. I won't be able to use my arms again for a month."

There were two more cannon shots, almost simultaneous. The enormous claw of the mantis reached over the edge. Genadie took Amalina and Aklan bodily down the trail.

"We're going back?" Aklan cried wearily.

"Back or die," said Genadie. When they reached the point of the switchback, Amalina's slippers were soaked through and she wished she had put on some underclothes because the wind was cutting up (and between) the parting of her robe and coat, which she tried to keep sealed with one arm. They looked down the hole Aklan had used to come up. Genadie noticed the neighboring depressions and then punched open the other tunnel entries. Amalina warned him the wolves had used them, but that didn't exactly explain who'd constructed them. "Where does it let out?"

"This one for certain opens where you crashed your sledge. Just before the streambed."

Genadie nodded. "Good. Excellent. These will get us down faster than the trail, surer than chancing a slide into the trees, and will keep our movements secret, eh?" Genadie pointed into the hole. "Ms. Dalc—ah, milady, take this one. We'll take the others."

"I'm not leaving the princess."

"If these end in different areas, all the better, little boy. We need to split up."

"Why?" snarled Aklan. "I'm telling you, you arrogant footman, you aren't giving any orders to me, and I'm not leaving the princess."

One of Genadie's eyes opened wider, but the other remained narrowed and focused. "You do what you like, you brat. I'm taking this one." Genadie pushed Amalina for the first tunnel. "You go that way. We'll try to find each other later when Master has won the fight."

Amalina stared at Genadie in disbelief. The mountain gave a shake, sending a cascade of rocks and snow down to Kyrgil, which got her moving.

"I'm going in first, Pretty Princess," yelled Aklan, budging in front and leaping into the hole. "I'll protect you at the bottom." A second after he disappeared there came a reverberating, joyous: "Wheee!"

The tunnel was wide enough for Amalina (inside her great fur coat) to fit with just inches to spare. Her legs felt like they were dangling as she entered. It was a very steep drop, indeed. She tried to pin herself to the sides with her arms. Aklan's joy could still be heard, but was fast losing strength as he hurtled further down.

"I'm going," Genadie announced, and holding the torch above his head, scooted himself into the neighboring tunnel. "Be safe, Ms. Dalca."

Amalina let herself go. By some marvel of physics, the hole had become a hardened gullet of ice. It must have been the heat of the incinerating village creating a melt, but not fast enough to collapse the tunnel before the cold, and the freezing winds of the storm channeling down through it, froze it solid. Amalina did not shout "wheee!" as Aklan had. She didn't say anything at first, as her stomach rose into her chest, and the rough bumps of the tunnel shook her back and forth and pummeled her bottom. The fur didn't even slow her. She gritted her teeth and groaned and tried not to think about how she was blinded by pitch darkness, encased in a tube of ice. On a sudden wrenching turn which spun Amalina's hips and caused her to feel like she was upside down, she began to scream.

. . .

"Where are we?" Amalina coughed, trying to close her fur coat, unhappy that she was in the open air with its solid breeze.

Aklan was visible as a golden outline amid the trees, the burning village as a backdrop. Pale blue light from the snow dimly filled in the rest of him. "Like I told you, near the stream."

Amalina ached all over, and her feet were freezing into blocks of ice inside her soaked slippers. She looked to the village and thought that might be the only logical place to go.

"Do you see Genadie? Where do you think his tunnel … Oh, no. Aklan, look!"

There was a glow several yards over. There the snow had blown off the icy tunnel. But the tunnel had sealed at the bottom. Instead of being thrown out the end, Genadie must have come to a crashing stop.

Amalina and Aklan scrambled through the snow and cleared away the thin top layer, trying to dig him out. They saw with a groan of despair that he was imprisoned. He'd been slowed along the way by a buildup of slush, and then came to the end of the tube, which was filled with runoff water. Genadie still held the sputtering torch above his head, luckily unable to lower it or it would have been snuffed out. But unable to lower it because, unluckily, the tunnel had narrowed to the width of his shoulders. He was wedged with one arm at his side, and one arm above. He shoved with his toes to bring his head out of the building water. He couldn't see them, but they could see him clearly, and the desperation on his face. He looked like a squirming, awkward, ugly butterfly sealed in a flooded crystal cocoon. His frantic cries were muffled.

"Genadie!" yelled Amalina as she slammed her fists uselessly against the ice shell. Her hands felt like they would break. "Get out of there! Keep your head out of the water! Oh, Genadie!" She turned to Aklan. "Go find a branch, or something we can dig with!"

Aklan had a dagger in his hand. He lay on top of the ice and began to chip away at it.

. . .

The battle raged for hours. As the sky began to lighten, and the village darkened with smoke as the fires settled and died, the deathly screams and the explosive violence raged on. Attila watched, not feeling the cold, with a spyglass held unwavering in one hand, and a weapon that felt by the second ever more useless in the other. What he witnessed was impossible, but he continued on, studying it dispassionately with his steady, scientific, calculating eye. He was of no use here.

The bodies grew and shrank with the blows. One second they were titans of mythological stature, dwarfing and treading on the castle, with lightning pulled from the sky to stab into silo-sized eye sockets or fierily rocket between tower-sized legs, the next moment they were nearly invisible ethereal spirits the size of a small birds zipping about. They threaded through the castle, and then mashed it, and then demolished it there on the mountain plateau, with bangs of cannons, the thunder of ancient stone, the cries of victory and agony. And while it was obvious they began to slow, as wounds were inflicted, they carried on like ancient knights in full battle armor (though they themselves were at times naked or naked beasts, or changed into outsized insects with brittle carapaces, or incorporeal banks of smoke or fog), ceaseless in their enmity and willing to last until the other dropped.

"The sun!" came a heavy cry, which echoed through the valley. "And no protection! You will burn!"

The ruins of the castle had been trampled nearly flat. One figure disappeared into it and reappeared in full armor. There was a laugh. Then the laugh was ridiculed by the other. "Holes and tears everywhere, son of a gypsy! You are not protected. You will still burn! Burn with me! Burn!"

They threw boulders from the castle at each other. Some hit, causing one to stagger. Some missed and detonated on the side of a mountain, or decimated a bit of forest, or crushed the smoldering remains of a Kyrgil structure.

"Ha! It's too late! You have no escape! No escape!"

This naked body was hammered down by a titanic shard of mountain which the armored knight ripped from it. The armored knight's enemy stumbled but then leapt free from a killing shot. It leapt and leapt again, looking like a tick abandoning a hound dog at the shoulderblade. It flew off the mountain promontory and bounced along the mountainside, set upon each time it landed by a sudden roaring pack of wild bears or howling wolves, their fangs claiming chunks of him, or pounced on by the numerous tribes of elks and deer and rams, their horns thrusting like so many daggers at his heart, these creatures seeming to be directed at the will of the armored knight above and always waiting there to receive him, until the armored knight itself was harassed into distraction by a wheeling, screeching, tearing storm of eagles apparently summoned by the bouncing body. The body flew high, took an erratic turn in the air and plunged into a hole in the side of a neighboring mountain.

The eagles broke off, and the knight in armor bellowed as it threw pieces of castle and mountain at the hole—the mouth of a cave. Expert shots, they plugged the hole. Then each successive blow further crushed the initial pieces inward. The next barrage of heavier stone was meant to collapse the mountain itself, and crush the enemy trapped inside.

But the mountaintop shook. Droves of birds sounded in protest and flew into the air like cloudfronts. Waves of pressure blew from the mountain, reigniting some fires in the village, felling trees, almost knocking over Attila. Lateral cracks formed along the mountain's side. Avalanches and rocklides poured in all directions. Then the peak of the mountain rose up, free of its base. Below it, looking like an ant hoisting a castle, was a man dressed in a heavy black cloak with blue clothes, and a large orange gourd atop his head. His pained, exhausted, but triumphant laugh, blasted through the valley. His legs shook, but he hoisted the mountain top ever higher, tipping it backwards at first, and moving this way and then the other, as if trying to keep steady under it, as if he might fall at any second.

The knight in armor rushed forward, but then backed away and held up an arm protectively, then scrambled into the unwelcoming debris of the razed castle, and in another instant began to run. But it was too late:

The enemy of the Knight of Ardeel had not intended to crush him outright. His goal was to shift the mountain to the side, and in one incredible burst from his legs that is what he did; opening the path of the rising sun to the clearing on the promontory. The knight stumbled and fell, his jagged shadow stretching out in front of him. Then came the wail, a high-pitched keen, as fire leapt out of the joints in the armor. Then the suit, and the body inside, exploded.

The enemy watched with a bent posture, hands on knees, almost doubled over with exhaustion. It waited to see that the body burnt to nothing, leaving only little metal rinds. Then he turned and retrieved the mountaintop, and lobbed it on top of the castle and his vanquished enemy. Because the Knight had already torn away pieces of the promontory, something in its structure had weakened, and at the introduction of so many new tons—a calamitous natural disaster, wrath-of-God hammerblow— almost half of the mountain fell apart. Sliding down into the valley, taking avalanches of snow and cathedral-sized boulders with it, crushing the parts of Kyrgil at its feet.

41

A New Beginning

Amalina felt like she was dreaming as she walked through the high castle of Netz. The air was calm and silent as it always was on a winter's day. But the violence still shook her body, the tremendous crash—the loudest sound she had ever heard, defeaning her for two days—still echoed in her mind's ears, and it was hard to believe that this castle still existed, that Netz still existed, that the world still existed after such a cataclysm. But she had been through this same thing before, hadn't she? Every time there was an act of shattering violence, and she was sure she would not survive, then came the quiet aftermath. The halls and rooms of Count Tepsji's high castle were always the place of renewal.

Last time there had remained troubling evidence of the struggle. Today, the only reminder was the throbbing in her arm and hand, and the wrap with a crude splint around them. All else was easily forgotten in the peaceful world of the Palace of Pleasure. And without Marosh's army, or Georg and Abraxa's family, it was as if time had truly turned backwards. Two years ago. Everything reset to their original places.

The tall man with the livid skin, large brown eyes, and slicked back hair limped slowly behind her as they walked through the *l'entrée grande* on the way to the Count's private study. When she turned to him and lifted her arm to show him in, his eyes rounded and took in everything.

"And here is the study," Amalina said in a soft voice. She pointed at the divan. "He would often nap on the couch there."

"Luxury," said the man. If he were the real Count Tepsji, he would have pulled on the end of his mustache. Instead he let the hair droop along the side of his mouth. He nearly collapsed onto the divan, then spread himself out on it like a slowly seeping stain.

"This isn't his inner chamber—"

He held up his hand. "*My* inner chamber."

"Not your real bedroom," explained Amalina. "It's just this way through to it—"

But he hadn't put down his hand yet, and he pumped it once in the air to let her know.

"Go away," he said. "Come to me a little later. See to our guests."

Amalina bowed to him. There were no *guests*, but she wasn't about to argue the point. She left the room quickly.

. . .

The collapse of the promontory on which the Kyrgil Castle once stood was a bit of a miracle. The lady princesses and their entire retinue, thinking they had been entombed forever in the crevice and caves, and suffering through the unexplained thundering devastation above, were released through a newly formed fissure that the collapse created; which led them out safely on the other side of the mountain. All safe and unharmed, except Gillette, who suffered an attack of hysteria. The nervous wreck had to be handled out by her servants.

They could not believe what had happened, but seeing all the wreckage and the rearranged scenery was good enough to allow them to accept what they were told: A volcano had formed, erupted, and capped itself within half a day. The early quakes in the morning hours are what had caused Amalina and Pia to become trapped themselves, and then Marosh, who had gone after them.

Marosh died heroically trying to save the two ladies. When things fell apart, Amalina and Pia were separated. Amalina could not tell them what happened to Lady Princess Pia Lampeda. She is feared lost.

Aria didn't believe the story. She was quick enough not to need the disquieting rumors from the Kyrgil slaughter to filter to her. She had eyes. But still, she looked ashamed when transports—sleighs suitable for a princess—arrived at the Kyrgil bridge and she and her people jingled off in the direction of home.

It was as the other princesses loitered in Netz, the closest decent village, and worried over Count Tepsji's fate, that they began piecing rumors together into an unpleasant tableau. Gillette and Isabeau didn't ask Amalina questions, but once Count Tepsji was found—terribly wounded but alive— they agreed to share costs and accompany each other back to France, leaving their minor servants behind to fend for themselves.

. . .

"Are you pleased to be back?" said Amalina.

Margeta made a lemony face.

"Oh, Margeta, after all we've been through, you aren't still going to stand on formality. All right, have it your way, *Princess Margeta*. Are you pleased to be back, Princess Margeta?"

"No, Princess Katarina. But as long as the foundations here are superior to the last castle, I will be satisfied."

"Your servants are bringing your belongings to your room—"

"May I have Princess Aria Ecci's room, since she has left us so suddenly?"

Amalina nodded. But was irritated by the stiffness of the conversation.

"Why did you mention this castle?" she asked Margeta.

"What do you mean?"

"Why did you mention this castle to the Count?"

"Why wouldn't I? Where else would we return to?"

"He has plenty of other castles."

"You don't like this one?" asked Margeta with a raised eyebrow. "It is the only one I've been, and it is *his* favorite. I don't understand your question at all, Lady Princess."

"You know that he might not be *the* Count," said Amalina.

"I don't undertand that one either. Perhaps you need a rest, Princess Katarina."

"There was someone he was fighting, Princess Margeta, during the eruption. I can't tell you positively that this man who was found in the valley is truly my uncle."

"You can't tell?"

"I know it sounds unusual."

"You've brought him into this castle. You've welcomed him as your uncle."

"That is true. Because he claims to be Uncle Tepsji. And despite the wounds—"

"He looks like your uncle."

"Yes."

"He acts like your uncle."

"Yes."

"People who have suffered a trauma have been known to become forgetful. That can explain the lapses in his memory."

"I've never heard of that."

"It happened to my grandfather on my father's side. He was hit on the head by a falling vase and he didn't know who he was for ten years. He didn't recognize his own wife."

"Well," exclaimed Amalina.

"If he looks like Count Tepsji, and he sounds like Count Tepsji, I don't know what more you could ask of him. I certainly am not. Let the other ladies believe what they want. They can be scared away like little mice."

"But still ..."

"Lady Princess Katarina, I don't know why you are abusing me like this. If a man of incredible strength and ability has survived the event in Kyrgil valley, and come forward as Count Tepsji, why would *you* or *I* question the validity of his assertion? I can only wonder. Do you not like me, Princess Katarina?"

"I invited you here, Princess Margeta."

"Then kindly allow me to claim my victory in peace."

"Are you pleased to be back?" Amalina asked Genadie, once Margeta's back was turned.

Despite the blackened skin of his cheeks, and his general downcast expression and scratchy voice, he said cheerily: "Of course. Never wanted to live in that castle. And I'll never have to spend all day risking my neck to clear a trail like that again."

"*You* know that *he* really couldn't be—"

Genadie brought his fingers to his lips, "Now, Ms. Dalca …"

"You *know*—"

"Ms. Dalca, Zeus is Zeus. And what Zeus does, and how Zeus chooses to present himself, ours is not to question. Oh, but I'm so glad to be back in Olympus."

"I can't believe you, Genadie." She didn't see an ounce of shame or remorse, and felt more alone for it.

"We should renew our language lessons, Ms. Dalca. French and Italian … and now, perhaps, some Greek."

• • •

It was nearing evening, the man claiming to be Tepsji was up again. Pils told Amalina with a profound sigh of regret she was wanted in the private study.

"You know most likely he isn't the *real* Count?" Amalina asked Pils, seeking an ally.

"What difference does it make?" he sighed again. His eyes were still blanked by the loss—the obliteration—of his *real* home. What did he care from monsters?

Amalina left him for the man in the study, who, she found, had risen only enough to be a bit of a pancake on the couch.

"Here I am, sir. What happened to your mustache?" asked Amalina.

"I didn't like it," he said, his eyes half-closed, looking woozy.

"Also, your hair is becoming curly again."

"Do you understand what it cost me to kill him? It will take me a good while to heal my wounds. Try getting hit by a cannonball or two."

"Yes, sir. I was only trying to help."

"It takes energy to keep this up. In time it will come naturally. But for the present, I should be allowed a curl or two."

"Maybe wear a hat or a hooded cape."

The man looked up at Amalina and then shook his head. "You said you will serve me faithfully, as you served him. It *is* true, isn't it?"

"You look like him. You have decided to live as him?"

"Why not?" the man smiled. "It's all been set up nicely for me. The servants. The castles. The obedient citizens. Why start from scratch?"

"The princesses, too," Amalina reminded him for some reason.

"I haven't decided if I like that or not. But I will give it a try. Don't forget, I've lived among those westerners for centuries already. Maybe we will try something from Asia. Or perhaps the New Americas. That intrigues me."

"And so … it's still the same for me, isn't it? Whether it is you or him."

"There *will* be differences," he said, yawning.

"You called for me? Are you ready to continue the tour?"

"I thought of going out tonight. But I am really too tired. Yes, show me to my bed."

Amalina pointed him to the cabinet. She showed him how to work the lock and open the secret door, which he accomplished with some effort as he was still limping and some of the scars restrained his movement. His eyes went wide.

Amalina showed him through the counting house, and the message center, then through the stone storeroom and the other passages and secret rooms until they finally arrived at the bedchamber.

He eased himself with a groan into the bed.

"Safe," he said. "Locked up under so much rock. No wonder he was afraid to come out. What an interesting fellow he was. Can't decide if I should destroy it all or keep it."

"There's some valuable art and lots of ancient books with interesting reading."

He turned his head and smiled. "Don't like to read, really. Not much fun. Always dreary. Never needed it in the old days. Don't see why it's become such an obsession now. Thought I'd try my hand at a book. Maybe I'll let it exist, see if it doesn't make some money. I'll publish anonymously, of course."

"Yes, sir."

"Is there anything else I should know?"

"He didn't tell me everything. This is all I know of. Here."

"But he definitely kept you close, the tricky fellow. To show you all this. But still, don't forget, he lied about many things. Never forget that. And who knows what he's kept back. I'll have to discover that for myself, I suppose."

"Yes, sir."

"I'm very happy to have you as my faithful servant. And you promise to serve alongside these other servants without getting into selfish strivings against each other. Pitting me against them and such. Hoping I will give you my gift."

"No. I mean, yes, sir. I won't do that, sir. I promise."

"Now that I think of it, do you still have that bone I gave you?"

"No, sir."

He looked surprised. "No? Why not?"

"It broke."

"How?"

"In the cave. I fell and it was in my pocket."

"Oh, well. You used it, though, didn't you?" he gave her a strange, haggard smile and stared at her through half-closed lids.

She nodded.

"It was probably running out of power. They never last very long."

"Can I ask something, sir?"

"You're curious about me?" He sounded exhausted and delighted. "I never tell a lie. Ask me anything."

"You could make more of those bones, couldn't you?"

"As many as I want. Would you like another? I won't do it. No need for it now."

"But when you came to fight with Count Tepsji—"

"Mmmm. The *former* Count Tepsji. But why don't we refer to him as the poor gypsy's son? Or The Fake. Or the Weak Conniver."

"Yes, sir. But when you came to fight him—"

"Fight, *who*?" Even fatigued, the man was as limitless as the old Count.

"Fight the—uh, um—The Fake?"

"Go on."

"Why didn't you use one of those bones? He never would have seen you."

"First, because I am not a weakling that skulks around like a frightened little spider. Second, because that kind of magic only acts on ordinary mortal bodies. Something about the makeup of our cells prevents our accepting it; the various electrical connections or something. It wasn't explained too well. But nevermind that, why would I want to do so when I should want to fight him directly?"

Amalina nodded, biting her lower lip.

"Well, don't feel sorry for us. The old gypsy magics are for your type. I'd rather be able to change myself at a whim." As he said this, the mustache popped out from under his nose like the flop of a horse tail. Then his clothes changed from cloak to a cardinal's robes to a suit of armor to an impeccably tailored dress. "Like it?"

"You can change your clothes?"

"Well, sort of. Do you like the dress?"

"It's very pretty."

He laughed and became nude. And when she made a face, so did he, and he was suddenly in his housecoat and turned over. "It's all me," he sighed. "You didn't know?"

"No."

"If you can turn into whatever you like—a cloud, let's say—why not give yourself some clothes while you are at it?" he hummed.

"But then how could you be protected from the sun when you change into those special clothes you wore? Why didn't you just burn up, if it's still just you?"

"Those were real clothes, little girl," he sighed. "Don't you get it? Really very uncomfortable and binding. But what are you going to do if you want to get around?"

Amalina thought of the many times she'd touched the Count's jacket or cloak. The thought that it was his skin was revolting.

"I'm so very glad I met you," said the new Count. "Let us celebrate this new beginning, as Master and servant."

"Yes, sir."

"Yes, what?"

"Uhm, yes, sir."

"Yes, *what?*"

"Yes … Master."

"When I get better we'll decide what to do with these princesses."

"Yes, Master."

"Then we'll set about pruning the world. It should be very fun."

"Do you really have to kill half the people in this country?"

"Oh, I've changed my mind on that. I am going to kill half the people in the world."

Amalina gulped.

"Actually, more than half. Probably about ninety percent. Not you, of course. Unless you give me good reason. But around ninety percent. Have you been to Paris? The stench is too much. Yes, it will be back to the Garden of Eden. Just a few things roaming around for my entertainment. See what they get up to. What they will do for me. That kind of thing. It should be very entertaining. And not as smelly and chaotic. Under control."

There was a very long pause. Eventually, he decided to fill it in: "I mean, I've had this idea before, but there have always been others who might judge me, you see? Now I'm the only one left of my kind. Why not treat myself the way I should be treated?"

Another long pause.

Amalina asked, cautiously" "Do you have to?"

His eyes came open. "I believe we have already learned I don't want to hear this kind of question, or the use of this kind of tone. I thought that you have already agreed, again and again and again, to serve me faithfully."

"Yes, Master."

"That broken arm didn't break itself. And I'm sure you don't want me to break the other one."

"No, Master."

"So you will never talk to me like *that* again."

"No, Master. I mean, yes, Master. Or, no. Or, whatever you say, Master."

"I'm going to kill almost the whole world, and you are going to help your master do it."

"Yes, Master."

"I thought I might go out tonight, but instead I believe I will sleep for the next week. Now, you had better leave. I'm tired and grumpy and if you don't get that damned torch out of my eyes you'll be lucky if I don't bite your head off before you reach the door."

"Yes, Master." Amalina bowed and left the new Count's side, not sure if she would see the next room.

. . .

She slowed and sighed when she reached the message center. She closed the secret door to the stone storeroom and sighed again. She considered the message center, which the Count had once treasured, being burnt. Centuries of correspondence, all destroyed. What a pity, she thought. But then she wondered why she felt nostalgia for any of it. It wasn't *hers*.

How much would the Strange Man destroy? The Great Library? The Grand Gallery?

He said he was the only one of his kind left. She hadn't told him of the woman on the wheel below the castle. She was a creature like him. But bound in silver chains. Starved. Probably easy for him to kill. He'll probably find her. Amalina could always claim she didn't know.

So much was going to be wiped out. And she was going to help him?

He might sweep across the world like a plague, she thought. But it was all going to be a matter of who she could help save.

The thought of smug Margeta getting the surprise of her quickly-ending life gave Amalina a pleasurable jolt. Which immediately made her feel guilty, for some reason.

Amalina spotted on the standing desk at the bottom of the stairs the book with the metal letters AXP. Amalina set the torch in a ring and then opened the book. She turned the pages idly and wondered if she shouldn't try to save it. The Strange Man couldn't object letting her have it, could he? She still hadn't broken its code.

On a thought, she pulled the pair of glasses from her pocket. The small vellum tags came into sharp focus, with their rough-torn edges and rich black ink. What she had first taken as smudges next to the writing were now plainly little portraits. The faces of the ill-fated young girls the Count had killed at the behest of an evil wrinkle of a man. Amalina turned to the last couple pages. At first she sensed it would be true, and then, of course, her eyes found the portrait she suddenly knew would be there: Lucinda Skeldar. A perfect study of the sad girl, in miniature. The Count had killed *her* in his murder service.

Amalina smirked and stared at Lucinda Skeldar. In the coming slaughter, Amalina would fight to save her father Dragomir, her cousin Jenna, her best friend Cristine, her beloved Lt. Ivanti Ion Vokent, and anyone else she cared for or thought deserving of life. But there was one ugly little man in Korr she knew deserved to die. And she would hunt him down, and she would swing the scythe of the reaper right at his neck.

Epilogue

In the Evening

That evening, while the rumors of a Kyrgil uprising (electric), or reports of a Kyrgil avalanche (tragic), or the word of Kyrgil's complete annihilation (wildly inconceivable) continued to spread through the mountains (like a certain mysterious fog); and Attila rested his head in the St. Grigori Cathedral without sleep, reviewing what he had seen, trying to convince himself a meaningful role still existed for him against such awesome power; Amalina was visited by a very familiar nightmare. She assumed it was because she had returned to the high castle where the curdled dream was a common feature, and also she'd looked into the leatherbound book of AXP's nasty plots and seen the face of Lucinda Skeldar. And so now it was a bright summer day, with blue sky, fluffy white clouds and buzzing bees, and Lucinda's head was bobbing up and down above the crowns of barley as she skipped down the sloping field towards Amalina.

But Lucinda did not sing that song that would set Amalina's nerves on edge. She spoke in the Count's voice: "You must kill my usurper, little mouse. Kill him for me."

"Please leave me alone, sir."

"Block the chimneys, little mouse, set a fire in the lower chambers and let the smoke gather. This will sow confusion. It will give him distraction should he wake, though he will not. He will sleep, deeper and deeper. And his senses will be dulled. Then you can kill him."

"No, he would kill me, sir. I saw your fight. It's impossible."

"But he is weak. Weak, and wounded, and so very tired … defenseless … He won't know what's happening if you do as I command: fill the chambers with smoke and distract his finer senses and keep him drowsy. This is what I'm telling you, little mouse. Then you just have to drive a dagger through his beating heart. And cut off his head. Do this for me."

"You're asking too much."

"I am asking to prove your loyalty."

"But you are dead, sir."

"Be the instrument of my revenge."

"To what end?"

"Don't you serve me, Ms. Dalca?"

"That I did, sir. But you are no longer—"

"It couldn't be that you care for *him* more than me?"

"Never. He is an absolute monster."

"And you *do* care for me, don't you?"

"Certainly, sir."

"Then kill him. Kill him. Kill him now, before it is too late."

Amalina began to cry: "Don't you see I can't? All this killing. All this death. All this murder. I can't take it anymore. I've never harmed anyone and I never will, and it has nothing to do with you, sir, I swear. But I can't kill and I won't kill, even something like him. Please, don't ask me anymore, sir. Please have mercy on me."

And now Lucinda was singing the song Amalina didn't like. And she was still coming straight for Amalina with a smile, but a fixed stare. But the Count's voice was gone and it didn't matter what the girl was singing. She was saying something else. Secretly. Demanding. As Lucinda always had before: *Kill the man responsible for my death, Amalina. Kill him. Give me justice. What are you waiting for, Amalina? It's been so long. Kill him!*

"He is already dead!" Amalina shouted at Lucinda, trying to dispel her, still wound up by the intrusion of the Count.

Amalina woke in a sweat, her covers knotted and thrown off the bed. Lucinda's song still haunting her ears.

"He's already dead," Amalina mumbled. "And the one who paid him to do it, who ordered him to do it, will die, too. Please ..."

She stretched out on the bed and wondered why in her dream she had been so kind to the Count. Somehow she'd become sentimental towards this creature? She couldn't believe she was still attempting to please him and placate him, even when he was gone. Her transition into Genadie-like sycophancy was depressing.

Or was the dream a secret part of her that was trying to communicate something she hadn't thought of? While the Strange Man was still feeble and vulnerable, strike him. Strike like she'd failed to do to the Count. If she did not kill him now, the Strange Man would only grow stronger. And he was readying himself to reap the world.

But she was too tired. To try was too much effort. And anyway, she didn't know if she could do it, mentally or physically.

And then, in another turn of thought, she decided the suggestion to set a fire to suffocate the Strange Man with smoke was just an abstracted memory of the Strange Man's mysterious fog, the destruction of Kyrgil, and her feelings of hatred and impotence toward the Strange Man; the associations mixing in an incoherent fashion.

And in a final turn of thought, she wondered if the dream hadn't been her fear: that the Strange Man was going to raze the castle. That he was going to burn everything in the lower levels—and destroy everything that was the Count's. Thus her secret sympathy—her unfulfilled curiosity—for all that was there, reached out to her, begged for her help.

She should have taken the AXP book from the message room. And the cypher sticks. She should have gathered everything that she wanted to preserve while she'd had the chance. There was no telling when he would start the great conflagration. He could be lighting the torches right *now*.

Amalina sat up suddenly.

. . .

Anka and Pils were sleeping in each other's arms in *l'entrée grande*. Amalina tiptoed past them. She held one candle to keep things simple, and had decided against using the bone because she didn't want to waste its power and risk getting caught with it, anyway. Better to save it for when it was needed. This action was simple enough: get the message book and cypher sticks. She needed to decode the shriveled little man's messages, to learn who he was and why he'd want these innocent young women killed. Then she would deliver justice.

She didn't bother to tiptoe in the study. The Strange Man would either hear her enter or he wouldn't. She'd have some explanation ready if he found her. The Count had been right when he'd said she was pretty capable fashioning lies on the quick. Or however he'd said it.

The secret door was still open.

She sensed something was wrong as she entered the counting house. It was hazy with a thin, almost scentless smoke. It thickened as she moved further in. Was this a new kind of fog? Or was the Strange Man already burning—?

"Who is that?" rumbled the basso voice. "Ah, I was just coming for you,"

Her candle was worthless in the haze. She only saw the tip of his nose. The smell grew acrid. She began to cough. Something *was* burning. Or had burnt already.

"Let's get away from all this. I'm afraid I'm still a little—well, why don't you come this way while I walk. I need to preserve my energy, you understand. It will be a day or so before I'm in the mood to hunt again."

As they moved to the lower level of the message center, she saw the smoke was thickest near the ceiling, with little swirling arms feeding into it and otherwise undulating like it was dancing in a current. The AXP book she'd come for was still on the desk, she saw it as they passed it. She tried not to stare.

He led her through the chambers and passages she'd just shown him hours before. And he limped and groaned and felt at the walls, as the thin sheet of smoke flowed above their heads in the opposite direction. As they passed into the tub room, Amalina was astonished. It was lit to nearly blinding by candles. Candles placed everywhere. And a board had been set over the basin of the tub, with a thick mattress and sheets and pillows laid on it. And resting in this makeshift bed was Pia Lampeda. Her white skin had a hint of gray that gave it an unhealthy, or deathly, pallor.

"Ahh, look at her," said the Count. "She is beautiful, isn't she? And with less care than a gardener takes, she will retain her beauty long after your children's children's children have sired and moved on." He rubbed his lower lip and looked as if the thought disagreed with him. "It is sad to think about, isn't it? Time, you know, and who lives and who dies. And who deserves what they receive. And what is the right thing to do and what is wrong. And can we ever learn? And should we ever care if indeed we can't? I have lived a very long time, Ms. Dalca, let me tell you. There are still questions—"

"Sir?"

He had sat in a chair to contemplate Pia, but now he turned fully toward Amalina. No curled locks. No features out of place. He just looked very old, and bruised, and burned, and his skin hung from his bones the way it did when he was exhausted. But he raised his eyebrow at her look.

"Sir," she said again. She wasn't sure if she should say anything. It could be some kind of trick. Or a test. The wrong word and the Strange Man could make sure it was her last. But then she ventured: "It's ... you?"

"I think that's a silly question. It should be obvious if you *really* cared."

"How?"

"Hallo, Ms. Dalca," Genadie's voice scraped cheerfully, as he entered through the door leading to the Count's bedchamber. He wore a rough cloth shirt and pants, which were soaked in blood, and he carried a large board. "Master, the smoke's cleared, but it's going to take me a while to get that bed changed out."

"Genadie," Amalina said needlessly. Genadie looked at her. He smiled a smile so large his beady eyes were sealed shut.

"*He* was willing," said the Count. He reached over and turned something that was sitting on a pedestal next to him. It was the bloody head of the Strange Man. Though from the mound of curly locks down to the manly chin, it was sticky with gore, the expression was calm and benign. "I told you it would be easy."

"It was!" chimed Genadie. "Very easy! And a great pleasure, Master."

"I—" Amalina didn't know what to say. Then: "I thought it was just a dream."

"It doesn't matter, Ms. Dalca. Time was critical. His trust in you was greater than Genadie's and so I came to you first. But I should have known ... understood ... Well, your response was very much you, Ms. Dalca. I shouldn't have bothered in the first place."

"Really, sir, I'm sorry. I didn't know."

"I've already forgiven you, Ms. Dalca," he said. "It's charming, that's all. The baker's daughter who wouldn't harm a fly, not even if the world counted on it. There's something pure in that. I think it explains how the princesses who have come to be my guests in my Palace of Pleasure are strikingly easy on their servants, considering their privilege and positions."

He winked at her, "I suspect you are subjecting my choice of guests to a filtering process of your own, Ms. Dalca. One programmed by your sweeter disposition. Am I right? Well, no matter. From now on you will be more liberal in your recommendations to me, I ask you. Servants have every right to suffer if they warrant, so don't cut from your reviews a princess who is easy with the lash, just because she is easy with the lash. More Margetas and Gillettes, if you understand. But do continue being as good natured as you are. I know I can't bully it out of you. And I wouldn't wish to. It makes my little mouse not only consistent, but dependable."

"Yes, sir. But, um, sir … I still don't understand what happened …"

"Genadie stabbed him in the heart and cut off his head."

"Yes, Master," Genadie agreed with an enthusiastic bob of his head.

"But, um, how are you alive?"

"I never died."

"You didn't?"

"I hid myself away. Until the time was right to make my move." The Count brought a finger to where his mustache would usually be and stroked the awful scab there, his lips turning up in amusement. "It was the only way really, Ms. Dalca. He'd fought and killed others. He knew too much of that sort of combat. And he was much stronger. Yes, I knew that. When he didn't die after his first attack; when I saw the fog roaming out from where he'd landed—no doubt his gypsy witchcraft—Oh …" The Count stopped and looked at her with tired but searching eyes. "You didn't believe the lies he told you about me. That I was some son of a poor gypsy who had stolen my lands and my titles, and assumed my noble rank."

Amalina shook her head.

"I should hope you would never believe such a thing. And you'll never repeat those falsities to anyone, will you?"

"Never, Master!" Genadie fell to the ground.

"I was speaking to Ms. Dalca."

"Why would I?" Amalina asked. She saw it wasn't a satisfactory answer. "Never, sir."

He picked up where he left off: "When I saw he hadn't died and he was working some magic, I knew he was stronger than me—"

"Never, Master!" cried Genadie.

"Leave!"

Genadie crawled out of the room, but there was no mistaking the smile on his face.

"He *was* stronger than me. So there was no possibility of my winning directly. It was going to have to come down to intellect and subtlety. Now, Ms. Dalca, this is how to lie, and this is how to win. When facing someone superior to you, you must use their own mind against them. He was experienced in killing his own kind, and he knew he was stronger than me. He knew that he would beat me and would not be satisfied until he did so.

And so I had to give him his victory in order to get the opening against him I could exploit. He had to see me die, Ms. Dalca. And he had to think he'd won against me in every sense, and that I had given him my all. And I did give him my all. Withdrawing when I could to preserve my strength. Using tricks and traps to confound him when possible. And hold things off until morning light. That is where he thought he was most superior to me, was it not? And so I gave it to him. And made sure to give him the idea to use the rocks in our battle. And permitted him the lee side of the mountain, like any fool would do. He naturally gloated at my idiocy. And he did not see, as he exposed me to the burning light, I had switched out with General Vezel, who—in his last act to preserve his rightful master—ignited the bombs within the armor. My suit of armor, which he was now wearing. It was enough to fool the fool. Yes, I was a liar, wasn't I? I lied straight to his face: told him he was smarter than me and cleverer. And that is an easy lie for anyone to take.

"Exhausted by our battle, he would seek rest and rejuvenation. It is not all blood, you see, Ms. Dalca. And he would be quite comfortable to put himself into a deep sleep, which he could do in order to heal faster, and because, in his arrogance, he felt he had no one else to fear. And then he installed himself in *my* castle, where he would seek to please himself by enjoying the richest, deepest sleep of all—the sleep of the conqueror. I only had to bide time by the princess' side until it all came to pass. And then call on my most trusted servants ... to strike!"

"I *am* sorry," Amalina said. "I really didn't understand."

The Count pardoned her with a shaky wave. He regarded Pia for a moment. She looked dead.

"Is she ...?"

"Oh, yes. I succeeded very well. It will only take some time for her to come through. Patience. Time is nothing. Let us leave her to her rest."

The Count pointed Amalina out the door. He followed stiffly after her, holding the Strange Man's head by the hair.

Amalina wouldn't be taking the AXP book after all.

• • •

The Count stretched himself out on the divan with a long sigh. He was now wearing a heavy robe of deep purple velvet. "Don't leave," he said. "Sit in the chair, Ms. Dalca, I would like to have a conversation."

He'd set the head on his desk. Amalina couldn't keep her eyes off it, so he nodded and put it out of sight behind the divan.

She sat, waiting for him to speak. Realizing this might result in them sitting there for days, and already feeling uncomfortable being at the center of his unblinking stare, she said: "You wanted to say something, sir?"

"I was saying before, Ms. Dalca, about what is the right thing to do. About the *fairness* of things. The passing of time. Who lives and who dies. Who truly deserves what they receive. You see, I have lived a very long time, Ms. Dalca, let me tell you. There are still questions ..."

"I remember you saying that," said Amalina.

He sat up and leaned forward and his heavy voice became low and confidential.

"I speak to you in confidence like this, Ms. Dalca, more so than Genadie, because it is gratifying to be able to speak to someone *openly*. It has been awhile since I've had someone I can speak to. To speak with. I had a friend once. But he grew very old. And died recently. Even his home is no more."

Amalina did not know he was referring to the old man and his castle in Kyrgil.

"I've heard that to be true to one person," said the Count. "True to one person alone—your whole life—makes you the strongest you can ever be." He gestured between them with his fingers. "A common teaching, for centuries. And this is *romantic* love I am speaking of. And every time you selfishly choose to love *another* person, beyond your first love, your heart breaks in two. Because, you see, your love never truly ends for the first one, nor for the next, nor the next, nor the next after that. So the more you love, the more your heart fractures, the more your soul is divided, and your *life*, like your love, is weakened.

"But knowing I cannot be bound by one love for life, Ms. Dalca," said the Count. "Being that my life is so vast, that I outlive the trees of the forest, and so how many loves must I necessarily have, from time to time to time ... I would be weakened eventually ... if this belief of men were true. I would be shaved down to nothingness, Ms. Dalca. So what is to be done? A life of loneliness?

"After studying my dilemma," he smiled, "I calculated a solution. If you limit yourself, you are weakened. If you love, and love them all, love as many as you can, so that your heart fractures and fractures and fractures again, until it can no longer break, because you cannot break something into infinity, it unites once more; harder than before, as in a mended bone; or like one great scar. And you can love as many as you ever want, because they unite as well. Not a single girl, but one vast tapestry that changes with the seasons; the colors more varied and richer. It is a good life. It is a good life that I have been granted."

He glanced over his shoulder, and then he went to the secret door and closed it. Then he sat even closer to Amalina. Almost touching his knees to hers, and bending so close, she tried to lean away without him noticing.

"I can tell you, I had my dissatisfactions. I was disgusted by the weakness of common men and their flesh. Had grown tired of making friends, of turning around and finding them gone. Or still hanging on, toothless and stripped of their natural hair and half their genius. And then turning once again only to discover they'd lost grip of the world at last, replaced by their inferior, middle-aged issue. But over time I grew to understand I'd have to get used to—and accept, and respect—their unacceptable fragility. But as you see, I had made my peace with it. Come to my conclusion—my satisfactory conclusion—of the lone-yet-multudinous heart of loves. And what should happen when I became sanguine with my destiny, and otherwise settled about my circumstance ...? What was I to think, when suddenly confronted with the amazing fact that, instead, I can now have— can make—someone as strong as myself? As eternal as myself? Hm? I could only ponder how fate is fickle; and humorous."

He said, lower than ever, and with a scent of having been wronged unjustly: "And now am I to revert back to the original belief of *one* love, now that I have an eternal woman? ... Well, I *can* write off all those who came before. Yes. *Yesss.* They were limited. Princess Lampeda is the first *real* one of my kind. Like me." He remembered the woman on the wheel: "The first one I *wanted*, that is. But still ... Shall I change my 'conclusion of the multitudinous-heart', which I came by so hard over the years? the belief I had come to *count on*, and to appreciate? to return to the notion of a simple, single love? No, I think not. Perhaps a shift. Perhaps an accommodation. Perhaps a slight alteration so I may satisfy both conditions. A *limited* love. But absolutely one love? No. No."

He sat there, his eyes looking both vulnerable and defiant. Maybe a little terrified, until he recovered himself and lowered his lids.

"You can do whatever you wish, I think," said Amalina, unsure how to proceed.

"The best number of wives, I've calculated, is nine," he said.

"Oh."

"If I'm to straddle eternity strapped to someone else. Nine seems fitting."

"I hadn't thought of that."

"But it seems fair to you, don't you think?"

"You love Pia?"

A flicker shot through his face. A guilty smile. "I developed my latest theory once it became a real concern, you understand."

"Oh."

"You like her, don't you?"

"She's very nice."

"And she's very fond of you. I can't see there being any trouble there."

"You seemed to favor Aria."

This cracked an even sharper grin below his stroking fingers. "Oh, yes."

"But she left," said Amalina. "Margeta's stayed behind."

"The process will sort itself out," he said, coming to, but retaining warm thoughts. "Princesses will come and go, and I will find the ones that will suit me, and satisfy me."

"And you satisfy them."

"That goes without saying," he mumbled. "But a blonde, and a brunette, and a readhead, and a moor, and a woman of olive skin, and a lady of cinnamon, and a lady of sunglower, and the rest. A brave one. A smart one. A bold one. A brash one. Tall and short, petite and plump."

"Young and old?"

"Please, Ms. Dalca."

"I'm sorry, sir."

"Now, where was I?" He fondled his upper lip, and it seemed a mustache might want to grow through the scab. "Plain and pretty. Fair and Freckled. Scentless and tangy. But never too religious, certainly."

"Certainly."

"And you will cap them off," he said with a clap of his hands, beaming at her. "My favorite. The most innocent of all. The purest of blood. The most opposite of me. As the strongest of magnets we will unite. You shall be mine."

Amalina was dumbfounded.

"I'm so happy you came into my life, Ms. Dalca. I'm thankful for it. I feel so fortunate." And though the Count's face didn't burst into flames when he said it, he growled contentedly: "*I thank God for it.*"